RANDOM ACTS
of
SENSELESS
VIOLENCE

RANDOM ACTS
of
SENSELESS
VIOLENCE

Jack Womack

GROVE PRESS
NEW YORK

First published in Great Britain in 1993 by HarperCollins Publishers
Published simultaneously in Canada
Printed in the United States of America

Library of Congress Cataloging-in-Publication Data

Womack, Jack.
    Random acts of senseless violence / Jack Womack.
        p.   cm.
    ISBN 978-0-8021-3424-0
    eISBN 978-1-5558-4761-6
    1. New York (N.Y.)—Fiction. I. Title.
PS3573.O575R36 1995   813'.54—dc20   95-38204

Grove Press
an imprint of Grove/ Atlantic, Inc.
154 West 14th Street
New York, NY 10011

Distributed by Publishers Group West
www.groveatlantic.com

FOR MY PARENTS
ANN TRUITT KARRENBROCK AND
JACK WOMACK, SR.

FEBRUARY 15

Mama says mine is a night mind. The first time she said
that I asked her what she meant and she said 'Darling you
think best in the dark like me.' I think she's right. Here I
am staying up late tonight so I can write in my new diary.
Mama gave it to me for my birthday today. I love to write.
Mama and Daddy write but I don't think they love to write
anymore, they just write because they have to.

I got a new bedroom for my birthday too. It's not a
surprise like my diary was. It's not a new room but the
maid's old room. We had to let her go but I don't know
where she went. Her name was Inez and she was nice but
she never said much to me or my sister Boob because her
English wasn't very good. Boob is my little sister and she
has her own room now too. Her real name is Cheryl but we
have names for each other that we've always used. Boob is
her name and Booz is mine.

My real name is Lola Hart. Faye and Michael Hart are
our parents. We live on 86th Street near Park Avenue in
New York City.

Mama and Daddy helped me move everything into my
new room this morning after my new furniture came. I have
a new bed and new lamp and new desk and chair. I also got
new sweaters and shoes and a dictionary for school.

I love my new diary the best of all my presents. I'd better
go to sleep now but I'll be back tomorrow. More birthday
treats then, Daddy says. I know he's telling the truth
because his face gives him away when he lies. Good night.

*　*　*

7

FEBRUARY 16

Today is Sunday and tomorrow is President's Day and I have a wonderful long weekend to do nothing. Daddy took us to brunch today at Rumpelmayer's as the extra birthday treat he promised. Rumpelmayer's is all pink inside like me and Boob. I used to like it more than I do now, it's not as good as it used to be. Boob likes it but she's still a kid. We had ice cream sundaes and naturally Boob got extra hot fudge. Daddy wanted to buy me a stuffie but I'm too old for those now, I think. I'm twelve. Mama says 'That's not old at all sweetie not at all' but it is. I already have more stuffies than fit on my bed now anyway. Boob started crying because she wanted a stuffie but Daddy said she didn't have a birthday so why should she get one? Then he bought her one anyway a little brown rabbit. Mama called Daddy a sucker.

Boob is nine and spoiled rotten but I love her anyway. 'Kiss it Booz' she said and then when I wouldn't she held her rabbit on her lap the whole time we were there. It has fudgy ears now. She wanted to wear her My L'il Fetus pack when we went to brunch but Mama wouldn't let her. Aunt Chrissie who lives in California sent it to her as a Hanukah present. My L'il Fetus is a doll baby that fits in a pack Boob ties around her stomach. When you press its button it kicks her like a real baby would. Mama and Daddy don't like it but Boob loves it. She'd even wear it to school if they let her but they won't.

I hate babies. They're messy and squirmy and smell bad. I never want to have one. The more I write the more I think about what I want to write. I'm tired though. I have a lot of time tomorrow and think I'll write a lot more.

FEBRUARY 19

I never wrote you on Monday because I wasted too much time thinking about what I should write. I think years from now a diary will be interesting when you can read it and see what you were doing that you forgot about later. If I'd had a diary when I was five or six it would be something to read now. I think I'd be embarrassed but I'd want to read it anyway. I asked Mama if she ever kept a diary. She said 'Yes darling but I stopped and I'm sorry I did.'

'Why did you stop?' I asked.

She said 'I was a foolish girl.'

'Who said so?'

'My mother darling my mother always told me I was a foolish girl. All mothers tell their daughters that.'

'You never told me that' I said.

'That's because you're not a foolish girl sweetie.'

'I know' I said. 'If I never stop writing in my diary then I'll always know what I did.'

'Yes darling that's why your father gave you your diary. So you could remember how sweet life is even when it doesn't seem like it is anymore.' I wanted to talk to her longer but she was working on her résumés and had to get back to work so I left her alone. Daddy was downtown talking to a director. I was bored so I went in the bathroom where Boob was taking a bath. She was sitting in the tub trying to squeeze water out of her baby. 'You're drowning it' I said.

'I'm not' she said and splashed water on me. 'Don't get wet Booz' she said. I brushed my teeth. Boob started washing her hair and stuck her butt in the air so she could get her hair wet and when she did I goosed her. She jumped and hit her head on the tub and started crying.

'Don't be a baby Boob' I said. She yelled for Mama but finally stopped when Mama didn't come in. Boob's only really upset when she isn't crying, she's Niagara Falls most of the time but it doesn't mean anything and we know it doesn't. It only works if you don't know Boob. When she got out of the tub she smacked me with her towel but I ignored her and then she went away.

A typical day. Now I'm lying on my bed wondering if I want to remember everything I do. I don't see any reason why I shouldn't.

9

I'm sticking to my writing schedule much better now and here I am writing you again two days in a row. I've decided I'm going to give you a name so I don't think I'm talking to a wall like Daddy says he feels like when he talks to us sometimes. Your name is Anne, that's a good name for a diary and I'll never show you to anyone else. What I tell you is just between you and me.

Let me tell you more about myself Anne. As you know I'm twelve and Boob is nine. We were both born in New York at Lenox Hill hospital but our parents are from other places. Mama is from Los Angeles and Daddy is from Chicago. They've taken us to both places on vacation. I don't like Los Angeles or Chicago. They're horrible places and I'm glad they're burning down.

Mama was an English professor at New York University until they let her go last semester. She teaches 20th Century Literature when she teaches. Right now she's trying to get another job at another school but isn't having much luck. She also writes books and papers on what writers were really doing when they were trying to do something else, that's the way she explains it. Students aren't very good any more she says. 'Darling they're so dumb you want to pinch them to see if they're asleep. But sweetie they're so sweet too and they do try and they have so many problems you have to let them get away with murder sometimes.'

Mama says even when they read something they really don't. She says it's because TV erases their minds. But she and Daddy watch TV all the time. Daddy writes for TV. When she was still teaching I asked her if Daddy distracts her students. 'Oh darling he writes good things they'd never watch anything like that nobody does' she said. She misses going to work and I hope she gets to go to another college soon. Doesn't look good so far, that's what Mama says.

Daddy belongs to the Screenwriters Guild. He wanted to be a novelist but Mama says he's no Charles Dickens. He writes scripts for movies. They haven't produced any yet but he gets paid for them anyway. He's had shows on TV. Last year he made a lot of money but not much this year. That's the way it's always gone before. Mama and Daddy aren't so good with money I don't think. Sometimes we have more than they know what to do with and then the next month we'll be broke. It doesn't matter. Somebody always owes Daddy money but never as much as he owes somebody else. Whenever Mama and Daddy talk they always start talking about money if they talk long enough. They've been talking a lot lately.

Boob tried to put her silly My L'il Fetus on me tonight to see what I'd look like pregnant. I threw it on the floor so she said she was going to turn me in for child abuse. Boob can be so immature. She was fun to play with when I was younger but I don't want to play dolls with her now. It makes her mad but I can't help it. I love her but she's so crazy. When we had the same room she sometimes would crawl in bed with me before I went to sleep to tell me all the nice things Daddy said to her.

'Daddy said I was the best girl he knew' she said. 'That's what he told me Booz. The best girl he knew.' 'Go away Boob' I say. 'He's going to take me to the circus when it comes to town.' 'Good now go away Boob.' 'You want to go to the circus Booz?' 'I want to go to sleep.' Usually I have to push her out before she'll leave. Once she fell on her arm and we thought she broke her wrist. She was crying too much so I figured she hadn't and she didn't.

Sometimes even if Boob doesn't bug me I can't get to sleep Anne. Seems to me though I can if I write you before I try to sleep. That's not the best reason to write you but it's a good one. I want to go to sleep now, I think. I don't know what I want sometimes.

FEBRUARY 21

Today at school our gym teacher Miss Norris showed us a video about sex diseases. What can happen to you if you do.

It was a heaver and my best friend Lori and some of the other girls got sick but I think they just pretended so they could go to the bathroom and smoke. It was really boring in school today. If it was spring we could go on the roof and play games. Last month it got up to eighty for a week and Miss Norris put up the volleyball net and we had a great time until it got cold again.

Boob and I love school. We go to Brearley which is a girls only school. Some of my classmates say they miss having boys around but I don't see how. Boys are really stupid and I don't know why anybody would want to be around them they're as bad as babies. Mama asked me last year if I minded going to a girls school and I said not at all, I wasn't interested in boys. Mama said 'Boys are awful scamps and worse my darling but you'll be thinking about them soon enough.'

'Why should I?' I asked her. She gave me a big hug and kiss.

'Angel that just happens and by the time you realize your error they have you hooked my darling because boys are very cunning that way.'

'Daddy was that way?' I asked her. She shook her head. 'Why didn't you know?'

Mama said 'They get more cunning as they get older my darling.'

I'm sure that's true but I can always outsmart them. I'd much rather write to you Anne than worry about what some stupid boys are doing. It doesn't make any sense to me. I know you understand.

At dinner tonight Mama and Daddy were talking. She was asking when he'd be getting money from the producers. Daddy said he thought he'd be coming back with a check when he got back from Los Angeles. He has to fly out there tomorrow to meet with them. Mama said 'Oh darling they're not hiring at Yeshiva they're cutting back just like the city I heard from them today.' They talked about tenure and why she didn't get it. I wasn't sure what they

12

were talking about and Boob was hopelessly lost like always. Boob asked 'What's tenure?' 'Sweetie if you have tenure you're always a teacher no matter how bad you are.' 'Why didn't you get tenure?' I asked. 'I wasn't bad enough' she said and she laughed but later she took a Xanax and I don't think she feels very good.

Daddy never comes in to check on me in my new room and I'm glad. I don't want to be tucked in anymore. I was able to write as long as I wanted tonight. He was in with Boob for a long time talking but I couldn't hear what they were saying. Once I asked Mama if Daddy wishes Boob was their only child and she said 'Don't be silly darling he loves all of us.' Boob's talking in her sleep now. She jabbers on all the time. I can hear her through the door but at least I can sleep through it now. Our rooms are separate and I'm GLAD, GLAD, GLAD. I like having my own room. Weekend's almost here! Night night, Anne.

FEBRUARY 23

Today my friends Katherine and Lori came over. We almost always do something on Saturdays. They're my age and go to Brearley with me. I've known them since first grade. They're my best friends.

Daddy flew to Los Angeles yesterday and so Mama slept late because she knows I can fix breakfast for me and silly Boob. Sometimes Boob goes along with us when we go out on Saturdays but not today ha! ha! she had homework to do. It was so warm out today we thought we'd go to the park. Mama said to us 'Be careful little geese and don't go far past the museum. There's perverts in every bush.' Mama calls us geese but Daddy always calls us the vipers because he says we're always up to no good.

We went to the park and we weren't going to go far but Anne you know how it is when you start walking and talking. There were hundreds of people in the park and the next thing you knew we'd walked down to the lake around the ramble. There were men down there sunbathing in their bathing suits. One of them that was hairy like a gorilla gave another one a kiss. 'Look at them they're bendover buddies,' Katherine said. Lori started giggling. I asked 'What's so funny?' 'How do they walk?' Lori said. She meant with their things between their legs. 'You'd know,' Katherine said. Lori went out with a fourteen year old boy named Simon Norris last Halloween. He was a brother of her brother's friend. They didn't do anything, she told me. She said they kissed for a while and he tried to take off her bra but she wouldn't let him so he stopped. 'You'd know, Lori' Katherine kept saying. Lori said 'Shut up Kat you're so stupid.' They're always arguing.

I finished my Coke so I took the can and stuck it between my legs and walked around all straddle legged. 'They walk like this' I said. Lori fell down laughing and Katherine acted like she didn't know us. 'That's so disgusting' she said. She's a real prisser.

We walked back to the east side of the park because Mama says it's safer on that side. When we got ready to cross the road we smelled something burning. There was an ambulance and some people and policemen were standing by a tree and we ran to see what happened. Somebody set a homeless person on fire a rollerblader woman told us. Katherine got sick and said she was going to spew. Lori and I tried to see if he was all burned up but they already put him in the ambulance. 'That's nothing you want to see' an old man said to me and I wanted to say how do you know but I didn't. Katherine was all green and shaking but she didn't blow. Lori called her a sissy but Lori didn't look like she felt good either.

On our way back we saw some black and Spanish girls breaking bottles on the wall of the park. From the way they were laughing I just knew they set the man on fire. 'You're racist' Lori said when I told her what I thought. 'I am not' I said but she said I was. I think Katherine thought I was right but she didn't say anything. I'm not a racist but I'm sure those kids did it, I don't know how I knew but I do. When we walked by the homeless people we saw on 86th Street Anne I wondered how many times somebody tried to hurt them or set them on fire. Mama and Daddy always give money to homeless charities but there's still homeless everywhere.

We went back to Lori's apartment and hung out in her room for awhile. Lori and her parents live on 83rd between Park and Lexington. Katherine said she was worried because her mom said she should be getting her period soon but she hadn't yet. Lori said don't be in any rush. When granny comes to visit me it's not so bad. I think I came out lucky, it only hurts the first day and then not anymore. Katherine says she doesn't want to use tampons, she tried to use one and it hurt. 'Then you'll have to use mouse mattresses' Lori said. 'No tampons for sissies.' Katherine got mad again but not for long. We listened to music and then I came home.

There wasn't anything about the man on the news tonight. I remember there used to be when they set people on fire. I didn't tell Mama or Boob about what we saw in the park because it gets Mama upset to hear about things like that. Boob gets so mad when I see something and she doesn't that I'd never tell her. So there, Boob.

FEBRUARY 24
Daddy's in Los Angeles. He comes back tomorrow. Mama said he called late last night after we went to sleep. I asked her what he said and she told me he sounded happy. She didn't say if he had his check or not. I bet he doesn't.

It was raining out today so I did my homework this morning instead of tonight. I'm supposed to read Silas Marner but it's so awful. Daddy calls it Silas Mariner because he says George Eliot must have written it underwater. I think if Miss Dudley gives us a pop quiz on it I can handle it but I wish we had other books to read in school. I read Life Among the Savages by Shirley Jackson again tonight. I've read it a dozen times before, I love it so much. It's all about this crazy family. I love to read stories about crazy families. Like I don't know any! Daddy says he knows people who knew the people in the book and they were even crazier than the book says. I wish I'd met them. We'd have a lot of fun.

Boob got one of those silly magazines somewhere and asked me if I thought the guy on the cover was cute. 'You think he is?' I asked.

'He's cute cute cute' she said. 'Here's a picture of him riding a horse. He could take me for a ride.'

'You'd fall off' I told her. 'Go away Boob.'

We watched TV while we ate dinner. Mom sent out for Chinese. I had noodles. The news was on and the TV people were talking about riots in Miami. They said there wouldn't be riots in New York. They don't know, they're always wrong though they act like they know everything. I hope there aren't any riots here.

FEBRUARY 25

Daddy came back this afternoon before we came home from school and when we got home he was in his office making some phone calls. Mama said 'They gave it the old thumbs down darlings.' She meant they didn't buy his idea so it's going to be harder than it's been around here because I think he was counting on signing the deal. I know there's been a lot more bills coming in lately than usually and Daddy's accountant was over last week talking to him about taxes. It's all making him and Mama a lot more upset this time. After he finished talking to people he went for a walk down 86th Street and while he was gone Boob and I asked Mama if we were in bad shape.

'No no no darling' she said but I could tell she was fudging. I can always see it in her face. 'Michael's a sweetie but he's such a spendthrift. I guess we both are but what

16

can you do. He has to come up with something new but he doesn't know what yet and here the wolves are at the door.'

Boob went to look. 'I don't see them' she said. Mama laughed.

'Why doesn't Daddy save more money?' I asked.

'Angel we try but it's very hard with prices going up all the time. They go up every week the way it is now and devil take the hindmost. New York's not an easy place to live in the best of circumstances.'

'I wouldn't live anywhere else' I said.

'No sweetie and we wouldn't either but living in New York means you're going to have to spend a lot of money you ordinarily wouldn't spend.'

'Unless you were Daddy' I said.

'We're going to have to think what to do' Mama said. 'Get a plan of action. It may be a little hard around here for a while but not for long my darlings.'

'How long?' asked Boob.

'Not long' said Mama. Then Daddy came back and he called the Chinese restaurant because Mama got distracted talking to us and forgot to fix dinner. I think she took too many Prozac it makes her forget things too easily. The fellow brought our food and we ate dinner. I had shrimp with cashew nuts and Boob had beef in garlic sauce and Daddy and Mama had sesame noodles because they said they weren't that hungry. While we were eating we watched the news. The President said things aren't as bad as they seem so nobody should worry. He's such an idiot said Daddy.

'A buffoon' said Mama. 'If I went to school with one of him there must have been a hundred. Now they're in charge of everything.'

Everything, Daddy said.

'But you say things aren't as bad as they seem so don't worry' I said. 'Just like him.'

'He doesn't know what he's talking about darling' Mama said. 'He hit himself over the head with that golf club one

17

time too many.'

The President blinks his eyes like Mama and Daddy do when they say everything's fine so I bet he's fudging too. Somebody asked if he was going to do anything and the President said people have troubles because they make their own reality and there's nothing you can do about it. Then he got in his helicopter and flew away. There was a riot in Detroit and one in Seattle and in Miami. Not to mention Chicago and Los Angeles. There's too much reality these days, said Daddy.

FEBRUARY 27

Yesterday wasn't a good day Anne. Whenever Daddy's upset Boob flips and she could tell as soon as she saw him something upset him really bad today. I asked Mama what the matter was but she said 'Nothing sweetie don't worry.' At dinner Daddy and Mama started talking and before you knew it Anne they were talking about money like they always do. Daddy said he didn't know where to get any.

'Get the bank to give you money' Boob said. 'Go in and say give it to me now.'

Daddy told her they wouldn't let him in the door at the bank anymore. Mama said 'Darling you worry too much you shouldn't.' Daddy said he had some ideas but nobody was buying anything right now with the way things were. He looked at me and Boob and said he wasn't sure what we were going to do.

'What can we do to help?' I asked. I figured he'd say nothing because that's what he always says and sure enough that's what he said. 'Are you sure?' I asked. He shook his head.

'Darlings there is one thing we've been talking about' Mama said. 'It probably won't be necessary but we thought I should talk to you about it.'

'About what?' Boob asked.

'About moving somewhere for a while. Not long darlings

just while we're in such perilous straits.'

Boob didn't say anything but she kept looking at Daddy while Mama was talking. 'Moving where?'

'We'd stay in town darlings but we'd get a smaller apartment for a while. We'd rent this one out. Just a couple of months over the summer or even in the fall. Not for long though sweeties, not for long. And it's just maybe.'

'How long?' I asked.

'Not long.'

'We're not going to Long Island this summer?'

'Oh darling that's out of the question even if we had money you know it's a bit rough there what with the accident and all the Chrissies out there in a tizzy.'

'We wouldn't move out of New York would we?'

No, Daddy said. That would cost too much money. We'd just find a smaller place in Manhattan for a little while he said. He said he just wanted to know how we'd feel about it if some things had to change.

'What other things?' I asked. He shook his head and said probably none but they'd be big things if they did have to change. 'How big?' I asked. He said he wasn't sure but he asked if I thought it would upset us. 'Depends on what the big things are' I said. 'Are you and Mama getting divorced?' Boob didn't say anything but the way she looked I could tell she was real upset. No no no he said not at all. 'I didn't think so. I'm glad' I said. He said whatever happened it would be the four of us sticking together there wasn't any question about that.

'When do we have to move?' I asked. We may not have to he said so don't worry about it yet.

'Don't worry about anything my geese not anything at all' Mama said and then we finished dinner. Well of course I'm going to worry about it. I don't want to leave here even for a little while Anne, I've never lived anywhere else. Boob wants to leave here even less than I do.

Just as I was getting ready to write you last night and tell you all about what happened Boob knocked on the door and asked if she could come in and sleep with me. I told her sure and so we went to bed. 'Are you all right Boob?' I asked. She nodded and didn't say anything and I knew she wasn't. Usually she keeps me up half the night talking if she gets half a chance but she didn't tonight. She was so hot it was like having a fat puppy in bed with me and I kept pushing her off in the night and she kept rolling back. Poor Boob.

Anyway that's what happened yesterday. Today everybody acted like nothing happened at all so I'm not going to worry about moving yet. I don't want to worry about it. I may not write you tomorrow I should wait and see what happens.

MARCH 1
Nothing's happened so far Anne so I thought I should write you before you forget I was here. Daddy and Mama haven't said anything else about moving so maybe they were just getting crazy and worked up about something. They do that all the time. They worry themselves crazy and then they act like there wasn't anything wrong like it never happened. When I was little it used to upset me but now I'm used to it. Poor Boob she's not used to it, she's been sick ever since we talked, or at least she says she's sick but she seems fine to me. I think she's just got herself all worked up. I'm glad I'm calm. Somebody has to stay calm around this place. Not much else to say tonight Anne so night night.

MARCH 2
Katherine stayed over with me last night and after we ate dinner we watched a video. She wanted to watch <u>Fantasia</u> so we did. She really likes it though I think a lot of it is awfully stupid. The devil at the end is really good though but then it gets so silly again. We had a good time.

20

Katherine is fun when she's not at school or around Lori. I don't know what it is but she's not as nervous or something. After we watched the movie we went into my room and got ready for bed. Katherine was putting on her pajamas and I saw a big bruise on her bottom. 'What happened?' I asked. 'I fell down' she said. 'Doesn't it hurt?' I asked. 'Not a lot' she said. Earlier I saw she wasn't sitting all the way down on the couch but propped herself up on her legs. I didn't know why until I saw the bruise. She must have fallen awfully hard when she fell.

I asked if she wanted me to sleep on the floor but she said she wanted to sleep with me and I was glad so I said get in. We talked for a long time. I did most of the talking at first even though when it's just us together Katherine isn't so quiet as she is around her parents or Lori or at school. We talked about our teachers and some of the girls we know like Icky Betsy. I told her that Mama and Daddy were saying we might move but I didn't believe them because they were probably just imagining it. My fourth grade English teacher Miss Wisegarver told me I had a great imagination and I told her I couldn't help it I inherited it. But I know when something's real or not at least, sometimes I think I'm the only one in my crazy family who does.

Anyway after a while Katherine and I started playing make believe. We hugged each other like we were in a sleeping bag. 'Make believe you have an imaginary family' she said. 'What's it like?'

'We'd live in Vermont' I said. 'Daddy would write at home. Mama would be just wonderful and sweet and take care of us all the time. She'd be like a nice Junior League lady. There'd be three or four towheaded kids. We'd have a big house with fireplaces and four white columns out in front.'

'That's nice' Katherine said. Her father is an investor. He works for a bank downtown. They live on Park at 78th Street. I don't go over to their house very often because she says her parents don't like too much noise.

21

'Your turn' I said. 'Make believe you have an imaginary family. What's it like?'

'They stay in their rooms and I stay in mine' she said. 'I read all the time and sometimes I watch TV. Dad works in another country and Mom calls him on weekends. He only comes home once a year. I have three older sisters who are all beautiful and love me. Make believe you have a boy-friend. What's he like?'

'I'll never have a boyfriend' I said.

'You will' she said. 'And what's he like?'

'He's not too tall and he has a beard. He wears glasses. If I ask him to bring me something he always does.'

'That's your father' she said and laughed.

'It is not' I said. 'Make believe you have a boyfriend. What's he like?'

'He's got blond hair' she said. 'He looks really cute and wears bicycle shorts. He swims really well and takes me out to dinner every night. He always remembers my birthday.'

'And his name's Corey' I said. I was laughing.

'No it's not' she said. 'It's Paul.'

'Make believe you could go anywhere you wanted to go' I said. 'Where would you go?'

'I don't know' she said. She put her leg on mine and I put mine on hers. It was nice and warm. 'I don't know where I'd go. Somewhere.'

'Florida?' She shook her head. Katherine and her family go to Florida every year. 'If I could go anywhere I wanted to go I'd go to Europe. I'd want to see where my grand-parents were from' I said.

'Where were they from?' Katherine asked.

'Prague' I said. 'I'd like to go to Prague. What next?'

Katherine rolled on her back and put up her knees like she was going to do situps. 'Lo' she said. 'Make believe you're a boy and you're raping me.'

'Why would I rape you? That's an awful thing to say' I said. 'Go on make believe' she said. 'If I was a boy I wouldn't rape you' I said. 'Why do you say that?' 'That's what they do' she said. 'I don't want to pretend that, Kat. We better go to sleep' I said. She rolled back over against me. 'If I snore just smack me' she said. 'I'll kick you' I said. 'Okay.'

I didn't go right to sleep because I thought about what she said to me for a long time because it bothered me. I didn't mind making believe I was a boy because I think I'd be a better boy than most boys but rape's bad and I don't know why she wanted me to pretend that. Katherine's really weird sometimes. She didn't snore at all and I don't know who told her she did. So I lay there for a long time listening through the wall to Boob talk in her sleep and I wished I had been alone because if I had been I'd have gotten up and written you Anne. Well better late than never.

MARCH 3

Granny's here and so are the crampers. The first day's the worst though so I know when I wake up tomorrow morning I'll feel better and that's good to know. I've only been having my period since last year but I'm already tired of it. Mama says 'Oh darling it's a terrible affliction for us poor women but what can you do?' When Granny's here I always think I smell bad and I get zits and I know I look funny. They tell you all about it in the movies they show you but they never tell you how much it hurts. I warned Boob because she said she wanted to have periods too and I said that's what you think. 'You just want to have them all for yourself' she said. 'I want them too.' Boob's so crazy. She still ties on her My L'il Fetus every day when she gets home from school. I think it needs to go in the laundry.

Katherine was acting weird again in History class today. Lori and I said hello and she blushed and ran away. I think she thinks I'm mad at her for her asking me to pretend I was a boy the other night. That's so ridiculous but you never know what people are going to think Anne. I think she'll get over it.

Lori was smoking again at lunch today. I could smell it on her breath when I saw her. I asked her if she was but she said she wasn't. I don't care if she smokes or not but she'll get in so much trouble when they catch her again. I know they suspend girls they catch smoking the second time and her parents would just kill her. She says they've been really after her lately about a lot of things but she doesn't say what things she means. Daddy says they should ship her off but he's not serious because that's what he always said he was going to do to us and we never believed him.

We listened to music by Ralph Vaughan Williams in Music class today. You don't say Ralph you say Rafe. We listened to <u>The Lark Ascending</u>. It's so beautiful and sad. I think if I ever have a funeral I'd like it to be played while everybody's crying, it'll make them feel even sadder and they'll miss me even more.

Finally finished <u>Silas Marner</u>. Yuck!

All for now, Anne.

MARCH 4

The weather's so crazy. It went up to ninety degrees today. It was so hot this afternoon Lori and I went to our favorite luncheonette at Lexington and 83rd for milk shakes after school. It's a real old place that's been around for almost a hundred years, I think and it's great fun to go in. Well Anne there we were sitting there when who should walk in but Mimsy Porter. She used to go to Brearley but now she goes to Chapin, she got kicked out of Brearley because her grades were so bad and her father didn't know anyone he could lean on.

Let me tell you how the schools are because otherwise you may not understand. Chapin is where the dumb girls go. They're not really dumb but they're dumber than the girls at Brearley. The society girls go to Spence. You don't have to be smart to go to Dalton but you have to have money. The girls who go to Marymount are so dumb they're remedial. At the other schools of course they all say the dykes go to Brearley but they're just jealous and you'd expect them to say that because our school is the very best one.

Anyway so Mimsy comes in all fancy shmancy wearing a new dress and pretty patent leather shoes. She walks over to where we're sitting and she starts acting like she's at cotillion. She says oh it's sooo good to see you and how have you been. I think Mimsy is annoying and really shallow but I can put up with her. Lori can't stand her. 'How are you doing, Mim?' Lori asks. Fabbbbulous says Mimsy. Her head's gotten so big I'm surprised she got it through the door. Anyway Lori asks 'What classes are you taking?' and before Mimsy can tell her Lori answers. 'Abortion 101? How to Be a Slut?' What are you talllking about Mimsy says. 'How much homework they make you do?' Finally Mimsy figures out Lori's making fun of her and you can imagine what she had to say to that. Lori just laughed and said 'Go away, somebody might think we know you.' Mimsy looked like she was going to slap Lori but Lori's bigger than she is so instead she turned around and flounced out and that was that. 'Why were you so mean to her, Lori?' I asked. 'She's silly but there's no need to be so mean.'

'Yes there is. She's so stuck up she drives me crazy' Lori said. 'They must be paying her to go to Chapin.'

'She's not worth getting upset about' I said. 'That's what I think.'

'You know we had a dance with those boys from Walden last year' Lori said. 'She snuck off with one of them and made out. I heard all about it later.'

'Like you and Simon did?' I asked. Lori got mad but didn't say anything because she knows I can handle myself better than Mimsy or Katherine can. Lori's kind of a bully but she's been one of my two best friends since first grade. We hated each other at first though. We were making clay sculptures and I made a pot with a little person in it. She asked who it was and I said 'It's you. It's an ogre in the pot. I'm making ogre stew.' Lori hit me and I hit her back and then we got into a big fight right there in class. We made up after we got out of the office though and we've been the best of friends ever since. Me and Lori and Katherine are the founding members of the Ogre Club though we're not as bad as we used to be except for Lori of course.

On TV tonight they showed the President meeting with the cabinet. I looked at his face and it looks like Mama's, I don't mean they look anything at all alike. I mean sometimes there just isn't anything there and I think he's on Xanax too.

MARCH 6
Anne I'm sorry I'm not being as diligent as I should be in writing to you every day but you know how it is with distractions like parents and sisters and school. Sometimes I just never get any time to myself! I'll try to do better.

Some days there's not much to say, though. Daddy says he has a new idea and he's been working on it for the past two days though he's not saying what it is yet. He always says it's bad luck to talk about what you're writing on before you're finished except to the people you're working with and sometimes not even then. Mama says 'Darlings your father is such a primitive at heart he has any number of personal hoodoos' and Boob and I think it's funny but I hope he has good luck this time. We'll see what happens. Once he worked on a script for three years before they finally turned it down but usually it doesn't take that long.

MARCH 7
Before you know it here it is Friday and it's the weekend again. Lori's having a party over at her house tomorrow night and I don't really want to go because I don't like parties but I want to see Lori so I'll go. She's invited some

boys she knows from Walden and friends of her brother's from Trinity and I'm not looking forward to putting up with them. I'm sure they'll be as stupid as they always are, the stupider they are the more they get away with. They're not cunning at all.

We went to a movie tonight that got good reviews but Daddy kept talking about how bad the script was until finally the people behind us asked him to be quiet. He made some sarcastic remarks and we thought that the man was going to get up and start a fight but he didn't. Daddy was quiet for a while after that but then started groaning again and kept groaning till the movie was over. This always happens Anne whenever we go to the movies. Even though he says he wasn't Daddy must have been awful when he was a little boy. I love Daddy but I think when boys grow up they stay the same.

After the movie we went to Falafel and Stuff over on First Avenue and had dinner. Boob asked Mama and Daddy if she could get a new dress. I've told her we shouldn't be asking them for things now because they can't afford it and they'll get it anyway but she never listens to anything I say. 'Oh darling do you need it for some sort of affair or something?' Mama asked.

'I need it because I need it' said Boob. That's not the most convincing reason I've ever heard, said Daddy. 'I need it' said Boob.

'Darling do you need it or do you want it there's a difference you know' said Mama.

'I need it because I want it' said Boob.

'We always want something sweetie but there's only a little bit we really need. If you really need it we'll see but if you just want it we'll have to wait awhile.'

'I need it' said Boob. I know they'll get it for her tomorrow. She'll wear it to school and somebody will say something about it and then Boob won't want to wear it anymore. Anything Boob wants she needs. I never know what I want or what I need. Sometimes I do but not usually. I think I can get by with a lot less than Boob but I wouldn't say that's bad for either of us, we're just different, that's all.

Granny's gone home. Hooray!

MARCH 8

It's so late but Anne I need to write you because I don't know who else I can talk to about what happened. Lori's party was tonight and even before I went I was afraid it wasn't going to be any fun. I was so right. It was just getting dark when I was getting ready to leave. Mama and Daddy let me walk down by myself since it's only three blocks away. Boob was a howler, crying when I told her she couldn't come, it wasn't a party for little kids.

'I never go to parties' Boob said. 'You just went to Sherrie's house for her birthday party last month' I said.

'I hate Sherrie' Boob said.

'You're a baby Boob' I said. She was wearing her new dress by the way.

'Oh my darlings you're both our babies' Mama said and she hugged us. 'Be careful walking down the street sweetie and don't turn off Park till you have to. The creeps are out and about.' 'Where else would I go?' I asked. 'China' said Boob. 'I want to go to the party too.' Daddy told Boob if she didn't stop fussing he was going to sell her to a Satanic cult. 'They'd want a refund' Boob said and then they both laughed. 'I want to go though.' 'But you don't need to go do you?' I asked. 'Yes' Boob said. She stopped crying. 'I want to go to China' she said.

I was so glad to leave the house. Boob was boohooing so much. Mama's really depressed because no one wants her to teach for them and Daddy's still working on the project he won't talk about. He says it's about done but he's still fiddling. My family drives me crazy all the time sometimes.

Anyway I think I looked very chic for the party not that anyone noticed. I wore barettes in my hair to pull it off my

28

face and my pretty blue dress with the white Eton collar. Mama calls it a baby doll dress though I tell her not to call it that. I wore my blue knee socks and my black patent leather party shoes. It was cold out so I wore my green coat. I walked down Park to 83rd Street as I promised I would. The only creeps and perverts I saw were the ones who live in our building though there was a man lying in the street near the curb on Park. There were fire trucks whizzing uptown but I didn't see anything burning so it must not have been major.

Lori and her parents have a duplex and a garden in a townhouse. The party was downstairs in the living room and the kitchen. Her father stayed upstairs but her mother came down sometimes to look in on us. Besides me and Lori and Katherine, Susan, Icky Betsy, Tanya, Whitney and Edie were there, and some other girls. Lori's brother Tom was there too and ten or eleven stupid friends of his. They're all fifteen or sixteen and think they're real grown up. They kept acting like they owned the place showing off but they didn't impress me. Simon Norris who I told you about before was there. Lori likes him a lot. He's fifteen but he has an evil baby face so her parents don't know he's as old as he is though they still don't like him she says. Lori looks older than she really is so they look like they're the same age.

Well Simon Norris has a friend named Clark and he must have thought I wanted to be around him as much as Lori wanted to be around Peter. He's a slimy toad. He followed me around all night like he was a baby duck who thought I was his mother. He kept telling me how rich his family was like it was a big deal. Our apartment's so big Dad pays two hundred dollars a month just on gas bills he said. 'He'd better find another doctor' I told him. He didn't get it of course he's such a fool. He even tried to paw me with his toad flippers. Finally I told him 'Would you stop bothering me' and then he <u>finally</u> did.

It was a stupid party because it wasn't anyone's birthday

29

or anything. Everybody was just standing around listening to music and acting like they were brain dead. The younger boys from Walden looked at us like they wanted to eat us up but none of them tried anything with their paws, they're still tadpoles. Tom's friends from Trinity except for Simon and Clark stood around like they were too cool to breathe.

I ate half a bowl of potato chips and dip and listened to Whitney tell me about her headaches. Then Icky Betsy came over and started talking and I just had to get away because she'd been eating. Every time she eats something she goes and heaves it right up afterward and then she smells like vomit even though she washes her face. I wanted to talk to Lori but she was gabbing with Simon. I think the only reason she had the party was because that way she could get together with him whenever her mother left the room. I went over to where Katherine was standing by herself looking geeky.

'What's the matter?' I asked. 'Nothing' she said. 'Do you think he's cute?' she asked and pointed to a Trinity boy who was bigger than the others. He looked a lot older than his friends and he was the dumbest looking one of all. His face looked dirty but it wasn't. He just didn't know how to shave yet not that he seemed smart enough to ever learn. His arms were hairy like a dentist's and he wore a sweatshirt that was cut off so you could see his hairy stomach. You could tell he thought he was hot hot hot.

'He's the Abominable Snowman' I said. 'What are you talking about?' Katherine said. 'I bet when he takes his shirt off he looks like he's wearing a sweater.' 'You mean like hairy shoulders?' Katherine asked. 'Like hairy everything' I said. Well sure enough a few minutes later she went over and started talking to him. He was at least a foot taller than she is and she acted more shy than she really is. My friends act so dumb around boys sometimes you wouldn't think they had any sense at all. I ate more potato chips and some Triscuits and then I went to the kitchen to get a Diet Coke.

Simon and Lori were in there and nobody else. They

were standing between the refrigerator and the door to the garden.' 'Close the door behind you Lo' Lori asked me and I did. 'Why?' I asked. 'Just circle and don't let anybody come in' she said. I did but a second later I looked behind me and sure enough Anne there they were like kissing fish slurp slurp slurp. He had his hand down the front of her pants. When I saw that I got out of the kitchen right away. Katherine was back over in the corner and she looked like she was trying not to cry.

'What happened?' I asked but she wouldn't tell me. The Snowman was with his buddies laughing. 'Did he say something mean to you?' I asked but she didn't say anything. 'Do you want to go home?' She shook her head and I said okay. I hate it when you know something's wrong with your friends and they won't tell you what it is. When something bothers me I usually tell whoever's around. But not always, really. Even though what I saw Simon and Lori doing bothered me I didn't tell Katherine. I wasn't going to say anything to anybody. Then Lori came out of the kitchen. She walked over like she was going to hit me but didn't.

'What's your agenda?' she asked me. She whispered so nobody would hear but of course Katherine did. 'Nothing' I said. 'Did you look?' Lori asked. 'I didn't want to be in the room while you were doing that. You were almost doing it.' 'I didn't know he was going to do that' she said and I knew she was telling the truth. Lori hides what she thinks in her face worse than Mama and Daddy do. Simon was back over where his buddies were and they were all laughing and I was mad because I could tell they were laughing at us. Boys always laugh at girls no matter what they do.

'Oh sure' I said. Even though I believed her I was so mad at her. 'It hurt so I told him to stop. If you'd have stayed in there he wouldn't have done it.' 'He would have.' 'You were watching then' she said. 'Saw it all' I said. 'If I'd stayed in there he'd have wanted to do it to me too' I said. That made her go post office. 'You think you're treat city'

31

she said. 'Well I wasn't going to stay in there while you two were fishfacing' I said. 'I'm going home now.' 'Go ahead.' So I went into the hall closet and got my coat. Katherine came over while I was there and got her coat too. 'Can I walk with you' she said, she didn't ask because she knew I'd say sure, which I did. 'Bye' I shouted at everybody as we left.

'Say goodbye to the queers everybody' Lori said and that made me pipe so I almost ran back in to hit her. Then I thought that would just make things worse so I didn't. Nobody else said anything anyway. The boys laughed, but I don't care what boys do. They may hurt some girls but not me.

It was nine-thirty and I didn't have to be home till ten so I was happy walking Katherine home. 'Lori's so stupid' I said. 'She's always telling on what other people do and then she does the same things herself. I hate her.' Katherine didn't say anything and I could tell she was still upset. 'What's the matter?' I asked her. 'Nothing' she said. 'Did the Snowman say something mean to you?' I asked her. 'He was just stupid like you said.' 'What did he say?' 'Nothing' she said but I know he did but I'll never know what he said unless she tells me and she won't.

We walked down Park to her building. I looked down 78th Street and saw searchlights in Long Island and I wondered what was doing over there tonight. Katherine asked me something but I couldn't hear her because of the sirens. 'Will you go upstairs with me?' she asked again and I said okay. She looked like she was ready to flood. 'If something had you racked would you tell me?' I asked. 'Sure' she said but she fudged and didn't look at me. We rode in the elevator which opens up at her front door. Before she got out her keys her father opened the door. He's tall and skinny with gray bushy hair and looks like a mushroom. He stood there with his arms blocking the door and then he started screaming like I wasn't there. Blah blah blah blah. Didn't I tell you you could only stay out an hour he said. Can't you tell time? What am I supposed to do with you?

'You're supposed to hit me' she told him and she ran inside under his arm. He turned around and slammed the door. I didn't know what to do Anne so I rode back downstairs. When I got outside I looked up but I couldn't see the lights in their windows because they live in the rear. I stood outside for a long time until the doorman said something to me and then I walked away. I walked up Park as fast as I could to 79th and then I crossed the street. There were only a few people out and they didn't pay any attention to me. At 81st this bum came around the corner. He was talking to himself and I don't even know if he saw me but I ran up the street anyway until I got to the next block. I had to wait to cross at 86th because of all the fire trucks going downtown but as soon as I could I ran and then got to our building and went inside. The man in the gutter was still there.

Mama was sitting in the living room staring at bills. Daddy wasn't in his study and I figured he'd gone to bed already. I could tell Mama had had a couple of somethings because she could hardly keep her eyes open and it wasn't ten yet. 'My darling you're home by yourself you should have called and I'd have come down and walked you home.' 'I'm all right' I said. 'Did you have a good time with your little friends sweetie?' 'It was all right.' 'Oh darling you must be starving come in the kitchen so we can put some more meat on those little bones.' She fixed me a cheese sandwich and a glass of apple juice and sat with me while I ate it, though I wasn't really hungry and just wanted to be by myself. But I didn't want to upset her so I stayed up until she got sleepy which wasn't long.

Anyway Anne I've been writing for over an hour. I want to go to sleep now too. I'm so tired I bet I just drop right off. So night night.

* * *

33

When I woke up this morning I didn't know where I was even though of course I was in my own bed in my own room. Before I got up I lay there for a long time thinking how I was still mad at Lori and wondering why Katherine's father seemed so mad. I don't know why Katherine said what she said to him except to make him mad. I'm glad I have my parents and not hers. Daddy never would hit me but if he did I'd hit him back.

Mama finally knocked and came in and 'Darling you must be so tired you're just lying here like a lox all morning.' 'No I feel fine' I said. 'Boobster says she's got something and I was afraid you might both have come down with whatever plague it is. Nothing's the matter sweetie?' she asked. 'No' I said and got up. I didn't really lie to her Anne because there was nothing wrong that I wanted to talk about.

Lori called at eleven. 'What do you want?' I asked her. She said she was sorry she yelled at me and called us queers in front of everybody. 'If you're scoring me that's one thing but there's no reason to cut Kat' I said and then I told her how Katherine's father acted. I didn't tell her about the bruise I saw on her because then she'd want to know how I saw it and it's none of Lori's business. 'I think we should do something' I said. 'There's nothing we can do Lo if that's what's happening and she wanted to spill she would' Lori said. 'Kat never spills anything' I said. 'That's her cross' Lori said.

I accepted her apology after making her squirm a little longer. I told her she better be careful with Simon because if her parents ever caught them she'd be in trouble. Lori can be so bad, she's always getting into something and I know Miss Taylor's threatened to suspend her before. She really is a viper. 'Well you seem awfully obsessed about it' Lori said and I didn't say anything because I didn't want to get into a fight all over again.

Anyway so we talked some more. We agreed that Icky

Betsy is as icky as they come and how dumb Susie acts and how Whitney thinks she's really mature and she's not. Lots of fun but then she had to get off the phone because she had to call somebody and she had to make the call outside. I know she meant she was calling Simon. If Lori keeps sneaking around like she's doing she's going to get the chair.

After I talked to Lori I tried calling Katherine but the answering machine was on. She never called me back though I left my usual message. This afternoon I kept thinking about what happened, how triple crazy her father acted and the way Lori acts around Simon and those stupid boys including Mister Toad. People go twisto when they get wrapped up in each others life. I guess that's the reason they go post office sometimes. It's so crazy.

Daddy finished his new story and he'll be going out to Los Angeles tomorrow to see if he can find any suckers. He still hasn't said what it's about. If they buy it by the time he finishes rewriting it for them it'll be another movie anyway. Aunt Chrissie called Mama from California and that did Mama in as usual. They hate each other but talk once a week. Chrissie always calls but Mama never hangs up, she just sits and listens to her blab. 'What did Chrissie have to say?' I asked when Mama got off the phone. 'Oh darling it was grotesque as always she said she and goofy Alan (that's her husband) were buying semiautomatics because they think there'll be an uprising of the maids and gardeners' Mama said. Daddy says they've seen too many movies.

Boob isn't feeling well. She has a cold so naturally she acts like it's pneumonia. Daddy brought her lunch and dinner in bed. I got to help him wash little Queenie's dishes. She keeps saying she has TB because she's coughing but there's only been ten girls at Brearley who have it, all in the older classes. When Mama recovered from talking to Chrissie she ran into Boob's room going 'Darling you don't have a fever yet but you might sweet sweetie.' Boob coughed louder of course. 'I do' she said. 'It's beri beri.' Please. Well that's all for now Anne.

P.S. I'm writing you again late tonight Anne. What happened last night still bothers me and I couldn't sleep. I went into the kitchen and turned on the TV to watch with the sound down before I wrote you again. Channel 9 had on the Dead Baby Hour. That's what I call it. It's an infomercial that shows pictures of dead babies in buckets while the narrator talks about liberal homosexual baby killers. It's so gross but you just keep watching it because you can't believe how disgusting it is. There's one baby that looks like a codger with an axe in his head. They keep showing it till you want to heave but you keep watching. Mama and Daddy saw the infomercial once about a month ago and couldn't believe it. Mama's sister Chrissie gives money to the Tombs of the Unborn Babies foundation and goes to protests constantly. That's one of the reasons she and Mama hate each other. Mama looks at Boob with her My L'il Fetus and says 'Oh Cheryl darling you little Boob you're going to grow up and be one of those awful people too throwing your children in front of cars at clinics like Chrissie does.' But Boob says 'I won't kill my babies just other peoples' and laughs. She would, too.

MARCH 10

Monday again. Daddy went out to Newark to fly to Los Angeles after I left for school. Boob stayed home with her double pneumonia TB. Exams and worse this week. No problem for me but they're so boring. Today I saw Katherine at lunchtime when I went to the cafeteria. She was sitting by herself reading a book. I figured she wanted to be left alone. She waved at me but then started reading again. Then Ms Cutler told her to sit with other girls because it wasn't good to be by yourself even if you were studying and wanted to be left alone. She walked over to where I was sitting and sat down with me but didn't say anything. 'How are you?' I asked and she just nodded. She hadn't combed her hair this morning. 'Aren't you going to talk?' I asked.

'I'll see you later' she said and then she got up and left. I think she might be worried that the people who heard Lori call us queers are running around telling everybody that we are. Maybe that's why she didn't want to sit with me very long but I hope not.

Lori was coming in as I was leaving. 'See you in Algebra tomorrow' I said. 'Oh no you won't' she said. 'Why?' I asked. 'I won't be coming in. It's done I already told Miss Taylor' she said. 'Why aren't you coming in?' 'I'll be busy' she said and smiled and wouldn't tell me anything else. I'm sure Simple Simon is involved. They'll probably both skip and go hang. It's spring break next week, I don't know why she just doesn't wait till then to see him unless she's going somewhere with her parents. If she's going to skip she'll get caught again, Anne, I know she will. The last time she tried she forged her mother's handwriting but she misspelled half the words so Miss Taylor didn't fall for it. I don't know what she told Miss Taylor this time.

After class we all had to get cholera shots because of the mess in the river from Long Island. Brearley is right by the East River with only the FDR in between. When we look across the river we can see the smoke and helicopters. My arm still hurts like it's on fire. Two of the girls in tenth grade got sick, they had an allergy or something. Melissa Cassidy told me one of them died but she believes anything she hears. I think Boob pretended to be sicker than she is so she could avoid getting her shot today. She's not dumb that Boob.

That's all for today. Time to study. Some people are actually rereading <u>Silas Mariner</u>! They're even crazier than my family.

MARCH 11
Lori wasn't in school today so she must have been telling the truth. I hope she knows what she's doing but I doubt it.

Boob's feeling better now. Of course she's still playing up

being sick for all it's worth. I asked her if she needed an iron lung. 'What is it?' Boob asked. 'I want it I need it' she said. Daddy is still in Los Angeles. He called her this morning to say he hoped she was feeling better and he'd be home at the end of the week. He'd be home sooner he said but he hadn't been able to meet with the producers. They couldn't leave their office because of the gunfire. Daddy said they were calling from underneath their desks.

'He didn't call Booz' Boob said. 'He called me because I'm el numero uno. No calls for Booz. She's a dumpster baby.'

'Shut up Boob' I said. 'He called you because you were home and you stayed home just so you wouldn't have to get a shot.'

'Show me where they poked you' she said. I pulled up my sleeve and showed her. My arm's all bruised green and yellow and looks disgusting. It still hurts. 'Booz can take my shot for me. A double shot for Booz.'

'And an Army physical for Boob' I said, jumping on her bed. I grabbed the candle out of her candlestick on her bed table and rolled her over and sat on top of her back so she couldn't get up. 'Time to take Boob's temperature' I said. 'Get the vaseline.'

'No' Boob screamed and I shoved her face in her pillow. She started kicking her feet like she was swimming.

'It's a very high fever' I said and spanked her with the candle. 'Jungle rot too. We'll have to operate.'

'Get off' Boob shouted and kept kicking. She almost stopped crying so I got off.

'Who's numero uno' I said.

'You're looking at her' Boob said and laughed.

Mama knocked and came in and said 'Oh darling I heard you two laughing are you helping poor Boob get better?' she asked. 'She's trying to kill me' Boob said. 'My sweeties you're both so comical what do you want to eat tonight?' 'Food' Boob said. 'Lots of food' I said. 'But then I have to study.' 'Oh yes you're so smart you both are.'

Boob put on her robe and sat at the kitchen table with me and Mama. She put away the food like we'd been starving her for years. I asked Mama if Daddy said anything about how the director liked this script when he called since I knew the director met him at the airport. 'No my darling he was suspiciously vague about it' she said. 'That's not good' I said. 'It's not sweetie but you never know. I hope he comes home soon I'm scared with him out there with all those loonies.' 'How come nobody's making movies now?' Boob asked. 'Everybody likes movies.' 'I know sweetie but everything's in such an uproar. And movies cost so much money now and nobody has money even in Hollywood. They spent it like water and now they're thirsty.' 'Everybody's thirsty' said Boob. Mama said 'I know I know, your father says things aren't really so bad but it just seems that way because it's been so long since they've been good he has no basis for comparison anymore.' 'Are things getting worse?' I asked. Mama nodded.

We turned on the news and they were showing pictures of the fires in Beverly Hills. We watched but we didn't see Daddy. They said no one was killed today. 'Nobody important was killed today' Boob said and smiled.

MARCH 11

Daddy called Mama today to say he was fine and there was no problems near his hotel. The producers finally got out of their office once the Guard came into the neighborhood. He was going to meet them this afternoon. He said he'd be back tomorrow because the trouble was all quieted down around the airport. 'He says it looks worse on TV but sweetie everything does' Mama said.

Bigger news here Anne. I can hardly believe it. At lunch Whitney told me she was in the office this morning and Lori came in and went right into Miss Taylor's office. She couldn't hear what they were saying. After a few minutes Lori ran out and left the building.

This afternoon when I got home before she told me about Daddy Mama said 'Oh sweetie you haven't seen or heard from Lori have you tell me you have.' 'I haven't' I said. 'Miss Taylor called Lori's mother this morning and told her she'd suspended Lori and now Lori hasn't come home.' Mama said. 'Why was she suspended?' I asked. 'Darling she tried to pull a fast one. She wasn't in school yesterday was she?' 'No' I said. 'This morning she came in and gave Miss Taylor a note but it was a forgery and not a very good one it seems. She suspended her right then and there and Lori didn't go home and now nobody knows where she is.' 'Is Lori in trouble?' I asked. 'The biggest sort of trouble' Mama said and her eyes were wide as mine.

Well Anne if you're going to skip school you have to figure out how not to get caught. I'm sure Lori thought she had but obviously not. Anytime she's caught she tries to lie and she's the worst liar. I've never skipped school myself. I don't see why I would but if I ever did I wouldn't get caught. They always believe me at school when I'm fibbing but they never believe Lori even when she's telling the truth.

So now nobody knows where Lori is. I called Tanya and Susie. Whitney had told them what happened but nobody's heard anything from Lori. Maybe she's gone home by now. I hope nothing's happened to her but you never know. Like Mama says it's hard to believe how many perverts are out there waiting to get their hands on tender geese like us. She was probably with Simon if she could find him and get her paws on him.

Boob went back to school today and they gave her her shot. She's got a bruise twice as big as mine and it's swollen a little. She's such a baby. 'It'll fall off Boob' I told her. 'Quit it hurts' she said. 'It'll stop hurting once the gangrene sets in. It'll turn all black and fall off unless you die first' I said. 'Stop' she started yelling and then she stopped crying. Then I did stop. It's a good thing the swelling started going down because if it had kept getting bigger we'd have never heard the end of it. She'd have wanted us to amputate it after all.

A credit agency kept calling us tonight. Mama looked very sad when she got off the last time they called. 'Did they say something mean to you?' I asked. 'Yes darling but that's what they're paid to do so you can't take it personally' she said. 'Why not?' I asked. If somebody says something mean to me they don't get away with it that's for sure. She just shook her head.

Tonight I studied civics and how the government works even though everybody says it doesn't anymore. I haven't prayed for a long time but I prayed for Lori tonight. Night night Anne.

MARCH 12
After I wrote you last night I went to sleep. Then about an hour later I heard loud noises outside so I got up and looked out the window. A huge gang of kids were running down 86th Street with policemen and cop cars coming after them. When they got to Lexington they ran north. They broke out windows in HMV and turned over the newsstand in front of the movie theater. The police kept chasing them and I guess they caught some of them though there wasn't anything about it on the news. The stores were boarded up this morning but otherwise it looked normal. Last night though it made me scared. I started thinking about Lori again and I didn't get back to sleep for a long time.

I'm glad I've only got one test tomorrow that I had to study for because I'm going to sleep early tonight, I'm so tired and it hasn't been a good day Anne.

Lori was already home by the time I saw the street gang as it turns out. An older girl who knows Lori's brother Tom and talked to him last night told Tanya's sister and she told us this morning. So Lori wasn't murdered in the street after all. But what is happening to her is almost as bad we all think. Lori's parents are putting her in a toughlove camp in

41

New Jersey. They've been threatening to do it for ages but I never thought they would.

'What do they do to you there?' Icky Betsy asked. She ought to go to bulimic camp.

'They shave your head' Whitney said. 'They tie you to your bed at night with big belts and they sharpen the buckles on the belts.'

'How do you know?' I asked. 'Because I know' Whitney said. "You weren't ever in one' Icky Betsy said. 'No but I've read about people who were and heard stories.' 'Why do they sharpen the buckles?' I asked. 'Because when you wake up in the night and have to go to the bathroom you not only cut yourself when you try to sit up then you're pinned down' she said. 'How do you go to the bathroom?' Icky Betsy asked. 'You don't they electrify the bed springs and when you pee you get electrocuted.' 'You don't know that' I said. 'I do' she said. 'Then everybody would die' Tanya said. 'It's not a strong electrocution just enough to hurt' Whitney says. I still don't think she knows what she's talking about.

Daddy came home from Los Angeles this afternoon. Me and Mama and Boob were so glad to see him. He brought necklaces he bought for us, pretty gold strands. They're not real gold I don't think. We put them on right away and of course five minutes later Boob's fell off and she lost it. We found it though. At dinner he talked about his trip but mainly about how everyone was handling the riots. I asked if his producers ever came out from under their desks and he said they did. They think the air force should bomb the neighborhoods, Daddy said. He didn't think that was a good idea. On TV they said that's what they were thinking about doing though so I bet they do. We asked if they bought his movie and he didn't say they did. He said it was under consideration but that almost always means no. He didn't act like he was sad or anything but he was fudging. Daddy was real jetlagged and he went to bed early tonight.

Then a really bad thing happened Anne. I tried calling

Lori's house. Her mother picked up the phone and when I told her it was me she said I wasn't allowed to talk to Lori anymore. 'Why not?' I said but she hung up on me. 'That's so incredibly rude my darling let me take care of this' Mama said when I told her. An hour later she called Lori's house. When Mama got off the phone she told me what was going on.

'She said she was sorry for hanging up on you sweetie but it's what she's been told to do' Mama said. 'Who told her?' I asked. 'The toughlove goons angel they say when a child enters their programs they have to stop talking to all their friends because it's impossible to tell which one led them astray' she said. 'I never did' I said. 'Oh sweetie I know but that's what they tell them to do.' 'She can't even talk to Katherine?' 'No angel no you're all heathens in their eyes.' 'That's not fair.' 'No angel' Mama said. 'Can she talk to us when she gets out?' 'I don't know sweetie I gather they give you such a brainwashing in those places you don't even know who you are anymore.' 'Lori may not ever talk to me again because she did something her parents didn't like?' I asked. Mama nodded. 'That's not right' I said. 'No sweetie' said Mama.

I tried to call Katherine again but naturally nobody answered the phone. I didn't even leave a message this time. After Boob went beddybye Mama told me Daddy said it doesn't look like anything's going to sell anytime soon. We'll have to figure out something else to get by. 'What kind of something else?' I asked but Mama didn't say.

MARCH 13
Friday the 13th has always been my lucky day Anne and this was no exception. This morning I took my Music test and zipped right through it. Now it's finally Spring break! Hooray!

Then I hadn't been home five minutes when Lori called!

Her father was at work and her mother went to the bank. Her brother Tom let her call me because he thought it was bone that she wasn't allowed to talk to anyone. 'Are you all right?' I asked her. 'No' 'When are you leaving?' 'Tomorrow morning I'm scared' 'How long are you there?' 'Six weeks' 'Can you talk to me when you get back?' 'I better' she said. Then her mother came home and she hung up before her mother could tell that she was on the phone with anyone. I wish I could have said goodbye but we didn't have time.

Mama said the name of the place they're sending her to is the Kure-A-Kid Rehab 12 Step Center in Upper Montclair, New Jersey. 'Will they shave her head?' I asked Mama. 'Probably something terrible like that sweetie they're nothing but concentration camps with video games from everything I've read.' 'You and Daddy wouldn't ever send me to one would you?' 'Oh my darling never never in a million years no matter how awful you were' she said. I'm sort of curious as to what one of those camps is like but I wouldn't want to have to go to one.

Boob was sitting there fiddling with her My Li'l Fetus. It lost one of its arms somehow. She kept getting up and looking in the refrigerator. 'What are you doing Boob?' I asked. 'I'm looking for Lori on milk cartons' she said. 'She came home already they're not putting her on milk cartons' I said. 'Maybe the one they've got's an impostor' Boob said. 'You're crazy Boob' 'How are they brainwashing her?' Boob asked. 'They're changing her sweetie' Mama said. 'How?' 'I don't know' Mama said. 'Are they washing her brain with soap or detergent?' 'Shut up Boob' I said. 'They're sticking her head in the washing machine' Boob said and laughed. 'Lori's in the spin dryer.' 'It's not funny Boob' I said. 'My darlings you're both such funsters' Mama said. Then she made us go in the living room so she could finish dinner.

Boob hopped up in Daddy's lap when he came out of his study and sat down. That was always fun. I've gotten much too big for that now, I'm almost as tall as he is. He hugged us. Things could be better, he told us, but the weekend's here at least and we should really enjoy ourselves. Boob squealed like a piggy and I was glad too but Daddy seems so sad. He's not telling us what's really going on. I don't know if I want to know. But he's right the weekend's here and Spring break too.

MARCH 14

Today should have been a great day Anne but it wasn't. This morning I was the first one up as usual. The phone rang and I answered it on the first ring. I thought Lori might have gotten away long enough to call me again but it wasn't Lori.

It was a man from Guaranteed Credit Associates. He had a voice that sounded like he had a mouth full of rocks. The first thing he said was when were we paying? 'You want to speak to my parents' I said. No I want to speak to you he said. Why aren't you in temple? 'We don't practice' I said. 'Let me get my father.' Do you like where you're living? he asked. 'Of course I do' I said. If your parents don't pay their bills we can put you in a foster home he said. 'You cannot' I said. We can he said we'll put you in a foster home and you won't see your parents or brothers or sisters ever again. 'I don't have a brother' I said. You know what happens to little girls in foster homes? he asked. I hung up. The phone rang again and I knew it was him again but I answered because I didn't want him to wake Mama and Daddy up. They're raped he said little girls are raped in foster homes your parents better pay their bills. Daddy picked up the phone in their room and I heard him say Who is this? and then I hung up. I heard him yelling and then I heard him slam the phone down so hard I thought he broke it. Mama came out of their room right after that. I was sitting on the couch.

'Oh sweetie what did he say to you?' Mama asked.

45

'Nothing' I said and I should have told her what he said but I didn't. 'Look at me sweetie what did that awful man say to you?' 'Pay the bills' I said. 'He didn't say anything else was he threatening?' I shook my head. I don't know why I didn't tell her what he said about being raped in a foster home. The way he said it made me feel real bad and I bet that's what he used to do to girls in the foster homes he was in. Mama hugged me and said she was so so sorry. 'Why don't you declare bankruptcy?' I asked. 'Oh my darling if we did that again we'd lose everything this time we couldn't' Mama said. 'Then they'll keep calling' I said. 'Michael took the phone off the hook sweetie they won't call again this morning let us answer the phone from now on' Mama said. 'Okay' I said.

She went back to their bedroom and shut the door behind her. I heard them yelling but I didn't want to listen. I turned on the radio and listened to music for a while. Boob woke up and came out and started doing silly dances. 'I'm hiphopping' she kept saying. 'Bad enough.' 'That's not rap it's classical music' I said. 'Get down I'm Rap Queen Cheryl Cherifah' Boob said and she kept dancing until she finally collapsed on the floor. She's recovered completely.

Then Mama came back out and fixed breakfast. We had toasted English muffins with strawberry jam and glasses of milk. After breakfast we got dressed. 'We'll have a wonderful time today my geese we'll ignore the cares of this cruel world.' Then Daddy came out and it looked like he and Mama had made up because they were hugging each other like always. Daddy put his hand on my shoulder and said he was sorry. 'It's all right' I said. It wasn't though. What the credit guy said really bothered me but there wasn't anything Daddy could do about it. Nobody is going to put us in a foster home. I wouldn't go even if they forced me.

Before we went out Mama put the phone back on the hook. It started ringing as we were going out the door.

Daddy answered it in case it was anybody he was waiting to hear from but it wasn't. It was the credit guy again and Daddy hung up.

We went for a walk through the park. It really was a beautiful day today. We went to the Met and saw the exhibit of Moorish art that's going on there. Boob was well behaved but then she always is when we go to museums. I looked around at the other people visiting the museum and wondered if they were having as bad a time as we were. Most of them looked like they were but you can never tell.

We went upstairs to the roof garden. Everybody there was over by the part of the balcony that's closest to Fifth Avenue. Down the side streets and over the buildings we saw big clouds of black smoke coming up from Brooklyn and Queens. The sky was dark like it gets before a bad storm. Nobody could see anything but everybody was looking. We saw flames that looked like fireflies they were so far away from us. 'What is it?' Boob asked. The civil disturbances a man said. They're animals someone else said they oughta blast them. 'Is that thunder?' Boob asked. Guns, Daddy said. Cannons and mortar someone said. The Army will have to come in if the Guard can't handle it another man said. They can't a woman said. 'A civil disturbance is a riot, isn't it?' I asked. Depends, Daddy said. When they said there wouldn't be any riots here I knew they didn't know what they were talking about. 'What are they rioting about?' Boob asked. Everything, Daddy said. Our eyes started stinging so we went back inside.

We had lunch at the coffee shop at Madison and 82nd. I've never heard us be so quiet before. It was the oddest thing Anne, we were quiet like we were still in the museum. I didn't feel like talking myself. I guess no one did, not even Boob. Then we walked down Madison as far as 59th looking at all the stores going out of business. I couldn't remember what half of them used to be and I was almost afraid I had Alzheimer's since I couldn't remember. Mama wished she could still go to Bloomingdale's. You couldn't hear the guns and cannon from where we were on the street because of the traffic. The smoke blew over Manhattan. It got dark like it was going to rain big black drops so we decided to go home.

We rode the bus back. It was crowded. We stood by the back door where we could get on and off fast. I'm GLAD GLAD GLAD we did because at 72nd a crazy man got on. There're crazy men all over but this one was really scary Anne. When he first got on he looked like anybody except the bottoms of his pants legs were torn and muddy and he had a big runny pimple on one cheek that was disgusting. He was five feet away from us. Boob was singing more silly songs to herself and Daddy told her not to attract attention. All of a sudden the crazy man started hitting a little old lady, she was sitting in one of the single seats. She was screaming and he knocked her glasses off and her mouth was bleeding. She hadn't said a word to him, he just picked her out. Mama and Daddy put their arms around us and pushed back against the people standing behind us. The people on the bus grabbed the crazy man and he started hitting them too. The bus driver pulled the bus over and stopped. We buzzed getting off then once we were safe we stopped to watch what happened. A cop car was already there. The cops got on the bus and a few minutes later dragged the crazy man out. They hit him with their clubs. Then Anne this man on the street wearing a suit saw what was going on and he ran over and kicked the crazy man in the head as hard as he could. Boob started crying. People on the street applauded like it was a movie. The cops pushed the man in the suit away and picked up the crazy man and threw him in the back of their car. It was all over then so we left. We walked home and it was such a weird day, we all went to our rooms and shut the doors like we'd been bad. I lay down on my bed and just wanted to go to sleep and I did take a nap. The phone rang a few times and Daddy got it every time but I don't know if it was the credit guy or not.

We watched the news later and naturally there was

48

nothing about the crazy man on the bus who almost killed everybody. They wouldn't let news helicopters fly over Brooklyn and Queens so none of the reporters could say what was going on. The Mayor said everything was under control. ABC news showed the President at his vacation house. Some people on TV said he hasn't been President long enough to know what he's doing but I think he's on Xanax.

If Lori hadn't been sent to Kure-A-Kid I'm sure we'd have spent the day together having loads of fun. I wish we hadn't had that argument. I wish I'd talked to her more. Now I think I'll never get to talk to her again but maybe I will. It's hard to tell, you hear so many stories about what they do to people and what happens when you're not the same person anymore.

Thanks to that nap I couldn't get to sleep again tonight so I thought I'd write you a long story of what happened. You must wonder when if ever I shut up Anne but you're so easy to talk to once I get started I just can't stop. Before I started writing tonight I was watching TV again late and I saw an ad for Kure-A-Kid. It showed a teenage boy goofing solo. He's wearing a heavy metal jacket with a skull on it. He's got pepperoni acne. He's smoking a joint. He starts laughing like he's crazy and then he runs out in the street in front of all these cars. Most of them miss him but then a big truck runs right into him. The actor playing the boy is a stuntman because then they show him being dragged under all the wheels of the truck and getting processed and all this blood spurts like it's hitting the TV screen. When the screen's all red words come on saying Put on the Brake Before it's Too Late. It was a heaver and double bone but they had a commercial on the other night for Drug Free America that was so gross I thought Daddy was going to faint.

I've almost worn myself completely out now Anne so I think that's enough for now. If you had ears you'd be deaf thanks to me. Six weeks from today is April 25. Night night.

MARCH 15

I don't feel like writing today Anne. I'm sorry but that's just how it is sometimes. I'll write you tomorrow I promise.

MARCH 16

It's terrible Anne. Somebody from the realty company came by the apartment and taped a note on the door this morning. I found it when I went down to get the mail. I gave it to Daddy. He took it into his study and didn't come out for a long time. When he finally did come out he didn't say anything. 'What is it?' I asked. Nothing, he said. Later after I made sure Boob was distracted watching some stupid movie on TV I went to Mama and asked her what was the matter. She looked very tired and I think she was taking more something today than she usually does, more Xanax or maybe she's on Prozac again. Her doctor has her take about six different kinds but all any of them seem to do is make her sleepy.

'The landlord's after us my darling making all sorts of threats' Mama said.

'What kind of threats?' I asked. 'Landlord threats my angel' Mama said. 'But don't you or Boobie worry about that Daddy's calling around and talking to some people he knows' she said. 'About getting some work?' I asked. 'Yes sweetie I'm afraid serious steps will have to be taken.' 'Is the landlord mad at us?' 'He wants the rent' Mama said. 'I thought Daddy just paid the rent' I said. Mama nodded her head and said 'November's rent darling we're a little behind.' That was a million years ago and I couldn't believe it. 'What's going to happen then?' 'Oh oh darling don't you worry we'll always take care of you we always will always' Mama said. 'It's a mess but believe me your father has infinite resources.'

I believe her. Right after I talked to Mama Katherine called me and asked if I wanted to do something tomorrow now that it was Spring break. I was so happy to hear from her. Okay I said but I didn't have any money for movies or eating at coffee shops so I asked if she wanted to come over tomorrow and she asked if she could stay over tomorrow night. I asked Mama and she said 'Oh darling any time she's probably all broken hearted about Lori too have her come over and you can commiserate.' So I told her it was okay and she'll come over tomorrow in time for dinner.

Tonight Mama and Daddy went into his study and closed the door and were in there a long time. Boob wore herself out somehow today so I put her to bed early and waited for them to come out. I waited till eleven but they were still in there so I knocked on the door. 'Oh sweetie it's so late come and join us' Mama said. When I went in I saw them at the computer adding up figures and doing math problems. 'Are you making a budget?' I asked. I'd never seen them do it before and I thought it was interesting. 'Oh yes darling and it's a struggle but not a hopeless one' Mama said. Everything was going to be fine, Daddy said. We'd just have to adjust a little.

'Adjust to what?' I asked. 'Changes darling' said Mama. 'If we get evicted are they going to put me and Boob in a foster home?' Daddy got up from his computer and sat next to me on the chair and held my hand. Never, he said, and we weren't going to be evicted. 'You're sure?' I asked and he nodded. 'But how will things change?' I asked. 'We're not completely sure yet sweetie but it won't be permanent' Mama said. 'Not at all. Not at all. Get to bed now baby it's so late. You'll be a little tired duckling in the morning and you won't be able to quack your way around' Mama said. 'Yes I will' I said but as usual that did no good.

Anne now that I've been thinking about it I bet they spent the rent money on Hanukah and Christmas presents for us. I wonder how much all my new furniture and Boob's stuff cost. I wish they hadn't done that but Anne I guess they wouldn't be Mama and Daddy if they hadn't. They're just like Boob, if they want something they just won't feel good until they get it. I'm writing you while sitting at my desk and I'm thinking maybe if they hadn't bought it we'd have the rent. And now I'm here in my room and I'm writing to you on what might be our apartment rent. Night night. I can't wait to see Katherine tomorrow and I'll be writing you the day after I'm sure.

MARCH 18

Daddy was out all day today and yesterday doing something but he didn't tell us what. I think he's trying to line up some work. I'm not sure if he's having much luck. The phone rings all the time but we just let the answering machine take it and Mama turned the volume down so Boob and me don't have to listen to the credit guy or the landlord or anyone else getting after us.

Mama went out for a while this afternoon and then came back looking a little happier. At first I thought she got a new prescription. She was carrying a big box and I asked her what was in it. 'People I know at a publishers gave me a bundle of manuscripts to proofread angel it's a paying job' Mama said. 'Is it a lot of money?' I asked. 'Oh no but it's a help' she said.

Like I warned you I didn't write you yesterday Anne because as I said Katherine came over and spent the night. She was wearing a little green hat and a button that said Kiss Me I'm Irish because it was St Patrick's Day. She'd gone to the parade which is why she didn't come over earlier during the day. Katherine's mother is Irish and it's like being Jewish in that regard, that makes her Irish too. Her mother has beautiful auburn hair and green eyes. Katherine though took after her father sadly. She has mousy brown hair but hers hasn't turned gray yet. I bet it will before she gets to college, she's always so panicky.

Mama worked on the manuscripts she brought home and Daddy watched a movie with Boob in the living room. Katherine and I stayed by ourselves in my room listening to the radio. We talked about Lori and what happened.

Katherine heard for sure that Lori met Simon the day they skipped and they went to Central Park. All they did supposedly was hang out until the middle of the afternoon like they'd been at school all day. Katherine didn't know where Lori hid out the next day after she was suspended but Katherine said she figured she just went to the movies or something, nothing real bad. We both bet that Simon didn't get in trouble.

'Did you ever hear stories about Kure-A-Kid camp?' I asked her.

'Not that one but I heard about another one upstate' Katherine said. 'This girl I knew had an older sister and she had a friend who was sent away.'

'What was it like?' I asked.

'It was awful' Katherine said. What she told me is so amazing but true I have to write it all down for you Anne. 'They locked her in a prison cell the whole time she was there and it didn't have a window. They took her clothes away and then sent over the boys to look at her. Every time they brought her food they said this could be your last meal you better enjoy it. It was always rotten and with worms and things too.'

'That's so gross what happened to her?' I asked.

'The head guard came in with a rope and showed her how to hang herself. They showed her how to tie the knot and how she was supposed to tie it around a pipe in the ceiling. They told her they have to give the parents their money back if the kid doesn't get better but if the kid dies they get to keep the money. They told her if she didn't hang herself they'd come back and hang her themselves and tell her parents she did it. They came back four times that night but she wouldn't hang herself. They got so upset that in the morning they made her go home. They had to give her parents their money back.'

'What happened to her?' I asked.

'She waited till she got home' Katherine said. 'Then she hung herself in her room so her parents would find her and

53

when they did they cried and gave her a huge funeral.'
'That's awful' I said. 'It's a true story it happened to her'
said Katherine. We both hoped that nothing like that
happens to Lori. Maybe Kure-A-Kid isn't as bad as that
place but I bet it is. 'What if you were dead' said Katherine. 'Who would you want to come to your funeral?' 'My
parents and Boob and all my teachers and my friends and
you and Lori' I said. 'And everybody else at Brearley and
the Mayor. What if you were dead then who would you
want to come to your funeral?' I asked. 'I'd want to watch
it' said Katherine.

We got ready for bed because it was getting late. While I
was taking a shower Katherine came in and asked if she
could sleep with me again and I said sure. She sat on the
toilet brushing her teeth while I was washing off. I wondered if she still had that big bruise but she'd already put on
her pajamas and I couldn't see if she did or not. We went
out and told Mama and Daddy and Boob goodnight and
then we went back to bed. As usual we talked and talked
before we went to sleep. I was so happy to see Katherine
again.

'You can tell me now what happened' I said. 'I won't tell
anybody.' She pulled the covers up to her neck so she was
almost completely hidden underneath. 'Tell you what
happened about what?' she said. 'What happened with
your dad after Lori's party' I said. 'Why you've been a
stay at home.' 'They didn't want me to go out for a while
after I came home late' she said. 'Was your dad really mad
at you that night?' 'Yes' she said. We'd already turned the
lights out so I couldn't see her face. 'What did he do to
you?' I asked. She rolled over on her side and faced away
from me. I pulled her back but I still couldn't see her face.
'Don't clam. Did he hit you?' 'Why do you think he hit
me?' she asked. 'When he asked what was he supposed to do
with you you said he was supposed to hit you' I said. 'Why
did you say that?' 'I was mad' she said. She rolled over
again but she kept her head on my pillow. She curled

herself up like a kitten and pushed her butt against me. She was much warmer than Boob and I wondered if she had a fever.

'You were mad because you couldn't stay out longer without getting yelled at?' I asked. 'That's it good night' she said. 'Don't get upset' I said. 'I'm not upset I'm just tired' she said. 'I thought you wanted to stay up' I said. 'I'm really tired Lo good night.'

Like I wrote you the other day Anne it's a pain when you know something's wrong with your friend and she won't tell you what's wrong. Before I fell sleep I thought about what it would be like if I couldn't tell anybody something that happened to me, not like what the credit guy said but something really important. It made me feel creepy and I got scared and I fell asleep before I knew it. In the middle of the night I woke up again. Katherine was lying right against me with her face next to mine. My arm was under her and it was asleep so I pulled it out without waking her up. It was nice having her face there and I kissed her on the cheek. That must have woken her up a little bit because she said don't don't and she rolled away from me all the way. I turned over on my side sorry that I kissed her.

MARCH 19

So much happened today Anne. I'm going to tell you everything because the only way I'll believe it is if I write it all down. Here's what's up. Daddy was out all day. He looked serious like someone died but not as sad this after-noon when he came back in. Mama fixed dinner for us, we had broccoli and chicken and new potatoes. We asked if we could watch the news like we usually do but Mama and Daddy said whatever was going on would only make every-thing else seem worse. Well Boob didn't think anything about that but I knew something must be really the matter because we always watch the news. I could hardly eat I started worrying so much but finally finished.

55

After we ate Daddy said let's go to the living room, we need to talk. 'Talk about what?' Boob asked. Daddy said he'd finally worked some things out and that it was going to be tough but not as bad as he thought it could be. 'You get a contract?' Boob asked. Daddy said no he didn't think he'd be getting any contracts anytime soon though of course you can never tell with Hollywood. 'Things will be very different for a while my darlings' Mama said 'but they won't be different forever no not forever.'

'How different?' Boob said. Then they started telling us. The first thing is that we don't have as much money to spend and they really mean it, they're not just blathering and fudging like sometimes. We're all going to have to cut back where we can. I'm going to sit down with Boob tomorrow and we'll figure out what we don't need. She doesn't know it yet of course. That's not going to be easy because Boob always needs something but if things are as bad as I think it's too bad, she's just going to have to suffer. The next thing Daddy told us is so unbelievable I still don't believe it but it's true. He actually got a job job! He'll be working at the Excelsior Bookstore on 57th Street. He'll be one of the store managers and he'll start work on Monday. Daddy worked in bookstores while he tried to sell what he wrote before me and Boob were born, even before he and Mama were married. 'I thought you said you hated working in bookstores' I said. Daddy said that was true but he's been away from it so long he doesn't think he'll mind doing it for a little while too much. He says he'll quit once the studios start buying again. 'What's the big cheese like?' Boob asked. Daddy said the boss acts nice but he looks like an explosion in a pubic hair factory. Mama laughed a lot. I still can't imagine Daddy working in a store.

'And darlings I'll keep editing horrible manuscripts' Mama said. 'I'm dumbfounded how illiterate writers are these days.' Speak for yourself Daddy said and they both laughed again. 'What's a pubic hair factory?' Boob kept asking and she was laughing too. I started feeling upset because things are obviously really bad Anne but every-body else in my family is acting like there's nothing to worry about. If they just wanted to make the best of it that's okay. But they go manic depressive, everything will be whoopdeedo until it's not and then everything's gloomy-doom. They're so crazy. All I can do is prepare for the worst and that way I won't feel as bad when they crash and then I can cheer them up, maybe.

Then Daddy said remember I told you we might have to move somewhere else for a few months? Boob stopped laughing and got real quiet. Here I thought we weren't going to have to because they never said anything else about it. 'Oh darlings it's as I said it'll just be for a little while' Mama said but I don't think she knows. This is the way it'll work. Daddy says we'll sublet our apartment until he gets his next contract. He was able to get another loan from someone he knows to pay the back rent. Another writer who's in the Western Guild will live here and pay the rent on our apartment plus extra for our trouble. With that and what he makes at work Daddy'll pay the rent on our new apartment. They've already signed the lease. Daddy went to Columbia and he rigged something with them that lets us move into one of their buildings. Not one of their dorm buildings but a regular one. Daddy says it's a safe neighborhood and we'll be able to live cheaper there. Me and Boob will have to share a room again of course. 'Booz and me together again' Boob said. That doesn't make me happy but I expected that might be one of my sacrifices. 'Will we have to leave school?' I asked.

'Oh sweetie never not until they throw you out' Mama said. Daddy says he's paid our tuition for this year and he's sure there'll be money to pay for it next fall. He said he'd talked to Miss Taylor and he thinks everything's worked out. 'What did you tell her?' I asked. He told me not to worry about it. 'I'll keep looking to see if anyone wants to have me as a teacher' Mama said.

Daddy says we're going to have to start packing. We're

going to have to move out next weekend! We'll be leaving a lot of our furniture here but we'll take our beds and the couch and some of the chairs, also chests of drawers and dressers. Daddy says I can take my new desk. Some of our stuff we'll put in storage but everything we need we'll take with us when we move. 'We're not nomads darlings we'll just be carrying our worldly possessions on our slight backs because we won't be gone that long I'm sure of it' Mama said. 'I believe you' I said. 'I'm sure of it darling oh don't worry' Mama said. Then I knew she was trying to convince herself and not me so I didn't say anything else. 'I want to see the new apartment' Boob said. Daddy said we could go over this weekend once the old tenants were out. This weekend is the day after tomorrow.

Mama and Daddy gave us hugs and kisses. Daddy said it'd be tough but it was a good thing not to get too spoiled. 'Were you spoiled?' I asked and Daddy said no. 'Darling he was so rotten you couldn't stay in the same room with him his mama said' Mama said. 'We're not spoiled either we're precious jewels' Boob said and then it was hee hee hee all around again. When we finished talking Boob went into her room to go to bed and didn't come out the rest of the night even when I knocked. I wanted to talk to her tonight to see how she felt. When I opened the door I saw she was already asleep. She was wearing her My L'il Fetus which now has no arms. She doesn't know what happened to them but I think she probably ate them in her sleep.

The only thing I can say about how I feel is that I don't feel good. I always have had this fear Anne that we wouldn't be able to live as good as we do forever and I'm afraid I'm being proven right. Once we move I guess I'll have a better idea of what it's going to be like living some other way. I'm lying on the floor to write this. I hate my stupid bed and desk and I don't want to take them along. I know that's childish but it's the way I feel right now and I'm not sorry. I don't want to move Anne I don't.

Night night.

Today was Friday and the last week of Spring break. When I woke up it was early so I went in Boob's room. She was still snoozing away so I sat down and shook her. 'Scram' she said when she saw it was me. 'Are you okay Boob?' I asked. 'I want to sleep' she said. 'We have to get up so we can start packing Boob so get up' I said. 'Don't want to get up.' 'You have to.' 'Don't want to.'

As you can imagine Anne it went on like that for some time before I finally got Boob sitting up conscious. 'How do you feel Boob?' I asked. 'About what?' 'About having to move' I said and she lay down in bed again. 'Too sleepy' she said. 'I mean move out of the apartment somewhere else' I said. 'We'll be back' she said. 'It's like when we went to London. We had another apartment then.' 'That was just for the summer Boob and of course we came back then' I said. 'This is different.' 'No it's not' she said.

She never would look at me while we were talking and finally I gave up. If she's not upset there's no sense trying to make her upset, it'll happen soon enough. Anyway once everybody got up and we had breakfast we spent the whole day packing and getting rid of stuff. We cleaned out the foyer closet and the hall closets and everything in the laundry room. Mama had Boob sorting piles into other piles to keep her busy. Once we had the closets done Mama went back to editing manuscripts. I can tell she's upset but she's acting like nothing's wrong at all.

On the news tonight they said everything is calmed down in Brooklyn but they have other riots in other places in Long Island. The Mayor was saying he was going to ask the President to bring in more of the Army. They said the President was busy and didn't say if he would or wouldn't yet.

Tonight I can't write you as much as I've been writing. It's very late and I'm about to fall over. Every muscle I've got is ripped and I can hardly walk I'm so tired. More packing tomorrow. Will write tomorrow unless I have a complete breakdown.

I woke up before anybody else did this morning. I was so stiff I knew I should move around and get loosened up. I went in the living room and was doing exercises. This being Saturday morning the credit guy called again. I recognized his voice right away and tried to hang up on him before he had a chance to say anything mean. Didn't work though because he recognized me and said ooh they're going to get you. 'Shut up' I said and hung up and took the phone off the hook. I thought at first Daddy hadn't paid off all the bills yet, but then I wondered if maybe the credit guy was calling back trying to get me like he was making obscene phone calls. It wouldn't surprise me.

After twenty minutes of exercising I felt much better. My gym teacher Miss Norris told me I'm very strong for my age and should think about going out for tennis or even fencing. I'm almost as tall as Daddy is now and I'll probably be stronger than he is before you know it. Daddy isn't exactly macho after all. I'm glad he's not, I couldn't stand him if he was. He'd be like those stupid boys at Lori's party that we're always having to fend off. He went to a mixed school and not a boy's school and I think that helped. Going to a boy's school just makes them worse, I think.

When I got dressed I came back in the living room and sat on the couch for a while watching the light come in the window as the sun came up. The fireplace got all gold first and then white again. Where Daddy took some of the paintings down the wall is much lighter and I can't believe how dirty the paint is. Our living room is ours Anne, it's nobody else's. I'm going to miss it so much even if they're all right and we do come back soon. I've never even thought about living somewhere else forever before. Even when we lived in London that summer I knew we'd be back soon and the last week we were there I couldn't wait to come back.

Nobody was up still so I went into my room and started going through my chest of drawers. Luckily I threw out a lot of junk when my new furniture that I hate so much now came last month, so it wasn't hard sorting it out. Daddy brought home boxes from the liquor stores on 86th yesterday and so I started packing away like a pack rat. When everybody else woke up they got to work too. I can't believe how much we're throwing out that I've never even seen. I don't think Mama and Daddy have ever cleaned out any of their stuff before.

This afternoon Daddy boxed up six boxes of his books and took them to the Strand downtown. He has thousands of books so that doesn't seem that many Anne but I've never known him to get rid of any before, he loves all of his books so much. 'Oh darling they're nothing they're just old college textbooks and full of silly nonsense now we went to school so long ago' Mama said. But I've looked for books for school when we've gone to the Strand before and they don't sell textbooks. So they must have been real books.

I love my books too but I don't have nearly as many as Mama and Daddy. I'd never get rid of any of mine either, unless I had to like I think Daddy has had to. Mine are all packed up now and ready to go and so are my summer clothes and my old stuffies and so much of everything of mine. Boob and Mama went through everything in her messy room today and tried to straighten it out. Boob wasn't goofing like usual, and I asked her if she was feeling all right. 'Tummy troubles' she said and slapped My L'il Fetus like she was trying to hurt it. 'I got an ulcer.'

Anne I'd write more but I'm too too tired. Maybe I ought to exercise more like I did this morning. We're going to go over to the new apartment tomorrow. I'll let you know everything about how it looks.

MARCH 22
Today Sunday was the first day we saw the new apartment where we'll be staying. I can't call it our new apartment because it'll never be ours like our apartment is. It's not

new at all, it's much older than ours. It's in an old red brick building at the corner of Tiemann Place and Broadway right below 125th Street. It's the most northern part of Morningside Heights. Boob calls it Alaska. Above 125th Street is Harlem. The subway is an el on Broadway at Tiemann and goes over a gigantic iron bridge that's all rusty and dirty. Old broken down cars are parked underneath. Mama and Daddy say we shouldn't catch the subway there. We can catch the bus to the east side on Broadway at 123rd and then ride over to Fifth Avenue and then we can catch the 86th Street bus to East End and then walk down to Brearley. We have to leave for school an hour earlier every morning to get there on time. I'll never get enough sleep again!

Daddy says the neighborhood looks worse than it really is. A lot of Columbia people live there and some of the buildings on the north side of Tiemann are even co-ops though I can't believe it. The people on the street all look poor and unhappy. Tiemann Place only goes two blocks and then it ends at Riverside Park. Daddy says we shouldn't go in, it's much more dangerous than Central Park which is much nicer anyway.

The apartment itself is really bad Anne and I'm not just saying that because it's not ours. The floors are all worn out and the walls are cracked. It's sort of big but not nearly as big as our place and not at all as nice. There's a living room and a small room like a dining room and two bedrooms and a kitchen and a bathroom. Daddy is going to use the small room to write in. A long dark hall connects everything. It seems like it'll be really hot in the summer though we're bringing air conditioners to put in the windows in our bedrooms. There're only two closets in the whole place and they're all crumbly inside.

'It's a slum' Boob said and Daddy said it wasn't, it was student housing. He said we were getting a bargain because they always charged students more. Mama didn't look very happy with the place but she didn't say anything. I think

62

she was doing more medication today than usual because she was very quiet and seemed to drift off all the time whenever she sat down. After we saw the apartment we walked down Broadway. Nobody I saw looked much like a student until we got closer to Columbia. The buildings along Broadway where the campus is are all being strung up with barbed wire because the crime is so bad and the people at the gate looked like real policemen with machine guns like at the airport. Even the students didn't look much like students somehow.

We took the bus home catching it at 110th and riding over and then down Fifth. When we got back to our apartment we heard an echo when we walked in because some of the rugs are already rolled up and the curtains are down in Daddy's study. He says they were expensive enough and he doesn't want anything to happen to them while someone else is living there. The walls are covered with lighter spaces now like they have measles. We've been stacking the boxes in the front room where it'll be easier to get them when it comes time to move.

Daddy went to bed early as he has to go to work in the morning. Mama says it's the first time he's had to go to a job since he was thirty-five. He's fifty now and Mama's forty-seven. It seems to me that they're getting pretty old for all these changes and that's strange because I never really thought of them as old before. I sat in the living room tonight with Mama while she cleaned out a chest of drawers. It was very sad. 'Oh sweetie look at this silly picture of Michael and me' Mama said and she showed me an old photo of them in Rockefeller Center. It was Christmas and the tree was up behind them. 'If your father was taller it'd look like the star was coming out of his head' Mama said. 'Were you married then?' I asked. 'Were we?' she asked looking at the photo. 'I think we were darling but it's hard to tell with old pictures it could have been taken anytime.' She threw the photo on the pile of stuff she was throwing out. 'Don't do that I want it' I said. 'Oh angel I didn't mean to throw it there so certainly rescue it and if you want it sweetie you keep it next to your heart' Mama said. 'I'll keep it in my diary' I said and here it is right now, tucked in this page. Then we talked about you Anne.

'Have you been writing something every day?' Mama asked. 'Just about' I said. 'Oh sweetie there's been so much bad news lately it must be a tearjerker of a book' she said. 'No it's just what happens good and bad nothing else' I said. She pulled out an old ashtray that was in the shape of a big red foot. 'Look at this silly thing darling Michael used it when he used to smoke look what it says' Mama said. I read what it said which was I Get A Kick Out of Rhode Island. 'I can't remember what we were doing up there but it must have been interesting' Mama said. She got up to throw it in the glass recycle garbage in the kitchen and I followed her. All the pots and pans were down on the countertops but she hadn't boxed any of them up yet.

'Are we really going to come back here?' I asked. 'You mean to the apartment sweetie?' she asked. 'Yes' I said. 'Oh yes my darling don't worry we will I just don't know when' Mama said.

I don't know Anne. I don't think we are coming back here. I don't have any reason to say that except that I think it's true. We'll be here ten more days and then that'll be it. We move into the new apartment that will never be ours April Fool's Day. The weekend before actually but that's close enough for us fools.

MARCH 23

Back to school for us. Boob was whinola this morning before we left but as soon as we got inside she was running around like she owned the place again. Everyone who likes me was glad to see me. I asked Katherine and Whitney and Susie and everybody, but nobody had heard anything from Lori. Her parents must and Kure-A-Kid must keep her lidded pretty good. Whitney said she had tried to find out from

Tom what was going on but no go. Lori's parents hired an answering service and it's impossible to get through direct anymore. She said she left two messages but they must burn them.

None of the teachers said anything about Lori being gone. I asked Miss Wisegarver if she'd heard anything from her, Lori was always a favorite of hers. 'Take your seat, Lola' was all she said just like I hadn't said anything and like Lori never existed. It was creepy strange. I don't know why they're acting so funny like that about Lori, it wasn't like she'd done anything that bad. Maybe Kure-A-Kid has something to do with the way they're acting. If someone goes there then they don't exist anymore.

That wasn't the strangest thing today though, Anne. What was most weird was that Boob and me were home hours before Daddy. He started working at nine because the boss Mister Mossbacher wanted him to come in early on his first day. Daddy said he found his being there so useful that now he wants Daddy to come in early every day though he still won't get off until six. Daddy'll be working Monday through Friday. He gets half an hour for lunch. Even me and Boob get an hour! Daddy says he thinks the job will be all right but he doesn't seem excited about it. We asked him what he did and he said he was on bag check all afternoon because three of the people who should have been there didn't show up and Mister Mossbacher didn't want him to handle money downstairs until there were enough people upstairs to watch out for shoplifters.

Daddy must have looked everywhere before he found this job. I took out a box of paper trash this afternoon when I got home that Mama had gotten from their bedroom. On top were copies of a hundred letters he sent out to places asking about jobs. I asked Mama if those were places that didn't answer him. 'It's very tough times sweetie' said Mama 'and certain to get tougher all the time.'

Boob was all kissy with Daddy when he got home and I was too but in my own way. We seemed to make him feel a

65

lot better. I don't mind giving him some sympathy but it spoils somebody if that's all you do, I think. Mama and Boob say I'm being very cruel but Daddy agrees with me, or at least he has in the past. He might feel different today. He's fudging when he says he likes his new job, I can tell.

MARCH 24

They killed the President today so they let us out of school early. They shot him while he was going from a building to his car. I didn't like him but he was the President so I should feel sad they said at school but I don't really. The new President is the guy everybody always makes fun of. 'Oh my angel all any of them know how to do is play golf it's such a horror' Mama said. Mama also said that when President Kennedy was assassinated everybody was sad but nobody else seemed especially sad today either so I guess I'm not the only one.

It's hard enough to keep packing this week now that Daddy's working and Boob and me are back in class. We can only do it at night pretty much and so I just want to warn you Anne you'll probably suffer this week because I think I'm going to be too tired to write much, especially if the other nights are like this one. Not that we were moving anything heavy or anything else really bad happened, but there's just so much stuff.

Before they told us the President had been shot I saw Katherine. She was crying at lunch today. I thought someone had done something mean to her again, but they hadn't it was just me moving away. 'But I'll still see you all the time' I said. 'At school and you can come over anytime.' 'You'll be so far away' she said. 'Don't be silly I'm just across town' I said. 'It's dangerous over there' she said. 'Who says?' 'My mom and dad' she said. 'They told me I couldn't stay over with you any more after you moved.' 'Because it's too dangerous? But it's not' I said though as I told you Anne the new neighborhood isn't nearly as nice as ours. 'That's what they say. You're my only real friend now that Lori's been sent up what am I going to do?' 'Can I stay over with you sometimes?' 'Maybe' Katherine said. 'Well it seems only fair' I said. She said she'd ask her parents. I really don't like her father so I wish there was some way she could stay over at the new apartment but if that's the only way it works then that's it. She was feeling better when lunch was over and I was glad to cheer her up.

Boob and me asked Daddy how work went today and he said smoothly enough. Mister Mossbacher showed him everything about how the deposits were supposed to be dropped off and made out and how to work out everyone's schedule when half of the people there are absent, which is often the case it seems. Daddy was lying down on the couch half the night instead of packing because he had to help carry in a two-hundred-box shipment of plastic bags.

On the news tonight the new President said there's no reason for anyone to worry about the situation. He didn't say which situation.

MARCH 25
School was closed today in memoriam of the President and will be closed tomorrow too for his funeral. Daddy has to go to work though. Excelsior never closes except on Thanksgiving and Christmas thanks to Mister Mossbacher. I'm not sorry I don't have to go to school.

Forgive me Anne for stopping here but I'm just too tired tonight. I'll write you a little more tomorrow night I promise.

MARCH 26
They buried the President a day sooner than they usually do because they couldn't secure the Capitol enough to let him lie in state. That's when they put the casket in the rotunda and everybody comes to see him. While we

watched the funeral today Mama said she remembered
with Kennedy they had a long line of limousines and a
horse with empty boots and they were drumming on drums
all day. This time they just drove out to the cemetery and
buried him because of security. The new President gave a
speech and said he doesn't plan on doing anything differ-
ently than the President because absolutely nothing is
wrong. 'They'll shoot him too next week then and not a
minute too soon if that's the way he feels' Mama said.

MARCH 27

Now that the President's buried it's like it never happened.
Nobody said anything and there's nothing on TV about it
anymore, it's all about the emergencies again. School had
to close early this afternoon today even though it was our
first day back and again Anne I can't say I'm sorry at all.
What happened was that smoke from Long Island blew
back over the river and came in through the ventilation
ducts so thick it was getting foggy in class plus it smelled
bad. It looked like there was a thunderstorm over there the
clouds were so dark and went up so high. We weren't doing
anything in class today this morning anyway just trying to
catch up on what we hadn't done.

Even though I'm sleepy let me try to catch you up on
what else is down. First of all some sort of good news.
Katherine told me she asked her mom and dad if I could
stay overnight with her sometime at their apartment. They
said they'd let her know once they thought about it. Why
they'd have to think about it like it's the end of the world if
I stay over I don't know but they're just like that. Katherine said it was good though because at least they didn't say
no right away. Usually they do when she asks them if she
can do something.

Mama acts like she's having a good time checking those
manuscripts though she's about finished with the first batch
she got. She says she hopes to get some more early next

week though the people she knows at the publishers weren't sure how many more they'd have for her right away. 'Darling I'm ready to work like a slave if they'll just have me' she said. I like it when she's working because then she doesn't have to take as much medication even if lots of other things like moving are going on.

Daddy's new job is going okay too he says. Daddy also says he remembers why he was so glad he left bookstores when he did. That sounded fishy so I asked him 'How could you ever forget if you hated it so much?' and then he admitted he was exaggerating. He says the people they hire as cashiers have to be taught how to add before they can work at the counter. Daddy's not even sure that everyone who works in the bookstore can read. 'How did they get the job then?' I asked and Daddy just said Mister Mossbacher likes to give people a chance. Daddy said he's sure half the people who work there can't write their names, only print them. He says he guesses this is typical these days. Can you believe it Anne?

Boob said she had a headache and Mama stuffed her with baby aspirin and sent her on to bed right after dinner. 'Sweetie go tuck in your sister and make sure she doesn't need anything else' Mama said. 'What do you need?' I asked Boob when I came in. She was under the covers with My L'il Fetus glued on her. 'Don't need a thing except take this vise off my head' she said. 'What vise?' I asked. 'The one you put on my head when I wasn't looking' she said. 'Shut up Boob and go to sleep I just wanted to know how you were doing' I said. 'Doing fine good night' she said. She sounded a lot like me when she said that I thought. Anyway then after I took a shower and said goodnight to Mama and Daddy I came here to write you. I'm lying on my bed writing this Anne. It isn't too comfortable but there're all these boxes stacked on top of the desk like a barricade. If Boob was on the other side I could pour boiling oil on top of her.

So this is our last night in our house and I can at least tell you how I really feel. I haven't told Boob or Mama or Daddy because I know they're having their own troubles about all this. Tonight at dinner Mama said 'Oh my angel please tell me are you doing okay?' 'No prob what's to be done about it anyway?' I said. 'Sweetie there's so much can be done and we'll do it' Mama said. 'All we can do right now is move so we'll do that and see what happens next' I said. Mama says I'm a pessimist but I don't think I am, I think I just don't see any need to fudge if I'm telling myself what's down.

I'm so sad Anne because I don't think we will ever come back here. According to them of course there's no reason to think that. But I just have this hunch and usually whenever I have hunches I'm usually right. I wish this time I wasn't and maybe I won't be, but like I told Mama what's to be done?

It's supposed to be a pretty day tomorrow at least, so we won't get rained on. Daddy is off this weekend, though now he's not sure how long that'll last. Mister Mossbacher told him he'd be off on weekends but Daddy thinks he's going to change his mind and if he does Daddy will have to do what he's told. Daddy hates that even worse than I do.

Night night Anne. I'll talk to you in the new place tomorrow.

MARCH 29
Here I try to be good and write you every day and look what happens. I didn't write you yesterday Anne because we didn't finish moving in until late. Moving was just so much more complicated and scary than we'd have ever guessed. I hope we go on better than we started.

To save money Daddy found an ad in the Voice and hired this fellow named VanMan. That's what he calls himself because he moves people in the van he drives. Anyway we were ready to go at nine o'clock yesterday morning but VanMan didn't show. Daddy called twice from the lobby and got VanMan's machine both times. We disconnected our phone in the apartment so we could transfer the number and so the new guy moving in could get his own phone. Anyway VanMan finally showed up at eleven thirty. I could hardly keep from laughing out loud when I first saw him and Boob was giggling so hard she couldn't stop. He was this ugly old hippie Anne and he was wearing a Grateful Dead T-shirt. Our doorman wouldn't have ever let him even sleep in the gutter in front of our building because he was too bummy. Daddy said he was late and VanMan said he'd hit a bad flow.

So he helped us carry the boxes and chairs out of the lobby and then he put everything in his old van. I never would have thought it held so much but it did even though toward the end VanMan started shoving things in where they wouldn't fit and we could hear stuff breaking. Daddy said be careful and VanMan said hey dude it's just settling. We decided we should go on. He was going to have to make two runs because we had to come back for the couch and our beds. Mama and Boob took a taxi over to the new apartment but I asked if I could ride with Daddy and VanMan. My mistake.

I crouched on the floor under the glove compartment because there wasn't enough room to sit between Daddy and VanMan. I didn't want to sit down there but I was glad soon enough. Daddy's knees kept bumping me in the head when we hit a bump which was every five seconds. VanMan didn't have paint on his van or door handles inside but he had a CD. He played Gregorian chants like we heard at school in music class. Daddy asked him to drive slower and VanMan said he'd try but he was having a religious ecstacy. VanMan would speed up whenever he went through the lights. Every time we turned we could hear more stuff break.

VanMan was braindead Anne and I wonder now if he was on drugs. I think he was. It got really awful then. We drove across the park and went north on Broadway and then we stopped and VanMan jumped out. I knew we weren't at the apartment yet and so I looked to see where we were. We were only at 92nd Street. VanMan was going through some trash on the sidewalk getting a chair loose. Daddy yelled out the window what are you doing? Van-Man said oh hey I can resell this great chair it's aces. Daddy said I'm paying you by the hour come back and get it on your own time. 'Daddy let him get the stupid chair he's crazy' I said but Daddy didn't listen. I knew he should have.

Everybody on the street was looking and laughing at us. VanMan finally got back in the van. Anne, when someone is <u>insane</u> crazy we say he's pissed for blood and that's what he was. When he took off he turned up the volume on the CD as loud as it would go and then he started speeding. He was running the red lights. Daddy said slow down my daughter's in here but VanMan didn't care. He kept going faster and faster it felt like. I sat up and looked over the dash once and saw we were heading right toward a bus. Daddy pushed me down. We didn't hit the bus. I kept thinking the police would arrest us but they didn't.

We got all the way to the new apartment before VanMan stopped. Mama and Boob were already there standing outside. VanMan jumped out before Daddy did and ran to the back of the van. I got out and ran back after Daddy. VanMan had a big crowbar that he kept hitting the side of his van with. He told Daddy to pay him the rest of the money before he'd let us get our stuff. When Mama and Boob came over VanMan swung his crowbar like he was going to hit them but he didn't. A lot of people stood around watching but nobody said or did anything. Daddy gave VanMan money and then VanMan unlocked the van. He threw everything in the street as fast as he could not even looking to see where he was throwing it. Some of the boxes hit other people's cars and they'd come over but VanMan would jump out and start waving the crowbar again and they'd back off. One guy was so mad though he pushed Daddy against the side of the van and called him a fucking asshole. I thought he was going to hit Daddy but then he walked off and got in his car and pulled out. He ran over a lamp of ours when he did and smashed it and then drove off. We tried to keep piling the stuff VanMan threw out of the van together but the boxes kept breaking open and everything was spilling out. Then VanMan finished throwing everything out and he got back in and he drove off. I guess he went back to get that chair on 92nd Street, he must have wanted it bad. Some of the people watching started helping us once they saw VanMan wasn't going to bash them. Some Hispanic ladies and two older black men carried boxes over from where he pitched them. Younger girls that looked like my age watched me and Boob like they were sizing us but they didn't do or say anything. Eventually we got everything sort of together. Mama and Boob stayed with our stuff while me and Daddy carried it into the lobby. Finally we got the elevator loaded and we rode up to the new apartment.

Daddy called another guy named Man With Van to rent another van but he wasn't available until today. He also called the doorman at our building to let him know what happened and when we'd be back to get the rest of our things. Daddy looked pale and was breathing hard like he'd been running. I was afraid he was going to have a heart attack but after he sat down he looked a lot better.

Once we got everything inside we looked to see what got smashed. Besides the run-over lamp there were broken dishes and glasses and our turkey platter. Mama's favorite flower vases were just little bits and a small chest of Daddy's he kept on his desk was splintered. Nothing expensive got broken which is a miracle. Daddy held onto his computer so it didn't get thrown out and I grabbed the TV before VanMan got his paws on it. I asked Daddy if he was going to report him and he said he didn't think it would do any good.

After we got everything sorted this morning we found out

that not all of our neighbors were neighborly. Some of them must have stolen things from us while we were fighting with VanMan. Nothing was left in his van when he peeled and there's nowhere else the stuff could have gone. Mama can't find the kitchen knives or the coffeemaker. Daddy says some of his shirts were lifted and a box of his books though he's not sure which ones yet. Boob didn't lose anything she doesn't think. A box of my books got stolen. It had my Pooh books and Oz and Life Among the Savages which was Mama's copy. She says it's been out of print for years and she doesn't know if we'll be able to find another right away if at all. I feel so awful Anne that was one of my favorite books and now it's gone. It makes me so mad some fool just came up and stole it. I bet they just threw it in the trash once they saw it wasn't money. Thank God nobody stole my purse which is where I had you for safekeeping and at least VanMan didn't kill us which is what I was sure he was going to do, he went post office so fast.

When Daddy tried to plug in his computer and printer today we blew a fuse. It was a couple of hours before the super brought up a new one and put it in. Daddy watched him to see how it was done and he says he'll change it the next time. Daddy's all thumbs when it comes to handyman work though so I guess the super better get used to it. Daddy says we'll have to turn something off whenever he's using his computer but we haven't figured out what yet.

Today Boob and I helped Mama put up the curtains and shades and then we swept out the kitchen. There're icky cockroaches in the bottom cabinets so we put down roach motels and boric acid. There's nothing I hate as much as bugs and roaches. Boob of course loves them or at least claims she does. I don't see her picking them up and playing with them though. She doesn't like mice for sure because she thinks they're baby rats in disguise. Last night she said she heard noises in the wall that sounded like scratching. Since our beds weren't here we slept on the floor last night on blankets. Boob kept kicking me and saying 'It's rats Booz do something.' 'It's not Boob go to sleep' I said. I think I heard something too. Maybe it's just the way these old buildings groan. We haven't seen any mice yet.

Today also Daddy went back to our apartment and met Man With Van. They brought over the rest of the furniture this afternoon. Man With Van was younger than VanMan and not as seedy. Nothing happened except Daddy had to spend twice as much money as he'd expected to, but Man With Van didn't pull an insaner or anything. I didn't go along this time because I'd had enough driving for a while but I sat outside to keep an eye out for thieves while they brought it upstairs. I looked at the people walking by and standing around. Some of them were there yesterday and now I wondered if any of them had stolen from us. They looked innocent mostly but I knew better. I tried to figure out who looked guiltiest and I finally decided they all looked as guilty as they did innocent.

While I was thinking about who looked the most guilty a black girl walked over to me. She looked my age and was very dark. She wore tight bike shorts and a dirty sweat shirt with a puppy on the front. When she spoke she didn't sound like a black girl. 'Moving in?' she asked. 'Yes' I said. 'You Columbia?' she asked. 'No' I said. 'Columbia building' she said. 'How do you know?' I asked. 'They awning the windows' she said. The grocery in the bottom floor has a big awning and I guessed that was what she meant. 'You gonna school here?' she asked. 'Public school?' I asked and she nodded. 'No I go to Brearley' I said. 'Private?' 'Yes.' 'What's name?' she asked. 'Lola what's yours?' 'Is.' 'Is what?' 'Is. Isabel. Call me Iz' she said. 'Okay.' Daddy and Man With Van came back downstairs. She looked at them and I saw this big bruise on her neck like somebody hickeyed her. She wore four pairs of earrings and a nose ring and has a mouth so big I bet she could put a whole tomato in at once. 'He wildeyed too?' she asked. 'The van guy?' She nodded. 'Not this one. You saw us yesterday?' 'Mmhmm' she said. 'Man oughta dillinger his ass second he

75

blindside' she said. 'What?' I asked. Iz smiled and held up her hand and made her thumb and finger like it was a gun. She put her finger on my forehead and wiggled her thumb. 'Dillinger like that' she said. 'BaBoom. Later' she said. Then she turned around and walked up Broadway. Was she bothering you, Daddy asked and I said no not at all. So that was my first conversation with somebody in the neighborhood Anne.

Today it finally looks almost like somebody lives here. This apartment is so much emptier than our old place even though it's smaller. We don't have any rugs here because we put ours in storage, and also the furniture like the dining room table and cupboard. All the pictures we had hanging up are in storage too so we're going to have to look for posters to put on the wall. Boob in fact did a drawing with crayons this evening before we ate dinner. It's the four of us sitting in a big yellow square. We're all smiling and happy. Outside the square are these thick black swirls like in a storm or fire. She showed it to us and then Mama pinned it up on the wall in our room for her.

Everyone but me went to bed early tonight. I'm staying up not because I'm less tired but because I missed writing you and telling you what happened. Lately it's so hard to tell if I'll get the chance to write when I want to what with Boob so close by and so I'll try to take advantage of every opportunity. It'll be harder in some ways now. I'm writing this at the kitchen table because I don't want to wake Boob up by keeping the light on in our room, and I can't turn the TV on to provide distracting noise because the walls are so thin it'd keep everybody up. Outside I hear siren after siren and loud music. The subway goes by on the el every ten minutes and it's incredibly noisy. I never knew how quiet our part of town was. I'll be glad to go to school tomorrow Anne and get away from here.

Well now we're all moved in and we'll see what happens next. Night night.

* * *

Great start to the week LIE. Boob and I left this morning at eight right after Daddy. We wanted to try to get to school before nine. When do you think we got there? Nine thirty. Everything went wrong of course.

The bus didn't come for ten minutes. Then when it finally did it was one of three that showed up all at the same time. Two drove on and the most crowded stopped for us. Since it was the most crowded it was also the slowest naturally. The bus just inched along but by forcing our way to the back we at least got seats for a few minutes. We didn't get to keep them long though because at 108th a man in a wheelchair got on. The bus driver made us get up so he could put up our seat and make room for the challenged guy. Then he lowered the bus and helped him roll on. He started yelling at the bus driver saying two or three buses had passed him claiming that they didn't have room. Before the driver could get back to the front the challenged guy started asking for his name or number so he could report him. I don't know why he was going to report the driver who stopped but I think he was crazy even though he was in a wheelchair. He sat there cursing the whole time. Boob accidentally bumped against his chair as we were getting off and he slammed his hand down like he was trying to hit her. We were so glad to get off that bus. We transferred to the crosstown and of course it took ten minutes to get there and then it crawled too, all the way across the park and down 86th to where we got off. We ran down to Brearley but it was no use, we were already a half hour late.

We had to go to the office to get excuses from Ms Cutler. We didn't get serious damage but she said we should start leaving a half hour earlier in the morning since our commute is so much longer. None of their buses go up that far anymore or they'd send someone to pick up Boob, she said. I'd still have to go the way I do now so no extra sleep for me in any event. Great! If the buses keep showing up on time like they did this morning maybe soon I'll start having to

77

wake up before I go to sleep. Ms Cutler acted psycho this morning when she was talking to us, staring at us like we were going to bite her or something. 'What's wrong?' I asked her as we got ready to leave her office. 'What do you mean' she said. 'Nothing' I said. It was the way she was looking at us, like we were dirt or something. I didn't know how I could say that without her blowing so I didn't. Maybe she thinks I'm getting too Loriesque all of a sudden.

I hope Lori's all right, I miss her so much. None of us have heard anything more so I guess she's still in treatment.

This evening I asked Daddy why he leaves so early in the morning since he takes the awful but much more speedy subway. He said Mister Mossbacher is very strict about people getting to work on time. He's worse than Ms Cutler Daddy says. Mister Mossbacher tells his workers that if they're five minutes late they'll be docked an hour's pay. It doesn't matter if they're managers or not. Mister Mossbacher says that if you know when you're supposed to be at the store you shouldn't have any excuse for being late no matter what happens, Daddy says. 'Don't you get there way early?' I asked. Yes Daddy said but he's able to get more work done before the store opens. When Daddy talks about Mister Mossbacher he sounds like he wants to hit him.

I saw Katherine at lunch today and she told me great news. She says her parents said it was okay for me to stay over there. We agreed that Friday night would be good to try. She's going to doublecheck to make sure it's done. If I do stay over I won't be writing you that night Anne, so I'll warn you now. I asked Mama and Daddy if it was okay and they said it was fine.

Mama got more manuscripts today but only a couple. She says they're short ones and it won't take her but a few hours and as she gets paid by the hour that's not so good. 'Sweeties I'll read as slow as I can though to try and boondoggle my time' she said. She's already finished one tonight though so I don't think she can doggle much longer.

In case you wondered Anne the trip home takes as long

78

in the afternoon as it does in the morning. Tomorrow I'll
see if Boob wants to walk after school and how far. Maybe
we can go through the park before we catch the bus. She'll
probably feeb out though or else it'll rain. Something will
happen I'm sure of that.

Nothing else for now Anne. I'm very tired and achy but I
can't get to sleep. It's so noisy over here and I don't think
I'm ever going to get used to it. Last night someone outside
the window on the street was screaming for ten minutes
until I heard glass break and then they didn't scream
anymore.

MARCH 31

Granny's back already! I had cramps yesterday but I
convinced myself it wasn't time for her to return already.
I was wrong though. Mama asked me why I was so grumpy
yesterday and now we know. 'Oh sweetie it must be the
stress' she said. 'I don't know what it is' I said. 'If I was still
beset with it I'm sure the same would happen to me but I'm
just an old dried out husk of myself now' Mama said. 'No
you're not' I said. 'My angel you may not think so but I
must be' Mama said.

So we didn't walk back this afternoon after all. I wasn't
up to it and I knew something would happen and it did. We
got to the bus stop early this morning and wouldn't you
know it there was no problem. The buses showed up when
they were supposed to and we got to school a half hour
early. It was all right just the same. I saw Katherine before
we went to class. She said her dad said it would be okay if I
stayed over Friday night. We're both looking forward to it.
The big news at school today was that Icky Betsy had to go
to the hospital. Apparently she must have heaved so much
during Spring break that she tossed up something she
needed. She's at Lenox Hill and we sent her a card that
everyone signed. Maybe she'll be treated now but probably
not.

Something happened at work today that got Daddy upset but he wouldn't say what it was. He was so quiet all through dinner, it was very bothersome because that's just not like him. Boob started playing with her food and singing silly songs and he smiled but that was all. We asked him what was the matter and he said nothing. He's more than fudging, he's lying. 'I don't know what happened sweetie but I have the idea someone was unpleasant to him I don't know who' Mama said when I asked if he'd said anything to her.

We watched TV while we ate. We don't have cable here and the reception's bad but we can get channels 4, 7 and 13 without too many ghosts. There were riots in Brooklyn again last night and then this morning too. What's even worse because it's closer is that they think there're going to be riots in Harlem and Washington Heights too and that's right next to us up here. The Mayor says that the Army has to come in if that happens because the National Guard is too busy in Queens and Long Island and upstate too. The President says he can't bring any more soldiers back to America to take care of problems local police and the Guard should be able to handle here. They said two thousand people have been killed in Los Angeles last week. Daddy said he hoped some of them were people he knew.

As if it's not noisy enough around here there's something else we've all discovered tonight Anne. Tonight about an hour ago just as I was getting ready to start writing you we suddenly heard this recorded voice blaring. At first we couldn't tell what it was saying because it was speaking Spanish and then Creole. Then the voice started speaking English saying 'Warning Warning Warning You Have Violated This Building's Perimeters Please Leave Immediately Or Response Will Be Called For.' Then it started in Spanish again. It's as loud as a jet at the airport and it went on for fifteen minutes before it finally stopped. Daddy thinks it's an alarm for the co-op across the street where they have the security guards out front all night. Why they need that alarm unless it's to keep the guards awake is beyond me. Anyway this is just one more obnoxious noise to drive us all crazy.

APRIL 1

We moved back to our apartment today and I got all As in my tests last week. April Fool to you Anne! I did get As though in everything but algebra and that was a B minus. I hate algebra and all math.

When Boob and I left the building this morning we saw somebody wrote EARTH IS HELL on the side in big white letters. Probably that stupid alarm kept whoever wrote it awake too. It went off three more times last night going Warning Warning Warning and woke me up every time. I can hardly keep my eyes open while I'm writing you.

This afternoon when we got back from school we walked over to the co-op and saw a new sign on the wire around the building saying ALARMED. Daddy was right about who the culprits are. The building's not any different from the one we're in but it's fixed up more so it's not like it's River House or the Dakota or anything. The day guard was out front. He's this little skinny Indian guy. 'Why does the alarm have to make so much noise?' I asked him. He told me and Boob to leave immediately or response would be called for. 'What response are you talking about I was just asking' I said. He had a gun and he started patting it like it was his buddy. I was almost as tall as he was but he could tell I'm not a murderer or anything. I could tell he scared Boob though so I walked away and pushed her ahead of me. I looked back and he actually looked like he wanted to shoot! What were we going to do Anne, tease him to death? When we got across the street some of the Spanish guys standing around outside the grocery store started whistling at me and saying hey culo culo which means my vagina I think. That really pissed me but I didn't say anything.

81

There's no point, it won't make the toads stop croaking.

The halls in this building smell like lentils cooking all the time and I hate lentils. People pee in the entrance too and it smells like the subway. This morning it was so bad I nearly heaved and my eyes burned. 'It's like walking into Saks and having them squirt you' Boob said but of course it's much worse than that.

Daddy was in a better mood today so I think nothing happened too serious yesterday. Mama finished those manuscripts though and now she's waiting for more and in the meantime she's back on Prozac. She left the bottle out in the bathroom this morning. We only have one bathroom here so it means one of us is always waiting for the others. Tonight Daddy was in there so long I had to go downstairs and pee in the entrance myself.

April Fool! I'd never do that.

APRIL 2

This commuting is killing me, Anne. I don't think I'll ever get enough sleep again. The buses were late and we had to run all the way from 86th down to Brearley and we just made it as the bell rang.

Mama Prozacked out tonight so Daddy unthawed dinner. When I was helping him clean up I saw that his shirt had a hole burned in it and I asked him what happened. Daddy said a customer came into the store this morning smoking a cigarette even though it's against the law. If Mister Mossbacher sees someone smoking on the street or in his store Daddy says he starts screaming until he's scared everybody to death. Mister Mossbacher was right up front dusting underneath the cash registers so Daddy told the man he'd have to put out his cigarette. The man flipped it against Daddy and then stomped out. Daddy put it out before Mister Mossbacher saw it because otherwise I think he'd have screamed at Daddy. He said the man was wearing a nice suit and looked perfectly normal but you can never tell who's psycho and who's not.

The rioters attacked an armory in Brooklyn last night and took it over. The Mayor was on TV telling everybody who lives over there what to do to protect their homes while they're out rioting. He's got police guarding the bridges and subways to make sure they don't all come over here. I don't like where we live but I'd rather live here than Brooklyn. The President told the Mayor he wasn't going to be able to send in the Army to Brooklyn because of the situation in Washington, not to mention everywhere else.

There goes Warning Warning Warning again. That's the eighth time today since I got home. I think the guards set it off deliberately just to make it seem like they're busy.

APRIL 4
Now that I'm back Anne I have to tell you what happened last night over at Katherine's.

Everything started out like it was going to be a wonderful time. After school Katherine and I walked down 86th and first we stopped for slices of pizza. Granny's almost gone but I'm still constant starving and I had to get something. Then we went in Elk Candy and each of us bought a marzipan fish to eat later. We aimed to cruise but there were gangs of older kids roaming and they looked like they were ready to wolf and we didn't want to be surrounded so we flew.

We went back to her apartment. Katherine's parents weren't home yet so we sat in the living room and listened to tapes on the good player. At five she started getting nervy and said we better stop because they'd be home soon and she didn't want them to catch us. 'Catch us what?' I asked. 'Doing anything in here' Katherine said. Well as it turned out her mother didn't get home until almost six. She fixed us Lean Cuisines in the microwave. We hadn't eaten dinner because we were still full of pizza. I had chicken cacciatore and Katherine had chicken amandine. They were awful but I've had worse.

83

'How are your classes Lola?' her mother asked me. 'Fine' I said. 'Do you like your teachers?' 'Very much' I said which isn't <u>true</u> true but close enough. 'Looking forward to summer?' 'A lot' I said. 'Going anywhere?' she asked but then she answered herself before I could. 'Oh you wouldn't be would you' she said. Then she didn't say anything else to me the rest of the evening. It was like she'd done her duty and she could get back to the real world.

Katherine's father came home at eight. He works late every night Katherine said and I know she wishes he worked later. He looked at me when he walked in but he didn't say hello, he just went into the kitchen. Katherine and her mother got even edgier when he came in. Pretty soon we went to her room and she shut the door. 'I'd lock it but it won't' she said. She lay down on the bed and sighed like she was going to cry. 'What's the matter?' I asked. 'Nothing' she said and so I dropped it knowing she wouldn't answer. Katherine turned on her stereo but kept the sound down. Her father hates any sort of noise and so her mother and Katherine get so quiet that you can hear pins drop if they're all in the same room. They're the jumpiest bunch I know.

We sat on her bed looking at Seventeen magazines. 'Would you wear that?' she asked every three minutes. Every time I looked she'd show me some doof wearing a topless bikini or leather chaps or silver eye shadow. 'Never in a million years would you?' I'd say. 'Maybe' she said. 'Well go ahead.' 'When are you moving back over here?' 'I don't know soon I hope' I said. 'Is it really slummy over there?' 'Not really you have to come visit' I said. 'I told you they won't let me' she said. 'Sneak over after school.' 'You sound like Lori.' 'I do not.' 'You do you won't admit it. They're right you know she was a bad influence' she said. 'She didn't influence you' I said. 'She tried.' 'How?' 'Trying to get me to stay out later than I should. Shoplifting. If I was ever caught doing anything bad' Katherine started to say but she didn't finish. 'She tried that all the time with me

84

but if I didn't want to I'd say no use and she'd let up' I said. 'You're meaner than I am' Katherine said. 'Lori's meaner than both of us put together' I said. 'She could be sometimes but you're pretty equal' Katherine said. 'We're not' I said and wrestled her down. All at once she got real worried but we weren't making any noise not enough to hear anyway. 'Stop please stop' Katherine said and I did. She'd have never said that if we'd been in my room.

'What else did she try to teach you?' I asked. 'How to drink a beer it was so gro' Katherine said. 'She taught me how to kiss I knew already but she wanted to show me' I said. 'How'd she show you?' 'She kissed me.' 'On the mouth?' 'Yes and she tried to use her tongue but I wouldn't let her' I said. 'She tried to use her tongue?' Katherine asked. 'Well Lori's got such a big mouth it has to go somewhere' I said.

'What was it like was it okay?' Katherine asked. 'Since there weren't tongues involved it was all right' I said. 'Show me' she said and sat up with her face near mine. 'Pucker up' I said and I kissed her. She sat there like she was tasting something she'd never eaten before. 'It lasts longer if it's with a boy isn't it?' she asked. 'Hours longer like for days because they're brushing each other's teeth with their tongues' I said. 'Lo!' Katherine said looking disgusted. 'Kiss longer so I can see what it's like' she said. 'No tongues' I said. 'Okay.' We kissed longer and it was nice but that was all. She smiled. 'How was that?' I asked. 'One more time just one' she said. 'Kat you're bad' I said. 'I'm not I just want to know what it's like' she said. 'Can't you tell?' I asked. 'Please.' 'Oh all right.'

Well that's when I should have put my foot down Anne. To shut her up I gave her a real face sucker and just as I did her mother opened the door. She didn't say anything at all but just closed it and walked back down the hall. 'Oh God oh God' Katherine said. 'You're the one wanted to keep kissing' I said but she wasn't listening. 'Oh God' she kept saying. 'What's going to happen?' I asked because she was so shaky I was getting all scared too. 'I don't know' she said. We sat there for a half an hour and didn't hear anything. Katherine just lay on the bed like she was paralyzed and I got up and sat at her computer chair looking through another magazine like I wasn't worried. It didn't seem to make her feel any better though.

Then there was a knock on the door and her mother said 'Katherine?' before opening it. 'Your father's turned in and Lola's bed is all made up on the couch. Say goodnight' she said. 'Lo can't sleep in here?' Katherine asked. 'You remember what we talked about' her mother said. When I looked at Katherine I knew she didn't know what her mother meant. Katherine said 'Okay' but looked so deepdown like she wanted to die. 'Lola knows where the bathroom is and has what she needs?' her mother asked. Katherine nodded. 'All right say goodnight' her mother said. 'Goodnight' Katherine and I said. I picked up my backpack and followed her mother into the living room where sheets and blankets were spread out on the sofa. 'Thank you' I said. Her mother just nodded and left.

I sat there a few minutes and then got up and went to the bathroom in the hall. When I tried to lock the bathroom door I saw the lock was missing and there was a hole where it had been. I stuffed up the hole with toilet paper and closed the door. While I was brushing my teeth I pressed my foot against the door so nobody could barge in. I didn't know why I thought someone would but I worried. Five hours in her apartment and I was getting as serious crazy as they are.

I got distracted popping a zit on my chin in the mirror and fiddled at the mirror for five minutes. After I washed my face I sat down to pee. I was putting in a new tampoon to be on the safe side when I saw the toilet paper wasn't in the lock hole anymore! Oh Anne it wasn't on the floor either. I stood up and went to the door and opened it but nobody was in the hall. It was dark and all the lights were out except in the bathroom and the living room down the hall. I heard Katherine groaning like she was having a bad dream. I almost went into her room to see if she was all right since I knew her door didn't lock. Then I got more scared and didn't. I ran back to the living room and pulled the blanket over me. It was too psycho but it was after ten and too late for me to go home unless I took a taxi and I didn't have taxi money. It was quiet the rest of the night but it didn't help me get to sleep. Finally I passed out but I don't know when, it was late.

The next morning I woke up early and got dressed. I had to pee so bad I was ready to pop and I decided to chance going to the bathroom there again. When I went in I stuffed the hole full of tissue and watched it the whole time I was sitting there but nothing happened. Katherine must have heard me and she came into the living room while I was packing my backpack. She looked sad and sleepy like a little match girl.

'I'm sorry' she said whispering. 'That's okay it wasn't your fault' I said. 'Are you leaving?' she asked. 'I better' I said. I really wanted to go home. 'You don't have to.' 'Were you having bad dreams last night?' She wouldn't look at me when I asked her. 'Every night' she said. She walked me to the door and was careful opening it so as not to make any noise. 'How are you getting home?' 'The bus to the West Side' I said. 'I'll see you at school Monday' she said. Then she grabbed my arm and kissed me again. I kissed her back and I shocked myself Anne. Even before I thought about what I was doing we Frenched and kissed with tongues. We were both shocked I think and she came out with me in the hall looking green. 'We're not queers because we did that are we?' Katherine said. 'No we just kissed because we wanted to' I said but maybe we were queers at least right at that moment. I don't know what anybody else would think, that's what I thought. 'Bye' we whispered and then I got in the elevator.

So I don't know which way is up Anne. Kissing Katherine doesn't worry me as much as everything else that happened does. Maybe it should but it doesn't. I know somebody was watching me in the bathroom last night and it wasn't Katherine and I'm sure it wasn't her mother. I don't think Katherine was dreaming when I heard her groaning because she didn't sound asleep. After I left I walked all the way up Broadway from 86th, it was so pretty out. I kept thinking about last night. Now I've spent all afternoon writing you Anne and I still don't know if I've said anything I've wanted to. But I'm glad I'm home now Warning Warning Warning and all.

Daddy had to work today I discovered because one of the other managers was fired. He has to go to work tomorrow at noon too. Mister Mossbacher is making out a new schedule for him Mama says. She didn't look very happy about it and she didn't say anything else about it.

APRIL 5
I was going to call Katherine today but didn't. I got as far as picking up the phone but before I could call her I stopped and went back to my room instead. Boob was sitting on the bed rocking back and forth and looking out the window at the subways going by. 'What's the matter with you?' she asked me. 'I'm preoccupied' I said. 'What with?' she asked. 'A lot of things' I said. 'What things?' 'I don't want to talk about it.' 'Talk about what?' 'Shut up Boob' I said and she started laughing. I decided to go for a long walk by myself. Mama got another manuscript on Friday afternoon so she kept busy today which is good. 'Can I go too?' Boob asked. 'Watch TV Boob it's good for you' I said. 'It asks so much and gives so little' she said. She got that from Daddy, he says that all the time.

I walked down as far as St John the Divine which will be the biggest cathedral in the world if they ever finish it. They're not supposed to until the 22nd century. No one around now including me will ever know what it'll wind up looking like. After that I walked along Riverside Drive for a while though I didn't go into the park, which is down the hill by the river and seems much scarier than Central Park though it's probably not any worse. Then I walked up and down some of the side streets looking at things. At the end of 111th Street is a fountain next to St John the Divine. It's bronze and has a big moon grinning at you stuck on top of a crab and there's an angel and some giraffes standing on top of the moon. There's a devil's head hanging off of one of the crab claws. It's about the dumbest thing I've ever seen but I guess it's religious or something. On 114th Street is a big rock behind a fence where a building should be. Mondel's candy store on Broadway around the corner sells good fudge Mama says but I couldn't have bought any even if it had been open. This morning I found my marzipan fish that I bought the other day when I was out with Katherine. At first I thought I'd save it as a keepsake. Then I wondered what I'd really want to remember later on so I went ahead and ate it. Every time I think about what a weird night that was I keep thinking I did something wrong even though I know I didn't, I don't think.

Then I walked back up Broadway as far as 125th, just to say I'd been at the very edge of Harlem. I didn't want to go any farther because the news says there's trouble up there but they don't say exactly where. What I notice most about our new neighborhood Anne is how many people live on the street here. In the morning when Boob and I go to school there's always a lot of people sleeping in doorways and under blankets because there aren't any doormen to chase them away. A couple even have little tents they put up. And in the afternoon they're all still there, though they're all awake by then. There was a woman lying on the sidewalk at 125th but I don't think she was homeless, though you never know. Her blouse was unbuttoned and she had giant tits as big as watermelons. She was drunk I think. She kept shouting and then muttering to herself like she was

89

goofed. An old woman stood over her saying she should go to church and the drunk woman kept saying Fuck White Jesus.

Then who else should I see at the corner but that girl Iz I told you about last weekend when we first moved in. She was with another girl. 'Hi' I said. Neither one answered so I started to walk back over to my side of the street. I was on the Harlem side by the General Grant Houses which is a big ugly project though not as big and ugly as the one up the street. Before I crossed though Iz said 'You talking to us?' 'Yes' I said. 'You done moving?' she asked. I walked over to where they were standing. They were too cool to breathe but I could tell right away that Iz was just trying to impress the other girl, the way she was acting. 'This is my girl Jude' said Iz and Jude nodded. 'What are you doing?' I asked. 'Loosin' said Iz. 'Not much' she added. 'What happened to that woman?' I asked pointing to the lady in the street. 'Bugged big' Iz said. 'She flying the Wild Horse' said Jude who has a Caribbean accent which makes her sound like she's singing even when she's not. 'What they call you?' she asked me. 'Lola' I said.

Jude is even taller than I am, maybe five nine, but I don't think she's much older if at all. She was wearing sweat pants and high tops and a T-shirt with a skull on the front with a knife in the teeth. Jude's thin without being skinny. That is she has muscles like a runner. Jude has short hair like a boy and little tits but she has a plump sticky-out butt like most black girls have. She's one of those black people that look like they could be a boy or a girl and look good either way. Iz is darker and fatter than Jude and has dreadlocks like Whoopi Goldberg so you can tell what she is right away. Black girls are prettier than white girls I think.

'Habla Espan?' Jude asked me. 'No' I said. 'You look PR. You not?' 'No.' 'Why you living up here then?' she asked. 'To save money' I said. Jude laughed. She has big pretty white teeth that look sharp. 'One hand save the other take away. Always be paying, no saving here' she said.

'That's right' said Iz and they both laughed. They were making fun of me I thought and it pissed but I didn't say anything. 'You school with us?' Jude asked. 'No Jude she down over the wall she schools down here' Iz said. I didn't want to say I went to private school if I didn't have to and I didn't. Kids who go to public school usually think I think I'm too good for them if they find out I go to private school and hate me for it. Once in second grade some public school girls chased me trying to beat me up when I told them and ever since then I try not to say. 'You loosin too?' Jude asked. 'Walking around. I'd better go back now though' I said. 'You better' Jude said. 'Bye' I said. 'We see you around' Iz said. Then I came back home.

Mister Mossbacher told Daddy his new schedule. He'll be working weekends during the day twelve to eight and during the week from four to midnight. He's off on Tuesdays and Fridays. Daddy says it should work out fine because he'll be able to get more writing done but I don't think he believes it. I know I don't. Mama didn't seem happy about it but she didn't say anything. What could she say?

I think Iz and Jude like me Anne but I can't tell for sure. They're different from my friends at Brearley, even or especially the black girls who go there. They're what some snobs I know call street girls but that's just because they go to public school. Iz and Jude act so much older than me though they're not I don't think. You can tell it in Jude's eyes though, Anne, in her eyes she looks very old.

APRIL 6
Usually you get short shrift from me during the week Anne but not tonight. I have to write and tell you what happened today because I feel like I'm ready to explode if I don't. I hope Daddy gets home soon but it's only eleven and with his new schedule he won't even finish working for another hour.

At school today Katherine saw me across the room at

lunchtime but pretended she didn't and so we didn't talk. Even though I wanted to talk to her I was glad she acted like that because then I could pretend I didn't see her either without feeling bad about it. It's not weird her acting like that though it's just Katherine. What was strange was that I saw Tanya and Susie in History class this afternoon and when I said hello to them they acted like I wasn't there. Nothing makes me madder than when that happens when you're standing right there and it's people you know. 'Are you deaf I think I said hello' I said. Then they said oh hi and looked around like they were embarrassed or just too bored to have seen me. 'Why are you acting so weird?' I asked. They didn't say anything and then class started so we had to take our seats. I don't know what their problem is but I've got enough of my own problems to worry about without worrying about theirs.

Mama acted like she was in a good mood when Boob and I came home from class. 'Oh sweeties there's a reference book I need to get and Excelsior has it will you come down with me and get it we'll say hello to your poor harried father as well' Mama said. 'Will he give us the book free?' Boob asked. 'No my angel but he can get us a discount and that's the next best thing' Mama said.

We walked to 116th and caught the subway down. Nothing happened on the way except two bums who almost got into a fight. A bum who only had one leg came through hopping and started telling everybody how he'd been pushed onto the tracks and lost his leg now he was homeless and had AIDS and wasn't able to eat. Then another bum who smelled even worse than the first one came in while the first one was talking. He stood at the other end of the car listening and finally he said are you finished yet go on shut up man nobody wants to give you anything. The first bum left and then the second bum started saying he was in Vietnam and now he had AIDS and he needed to get something to eat too. Nobody gave either of them any money.

We got to Excelsior at four thirty. It's a big store but it was packed like Christmas. Before we could go in we had to stand in line with everybody else while the guards looked in everybody's bags and purses. People were complaining and whining. One man was yelling at the guards and they just looked at him like he was crazy. Finally we got inside and we found Daddy at the information counter where he and another fellow were surrounded by shouting customers. Eventually he got somebody to replace him at the counter and he came out with the book Mama wanted. 'Oh Michael dearest thank you can we take it right up to the cash register?' Mama asked but Daddy said no he had to take it back to Mister Mossbacher to have the employee purchase forms he'd filled out signed or otherwise he couldn't get her the discount. So we followed Daddy down the aisle toward the back of the store.

'Dears your father has told me stories I'm sure he's exaggerating but don't say anything if anything odd happens' Mama said. 'Odd like what?' Boob asked. 'Well I don't know sweetie just anything peculiar' Mama said. It wasn't just odd or peculiar it was horrible. In the back of the store is a big concrete box with a dumbwaiter in it where they send up books from the basement. Standing by the dumbwaiter was a skinny little man with a bushy pubic hair beard looking exactly like Daddy said it did. Yes the man was Mister Mossbacher and he looked like a real bum wearing a dirty old T-shirt and jeans. He looked like the kind of bum that when he gets into the same subway car as you you get out at the next stop even if you don't have to. It was so scary Anne he was standing there hitting his head on the side of the dumbwaiter over and over again saying fuck me fuck me fuck me every time he hit his head. Anyway he stopped when Daddy walked up to him and said something. He shouted at Daddy what the fuck is it now? Mama put her arm out so as to keep us from getting closer. Boob was already hiding behind her.

Daddy handed Mister Mossbacher the pieces of paper

and he scrawled his name on them with a pen and said hand me those books. There we were surrounded by thousands and thousands of books and Daddy didn't know which books any more than I did, I could tell because he got all fidgety. Mister Mossbacher went total post office. If he'd had a gun there wouldn't have been anyone alive. He kicked over a stack of books and threw the one he was holding down the aisle and it almost hit a customer. Can't you fucking do anything can't anybody fucking do anything around here Mister Mossbacher screamed at the top of his voice and then he got all quiet again like nothing had happened and he wondered why everyone was staring at him. He grabbed a different stack of books that was on the other side of the dumbwaiter and started sorting them out by title and acted like Daddy wasn't even there. Another customer started to ask him where something was and Mister Mossbacher said to the customer do you see the sign that says Information can you read it if you can't read what the fuck are you doing in a bookstore? he asked. The customer looked frightened and walked away without saying anything.

'Is he on medication?' Mama asked when Daddy came back over to where we were standing and Daddy shook his head. All the way back up the aisle Boob and I kept looking behind us to see if Mister Mossbacher was going to pull any more insaners but he just kept checking in books. At the checkout a customer was telling a cashier that there was a crazy man in the back of the store throwing books at people and screaming. 'That's the owner ma'am' the cashier said. The customer said fuck you to the cashier and started to walk out, but he was moving so fast the guards must have thought he was trying to shoplift so they threw him down on the floor.

Then the ride home was just as bad and even scarier. It was right in the middle of rush hour. The subway was so crowded it was hard to breathe. I got a seat and Boob sat on my lap and Mamma stood in front of us hanging onto the bar. Between 66th and 72nd Street the train stopped in the tunnel and the lights got dim and the air conditioning shut off. The conductor said something but the speaker was broken and he sounded like he was talking inside a drum. Then it got real quiet inside the car like it always does when the train stops. Suddenly a woman said 'Watch your feet' and a man said you watch. 'I said you watch' she said and he said his feet weren't in the way it was her baby carriage. 'My baby's not in the way' she said and he said the fuck it wasn't. They started cursing each other back and forth and getting louder and louder. 'Please quiet down' another lady said and the man said fuck you too. 'Don't talk to me like that motherfucker' the lady said and then a lot of people shouted no no and the crowd in our half of the car pushed back like they were being shoved and I thought Mama was going to fall on us. It was so crowded me and Boob couldn't see what was happening. 'He started it' one of the ladies said and then everybody was saying be cool be cool. The crowd stopped crowding and some people muttered and everybody got quiet again. Then the second woman said 'Dumbass motherfucker' and people started screaming real loud and everyone started pushing into our half of the car like they were getting ready to come through the windows. Everyone was shouting no no don't don't and it must have worked because no one did. Then the lights and the air conditioning came back on and after a minute or so the train started up again. When it got to 72nd about half the people in our car got out and then it was quiet again so I think whoever was arguing got out too. Mama looked really white and tired and Boob didn't say anything so I know she was scared.

It's just been an awful day Anne. I'm tired of writing but I had to tell you what happened today because it was so awful. Boob is throwing things at me and saying 'Turn out the light Booz' so I'm going to stop now. Mama took a couple of Xanax so she's in Dreamland now and won't hear Boob but we need to get to sleep too. 'Why does Daddy let

Mister Mossbacher talk to him like that?' Boob asked me when we got home. 'Because he needs to keep the job' I said. 'I wouldn't let anybody talk to me like that' Boob said. 'You would if you needed to keep your job' I said. 'Won't find me working' Boob said and then she said 'Daddy should hit him on the head with a shovel and bash his brains in.' 'It's not cartoons Boob' I said. 'I know' Boob said.

Daddy won't be home for another hour probably. Night night Anne.

<del>APRIL 8</del>
<del>Anne I don't know how much I'll be able to write you tonight I just</del>

APRIL 10
I'm sorry I haven't written you during the week Anne but I haven't wanted to or been able to until now. Wednesday night I tried but I was too tired and in too bad a mood. And why would anybody want to hear from someone who was going to yell at them for something they didn't have anything to do with?

Remember I told you how weird Tanya and Susie were acting on Monday. Well Tuesday they were acting like that again and so on Wednesday when I saw them at lunch I said 'What is it with you two?' 'Nothing what's the matter with you?' they asked. 'You act like I'm poison' I said. 'You're crazy we're not acting weird at all you're the one acting weird' Tanya said. 'Ever since you moved you've been so mental we've been thinking you're a committal' Susie said. 'In every way' Tanya said. Then they started giggling like they knew a joke on me that I didn't. I said 'What is it?' 'Oh nothing.' 'Yes it is it's something what is it?' I asked. When I started to sit down they stood up. 'Did we say you could sit down?' Tanya said. 'Who's mental now?' I asked. 'Come on Susie she's zoned all the time now that she lives up in crackworld' Tanya said and then they left.

After school I saw Katherine outside and I thought it was about time we talked about the night I stayed over. I wanted to ask her right out if her father was looking at me when I was in the bathroom. She didn't see me come up behind her and when I said hi she acted like she'd seen a ghost. 'What's the matter with you?' I asked following. 'Nothing' she said and started walking away from me. I grabbed her arm and she pulled away and lifted her books like she was going to hit me with them. 'Don't touch me' she said. 'Why are you acting like that?' I asked. 'You know why' she said. 'Leave me alone.' 'I won't if you don't tell me what's the matter' I said. 'I'll scream and they'll arrest you' she said and then she ran across East End and down 83rd Street.

Then I heard girls behind me singing Queer Queer Queer. I knew I knew them. When I turned around and looked I saw Susie and Icky Betsy of all people. They started laughing at me. 'Shut up' I said and they laughed some more. I saw Boob and walked over and said 'Come on Boob let's go home.' 'It's a pretty day let's walk' she said. 'Let's take the bus' I said. 'Watch out she'll get you' I heard Susie yelling. 'Who'll get me?' Boob asked. 'Shut up Boob let's go home' I said.

We caught the bus on 86th and rode across the park and then transferred to the one that went uptown. 'What's the matter with you?' Boob asked me over and over again. Finally I shouted at her saying 'Boob there's nothing the matter please shut up all right?' Of course by doing that it proved to her that there was something the matter but she could also tell I didn't want to be teased about it. But then she decided she should be my shrink. 'You know what Daddy says if you don't talk about problems eventually you blow up' she said. 'You got to hang it all out Booz' she said. 'Boob shut up I don't want to talk about it' I said.

97

'Whatever you say but you'll break out and get ulcers' she said.

But I didn't want to talk to Boob because she wouldn't understand and I didn't want to talk to Mama because I didn't know what she'd say. I wanted to talk to you Anne but Wednesday night it was hopeless. Boob kept interrupting as I was thinking about what to say shouting 'What are you writing now Booz?' She wouldn't stop and finally I gave up. There's nothing I hate worse than trying to write and being interrupted over and over again. Tonight Boob went right to sleep and so I'm finally writing you and telling you what happened. None of the girls spoke to me yesterday or today. This morning when we got to school I found a Playboy magazine in my locker, someone had shoved it through the slot. They wrote on it Something you can beat off to. I threw it right in the trash can.

I'm glad you have a lock on you Anne because Boob would try to read this if she could but she can't.

Katherine must have decided what we did the other morning was wrong I think and then she told the girls what happened even though she was the one who kept saying she wanted a kiss. I'm sick of them acting like this it's so immature. It makes me think we did something awfully wrong but I know we didn't but maybe we did. I wish Lori was back she was the only one who could make those girls shut up when they acted like babies without beating them up. She should be getting back next week and maybe then she can straighten them out.

Anyway that's what happened and why I haven't had a chance to write before now. Daddy's still not home. Even though Excelsior closes at midnight he has to be there for another hour until they finish waxing the floor and then it's another half hour before he gets home even if the subway shows up on time, which it hardly ever does that late.

I'm glad it's Friday. I always hated it when they acted that way to other girls and now it's my turn. I don't know why they're like that.

Even before noon it was ninety degrees today and so humid that everything was dripping like a sponge. Everything smelled like rotten garbage too like it always does in New York every summer. If I'm not in New York I love summer but I hate it when I am. When it's humid like it always is the back of my neck is always wet and I have to wash my hair twice a day sometimes just because otherwise it feels like I'm wearing bacon on my head it gets so greasy.

After Daddy left for work at eleven thirty I went outside. Mama had new manuscripts to proofread and Boob was watching cartoons. We all slept until ten since it's the weekend and it's so hard to get out of bed when you don't have to especially when it's this hot. I didn't want to be miserable so I just wore sandals and a muscle T and an old pair of cutoff jeans. 'Sweetie where are you going?' Mama asked me. 'Just out' I said. 'Bad boys will be whistling at you my angel you look like such a little cookie' she said. 'I'm not a cookie it's hot out' I said. 'Be careful sweetie don't fall prey' Mama said. 'I won't' I said.

It was like a party on the street because everyone had gone outside. The super and some of his friends had set up a card table and were playing dominoes. Some of the old ladies who live upstairs from us were leaning on the lightpost out front talking. A bunch of Spanish boys were standing at the corner of Broadway. They all wore caps and football shirts that came down to their knees. They were older than me which means they're at the very worst age, they think they're big like men but they aren't old enough to drive yet. I wanted to cross Broadway and walk on the Columbia side but the light was red and I had to wait. That's when they saw me and started in.

Anne they started hooting at me like baboons going Hey Baby Hey Baby Hey. 'I'm impressed' I said though now that I think about it that was probably just leading them on. They laughed and called me culo. Like I told you that's a really dirty word in Spanish, as bad as the really bad ones in English like fuck and cunt. One of the bigger boys walked over to me. He thought he was growing a mustache but it just looked like he'd been eating coal. He had a cane but he didn't have a limp he was just swinging his cane around like he was going to hit someone but didn't. He grabbed my arm and said yo queenie let me help you cross the street to my house. 'Let go of me' I said trying not to look at him and I pulled loose. His friends walked over to where we were standing. When I started to cross the street the big one pulled me back on the curb.

Why don't you talk to us? he asked. She too good to talk, another one said. She look like she good for something, another one said. 'I don't want to hang around with boys' I said telling the truth. You dress like you do baby what's this back here? the big one said and grabbed my butt. Another one who was missing a tooth in front put his hand under my shirt. Some of the men were speaking Spanish to them like they wanted them to quit but the boys didn't pay any attention. 'Let me go' I said but they didn't. You ought to go with us one of them said. Let's go to the park for awhile said the big one and then he squeezed my butt till it hurt. They were still laughing and I wanted to get away from them, I didn't think it was funny and I don't think they did either.

Then a girl said 'Yo yo yo yo Mico the maricon.' The boys let go of me and stepped back. I looked and it was Iz and Jude and another girl crossing Tiemann Place. 'Yo Mico two hands on the books please' said Iz. I walked over to them, away from the boys. Don't dog us we just saying hello the big one said. His name was Mico I thought. 'Dogs be dogged' said Jude. Slack us bitch nada's meant said Mico. 'Mighty mass boys think they be trumpin' said the girl I hadn't met yet. She was the one who said yo yo yo. She was Spanish too and wore seven pairs of earrings and noserings on both sides of her nose. Her pants were so tight that if you cut her she wouldn't bleed. 'You want hosin Mico go hose gangstagirls uptown you hear g girls spread they sorry ass to any old shit' Jude said. Chinga tu madre said Mico and Jude laughed. 'Find her first but don't be dickin this block.' He lifted his cane like he was going to hit her. 'No trouble getting that up' Iz said to him. Mico looked like he wanted to hit them both but they just stood there and then he backed off. 'Beat it moreno' Iz said. 'Hasta, jibaros' said the Spanish girl. The boys muttered and cursed and then walked uptown. 'Pansyass motherfuckers' Iz shouted and they looked back but didn't say anything.

'Thanks' I said. 'Go out lookin like you do they think you fishing with big bait' said the Spanish girl. 'What about the way you're dressed?' I said. Iz and Jude laughed. 'What about it?' she said looking very mad, but just for a minute. 'Don't funnyface her' Iz said and I didn't know which one of us she was talking to so we both shut up. 'Streethangers after you cause they deadhead' Jude said. 'However you look. They fuck anything room temperature' Iz said. 'Come with us we're on the prowl' Jude said. 'What are you doing?' I asked. 'Hanging just hanging' said Iz. 'Okay' I said. I wondered if those boys would have done anything if the girls hadn't come along. Probably not because the men were looking at them funny and I would have started screaming if they'd have kept pushing me. Just the same you never can tell what's going to happen with strangers.

We girls started walking downtown up the hill. We walked side by side and made other people walking toward us get out of our way. As we walked I saw the Spanish girl had a limp but didn't have a cane. 'What's your name?' I asked her. 'Weezie' she said not looking at me. 'You don't wanta know her real name' Iz said. 'You the new girl moved in?' Weezie asked. I nodded. 'You not Spanish.' 'No' I said. 'Jewish?' 'How could you tell?' I asked. 'I'm people literate' Weezie said. 'Only kind of literate' said Jude. 'I spy some cholo airin his heels I tell you which island he footed last' said Weezie. 'That's good?' She shook her head. 'Straight' she said.

Around Barnard were lots of college girls with their books. I always thought I'd go to Barnard or maybe Smith, they don't let boys go to Smith and that's a plus. The other girls looked at the students as we walked by but nobody said anything except Jude. 'Chumps' she said but then got quiet again. 'You go private school?' Weezie asked. I guess she could tell that too and I wasn't going to lie. 'Yes' I said. 'You like it?' Iz asked. 'It's all right. It's school, you know' I said. They nodded. 'Do you like school?' I asked and they laughed. At first I thought they were laughing at me but then Jude said 'Too deadhead for me.' 'Boys be dillingerizin the hall all day dag' said Weezie. Iz didn't say anything and I guessed she liked school but didn't want to say. 'Do they shoot people in your school?' I asked. 'They detectored but there's ways' said Weezie. 'She oughta know' said Jude. 'Show her Weez.'

Weezie was wearing shiny knee boots with electric tape on the toes. She reached into one of them and pulled out a Rambo knife a foot long. She grabbed my arm and stuck the knife point right under my chin and smiled and showed her gold teeth in front. I know I should have been scared Anne but it was the strangest thing, I wasn't. Iz and Jude didn't look worried and maybe that was why I didn't get scared. Weezie laughed and let go of me and we kept walking. Some people on the street looked at us but not many. Most of the people we saw wouldn't look at us as if we weren't really there.

'Dominican toothpick' said Weezie. She tossed her knife in the air and caught it before putting it back in her boot. 'You crazy Weez you get exed out some day sticking people with that' Iz said. 'Unless they gunnin nobody argue with this' said Weezie. 'Almost cut her foot off last month that's why she's hopping' said Jude. 'What happened?' I asked. Weezie blushed like she was embarrassed but Iz told me. 'Psycho Killer here she cruising with Charmin and Blood T one night trying to faze the Renegades' Iz said. 'Skying her blade like flipping heads with a quarter. Dropped it right

through her foot. That's why she tape those slut slippers.'
'You go to the hospital?' I asked. I wanted to see what her
foot looked like but since we just met I didn't think she'd
show me. 'Don't funnyface me they'd just hand me Tylenol
say see if it's poison' said Weezie. 'She didn't do nothing'
said Jude. 'Doctor girl just pull it out wipe it off she been
gimpin ever since. Shit' she said and laughed.

At 110th Street they headed down into the subway. 'We
gotta go to the bank' Jude said. 'Meeting folks downtown.'
'You around tomorrow?' Iz asked me. I nodded. 'Be outside
the Chinese place cross Broadway noontime' she said.
'Okay' I said and then she ran after Jude and Weezie. I
walked further downtown and then came back along Riverside because I didn't want to see those boys if they were still
hanging out on Broadway. I wanted to go to a movie or a
museum or something but where's the money so there
wasn't anything to do except walk around. Riverside Park
always looks so scary not like Central Park at all. There
were police cars parked along the street at 116th and there
were police all over the place. I didn't know what had
happened but I was glad it didn't happen to me.

'What did you do sweetie did you have a good time?'
Mama asked me when I got back. 'Just walked around with
some girls I met' I said. 'Do they live in the neighborhood
my angel?' 'Around here yes' I said. 'I'm glad you're
making friends sweetie I'm so glad' Mama said. 'We'll be
living here from now on won't we?' I asked. I knew it was
true that we would and I didn't see why we should all tell
lies about it. Mama looked sad when I asked her like I'd
told her I hated her or something bad like that. 'Oh darling
no no we won't we'll be back home someday you wait and
see' Mama said. 'It's all right if we don't but I just want to
know' I said because I could tell she was fudging like crazy.
'No my sweetie don't you fret we'll be back home before
you know it and Daddy won't have to work for that awful
lunatic any more and the trains won't keep us up at night'
Mama said. 'I'm used to them' I said. 'They don't wake me

103

up anymore.' 'Oh sweetie they shouldn't have ever woken you up at all.' She gave me a big hug and a kiss and then went back to proofing her manuscripts. I saw the check she got for the first one she did, it got here very fast she said. It was only for a hundred dollars.

I'm glad Iz wants to get together with me tomorrow. She seems really nice and not just because she was the first person up here to talk to me. Weezie seems dangerous even though she's friendly. Jude's all right but she acts like she's always thinking about something else far away. It's funny how you wind up with your friends, sometimes I think you always look for someone who's the most like you. That's probably why I like Iz the best even though it seems like she's so different, I don't think she really is.

Four more days till Lori gets back from the camp. I can't wait to see her. I wonder if she'd get along with Iz. Probably not though, I've heard her say nigger before even though she says she's not a racist and has worn buttons and everything.

Night night Anne.

APRIL 12
Our air conditioner isn't working so me and Boob boiled last night. Better get used to it though there's no money for a new one even if it wouldn't blow the fuses.

At noon I met Iz across the street who was already there. It was just as hot today as yesterday. Iz was wearing a halter and tight jeans that made her look fatter than she really is. 'Where's Jude and Weezie?' I asked. 'They partied bigtime last night and sleep like they dead' Iz said. 'Can't hang waiting on them daylong I got to do right with my time. You eat?' I shook my head. 'Come on then not Chinese though I don't want to eat cats' she said and pulled a ten dollar bill from her pants pocket. It was quite a struggle. We walked around the corner on 125th Street and went to a Spanish restaurant. Iz ordered rice and beans at the counter and got two Cokes out of the machine. We sat in a booth away from the window brushing all the crumbs from the seats. A cockroach crawled over the table-top and Iz squashed it with her thumb and wiped it on her jeans.

'Why you moved up here really you run out of money?' she asked me when the waiter brought our rice and beans. 'Yes' I said. 'My Daddy's a screenwriter but they're not making movies they want him to do right now so we're broke practically' I said. 'He makes movies?' 'Writes them.' 'What kind?' 'All kinds.' 'What's he doing if he's not writing movies?' 'Working at Excelsior bookstore in mid-town.' 'Dag I went in there solo one time to buy books for English class and they on me like flies.' 'The owner's such a psycho' I said. I told her about the time I saw him hitting his head on the dumbwaiter yelling fuck me fuck me. 'Crazyass motherfuckers crazier they act better jobs they get' Iz said. 'That's probably why they were following you' I said. 'They following me cause I'm black fuck em' Iz said.

After we ate we walked uptown toward Harlem but not actually in it. There're all these abandoned warehouses and burned out buildings where the subway runs above ground. Nobody said anything to us except a different group of boys we walked by saying the usual. Even though it was hot again today I wore loose jeans this time so nobody would think I was trying to be hot but it didn't make much difference because of the way Iz was dressed.

'You got to eye close up here' Iz said. 'Weezie almost cut you yesterday.' 'I didn't do anything' I said. 'You did you dissed her about her slut clothes' Iz said. 'That's how she was dressed' I said. 'Don't matter that's why she bladed you like that.' 'Why didn't she cut me then?' 'She wanted to fear you let you know she don't slack.' 'She'd have cut me for that?' 'Weezie's crazy' Iz said. 'I don't know what private school's like except on TV but you don't dis like that less you want cutting or worse.' 'Should I say I'm sorry?' I asked. 'No that'd just make her crazier it's done so don't ulcer yourself she let it slide' Iz said. 'You didn't look scared' I said. 'No she coulda had you head and nothing we could do about it if she wanted to move, Weezie fast. And I don't want to get it. She blade first think later' Iz said. 'Then why do you hang with her?' I asked. 'She's our friend and got big league talent besides' Iz said.

'Thanks for telling me I wouldn't have known' I said. 'You'd known when you got that blade in you neck' Iz said. 'Just lipstill round her though that's best. She almost got me one time cause I tell her she raising a pussy tickler like Spanish girls get sometime.' 'What's that?' I asked. 'Mustache' Iz said. 'Tickles. Took me months figure out which way to stand when she blowing. Me and my mom just moved up here last year when our name hit the top of the list, it was rough till I met Jude. Jude's my main. We girls together. It's handleable' Iz said. 'How old are you?' I asked. 'Twelve' she said. 'Jude and Weezie, they fourteen. What are you? Thirteen fourteen? You not fifteen are you?' 'I'm twelve too' I said. 'Dag you tall for you age then. That's what threw me. Can't tell from what you know' Iz said.

One of the big old warehouses we walked by didn't have any windows along Broadway and only a couple of doors. The wall was painted over with dozens and dozens of names in bright colors. Iz saw me looking at it and said 'That's who's dead lately. Drugs.' 'There's so many' I said. 'They painted over it twice since I been living up here, there's always more. The Pit, that's a block over going that way' Iz said pointing east. 'What's the Pit?' 'That's where they all hang selling they crack and whoring. Bad news. Don't ever go over there you can keep from it' Iz said.

We stopped at 137th Street. 'Eye that way' Iz said. About ten blocks up there was a lot of black smoke and police cars and fire engines with their lights flashing. There hadn't been anything about more riots on TV so I thought it must have just started. 'Going down like this a week now' Iz said. 'Let's head back.' Then we walked back down

Broadway. The subway kept going through like it didn't make any difference that there was a riot going on.

On our side of Broadway but further up is a huge building that's another housing project. It's so big it blocks out the whole sky and river for several blocks. 'I live on the twentieth floor there' Iz said. 'Is it nice?' 'Good view' she said. 'You ever been to Jersey?' 'Sure' I said. 'One day I'm going to go to Jersey. Just get on the bus go over see what it's like' Iz said. She made it sound like China. 'You probably been to Europe and all over like that' Iz said. 'Just once' I told her. 'What was that like?' she asked. 'Pretty' I said. 'Not like here?' she asked. 'No' I said.

There was something I couldn't figure out Anne. 'Why did you start talking to me?' I asked Iz. 'What do you mean?' she asked. I didn't know what to say because what I meant was why did she start talking to me when I was so different, she could have just ignored me or beat me up or anything but she didn't. But I didn't know how to say that without making her think I meant something else. 'I don't know' I said. 'You looked okay that's all' Iz said. 'Do Jude and Weezie like me too?' 'Jude thinks so Weezie I don't know I don't even know if Weezie likes me. Weezie's Weezie that's all' Iz said. 'We be Death Angels that's the name of our crew. We all got names for our crews up here, there's the Renegades and the Amsterdam Cheeseburgers and the Bad Boys and all of them.' 'Do I get to join the Death Angels?' I asked. She laughed and I think she was laughing at me this time but it wasn't bad all the same. 'We talk to you don't we?' Iz asked.

When we got to the McDonald's at 125th she said she was going to walk east and meet Jude and Weezie. 'You want to come up and see where I live before you go?' I asked. 'Sometime' Iz said. 'Remember what I tell you about Weezie. She no private school girl. Stay on her good side, everthing be all right. And don't ever get on Jude's bad side.' 'Why?' I asked. 'Cause you won't know that's where you be till it too late' Iz said.

Iz left and I went home. Anne it's so strange that people are so crazy. Weezie acted funny but didn't seem psycho. It didn't seem like she could really go post office and kill somebody but I guess she could. I'm glad Iz told me but now I'm scared I might say something and not even know what I've said and get cut with a knife for it. I'm glad Iz likes me even if I'm not sure of Jude and Weezie. I don't know if I want to be a Death Angel but maybe I do.

On local TV tonight they didn't say anything about the riots right up the street. They interviewed a radio guy who said the homeless should be killed and the newswoman said really killed? and the radio guy said really killed. Then it showed the dog show. On the national news they talked about containing disturbances and they showed machine guns in front of the Capitol and the White House. There's probably a lot going on that they're not saying anything about. I didn't say anything to Mama or Boob about how there was a riot going on just uptown because it would just get them all tizzied. Daddy didn't get home until almost ten tonight. He said that it took an hour for the cashiers to get the drawers balanced because they kept giggling and losing count. Then he had to walk home because the buses weren't running and the subway broke down because of problems they weren't explaining. He was worn out and went right to bed. Just like I predicted Anne I don't think he's getting any writing done at all.

Boob shivers in bed like she's cold. School tomorrow. I wonder if anyone I know will talk to me this week. Lori will be back to school on Thursday. I think she gets back home on Wednesday. I can't wait. Maybe she can straighten everybody out once she hears what happened. She's my best friend and I miss her so much.

APRIL 14
Daddy's day off was today and he was glad as can be. Mister Mossbacher screamed and worse than that at him

last night. What happened was during the evening rush somebody paid with a hundred dollar bill that was a counterfeit. All the managers are supposed to look carefully at the big bills to make sure they're real. Daddy must have missed this one. So Mister Mossbacher took a hundred dollars out of Daddy's paycheck to make up the difference and screamed at him. Mama said he made Daddy sit in a chair and then he called him idiot over and over again in front of the cashiers.

It's a good thing Daddy paid as much of the taxes as he could before now because this means we'll fall behind in this week's payment to the bill collector. Mama was furious and said she was going to call Mister Mossbacher and tell him he was keeping her children from eating. Daddy wouldn't let her because he said it might get him fired and Mister Mossbacher wouldn't care anyway. He said he'd make sure we didn't go hungry if it came to that.

Do you want to know what's typical Anne? Mister Mossbacher might have screamed and shouted and told Daddy what an awful worker he was but that didn't keep him from telling Daddy he was going to have to work on Friday too this week. He won't get overtime though because since he's getting paid a hundred dollars less this week it starts from that somehow and that way he doesn't work overtime.

I hate Mister Mossbacher.

Lori comes back tomorrow! I'm going to call tomorrow night to talk to her. I'll let you know what she says.

APRIL 16

Anne I didn't write you know yesterday to tell you what Lori said when I called her because when I called no one answered or called back even after I left messages on their machine. Today she came back to school. When I walked into Math class this morning there she was sitting in the second row from the front which was much closer to the teacher than she ever sat before. She looked the same as she did before she left except she was thinner and she had this smile on her face like she was posing for the photographer except there wasn't one. Class was starting so I didn't get to talk to her until after.

When the bell rang she walked out without waiting to talk to anyone. I caught up with her in the hall where she was talking to a teacher whose name I forget. 'Lori it's wonderful that you're back' I said. She looked at me like we hadn't been introduced and then turned around and walked down the hall. 'What's the matter Lori' I said but she acted like she didn't hear me. Nancy Featheringstone who wasn't a friend of mine but who still talks to me said 'That's part of the program.' 'What do you mean?' 'She's been rewired' Nancy said. 'That's silly' I said and I ran after her. She was already in her French class when I found her.

'Lori why won't you talk to me?' I said standing right in front of her. She just stared straight ahead smiling. I grabbed her shoulder and shook it but she still acted like I wasn't there. Tanya came over and said hello to Lori but not to me and Lori said hello but nothing else. The warning bell rang and so I said 'I'll talk to you later Lori' and ran. My next class was upstairs. The second bell went off before I could get there and when I opened the door everyone was already sitting down and I knew I was in trouble.

Miss Dieterle was mad and told me to go to the office and get a late slip even though I was only a minute late. When I got to the office they made me sit there for fifteen minutes before they gave me one. Miss Cooper came out and said 'Lola you're certainly not behaving as we're used to having you behave lately.' It's the first time I've been late to class in over a year but that didn't seem to make any difference. By the time I went to class I was almost a half hour late since I had to get a late permission slip. On the way back I wondered why I was even bothering, since no one would talk to me once I got there and I was being treated like I was dysfunctional or a challenged child or something. The doors don't lock on the inside and I figured I could have just walked out but I'd have really gotten in trouble then so I didn't.

Katherine and Icky Betsy and Tanya all had lunch together and ignored me of course when I said hello. Ever since they stopped talking to me I've been sitting by myself at lunch since nobody seems to want to sit with me that I want to sit with. Every day at school anymore just seems like a trial Anne I get so mad and lonely. I thought it would all be different again once Lori got back but I guess it's not going to be. After school I saw Lori again outside getting ready to leave. I ran over to her and stood in front of her and said 'Why won't you talk to me anymore we were best friends.' Some of the other girls were standing around and laughing. Lori kept smiling that zombie smile like she was deadhead. She took a card out of her little purse and handed it to me before walking off. I was yelling Lori Lori after her but she kept walking down 84th Street like she didn't hear anything, like I wasn't even there. I didn't think I would Anne but I started crying like a little baby. Boob wasn't outside yet of course and I had to wait for her. Everybody walking by was laughing and pointing at me like I was some goon. I wanted to stop crying but I couldn't. I've never felt so awful in my life Anne. They're all so stuck up, all of them.

Boob finally showed up and she must have thought I looked scary or something because she didn't say anything. She didn't look like she felt real good herself so we were both quiet. We walked up to 86th to catch the bus which took hours to show up of course. While we were waiting for it I looked at the card Lori gave me. The logo of Kure-A-Kid where they zombiefied her was at the top with the phone number. The only other thing it said on the card was from the Bible, we shall not die but we shall all be changed.

So I'm just miserable Anne and I'm so mad but there's too many people to be mad at. Sometimes I think I'm going to go post office like everybody else. Oh well. At least I'm making new friends in my new neighborhood. Iz at least.

APRIL 17
Friday!

It just keeps getting worse and worse at school. Today Miss Wisegarver asked me why I'd stopped dressing up for class and wearing jeans and khakis instead. I told her we'd had to cut back on our dry cleaning which is the truth. She shook her head and said that anyone who really cared about how they looked could always find the money for dry cleaning if they really wanted to. Last night we had baloney sandwiches with one slice of baloney only because that was all that was left over and she's saying we should use more money for dry cleaning. I didn't say anything though, just that I'd tell my parents what she said. When I told Mama she shook her head but she laughed and said 'Oh my angel it doesn't matter what you look like as long as you learn what sort of things are they teaching you in school?'

Miss Wisegarver also told me that she was very disappointed in my grades lately. The only test I've taken in her class since the midterms I've gotten a B plus on so she's right and I don't like it but it's impossible to study when Boob keeps telling me to turn out the light like she's doing right now. Excuse me Anne while I go to the kitchen and write. Mama does her proofreading in there because the light's better but she's gone to bed.

Okay now I'm in the kitchen and can continue writing. Anyway Anne it's just an awful mess. I'm so unhappy at school. One of those girls wrote DYKE on my locker with a pen I can't rub off and now every time I go to my locker I see it. They're all looking at me whenever I walk by and I know they're all laughing behind my back because they do it so often to my face. When Katherine sees me walking down the hall she'll turn around and go the other way

112

because she wants to avoid running into me so bad. She must have told everybody I raped her or something the way they've all been acting but sometimes I think it's something else. It couldn't be just because we had to move up here but maybe so, I've heard them talk about public school girls like Iz before and it's always like they were just deadhead trash. Maybe that's what they think I am now.

This evening I tried to talk to Mama or actually Mama tried to talk to me. She'd taken Placidyls to calm herself down, she's run out of Xanax and I think her doctor doesn't want to give her any more. It's a good thing Daddy's Guild plan still covers us or she'd have to go to the Pit to buy her drugs. 'My angel what's the matter why don't you tell me' she asked when I said I was sick of school. 'Lots of things' I said. 'But what sweetie tell me' 'Lori' I said because that's what really bothers me the most. 'You mean the way she's not talking to you? I told you honey they do peculiar things to people who have to go to those places they've probably been having her play with her inner child and who knows what nonsense' Mama said. 'It's like she's not even there when I talk to her' I said. 'You mean you talk to her and she just stares at you?' Mama asked. Like you do sometimes I almost said but didn't. 'What do your other friends say sweetie?' Mama asked.

'Nothing' I said. I've never told her about what happened with Katherine or the way the other girls are acting toward me now. It's weird but I'm scared she'd call me Dyke too though I know that's ridiculous. 'They're acting weird that's all' I said. 'Sweetie they're probably as puzzled as you by her odd behavior' Mama said. 'I wish we lived at home again' I said. I hadn't meant to say it but I did anyway. 'Oh my angel I know this is all so hard on you and sweet Boobie but it won't be forever it won't' Mama said. 'I think it will' I said. She shut her eyes for a second and I thought she was going to sleep. 'It won't' she said. 'It won't it won't it won't oh no.' She said it enough that she seemed to finally convince herself and then she didn't say anything

113

else. Neither she nor Daddy have gone to their shrinks since we moved. The way they act sometimes I think they should.

That was about all there was to say so we stopped talking. Daddy of course is working his extra day today. He got his paycheck with the hundred dollars taken out of it yesterday so the next week will be tough. I guess we'll have to cut back on the dry cleaning some more. I went into our room and started writing even though Boob was already in bed. This past week Boob has been going to bed earlier and earlier like she was a baby who needed to sleep more. Even so she doesn't sleep any more than she did before she just lies there awake under the covers. By the time she gets to sleep it's usually after I've gone to sleep and then she kicks me all night in her dreams. In the morning when she wakes up she sits there rocking back and forth with her My L'il Fetus in her arms without saying anything before she finally gets up. I ask her what's the matter and she won't tell me.

Anyway Anne that's all for tonight.

APRIL 18

Chrissie called Mama from California this morning while we were all still asleep. They're getting ready to hide out in the hills she told Mama. 'Hide out from what?' I asked when Mama got off the phone. 'From city people sweetie you know them they're so paranoid they think all the poor people are going to come hack them to death in their sleep' Mama said. 'You mean black people?' I asked. 'Yes my angel that's who they mean and Mexicans and liberals and everybody else who looks funny at them they're so crazy' Mama said. 'What else did she say?' I asked because Mama looked really upset when she got off the phone. 'Just the usual rantings and ravings of the mad sweetie' Mama said. 'Like what though?' 'Nothing my angel.' 'She did I can tell what did she say to you?' Mama looked like she was about to cry but didn't she doesn't cry any more often than I do even though I did earlier this week like I admitted. 'Oh sweetie she's very good with accusations and making me feel guilty she's like Gran' Mama said. 'What did she say?' I asked. 'She said everything we've done wrong is coming back to haunt us now she said we're criminals for keeping you both here in New York where we'll all be murdered in our sleep she said I was a horrible parent' Mama said and then she started crying. 'She's crazy Mama' I said. 'I know my angel' she said 'but it's the way she says it that counts she knows how to say it' Mama said. 'You're the best parents you and Daddy' I said. It's true even if they're goofy they're my parents and I'd die before I lived with Chrissie. Mama gave me a big hug. 'Oh sweetie thank you so much you're such an angel you and Boob both' Mama said. 'It's just a lapse on my part sweetie forgive me.' 'There's nothing to forgive' I said. 'What else did Chrissie say?' 'Oh that was the worst of it sweetie she said San Francisco is burning down nightly what with the riots but who knows if she's hallucinating or not it's altogether possible' Mama said.

I know I'll sound like I'm boasting Anne but I can't help it I'm glad I was able to make Mama feel better. Chrissie is such a psycho I can't believe she's in the same family as we are but I guess it's true. Anyway after crisis intervention this morning I stayed in most of the afternoon trying to read Tess of the D'Urbervilles but I can't get the drift. It's so hot and we have to keep the windows open and it's so noisy with kids yelling in the street and the subway going by all the time. I know I'm driving you crazy with all this complaining but I can't help it. The book's even more boring than Silas Marner and a whole lot more annoying because Tess is such a wimp so far. I knew Angel would act like he did right from the start he's such a loser. She should have just gone somewhere off by herself where no one knew her and start over again I think but I guess it would have been hard. Even so I think it serves her right whatever happens. Daddy says he doesn't believe Hardy should even be taught until graduate school but I'd probably feel the same way if I waited to read it then.

Late this afternoon I went outside to look for Iz. I wished I'd gotten her phone number or I'd given her mine. Hot again today so everybody was hanging outside. People in New York look so ugly when it's summer out guys run around without their shirts and old fat ladies wear the worst clothes. At least those awful boys weren't around they must have been somewhere being cool. I thought I'd walk toward her building and see if I saw her or Jude and Weezie. When I got to 125th Street I was all set to cross the street when suddenly I saw something amazing.

There were about ten dozen Army trucks and humvees and cars coming down 125th Street from the east. They turned onto Broadway and headed north to where the riots were. It looked like an invasion Anne I've never seen anything like it. I don't know if there was anything on TV tonight about it but there hasn't been before now. Everybody was stopping to look at them drive along watching to see where they were going. Some boys were cursing at them and saying traitor traitor whenever they saw black soldiers. I watched with everybody else and after I saw they were going to keep coming I went ahead and crossed the street into Harlem.

I didn't want to go too far into Harlem by myself but figured it would be safe enough if I went as far as Iz's building. Nobody paid any attention to me because they were too busy watching the Army go by. As it turned out Anne as I was walking up guess who I saw walking down? Iz and Jude and Weezie and another girl who looked younger than me. Even from a block away I saw how pregnant she was. It threw me because it was like seeing Boob really pregnant and not just with her My L'il Fetus strapped on.

Iz waved when they saw me. 'Girl you crazy what are you doing up here?' Iz asked. 'I wanted to see if I could find you' I said. 'You found.' 'What's going on?' I asked. 'Invasion' Weezie said. 'Greenasses comin to slam us sinful Harlemites' Jude said looking out at me from beneath her baseball cap. 'Are the riots worse?' I asked. I looked north but I didn't see as much smoke as there usually is over Long Island lately. 'No they just want to stick in the fear and twist it' said Jude. 'Curfew tonight at seven up here' Weezie said. 'You're going to stay in?' 'We better' said Iz. 'Wait see how often and where and who they be shootin' Weezie said. 'What are you doing now?' I asked. 'Running Esther to Mickey's feed her' Jude said. 'Esther say hello to Lola' said Iz. Esther wasn't as young as I thought but I'm sure she's not any older than me Anne. She was wearing baggy gym shorts and a big shirt but she still looked like she swallowed a basketball. She's as dark as Iz and has a little baby face except for a scar on one cheek. 'We on fetus patrol for Esther make sure it pop out all right' Iz said. 'Come with us.'

Weezie looked mad but didn't say anything so I couldn't tell if she was mad because I was coming along or not. I think she doesn't like me as much as Iz and Jude seem to. Ever since Iz told me about how she almost cut me with her knife I haven't trusted her. She didn't do anything today though. We walked down to McDonald's and went in. They got Big Macs for themselves and two fish sandwiches for Esther because she doesn't eat meat. I had enough money for french fries and a Coke. We sat at a table at the window so we could look out. The Army finished going by we thought and then it was nothing but traffic in the street for a while. Then some bigger Army trucks came along and hundreds of soldiers marching.

'Look PCs' Jude said. 'What?' I asked. 'Personnel carriers. Heavyduty action' she said. 'Lola you ought not be struttin solo up where we are' Iz said. 'Gangstaboys catch you drag you inside a wreck and poke you full of holes.' 'I'd run and scream like I would have done last week' I said. Weezie laughed but Jude watched me while I was talking like she was really interested in what I had to say. 'And like they'da raped you last week we hadn't come along. Scream all you like girl, better do more than scream' Weezie said.

'If I'd had your telephone number I'd have called first but I didn't' I said. Iz wrote down a number on a napkin. Esther still looked hungry so I gave her the rest of my french fries and she ate them up. 'That's my house you just call and I come meet you' Iz said. I borrowed her pen and wrote down mine for her. 'You don't habla Spanol, no use me giving you mine' Weezie said. 'I ain't phoneable where I bed' Jude said and I gave her my number too. 'Esther darlin your tummy still hollering?' Iz asked. 'Sure is' Esther said. 'Get some exercise Weez get up and get more food for this girl' Jude said. Weezie leaned over to pick up her bag from the floor. She was wearing a tank top that was too big. I saw she wasn't wearing a bra even though she should.

'When you rise and shine?' Jude asked me once Weezie went to the counter. 'On weekends not till ten usually' I said. 'Phone her noontime tomorrow Iz' Jude said. 'No good Jude Meemaw's bedding with us this week so it's churching for me' Iz said. 'Then less the Army smart bombs me tonight I call you tomorrow noon we hang together some. Cool?' Jude asked. 'Sure.' It made me feel important somehow that Jude was inviting me to come out. Important's not the right word but you know what I mean. 'Preacher gets drymouth by two' Iz said. 'Once we done holy rolling I run home change and fastfoot it over.' Jude nodded.

Weezie came back with another fish sandwich for Esther and a bag of french fries. 'Take some she eat all yours' she told me. I didn't feel right taking them from Esther because she seemed so hungry and pregnant besides but the way Weezie said it I thought I better have a couple. Then Weezie and Esther and Iz talked about boys they knew at school and the stupid things they'd done. I didn't pay much attention and I don't think Jude did either. She was looking out the window for a while at the people going by and I started looking too. After a minute or so I saw she was looking at me and I smiled. She smiled too. Jude's lost her top teeth on both sides but the ones she has in front are as big and white as Iz's. It made me feel good when she smiled at me, Anne. Right now's the first time I've been thinking about those stupid girls at school and that's only because they seem even stupider in comparison to Jude and Iz. It was six thirty when we finished eating. The Army went wherever they were going. 'I call you' Jude said and then the girls walked back uptown.

I went back home to watch the news to see what they said about the Army coming to town. Mama hadn't been watching so she hadn't heard anything. 'You said there were many many soldiers my angel and they were all marching north?' Mama asked. 'Thousands I'd say that's what it looked like' I said. 'Sweetie that's so unnerving what are they going to do do you think?' 'I don't know that's why I asked if you watched the news' I said. The local news had gone off so we switched the TV over to CNN. The style show was on though so they didn't say anything till seven when it was time for the national news. 'Chrissie's right' Mama kept saying and shaking her head. 'No she's not' I said because I knew how much Chrissie had upset her this morning. 'She is my angel she'd be sitting there all smug and happy like a fat frog if she were here saying look see I'm right as always' Mama said. 'She's not though and she's not right either' I said. 'I'm afraid she is my angel oh she is' Mama said so I didn't say anything else. Boob just watched TV looking really scared. I put my arm around her and she was shivering again, she shivers all the time now.

The national news came on and they talked about the emergency situation. They said the National Guard was being federalized. They said everything was so bad that the government was taking steps to make sure nothing like what was happening in Long Island happened anywhere else. They said the President would be on TV tonight and he was an hour later. We watched a nature show until then. When the President came on we watched him. I don't know what he was doped up on tonight Anne but it was something intense. He had glassy eyes like Mama gets and he looked like he didn't even want to be there. He was sitting in an armchair next to a fireplace like we had in our living room. He said that Operation Domestic Storm would calm everything down in no time and that there was no need to worry about the economy. He said the nation was poised for recovery like he always said. He also said on the advice of advisors mobs of animals in the cities would be shown no mercy. 'Does he mean us?' I asked Mama. 'No sweetie he means everybody else' Mama said.

We watched some more but he didn't say anything else but how great America was. 'How will they tell the difference between us and everybody else?' I asked but Mama didn't say anything like the answer should be obvious. Boob sat between us rocking back and forth and holding her doll. Daddy came home right after that just like it was a normal day, he said everything was like it always was at the store. He didn't say anything else. The store takes all the talk out of him.

That's all tonight.

APRIL 19

What a fun day today was Anne. Let me tell you what happened. At noon Jude called! She told me to wear old clothes and come out and meet her at 125th in McDonald's parking lot. I put on an old shirt of Daddy's and a pair of jeans torn out in the knees and went out. Mama was sitting in the kitchen watching the news. I asked her if anything happened but it hadn't.

Jude was there when I got there leaning against a truck. She was wearing really expensive running shoes and had her hair pulled back tight from her face. She has the best cheekbones you've ever seen. 'Let's go my house' she said and we started walking up Broadway. 'What happened last night?' I asked. 'What's meant?' Jude asked. 'With the Army what did they do?' 'Posed. Stancing flatfoot on street corners holding they guns like to beat off' Jude said. 'They shoot anybody?' 'Nobody worth mentionin' Jude said. 'Where are they now?' I asked not seeing any. 'All over further up. Not down here. In the Pit neither.' 'Iz told me about the Pit' I said. 'Just like blueboys they ain't trucking with Pit Bulls yet less they get a mighty cut. Ever want to clear the Pit they gonna have to napalm' Jude said. 'What's everybody doing?' I asked. 'Keeping shutmouthed and walking light till they figure the agenda' Jude said. 'Have they stopped rioting?' I asked. Jude pointed to a black cloud in the sky ahead. 'Long as there's going they went. Spilling down too. Check this out' she said.

Two blocks up at 140th the Army had blockades in the street. They parked their trucks crossways with only one lane open on each side to let cars and buses through. There were about twenty soldiers with their guns standing there checking everybody driving in or out. The stores and restaurants that were still in business were all closed with the gates pulled down. Broken glass was all over the street and a burned out car was in the center median of Broadway. Some of the stores had their gates pulled off and the windows smashed. A liquor store at the corner was completely trashed and on fire.

We walked east on 138th. It looks like the streets on the Upper West Side except most of the buildings are abandoned. A streetlight was lying on the sidewalk. Halfway down the block was a vacant lot full of bricks and garbage where buildings used to be. Next to it was an old tenement with the lower floor cemented up with concrete blocks. Most of the windows upstairs that weren't broken were covered with flowery decals like you see on buildings in the Bronx when you ride by. Jude looked to see if anybody was following us and then we walked through the vacant lot around to the back of the building. She pulled a big wooden board away from the wall. There was a hole there where a couple of blocks had been taken out of a basement window. 'Scared a holes?' she asked. It was dark and dirty inside but I shook my head. 'I'll light up once we're in. Me first, then you. Just follow' she said. She got down on her hands and knees and wiggled through headfirst. Once she was in I crawled in too. It was scary but I figured she knew what she was doing. The floor was level with the window which was good because I was afraid there was a drop and I didn't know what we'd be dropping into. Jude had a flashlight inside that she must keep there and she turned it on so we could sort of see where we were going. Broken wood and old wine bottles and cans on the floor were cleared off in front of the window so nobody would hurt themselves crawling in. Jude walked up a flight of rickety wooden stairs and I followed her like she said. I heard chirping sounds like birds and the air was full of dust and dirt. The stairs leaned down so it was hard to walk on them.

'Crack house onetime I spec' Jude said. 'I repossessed it after the heads gentrify the Pit. First time Weezie and Iz visit entrance was smaller, only one a them blocks was out to keep prying eyes blind.' Jude shoved open the door at the top of the stairs. We were in a long hall. 'Foot careful' she said. Some of the floorboards were pulled up with pipes sticking up. Jude held the flashlight down so we could see where we were walking. We made it to another stairway and went upstairs. 'I snaked in, out, no prob but Weez she just get halfway. Big Dominican culo stuck like a cork' Jude said and laughed.

On the stairs where we were walking and on the bannister where we had our hands the dust was gone but on the sides it was an inch thick. There was graffiti on the walls and places where holes were knocked through. 'Weez she cursed me blue and let me tell you girl I was rollin' Jude said. There was all this crunching under our feet when we got to the next floor and when I looked down I saw the floor covered with little glass things and envelopes you put crack in. 'Then we try unpluggin her and nobody laughing now. I pull, Iz push but Weezie, she don't budge. I say Weez how I get out if you blockin the door and she scream at me again' Jude said. She walked up another flight of stairs to the third floor. We had to be especially careful because the bannister was gone. I stayed close to the wall. There were scratching sounds and more chirping ahead of us and I knew it must be rats. I hate rats but Jude didn't seem scared and kept walking up.

'Weezie was stuck like Winnie the Pooh' I said thinking of how funny it was to think of them compared. Jude didn't say anything like she didn't know what I was talking about. On the third floor Jude pushed open another door and we walked into a dark room where it felt like it was a hundred degrees. 'Stand there' Jude said and then she took sheets of wood down from the broken out windows. There was a breeze when the windows were uncovered but not much. 'You finally got her out?' I asked. 'Looks that way don't it?' Jude asked. 'Iz she got Weezie's pants down and got her slippery with cold cream. Then we yank and yank and finally Weezie popped out like a fart. Before Iz tried getting in I knocked out another cement block make sure she could make it' Jude said. 'Weezie was stormin but I hashed her quick.'

The room was as big as our old living room. Jude uncovered three of the windows. They looked out on the rear toward 139th. An old mattress with sheets and pillows on it lay on top of bricks to keep it off the floor. There was a beat up suitcase on a desk that had been painted over a dozen times. Next to it was a boombox and cassettes. Hanging from nails on the wall were a blue recycle bag full of bottles and a bag stuffed with trash like McDonald's wrappers and old newspapers. There were holes in the walls, some punched in by people and some by the floor I thought were rat holes. Lots of candles like holiday candles were everywhere. They were from botanicas and each candle was in a glass container. On the sides of the glasses were drawings of pretty women wearing crowns and old men in robes and Jesus too. They all said something in Spanish on them.

'This is your house?' I asked. 'For now' said Jude. 'Where are your parents?' I asked. 'Somewhere fuck em' Jude said. 'You stay here all the time?' I asked. 'Sometimes.' 'Where do you take a shower?' 'Iz's sometimes, other places other times.' 'How long you been here?' I asked. 'February' Jude said. She put a rap tape in her boombox. The singers were bombers and rapped so fast I couldn't hear anything but blurs. Except for Bob Marley most of her cassettes were of Caribbean groups I hadn't heard before or whose names I didn't recognize. She had a framed certificate on the wall that said Outstanding Student Sixth Grade Judy Glastonbury. Jude sat down on her mattress and patted it so that I'd sit down beside her which I did.

'Are you from Jamaica Jude?' I asked. 'My parents from Barbados but I was born at St Luke's' Jude said. 'You have an accent' I said. 'You too' she said. I didn't know I did. Hers is so pretty. Whatever my accent is I know it's not an awful one like Long Island or New Jersey people have. 'What's private school like?' she asked. 'Same as regular school I guess' I said. 'Doubt it. You go to mix school or girls' school?' 'To Brearley. I wouldn't want to go to a school with boys in it' I said. 'I hear you. Boys be so constant deadhead and lowering the tone. Hell if you're actual schoolin and not just day-wasting like they' she said. 'Are you still in school?' I asked. 'Where else I be?' she asked. 'I don't know. You're fourteen?' Jude nodded. 'So's Weezie. Esther's thirteen. Iz, twelve but she's fast.' 'I'm twelve' I said. 'Known.' 'You have any brothers or sisters?' I asked. 'Two in the Army two dead' Jude said. 'What happened?' 'They exed out. Happens' Jude said.

She didn't say how but she didn't seem like she wanted to say. There was a cracked mirror leaning against the wall across from her bed. 'Do you think I look older than twelve?' I asked looking at myself. 'You tall but babyfaced plain' said Jude. 'I know' I said. Her room was good to hang in but it seemed like such a horrible place to actually live. What she did when she had to go to the bathroom I didn't have any idea and I was glad I didn't have to go. 'Where do you study?' I asked. 'School during class.' 'Your teachers don't say anything?' 'They keen on viability not homework' Jude said.

Anne where Jude lives is so awful but after a while I got used to it and it felt like a nice place. It's like our apartment now it's not as good as our old one but it's home just the same. It was weird though that you could adjust to something so quick and I wondered if I were Jude if I could ever get used to living in a place like hers. 'You like you life?' Jude asked. 'Sometimes' I said. 'School I used to like but I don't anymore. I probably will again. At home it's hard because we've gotten so poor.' She didn't say anything and I thought I'd said something bad because as poor as we are we still have more money than Jude does now. But she didn't act like she was mad or anything.

'What about you?' I asked. 'There's a lot more I want a lot more' she said. 'Yes' I said. 'Got to get it one way or other' she said. 'You don't sell drugs do you?' I asked. 'Never hook with junkies' Jude said. 'I know you thinkin you virg but they more white junkies than black. They find you if you look.' 'I know a couple' I said. 'Me too. Don't know em long though. Iz and Esther clean too.' 'Weezie?' I asked. 'Weezie shit Weezie do what Weezie wants. She be exed one day. I tell but she deafs' Jude said.

We didn't say anything for a minute or so. 'Boys too' she said. 'Top trouble.' 'Have you been with boys?' I asked. She nodded still staring out the window. 'Like you've kissed them and made out?' 'Oh yeah' she said. 'I've never kissed a boy' I said. 'I kissed a girl friend of mine. Then she told everybody I was a queer.' 'Bad news. Are you?' Jude asked. 'I don't know' I said surprised that I said it. 'We tongue kissed' I told her. 'That don't mean nothing.' 'How old were you when you first tongue kissed?' I asked. 'Six, seven. Don't remember' Jude said.

She said it like she didn't think it was anything strange. I couldn't picture Boob tongue kissing anybody and Boob is three years older. Jude was sweating through the front of her T-shirt and I was surprised to see how dark her nipples were. 'Bad girl. You eyeballin me like you eyeballed Weezie yesterday' Jude said. 'When?' I asked. 'When she lean over and her titties do a flipflop. I saw you. Careful when you scope.' 'Why?' 'When she think somebody queer Weezie don't just go post office, she go <u>G</u>PO. Sometime she hook with Intercrime, she want to be a gangstagirl. They zip down to the Village, go bash bigtime. And Weez already got a big problem with you cause you're white.' 'But she's Spanish' I said. 'Don't make her white' Jude said. 'Boys or girls make me no diff but if you don't know which send you don't let Weezie know.'

'Have you kissed girls before?' I asked. 'Kissin sure. You mean which do I hop when I want hoppin?' she asked. I nodded. 'Depends on who offers what when' she said. There was a whistle downstairs all of a sudden. Jude whistled the same tune back. 'That's Iz' she said. In a few minutes Iz came upstairs panting like she ran all the way. 'What's doing?' she asked. 'Looselippin that's all' Jude said. Iz had a big bottle of Pepsi with her that she opened and drank from before passing it to us. 'I'm overheating so scuse' Iz said and pulled her jeans and shirt off. She wasn't wearing a bra either and like Weezie she should have because she's full size. In her underpants she looks like a high school girl and older than when she has her clothes on. She lay down next to us. 'Looselipping who?' she asked.

'Weez' Jude said. 'What about Weez?' Iz asked. 'Her special craziness' Jude said. 'You see her?' Iz shook her head and said 'Weez running the Pit looking for Bad Conrad.' 'What for?' Jude asked. 'Debt collecting' said Iz. 'How did she get the name Weezie?' I asked. 'From weezin' Jude said. 'What's that?' I asked. 'You know' Iz said and huffed and puffed like she was still out of breath. 'Weez got TB. Don't slow her none.' 'When she take sick in third grade she be weezing daylong so we dub her Weezie' Jude said. 'Don't let her cough on you Lola. She say she got the TB beat out a her but she lying' Iz said.

We sat there drinking the bottle of Pepsi until it was all gone. I was so thirsty and so were they. 'How's church?' Jude asked Iz and tossed the bottle in the recycle bag. Iz rolled over on the mattress until her legs rested against me. It was so hot I scooted away but not far. 'Churchy' Iz said. 'You get saved girl?' Jude asked. 'Not yet' Iz said. 'Preacher preached till he was hoarse. Going on bout devils in the streets. Sunday School teacher be especial corny horny today, laying on the hands ever chance he get. Old ladies in hats be pinching my cheeks till I'm sure.' Jude reached across and gave Iz a real hard pinch on the butt. 'Damn you know what I mean' Iz said and kicked out her feet and Jude fell down on top of her. They wrestled on the mattress a few minutes giggling and laughing. I stood up so I wouldn't get kicked or hit and just watched. Finally Jude sat on top of Iz and pinned her arms down. They were soaking wet and both smelled stronger than white girls but they smelled good. 'Caribbean Crusher win again' Jude said. 'Two out a three' Iz said and they both laughed. Even though it was hot Jude didn't get up.

Then I heard a scratching in the corner and I looked. Agh! Anne it was a giant rat the biggest I've ever seen. It could have eaten a cat it was so huge and had a long ratty tail. I screamed and Jude jumped up. The rat knocked over a box of tampons trying to get away. What Jude did I still can't believe. She grabbed a piece of twine she had by her mattress. It had a noose tied in one end and she lassoed the rat around the neck! She jerked it real quick and caught him. She stood up holding the twine and pulling the rat up from the floor. I could hardly stand to look at it it was so horrible. 'Mister Ratty you holidayin the wrong beach' Jude said. 'Careful Jude' Iz said standing on the bed. The rat twisted around on the end of the twine and was trying to lunge at Jude even though it was choking. It hissed and snapped its teeth. 'Rats like people' Jude said. 'Out to get what's gettable.' After it tried to bite her again she reached into the desk drawer and took out a cigarette lighter. She lit it and adjusted the flame so that it burned real high and then she turned it on the rat's belly. 'Whatever they do to you to keep you away' Jude said. The rat pulled itself loose and fell on the floor but before it could run off she caught it by the tail. She swung the rat around and around and then let go and it flew out the window. 'But they get you endtime, just the same' Jude said.

I read in the paper somewhere or remembered from class hearing where a mouse or rat could fall from a high distance and not be hurt because they were small. A person though would be killed or at least all smashed up. Even though I hate rats I hoped it either got away or died. After a while Iz got dressed and we went back downstairs. We saw soldiers walking along Broadway south of where they had the barricade. They weren't doing anything but they looked like they were ready to. The ugliest ones made remarks to us but we didn't pay any attention. We reached the subway where it was elevated at 125th. 'We gotta go bank. Later' Jude said and they ran upstairs.

I went home. Mama was lying down on her bed. She'd been working on manuscripts but must have gotten tired and stopped. When I saw her I stood by the bed and listened to her breathe to make sure she was all right. Boob was lying down too. 'What's the matter Boob?' I asked. She was sucking her thumb and holding her My L'il Fetus and looked like a little baby except she was so big. I sat in the kitchen and wrote you and now I'm finished for today.

APRIL 20
Nothing worth mentioning happened at school today. I'll be so glad when the term is over and it's summer. Daddy was at work of course by the time we got home.

* * *

128

I'm really worried about Boob Anne. She's tuned out
completely. She doesn't say anything when we're going to
school and doesn't say anything on the way home and
hardly talks at all once we get here. Boob used to talk me
to death but now I wish she'd say anything, it's scary the
way she clams. I asked Mama but all Mama said was 'My
angel your sweet sister I think is just overwhelmed she's so
sensitive to changes she's like a barometer.' That's true but
it's scary all the same. When Boob was sitting on the sofa
watching TV with us I kept asking her if the cat had her
tongue and making faces to try to get her riled but she
didn't do anything, it was like I wasn't there. Sometimes I
think I'm turning invisible Anne.

APRIL 22
Maybe I ask for it sometimes Anne but I woke up this
morning so mad thinking about the way all my so-called
friends at school have been acting and treating me. I lay in
bed for an hour before I got up this morning just stewing in
my own juices and listening to Boob snoring. Once I hit her
so she'd roll over and she didn't so I hit her again. She
whimpered and then I got mad at myself for hitting her and
I finally got up.

When I got dressed I called Katherine's house. I wanted
to slam her, I'll be honest. Her mother answered the phone
and I didn't say who I was, I just asked if Katherine was
there. She must have recognized my voice though because
when she said she'd go get her I could hear them talking in
the background for a long time but I couldn't tell what they
were saying.

Finally Katherine came to the phone and the first thing
she said was 'What do you want?' like I was dogshit or
something. 'What did you tell everybody?' I asked her. 'I
didn't tell them anything' Katherine said. 'Then why are
they acting like they are?' 'It's your problem if they figured

it out themselves' she said. 'Figured what out?' 'The way you are.' 'What way am I?' 'I don't have to say it.' 'Yes you do if you're going to lie tell me what you're lying' I said. 'I'm not lying' Katherine said. 'You're telling people I'm queer aren't you?' 'No I'm not I never did' she said. 'Well somebody is.' 'You're just guilty because you know it's true.' 'It is not why are you telling people I am?' 'I'm not I told them you weren't' Katherine said. 'Who told them I was?' I asked.

She didn't say anything and I asked her again. 'Daddy saw us kissing in the hall' she said whispering so I could hardly hear her. 'Why was he spying on us?' I asked. 'Look he saw it I said we weren't queers and he said he knew I wasn't.' 'So he told everybody at school?' 'No' she said and then she clammed again. 'Who'd he tell then?' 'He's friends with Tanya's dad they play racketball at the health club he told him to tell Tanya so she'd be careful. He's talking about putting me in a mixed school next year so I'll be safe and I don't want to leave Brearley' Katherine said. 'So Tanya's dad told Tanya and Tanya told everybody?' 'Yes that's what happened and I'm sorry' Katherine said. 'Why won't you talk to me then?' I asked. 'Because then people will think we're both queer I can't talk to you' she said. 'You're no friend' I said. 'I'm sorry' Katherine said. 'And your dad shouldn't have been spying on me in the bathroom either which I know he was' I said. 'No he wasn't' she said. 'He was that's why I was leaving so early because I thought he'd spy on me more.' 'He wasn't.' 'Does he spy on you when you go to the bathroom?' I asked her. Oh Anne I'm sure he does. Katherine started crying and I said 'Don't cry talk to me' but she hung up the phone. I almost called her back but didn't. But I sat there for a half hour in case she called me back. She didn't.

If Katherine's telling the truth and I'm sure she is there wasn't any reason her father should have told Tanya's father I was queer. He doesn't know he just thinks that because he saw us kissing not that he had any right to look.

130

I wouldn't have kissed Katherine except she kept asking. I wonder if Tanya's father told everyone's parents about me. All the girls must think that at least they've got their minds made up about it. The girls at other schools all think Brearley is the queer school. It isn't though it might as well be in my case. Anne I don't know what's happening to my life. Everything seemed fine just months ago and now it's all falling.

Iz just called me so I'm going to go out and meet her. Public school is closed too. I don't know what we'll do but I'll let you know what happened. Bye for now.

Hello Anne I'm back even though it's not late. Iz and I had a good time though we didn't do anything. I'm in a much better mood now than I was this morning and I'm sure you're glad. I met Iz at McD's. They had a buy one get one free deal on Big Macs so we had a good lunch. Iz was so pretty today Anne she was wearing a black dress and black patent leather shoes and a black band around her dreadlocks so they hung down her back. She was so dressed I felt like a bag lady, I was wearing my jeans and an old shirt like always when I don't have to go to school.

I asked her why she was all spiffed. There was a special memorial service at her church for the dead President and her mother made her go to it with her. As soon as it was over Iz called me from the church and ran right down. 'No reason remembering him' Iz said. 'Never done nothing for black folk never.' 'What did they say at the memorial?' 'Preacher gassin up like he do ever Sunday going on about chickens homing where they roost' Iz said. 'Was everyone sad?' I asked. 'No more'n usual' Iz said. 'Do you have to go back home right away?' I asked. She shook her head and said 'Little while but not yet.' 'Have you seen Jude?' 'I holler up to her place when I pass but she either snoozing or out. Not dressed for crawling so I didn't investigate. Mama she stay after church to wail some more and then eat something with the ladies. I ran girl I ran.' 'What are the

131

soldiers doing?' I asked. 'Greenasses be toesteppin light. Locked their loads once they got they shootin orders. They spec nasty doings and if they don't get them I spec they give them' Iz said.

After we ate we walked down Broadway. Columbia and Barnard were also closed it looked like, we didn't see any students. There was a banner hanging across the front of Barnard saying PAY THE ARMY AND SEND THEM HOME. All the stores were closed further down. It was funny watching Iz walk so dressed up. She held her head up so high she looked at clouds the whole way. 'Why doesn't Jude get along with her parents?' I asked. 'Jude doesn't get along with just everybody' Iz said. 'Did they throw her out of the house?' 'Mutual tossup.' 'She said she had brothers and sisters but they were gone' I said. 'Jude had three brothers. Two oldest joined the 43rd, now they stuck warrin out on Long Island. They probably dead. Bodega owner in the Bronx shot Frederick last year when he tried boosting. Sister Gloria cracked up in March, she gone' Iz said. 'That's so sad' I said. Iz nodded.

We walked over on 106th Street to Riverside Drive, then we walked back up. No one was on the street but homeless people. Nobody was driving and buses went by only every fifteen minutes or so. It was quieter than Christmas and creepola Anne like everyone but us were dead. Probably they were in church or watching TV but that's how it seemed, all abandoned and all ours. Before now I always liked being around people like you always are in New York but lately I didn't and in a weird way I wished it was empty like that all the time.

'You ever go in Riverside Park?' I asked. 'No ho. Jungle-land over there' Iz said. 'You mean there's animals like wild dogs?' I asked. On TV last week they told how a little boy was eaten by wild dogs in the Bronx and all that was left was his head. It was the sort of thing that was so gross Boob would have laughed herself sick about it but when she saw it she just sighed. 'Animals like the Naturals' Iz said. 'What are Naturals?' I asked. 'Marginals gone wilding. Live on the railroad tracks run under Riverside Park. They nightcrawlers. Go butt naked even in wintertime' Iz said. 'No Iz, truth me' I said thinking she was exaggerating. 'Truthing plain' she said and the way she said it made me believe her. 'They tie leaves round they private zones. Paint like savages like with Army camouflage. Make spears from tree limbs. You be footing solo long here come nighttime, they be ghostin round till you blind, then they grab you and fade black in the bush.' 'What do they do to the people they catch?' 'Whatever they want' Iz said. 'When they done playin with the bodies they toss them riverways. Bad evilness Lola I tell you. Not even Weezie go in Riverside Park and she go everwhere.' 'Everwhere?' 'Ever WHERE' Iz said. 'Are they the scariest gang?' 'Naturals a loose gang, no bones to em. Scariest real gangs be the DCons.' 'Where do they hang?' I asked. 'Subway. D train mostly that's not why they called that. They an old gang' Iz said. 'DCon like the roach motels?' 'They cityroaches there no denying that. The DCons the worst there is. They A one terrorists' Iz said. 'What are they like? What do they do?' I asked. Iz shook her head. 'You don't nightcrawl. You won't see em. Pretend you never heard of em' Iz said.

I was disappointed because I wanted to know more about the DCons but Iz wouldn't say anything else about them. I looked over at Riverside Park but it was quiet over there and I didn't see any Naturals. Probably they were why all of those police were over there a while ago.

'Does Weezie hate me a lot?' I asked. 'Weezie hate everybody a lot' Iz said. 'Why?' 'Cause she can't read people like she claim. New people scare her white. Then once she get scared enough she come bladin. That's why we tell you to foot careful round Weezie, she's crazed.' 'Jude told me Weezie hates queers' I said wanting to see what Iz's reaction was. I wondered if she hated queers too. 'Yeah she hate everybody' Iz said. 'But why?' 'Why not?' Iz said. 'Some people just like that. I'm not, Jude neither.' She

133

looked at me and laughed. 'What?' I asked. 'No it's just you're so out a water up here. Goldfish out a the jar' Iz said. 'What do you mean?' 'You're not street, that's all. Me neither but you got to know what's curb and what's cars' Iz said.

We walked over to Broadway when we reached 120th Street. There was a big fire in front of Grant's Tomb with people standing around. It must have been a demo since no one needed to keep warm today. 'You said when you first saw me you talked to me because I looked okay. What'd you mean?' I asked. 'Mean you looked good' Iz said. 'How do you mean looked good?' I asked her. 'Like you was friendly. Like you didn't belong. Jude and me we pick up strays when they look like they need pickin up' Iz said.

'Was Esther a stray?' I asked. 'Esther my cousin' said Iz. 'How did she get pregnant?' I asked. 'Usual way I magine' Iz said. 'I mean who' I said. 'Think somebody raped her but she shamed to say. No need pressin it what's done's done' Iz said. 'What do her parents say?' 'Nada' Iz said. 'No father round and her mama had Esther when she was fourteen so what's she gonna say, you shoulda waited to next year?' 'When's Esther going to have the baby?' 'Couple months Jude thinks. Esther, she don't know how long she been pregnant' Iz said.

We were almost to our apartment when I said 'What do you mean I looked good?' Iz shrugged and said 'Pretty that's all.' She didn't say anything else and I wondered if she meant she thought I was pretty or if she thought I was pretty like she wanted to kiss me. The more I think about the way she and Jude were acting on Sunday the more I wonder if they've been queer together sometimes. If that's so then I wondered if that's why she first started talking to me and why they seem to like me hanging with them, that there's a way they can tell if I'm queer. Probably not because if they were Weezie wouldn't want to hang with them but maybe Weezie doesn't know. I didn't say anything else because I didn't want Iz to think I was queer if she's not.

'Would you like to come meet my mother and sister?' I asked when we reached my apartment. 'You look so pretty today you always do I mean' I said and I worried about saying that but Iz just smiled. 'Okay but then I got to run' she said. We went upstairs and I introduced her to Mama who shook her hand. 'Oh angel is this one of your new friends in our new neighborhood oh Isabella it's such a pleasure and honor to meet you' Mama said. 'Iz's ok' Iz said. 'Sweeties thank you for giving me such a welcome break from the mournfest can I fix you glasses of milk or something?' 'Yes please' I said. 'I can't drink milk but thank you anyway' Iz said. 'Oh darling why not it's so good for young bones' Mama said. 'I'm lactose intolerant' Iz said. Mama smiled and said 'Well some juice or something our home is yours too for any of Lola's sweet friends.' 'No ma'am thanks kindly but I be rolling' Iz said. I told her I'd need to stay in tomorrow to get some studying done but I'd see her on Saturday. Iz said we'd go out with Jude and maybe Weezie she thought it was time I came along with them when they went downtown.

They were going on on TV about security and bomb threats that proved to be false. 'Is lactose intolerance a black thing sweetie?' Mama asked me but I didn't know. 'Your friend seems very pleasant darling is she a lot older than you?' 'We're the same age' I told Mama but I don't know if she believed me.

A bad day to start with but it wound up good after all thanks to Iz. I'm glad I found out what happened with Katherine even though we're still not friends anymore. I'd feel a lot worse if I'd never known.

Night night Anne.

APRIL 23
Daddy will receive a full paycheck this week again so we get something to eat besides spaghetti. I studied what I needed to study today but probably for not as long as I should

have, I just couldn't concentrate. I wonder if I have a brain tumor or something.

Boob stayed in bed today with the covers up over her head. Mama was upset. 'Oh sweetie I don't know what we're going to do about your sister' she said. 'What do you mean the way she's always quiet all the time?' I asked. 'Yes my angel yes' Mama said. She told me one of Boob's teachers called her on Monday and said Boob was so withdrawn and depressed that we'd have to have her checked out by a shrink. Her teacher said that she could tell it wasn't child abuse like we were beating her or anything but that it was something just as bad. Mama held her head in her hands and cried and cried. 'My angel I just don't know how we can I'm trying to find someone who'll see her for cheap but no go. Will Boob talk to you sweetie do you think she will?' she asked. 'I keep trying to get her to talk but I'll try again' I said. 'Please do angel please do' Mama said.

So I went into our room and lay down on the bed next to Boob. 'What is it Boob you can't just stop talking like this you can't' I said. 'Yes I can' Boob said. 'What's the matter Boob you can tell me you know you can' I said. 'No I can't' she said. Then she rolled over and wouldn't say anything else. I stayed there a long time but she kept still and finally I heard her start to snore. I got back up and told Mama. Mama was still in the kitchen and she hadn't started working on her manuscripts yet. 'Don't worry though I'll get her to talk again' I said. Of course Anne I don't know if I can or not but I'll try. 'I'm sorry I'm such a bad mother it's just like Chrissie said' Mama said. It made me so mad that Chrissie upset her so much and it made me mad that she was letting herself be upset too. There wasn't any reason she should worry about what Chrissie had to say. I know there's no reason why I should worry about what the girls at school say either but I do, but Mama's old enough to know better.

'Fuck Chrissie' I said. Even when I said it I knew I shouldn't but I didn't care. Mama's eyes got big as saucers. I thought she was going to explode but didn't. 'Angel I've never heard you say that word before' Mama said. 'I don't say it often' I said. In fact even though I've written it before I don't think I've ever said it until today. 'But it's true' I said and then said it again. 'Fuck Chrissie.' Mama started laughing even though she was crying and then she was laughing and nothing else. 'Yes my angel yes' Mama said. 'Fuck old Chrissie' Mama said. 'That's what your father says and you're both right.' She kissed me and hugged me and then got right to work.

I was glad I'd at least made her feel better even if I hadn't been any help to Boob. Sometimes I think no one in my family needs a shrink they just need me. I need somebody but outside of you I don't know who Anne.

APRIL 24
Boob stayed home today. Maybe she's just been coming down with something and nothing else. I hope so.

I saw Katherine at lunch but this time I didn't even say anything because if what she said really happened then there's no point in slamming her about it. She looked really sad. No one's doing anything to my locker any more but they probably will again when I don't expect it. I saw Lori too. She walks through the halls like she doesn't even know where she is and maybe she doesn't.

Weekend's here.

APRIL 25
What a day today was Anne. This morning Iz called me and told me to meet them at eleven thirty. Now that Mama was able to go to the grocery again I was able to stuff myself like a pig for breakfast. I had a big bowl of cereal and three bananas and a cookie. Boob actually seemed to be feeling better, at least she said good morning and watched cartoons like she was all right.

137

I met Iz and Jude and Weezie at the entrance to the escalator at the 125th Street station. Iz and Weezie wore big baggy pants that they stuffed into motorcycle boots and T-shirts under jackets. Iz's had a number on it and Weezie's had a long list of names. Jude was dressed like for a track meet. She wore running shoes and a black halter top and black leggings that fit so tight you could tell she was only wearing a string. The way she dressed would have made the boys in the neighborhood go wild but they weren't around to comment and the way Jude was I bet they wouldn't have said the same things they would have to me.

'Aimed to step?' Iz asked. 'B n Ts be packin flush today' said Weezie. 'Mind when I pump and dime when we movin' said Jude who gave us tokens. 'Let's.' It was a beautiful sunny day and clear without being hot. Where we are the smoke hardly ever stays around even when you see it overhanging farther up or over on the East Side. We got in the first car when the downtown train finally showed up. 'Glue tight' Jude told us. 'Cruise to clear.' She led Weezie, I followed and Iz stayed behind me. We walked through the cars all the way to the back. It was fun swaying back and forth like on a boat while we walked though it was scary whenever we went between the cars while the train was going fast. It wasn't crowded when we got on but more and more people got on at every stop. 'Gangsta free' Iz said to me.

Six or seven bums were on the train shaking their cups and holding signs saying Have AIDS 4 years TB 5 years Cancer 6 years. The man without legs who rolls through the number one trains every day was on the train too with his cup asking for change. Asian guys sold fortune cookies out of boxes and a Korean man walked through with a suitcase full of toys. He played with a glowing yoyo and a little doll that peed when you pulled down its pants. Peepee he kept saying and holding the doll up to squirt down the aisle.

In the last car there were several men sleeping on the seats lying under raggy blankets. We turned around and

went back toward the front. Three cars up Jude stopped
and we grouped together. Iz and Weezie and Jude whispered into each other's ears. Jude looked into the car we'd
just left and nodded to Weezie. I looked where she was
looking and saw a bunch of people who got on at 96th
standing between the two sets of doors at the end of the car.
Iz whispered to me saying 'Shadow me don't say or do nada
shadow that's all.'

Iz walked into the car we'd passed through. I followed.
She stood beside the exit doors facing the door at the end
we just came through. She pointed I should stand between
her and the three seats at the end where old men were
reading newspapers. When we reached 72nd Street Weezie
came in and stood behind a man holding onto the bar
above the old men. When the train pulled out Jude came
through and stood in front of the guy between him and us.
Jude was as tall as he was and she gave him a toothy smile
and he smiled back. He was a middle age white guy in his
thirties wearing expensive orange pants and a short leather
jacket. Jude the man and Weez all stood looking the same
way with hardly an inch between them.

We got to 66th and no one got on or off where we were.
When the train started up Jude fell against the guy like
she'd lost her balance and he bumped into Weez. But then
she pressed her butt against him rubbing like she was a cat.
The man went goofy like cartoon people look when they're
hit on the head with anvils or safes. Iz nudged me so I
wouldn't stare. I tried not to but I couldn't believe Jude
going slut city just like that. Iz looked through the windows
as we pulled into 59th Street and winked at Jude and Weez.

'Yoyoyo scusi gettin off please gettin off' Weez said and
the man stepped out of her way. Me and Iz and Jude were
already off the train. Weez got off just as the doors shut and
the train took off. Jude looked at Weez and said 'Yeah?'
and Weez nodded. Iz started laughing and we walked to
the turnstiles. We went through and then upstairs where we
came out in the middle of Columbus Circle.

'Uglyass felt like he packin a turkey leg up his pants. What's scored Weez what the dog carry?' Jude asked. Weez pulled an expensive wallet out of her pocket and gave it to Jude who kept it close to her while she opened it looking behind the credit cards and in the compartments. 'Yo Mari save his lunch money to buy more fancy clown pants' Weez said. 'Hundred sixty seven' Jude said grinning when she finished counting the money inside. 'Payday' Iz said. There were eight twenties and Jude gave everybody two. The seven dollars left over she rolled up with her two twenties and shoved into her halter. 'Do dry cleanin with my percentage. He stain me?' Jude asked looking over her shoulder down at her butt. 'You dry Jude' Iz said. Jude threw the wallet into a trash can. 'Death Angels rule' Weez shouted. They put their money in their pockets and I did too. We crossed the street and started walking down Broadway side by side to make people get out of our way.

'You picked his pocket' I said hardly believing it. Iz and Weez were on either side of me and put their hands on my shoulders and laughed. 'No girl it drop in my hand' Weez said. 'How did you do that?' I asked. 'Timin and practice' Jude said. 'It pie easy' Weez said. 'Iz look out, I lift and Jude distract.' 'Weezie she used to bait too but no more' Jude said. 'Don't want no nasty on me' Weezie said. 'I rather strongarm.' 'You <u>lie</u>' Jude said. 'What happen was one day we go bankin and Weezie does the boost to this old man with sharp reflexes' Iz said. 'Seventy, eighty' said Jude. 'He reacharound Weez, octopus her titties and start humpin her right there in the car.' 'Nasty' said Weez. 'Jude laugh so hard she drop the wallet.' 'Nothin in it' said Jude. 'Weez she elbow back on that man like to break his ribs. He fall floorways rollin and groanin' Iz said. 'Nasty motherfucker' said Weez. 'Got to work em up enough to get em goggle eyed but not enough they gonna pull it out' Jude said. 'You didn't have to boost him Jude I pluck that boy first call' Weez said. 'Wish I knew' Jude said rubbing her butt like he was still back there. 'How much money you

140

usually get?' I asked. 'Not enough' Weez said. 'How do you tell who has money?' I asked. 'Cause people readable and we read' Weez said. 'Boys be doing the same when they go yoking' Iz said. 'But we subtle' Jude said and laughed again. 'You ever get caught?' I asked. 'Not yet' Iz said. 'Aren't you scared?' I asked.

I didn't expect it at all but Weez grabbed my arm like she was going to twist it off. She put her face in mine and said 'Bitch you do or you don't do that's all.' 'Freez Weez' Iz said. 'Fuck you' said Weezie letting go of me and limping along. Jude eyed us the whole time. 'What what what what what what why. Dag. Flapmouthin like you somebody and you lower than shit' Weez said to me. She had this look like she was going post office any minute and I knew she had that knife in her jacket. 'Cat tongue Weez don't dozen her when she's not angelled yet' Jude said. 'Never gonna angel with us' Weez said. 'Once she winged she will' Iz said. 'When she gonna wing? When Esther do? We gonna half-way house fuckass white girls now?' Weez asked. If she asked questions that was all right I supposed. 'Don't call me that' I said. I was sick of Weezie. Anne she spit right in my face when I said that. We stopped walking and she looked at me and laughed with her earrings jingling. I wiped her spit off but didn't say or do anything I was so shocked. 'That's crazy evil Weez' Jude said. 'Evil be me' she said. 'Weezie you a <u>Dominican</u> Republican racist' Iz said. 'Oh and who savin themselves for white boys cause black ain't good enough?' Weez asked. 'No boy I know good enough' Jude said. 'Guess not since you be bumpin each other all the time constant' Weez said. 'Better n hosin dogs like you do' Iz said.

Weez eyebugged and pulled her big knife out of her jacket. 'What Weez you gonna be bladin here?' Jude said. We were at the corner of 55th Street where buildings they were tearing down had collapsed on the sidewalk. People walking by looked at us and kept walking. Weez was shaking all over. 'Damn Weez freeze would you?' Jude said. Before I knew what was happening she kicked up her foot and knocked the knife out of Weez's hand. It fell on the sidewalk and the blade broke. She jumped on Weez and they both went down. Jude grabbed her nose ring and pulled. 'Said freeze' Jude said while Weez moaned and shook her head. Jude slammed Weez's head against the sidewalk. 'Mind girl. Hear?' Jude said pulling the ring harder. Weez started crying and she nodded her head and Jude let go. They stood up. Weez held the back of her head and I saw she was bleeding. 'Settle' Iz said. They looked at each other a second and then Weez and Jude hugged. 'AO then' Iz said.

For a minute nobody said anything because I think everybody was in shock. I couldn't believe how violent they got so quick it was so scary. Neither Weez or Jude looked at me though Iz did. 'My cutter' Weez said kneeling down and picking up the two pieces. She was still crying a little sometimes holding her nose and sometimes her head. 'Sorry Weez but you don't blade me like that never. Hear?' Weez nodded. 'Let's uptown. Too much harryin and investin's called for this week anyhow' Jude said. 'I gotta shop' Weez said. 'Shop then but we not not now too shaky' Iz said.

Weez threw the pieces of her knife in the rubble where the buildings were coming down and limped back to Broadway. Once she was gone Jude grabbed my shirt and stuck her finger at me poking me in the chest. I didn't know what was going on and wished I'd stayed home.

'You two'll deathpiece less you quiet her quick. Public defendin's not my job hear?' 'Hear' I said really scared that Jude was going to hit me. 'Weez bully you constant less you fear her' Jude said. Iz came up and pushed us apart. 'Damn Jude Weez's crazy it not Lola's fault' she said. 'Unmatters it's Lola trips her wire' Jude said. 'It's Lola's being not Lola's doing she can't help it' Iz said. 'Pointless tension stirrin just the same. Something gotta settle soon you know Weez gonna go hook a new blade' Jude said. 'Why does she hate me so much?' I asked. Jude shook her head. 'Like I say she hate everbody but some she respect she gotta respect you' she said. 'How?' 'You gotta roll her over that's all' Jude said. 'How she supposed to do that?' Iz asked. Jude shook her head again. 'What if Weez kills me?' I asked. 'Won't happen' Jude said. 'What if it does?' Jude shrugged and said 'You dead.'

I couldn't take it Anne. I reached in my pocket and took out the money she gave me and stuffed it in her hand. 'I'm not a Death Angel here take it back' I said. Jude looked at me like I was a street raver. 'I better go home' I said. 'Weez ain't gonna ex you she nothin but blowin wind' Jude said but I was already walking off. 'Lola wait' Iz said running after me. I stopped at the corner and she caught up with me. 'Jude adrenalized from tossin Weez she'll cool' she said. 'What do I do about Weezie then?' I asked. She didn't answer. 'Hear me I call tomorrow you be around?' Iz asked. I nodded. When the light changed I crossed the street and ran to the subway.

There you have it Anne. I don't seem to be able to keep friends very well. No matter what I don't do I'm still doing something. I came home and I felt awful but I didn't cry a lot at least not enough that Mama could tell. When I went in our room Boob asked 'What's the matter?' and I said nothing but she could tell I was fudging. She didn't say anything though and later I thought that if I hadn't been so upset maybe she'd have talked to me about what's been bothering her but it doesn't matter now. Boob's quiet again and she probably figures I'm just like Mama and Daddy when we'd ask them what was the matter and they'd say nothing.

Maybe Weez and Jude are too street and hard like they are but Iz doesn't really seem that way. I guess that's why she's still friendly but I can't tell anymore. If I still had friends at school that'd be one thing but it doesn't look like I do and I wish I did. I didn't do anything to them but I didn't do anything to Weez or Jude either and look at how they acted. Now I don't even want to be around them because of the way Weez acts. I still feel Weezie's spit on my face and I know I always will. It scares me Anne because when I think about what she did I get so mad I can't even think. That's not good because one thing I've always prided myself on is that it used to be I can think when everybody else is going crazy. It's getting harder and harder though. I just feel even more alone than before. It's one o'clock and Daddy's still not home.

Night night Anne.

APRIL 26

Tonight I feel better Anne because Iz and I had a good long talk today. After breakfast I went out and met her and we went walking. Iz didn't go to church today since the Army pacified her grandmother's block and she went back home. She was wearing a shirt with Bob Marley on the front and I remembered to ask her about the shirt Weez wore yesterday what the names meant. 'That's the boys killed on her block last year block association put em out to pay the guards' Iz told me. There must have been forty names on her shirt.

We wound up on Morningside Drive by Columbia sitting on the wall that looks out over Morningside Park and Harlem. Morningside Park is so dangerous that you can never go into it not even in daytime. Today was hotter than yesterday and there was finally smoke up here though it wasn't so bad we had trouble breathing. Over Long Island was nothing but smoke and further up in Harlem too. Every five minutes we could hear something explode somewhere. Helicopters kept flying over us going east. Flakes came down from the sky and made our combs black when we combed our hair.

'How's Esther?' I asked when we sat down. We hadn't been talking about anything major just how the Army was and what we had for breakfast. 'Middlin' Iz said. 'We stuff her when we see her cause her appetite lacks and she has to eat twice as much while she babying.' 'Why didn't she get an abortion?' I asked and Iz laughed. 'Can't afford coat hangers. No that's mean. She can't get aborted. Even if she believed in it she think she ready for mamming' Iz said. 'But she's so young' I said. 'That's Esther.' 'Would you want to have a baby?' 'I got schooling can't do that minding no baby.' 'I'd never want a baby' I said. 'Don't ever say never you never know' Iz said. 'You just said you never wanted one' I said. 'Did not said I don't want one now that's different' Iz said.

We looked at the biggest clouds of smoke looking for faces. I didn't see any but Iz kept seeing singers she knew that I didn't know. 'What's Jude doing today?' I asked. 'Working' Iz said. 'She has a job?' 'Not a job job but she pockets green' Iz said. 'What's she do?' 'Helping the challenged she call it' Iz said. 'Have you been stealing a long time?' I asked. It bothered me once I thought about the way they pickpocketed that man yesterday. It happened so quick and then there was the fight with Weezie and I didn't stop to think about it until this morning. I was glad I didn't keep the money Jude gave me. 'I just lookout' Iz said. 'But they steal and then you get part of the money' I said. 'You dead without money honey' Iz said and laughed again.

'Have you seen Weezie since yesterday?' I asked. 'I keep distance from Weez whenever possible. There's enough craziness.' 'Why do you stay around her?' 'It's Jude stays round her I could do without' Iz said. 'Are they old friends?' 'Since elementary school they pallin. Weez went greeneye when Jude took me up but Jude hashed her quick so no trouble accepting. Weez and me close but no closer' Iz said. 'She never bullied you?' 'Nothing fatal.' 'I don't know how to get her to leave me alone' I said. 'Earplay it see what happens. It's nothing you done' Iz said. 'I ask too many questions but there's nothing wrong with that.' 'That's so and that's not it. Weez ideas that somebody like you think natural you better than her' Iz said. 'I don't' I

145

said. 'Bet you do but don't know it. Everbody think they better'n somebody else otherwise they be more miserable than they is' Iz said and then corrected herself. 'They are I mean. Hear now listen when I around you I feel what Weez looselipping about but I know you don't mean it, it just the way it is. It's just' Iz said. 'But I don't act stuck up' I said. 'It's nothing you say it's the way you look sometime like something upsetting you the way they are or do.' 'Really?' 'I mean Lola I snobby that way too I admit it but I grew here so the look's different.' 'How should I look?'

Iz just laughed and combed Long Island out of her hair again. 'Look the way you look what's wrong with that?' 'If it upsets Weez it might upset other people though' I said. 'But you can't help it and that's not all you can't help. Like I say, you white. Weez don't like that. You help being white?' 'No' 'Course not. My mama same way but not as bad. Weez's daddy black see' Iz said. 'He rule their house like an iron man. Weez loves her daddy and he hate white people.' 'Is her mother black?' 'No her mother white. Her daddy's mother's white' Iz said. 'Why doesn't he hate them then?' 'They family that's different. You not a white white girl since you're Jewish.' 'Sometimes people think I'm Italian' I said. 'Sure but you could be three times darker with a suntan make Weez look albino and you still be too white for her. If she just stirred inside that'd be one thing but she got that hot Spanish blood so everthing come up' Iz said. 'Not all Spanish people have hot blood' I said. 'No but if they hot blooded to start with being Spanish don't freeze em' Iz said. 'She and Jude get by tight cause they so opposite. Jude freeze constant cept when she want to heat up.'

'Has Weezie always been like that?' I asked. Iz nodded. 'Jude says so. Thing is Lola she be dissin you till she thinks you deserve respect. She always saying she so good reading people but she can't read you. Can't read me either but that's different' she said. 'How do I get her to respect me though?' 'Don't know. If she beats you that won't do it. If

146

she keeps on like this, that won't either. If she blade you' she started to say and stopped. 'You think she will?' 'No' Iz said. 'You know for sure?' 'Something'll settle don't fret.'

Helicopters flew over so low that the trees in the park shook like in a thunderstorm. A soldier shouted something at us but we couldn't hear what he said over the noise the copter made. 'You allowed to sleep over with friends yet?' Iz asked. 'Sure' I said. 'This Friday then why don't you come to my house sleep over. We get up Saturday morning hang some meet Jude and we figure out what to do bout Weez.' 'It'd really be all right?' 'I tell mama nother friend staying over. It be troublefree, Jude all the time crashing with me though usually not weekends. Even if she need to that be fine.' 'Okay' I said feeling very happy not only that Iz was going to try and help me with Weez but that she wanted me to spend the night at her house. 'I really like you a lot Iz' I told her and held her hand without wondering until later if it worried her or not. She squeezed back with a really hard grip. 'I like you too' she said and we hugged.

Our eyes started burning since the smoke was getting worse so we started walking back over to Amsterdam holding hands the whole way until we got to Columbia. We would have cut through the campus but last week they put up new gates with heavier razor wire and now the guards only let you in if you have student ID or you're a professor. The guards are carrying bigger guns now too and there's a lot more police around. So we walked up to 120th and then went over to Broadway. I feel so much better now than I did Anne.

I asked Mama if it was okay if I stayed over at Iz's this Friday and Mama said 'Oh darling certainly that sounds like so much fun' and then she asked 'Why don't your other friends ever call or come over sweetie what's the matter with them?' 'I think they're scared of the neighborhood' I said not just fudging but lying but I didn't want to tell her what really happened. 'They're such silly geese the neighborhood is perfectly safe if nothing else' Mama said. I wondered why Katherine's father hadn't called Mama or Daddy to tell his lies. If he had they'd have given it to him no question but at the same time I was glad he hadn't because I didn't want to talk about it. They're worse than silly geese but I can ignore them now because I do have one true wonderful friend besides you Anne.

Tonight Daddy was home before nine. He was so late last night because another one of the drawers kept coming up short and he had to stay with the cashiers till they got it straightened out. He's sort of getting used to working now I think but he's not writing at all now. Boob was quiet again and looks so sad. I tried talking to her again but of course tonight she didn't want to talk, she just lay in bed holding her My L'il Fetus and sucking her thumb. I think something happened to her but I don't know what.

Anyway I can't wait till Friday Anne. Weekend's over and it's been rough but I think everything will work out. I hate it that it's school again tomorrow and that's sad because I used to love school so much. But maybe it won't be as bad now.

APRIL 29
Tonight I didn't have any homework so I'm able to give you a little time Anne. School's been about what you'd expect. Some of the girls I never talked to very often sat with me at lunch today and chatted but they didn't say much, they're so boring. I mean they're okay but still deadhead.

When Boob and me were riding up on the bus I saw Weez walking by herself down Broadway up the hill by Columbia. She had her hair pulled up under a bandana and was wearing sunglasses but I knew it was her. She didn't see me of course and I was so glad.

I still can't wait till Friday though I'm not looking forward to seeing Weez where I'll have to be around her.

* * *

148

Oh Anne the President was killed again. This time it was an accident though. His airplane collided with a helicopter in Queens as he was getting ready to land at Newark and they both crashed. On TV they say they don't know if it's a terrorist thing or not but they're checking. They'd tried to shoot down the helicopter but missed. Soldiers in Long Island haven't recovered the bodies yet but they think they will. The funeral's tomorrow so they don't have to close school this time which is too bad. The new President is probably the worst one yet Mama says since nobody knows anything at all about him.

Leaving that aside it's been sometime since I wrote you on Wednesday Anne. Here I go with my weekend catch up which is even more so than usual tonight. After I got home from school yesterday I packed an overnight bag and had a snack of bologna sandwiches. Friday at last! I was supposed to meet Iz at six at the corner and was ready by four thirty. Boob was taking a bath and Mama was in the kitchen proofreading a manuscript while the chicken they were having for dinner was in the oven baking. Daddy was off work yesterday and sitting in the front room looking through a picture book of Europe. Would you like to look at the places we've been with me? he asked when he saw me. 'Sure' I said and sat down next to him. He was looking at a picture of Berlin. Do you remember Berlin? he asked. 'Of course I do I don't forget everything like some people' I said and he smiled.

It was a color photo of the Kurfurstendamm at night with all the car lights trailing red and white. It was beautiful Anne I remember it well even though I was eight. The Brandenburg Gate was huge and lit up like the Reichstag and the old ruined church. Berlin was much prettier at night than in the daytime just like New York. We might have trouble there now considering Daddy said. He turned the pages and then we looked at pictures of Prague where we'd also been along with Budapest and

Vienna on that trip. We saw Kafka's house and the house where the golem lived and the old Jewish cemetery and there they were in photographs again. As much as I love New York I wish we lived in Europe Anne. They have troubles over there too but different at least.

'Will we ever get to go to Europe again?' I asked Daddy. He didn't smile but fudged of course he said certainly we will cookie we'll go next year maybe this year if any projects come through. 'Do you think any will?' I asked. At some point he said just maybe not as soon as we'd hope things were very bad and getting worse all over. 'Like with us' I said. No no with everything else he said. 'How's Mister Mossbacher?' I asked and he made a face.

Then he said has your sister ever talked to you about what's bothering her? 'No but I think it's because she's not happy here' I said. I can understand that Daddy said I'm not either. 'There's something else too but I can't tell what' I said and Daddy nodded his head.

I looked at his beard and remembered how when I was small he let me sit on his lap while he was reading and tie braids in it. Once I tied so many that he had to trim his beard really short because the braids all got tangled but he didn't get mad at me. I wanted to tie a braid in his beard then but I didn't because I've gotten too old to be doing things like that. Your mother and I are very worried about her Daddy said. 'I know I am too' I said. We're going to be sending her to a specialist soon he said. I've just about worked something out. 'You mean a shrink?' I asked and he nodded. 'If she won't talk to us why would she talk to a shrink?' I asked. People say anything to strangers he said even young people. I doubt it but if that's what he thinks it won't hurt to try. Are you unhappy here? he asked me. 'I'm not as happy as I could be that's all' I said. This won't last forever sweetie I promise you he said. I was glad Daddy and I had time together yesterday, he's been so sad lately and I was happy we could finally get together for a while.

When it was six I went and met Iz. We walked to her

apartment building. Anne the place is bad enough from the outside but you should see the lobby. There were bullet holes in the glass in the doors and half the lights were broken out. A pipe in the ceiling was broken and dripping water on the floor. There was a desk like for a doorman but it had been turned over and smashed like with axes. People wrote graffiti all over the walls. Half the elevators weren't working and had their doors pulled away like somebody tried to get in them with a can opener. Five or six men were sitting in broken chairs drinking beer and staring at us.

We rode up. On Iz's floor the halls are concrete block that's been painted green halfway up like in a basement. The windows at the end were broken out. She pointed to one door as we walked by and told me that was where Esther lived. Inside her apartment it was completely different, it was really nice though not as big as the one we live in now. There's a living room and a kitchen and two bedrooms. Iz and her mother have nice furniture and a big sound system and even some paperback books. We put my bag in her room which was cozy but pretty. Iz has flowered curtains on her window and a double bed with white ruffles and big pillows. On her walls she has a poster of Martin Luther King and a photo of her and Jude hugging and showing their teeth at the camera. Iz said come meet mama who was in the kitchen. Her mother didn't say anything but hello when she saw me and then she got up and went into the other room.

'You hungry?' Iz asked me fixing herself a sandwich. 'No thank you' I said because I didn't know how much food they'd have so I made sure I ate enough before coming over. Iz had just finished eating her sandwich when her mother said 'Isabel come in here I want to talk to you.' Iz rolled her eyes and told me to just sit and wait till she came back. I heard them shut a door but if they didn't want me to know they were arguing it didn't do any good. I could hear them yelling but I couldn't hear what they were saying. After five minutes or so I heard the door open and a minute later Iz came back in the kitchen with my bag and a plastic bag she'd stuffed some clothes into. 'Lola we going' she said looking at the clock on the wall. 'What's wrong?' 'Six thirty curfew soon come on' Iz said handing me my bag. I stood up and followed her through the living room. 'Don't you be stomping out of here like this' her mother was saying from her bedroom. 'We stay at Jude's then. I tell you it's not right' Iz shouted back. 'Jesus God child they'll shoot you on the street it's not safe' her mother said. 'I know' said Iz pulling me out by the arm. 'Isabel' her mother said but Iz slammed the door behind her.

'I'm ashamed' Iz said when we got to the elevator. She was so mad she was slapping her hand against the door until I touched her shoulder. 'I can't believe her girl I can't.' 'Why do we have to leave?' 'She bad as Weezie' Iz said and we got in the elevator. 'What did she say?' 'No mind Lola no mind' Iz said. 'Because I'm white?' Iz nodded. 'She don't like Weezie either. That a bitch or what?' Iz said. We got back to the lobby and went outside. There were chunks of concrete lying on the entrance plaza where they'd fallen off the building and Iz picked one up and threw it. 'Where are we going?' 'I'm going over Jude's. Not as homey but it mine too. You too you want to come too. You wanta go home I understand' Iz said. For a second I thought about going back. But I figured Daddy would be sleeping and Mama working and Boob not saying anything and I knew I could see them any time. But I wanted to stay over with Iz last night and so I said okay. 'Got to get there fore curfew then come on' she said.

We tracked Broadway. It was still light out now that the time had changed. Fire trucks with their sirens on whizzed uptown and police cars too. There was a big group of rough men at 130th standing in front of a bodega and we crossed the street so we'd avoid them. One of the men yelled at the others and they shouted back at him. Then Army humvees drove up and soldiers got out holding rifles. The men had baseball bats and sticks and started throwing rocks and bottles at the soldiers. I slowed up to watch but Iz grabbed my arm and dragged me along with her. Then there were some popping sounds and Iz said 'Run.' We ran. The soldiers were shooting at the crowd and the crowd broke up but then people started firing at the soldiers with their guns from windows over the bodega.

We saw more Army coming downtown. A subway train passing by grinding its wheels stopped on the tracks and people started throwing bottles at it which exploded and started burning. Lots of people started running down the street toward us screaming like they were being chased. 'Shit' Iz said and we turned east down 136th. Kids were playing on the stoops and in the street like nothing was going on and we ran right through. Iz knocked over a little boy she ran so fast and I was glad I keep in shape because she'd have gotten blocks ahead of me otherwise. She looked down Amsterdam and then we ran north again to 138th. On that street and on the blocks going east were more soldiers. They went from building to building yanking people out. One lady wouldn't stop screaming and a soldier hit her in the mouth with his gun and she started bleeding. I've never been so scared in my life Anne but we kept running until we got to Jude's building. We cut through the vacant lot over the bricks behind the building. We pulled the cover away from the hole and crawled through. 'Jude or Weez round one' Iz said when we got inside and pulled the cover back. She whistled and somebody upstairs whistled back. 'Jude' Iz said. 'You solo here this where she stash the flash' she said taking out a flashlight from a hole in the plaster wall. 'There three so there always one.'

Jude was kneeling on her mattress looking out the window when we got upstairs. 'Some target' Iz said. 'They not shootin stars just suspects' Jude said not moving. It was getting dark inside and hard to see. 'Should we light candles?' I asked. 'Keep it black' Jude said. We got beside her and peeked out. We couldn't see anything but heard more shots and sirens and screams.

'Thought you was campin over tonight' Jude said. 'Wanted to but Mama she see Lola and pull her Islam Nation rap and we booted' Iz said. 'You didn't tell her you hostin a white devil?' 'She got to adjust sometime' Iz said. 'Well Weez be here soon that keep the oven hot here too' Jude said. I knew it would happen soon that I had to see her but I didn't think it would be this soon. 'Is everybody rioting?' I asked. 'Seem so' Jude said resting her back against the wall. 'Everbody sick a these greenasses wilding our crowd. Take so much and no more' said Iz and I thought about the rat Jude caught. 'We saw them taking people out of buildings beating them up' I said. 'That's constant Army or not' Jude said. 'Why?' 'Crackhead round-up they claim but the Pit still overtiming' Iz said. 'That free enterprise' Jude said.

The room shook a moment later and plaster fell from the ceiling when a big explosion went off. I was worried they were going to blow up the building but Iz and Jude didn't even seem to notice. 'What if they come in here?' I asked. 'That why we keep dark inside, so they don't come knockin' Jude said. 'Front all sealed up place look dead gone' said Iz. 'We're really safe?' 'Till Weez get here' Jude said laughing. 'She better get here soon.' Iz looked over at me and I guess even in the dark she could tell I was still worried. 'Show her our defense Jude' Iz said.

'Operation Dead Motherfucker' Jude said reaching underneath the mattress between the bricks. She pulled out a huge rifle with handgrips and sights on the top. 'If you skinny this add twenty pound weight real fast. Lead weight. You seen them Russians hustlin little dolls and shit?' she asked. I nodded looking at the rifle. Jude held it like she knew how to use it before she slid it back between the bricks. 'Sell these too if you know how to ask' Jude said. 'Nobody touch that but me' she added. 'But if a bunch of them came in wouldn't they kill you too?' I asked. 'A squad yeah. One or two go nightcrawlin, they regret. If we beset we be strategic' Jude said lifting up a

154

rope. 'Hooked up to the wall. Drop it out, slide down, we gone' she said.

We heard another whistle and Jude whistled back. 'She beddin here too?' Iz asked. I was glad when Jude shook her head. 'Weez just drop in fore she go cattin. Might reconsider tonight though' Jude said. Helicopters flew over shining searchlights into the vacant lots. The noises outside were loud but distant enough we could hear footsteps on the stairs outside. 'Yoyoyo it hurricane weather out there' Weez said coming through the door. She carried a bag that she put on the desk. It was dark enough that I don't know if she saw me right away or not. If she did she didn't say anything. Reaching into her bag she pulled out a big bottle of beer and opened it. It fizzed all over her hand. 'You can't pass Weez where you get that?' Jude asked. 'Not no bodega no. Go downtown, Koreans sell anything anybody' Weez said. 'Maybe almost anybody. Deal me' Jude said. Weez tossed her another bottle of beer and opened a bag of potato chips. As you'd expect she ate them by shoving huge handfuls in her mouth and crunching them with her mouth open to make the loudest noise.

'It too dark for goodness now help me put the shades up Iz' Jude said. She and Iz got pieces of wood and metal sheets and covered the windows. 'Let there be light' Iz said lighting the candles on the desk. In a second the room was bright and we could see again. 'Take em down when we bedaway get air back in' Jude said. Now I knew Weez knew I was there but she still didn't say anything to me. 'How's the pacifyin goin?' Jude asked. 'They workin overtime not shootin the right ones' Weez said staring at me. 'No news there' Jude said. 'Otherwise calm so look I'm gone.' 'Where you runnin?' Jude asked. 'Out. Down' said Weez. 'They gonna shoot you out there Weez stay here' Iz said. 'I'm no spare' Weez said starting to limp toward the door holding her beer. 'Sit yourself' Jude said sounding threatening. Weez stanced there a moment. 'Rat die in here or what somethin stink' she said. 'Zip it' Jude said.

Weez sat on top of the desk. 'What?' she asked. 'I don't need attitude' Jude said. 'Look you're buggin and we're problematicked. You deadheadin Weez I know why you walkin.' 'Time wastin Jude speak up' Weez said. 'Why's Lola pick at you soul so?' I felt embarrassed but thought I'd better not join in just yet. 'Answer girl you jealous or what?' 'Jealous shit' Weez said. 'So level' Jude said. 'It flatline now nada level needin' 'You lyin' Iz said. 'You not the only one people literate Weez we read fine. There nough warrin outside' Jude said. 'Too much slummin round here to-night' Weez said. 'Too much trash blow in.' 'Freez Weez' said Iz. 'Look we booked full here cause Iz's mama dead-headed like so many no minds do and evicted unlawful' Jude said. 'Senseless to be cat tonguin when you keen to spit. Blow or suck, Weez. Hear me?'

Weez nodded her head without looking at us. She kicked her good foot against the side of the desk making noise. 'Some matter some don't' she said. 'What's meant?' Jude asked. 'Mean while you tradin up you tossin out good for bad' Weez said. 'No tradin up Weez' said Iz. 'It everbody for theyself these days' Jude said. 'Four of us make one big one. That reasons right Weez and there no call for your ballistics. Peace yourselves proper less you cravin death-peace.' 'Nobody hurtin yet' Iz said. 'Maybe that what's needin' Weez said sounding angry. 'You buggin Weez' Jude said. 'You dissed me. Broke my daddy's knife' Weez said. 'You probably already rebladed' Iz said but Weez shook her head and finished her beer. 'No sales. Everbody too tensed' Weez said. Then without warning she got up and swung her beer bottle at me. Jude knocked her arm down but she still hit me on the side of the head.

I heard Jude and Iz shout and I fell over on the mattress holding my head and wondering if she fractured my skull. She didn't because she didn't hit me as hard as she wanted to but it hurt. There were pink and blue flashes in my eyes and the longer I sat there the more it hurt. When I put my hand against my head it came away red with blood. It looked like more than there was I found out later. Weez was screaming and holding the bottle over her head waving it at Iz and Jude. 'She think she better'n me too I know she do' Weez said. 'Drop it Weez' Jude was saying. 'Fuck her fuck you fuck her fuckin scrawnyass blazer wearin hair teasin pastyface puta fuck' Weez shouted.

I had enough Anne. I kicked out my legs and hit her in both knees with my shoes. She lost her balance and held onto the desk. 'Watch the candles Iz watch em' Jude shouted and Iz caught one that was falling over. Sitting up and putting my fists together I hit Weez on the nose as hard as I could. She fell on her stomach on the floor with a crash. I jumped up from the bed and threw myself on her sitting down on her back like I do when I tease Boob. I didn't tease Weez though. I started slamming her face against the floor with one hand and with the other I grabbed her arm and bent it up behind her back. Anne I stopped thinking though I didn't realize it then only after. I had pictures in my mind of the way she hit me with the bottle and she looked at me and her stupid face and the noise she made eating potato chips. It made me madder and madder and I slammed harder and harder. She screamed but I didn't care.

Then Iz and Jude pulled me off. 'Enough enough enough' Iz said holding my arms tight with hers. Jude helped Weez up. I was shocked Anne. Her nose and mouth were all bloody and she wobbled like she could hardly stand. I was panting tired out of breath. I kept trying to get loose but Iz is very strong even though I'm taller. Jude wiped the blood off Weez's face with kleenexes. Eventually I felt like myself again.

'Damn girl you a mayhem specialist' Iz said. 'Thought we gonna have a nine oh one here' Jude said sitting Weez down on the mattress. 'I'm letting loose now. Safe?' Iz asked me. I nodded catching my breath. When she let me go I held my head where it was sore and leaned against the desk. Weez was breathing as hard as I was. 'Anything broke?' Jude asked Weez who shook her head. Then she pressed a kleenex over Weez's eye where she was still bleeding and wadded up some more and shoved it above her upper lip to stop her nosebleed. 'Evil craziness' she said.

Anne I felt really sad. I hadn't wanted to hurt Weezie I just wanted her to like me. I'd hurt her really bad without even thinking about it. Since she and Jude were old friends I was scared that now neither of them would like me and I didn't know what to do. It didn't seem like I could do anything right and now when I'm writing about it I'm feeling sad again. At the time though I was too tired and upset and my head hurt too much to feel sad for long. Iz got some kleenexes and found where I was bleeding and dabbed up the blood there. It hurt when she touched it and she was very gentle. 'Recoverin Weez?' Jude asked. 'You want to home it?' Weez nodded. 'It be brutal outside Jude ear up' Iz said. We listened. There were more gunshots and noises though maybe not as many as before. 'You better hang.' 'This no recovery room she need wrappin' Jude said helping Weez to stand by putting her arm around her waist. 'I say we got a casualty anybody ask' Jude said. As they walked by me she touched my shoulder. 'You settlin?' she asked and I nodded. 'Get her home nurse her up. Don't fret' Jude said. They left the room and went downstairs.

'Will they really be all right?' I asked. 'It rough out there but Jude no fool she'll play safe' Iz said. 'Does Weezie live far away?' 'Fifteen block. They make it easy less there's random senselessness.' 'I'm sorry Iz.' 'Don't apologize it happen' she said looking at my head while holding up a candle. 'Comb it out otherwise blood mat there and pull loose later' she said. I found my brush in my bag and combed my hair even though it hurt a lot when I did.

'Am I still bleeding?' I asked. Iz looked. 'No you dry.' 'Will I need stitches?' She shook her head. 'Me and Jude we figure you could come out even didn't know you'd decontrol like that' Iz said. 'Me neither.' I'd been in plenty of

fights with Boob and Lori but never hurt them like that.
But then I love Boob and loved Lori and would never want
to hurt them. I didn't think I'd ever want to hurt anybody.
'Is Jude mad at me?' I asked. 'No. How you feelin?' 'Tired'
I said. 'Understood. Here' she said and handed me Jude's
bottle of beer. 'Cheers.'

It was the first time I ever drank beer and it tasted awful.
It was warm and I felt sick at my stomach after a few
drinks. Iz drank what was left and we ate the rest of the
potato chips. There was less and less gunfire outside and we
heard some sirens but it was mostly quieter except for the
helicopters flying over. It was incredibly hot inside and Iz
took off her clothes. I was boiling but I felt shy so I stayed
dressed. 'Let's air the place' she said blowing the candles
out. We took the covers off the windows. The breeze was
warm but felt so good. 'Let's bedaway' she said and lay on
the mattress. 'You going somewhere?' 'No' I said. 'Why you
still dressed then?' Since it was dark I took off my shirt and
pants but left my underwear on unlike Iz.

The mattress was lumpy but it was nice to lie down. I
heard scratchings in the wall though and I started worrying
about rats. 'Do rats ever crawl in the bed?' I asked. 'Not
that I notice' Iz said. It was hard to get to sleep because of
the noise and heat and I lay there looking at the shadows on
the ceiling listening to sirens and helicopters. Their searchlights reflected in the room sometimes but they weren't
pointing them straight in. I was tired but not sleepy and
we just lay there quiet. I could tell Iz wasn't asleep. I didn't
know what time it was and Iz didn't have a watch but it
was late.

'How's you head?' she asked me. 'Sore but settling' I said.
'How you feeling otherwise?' 'Worried. Guilty' I said.
'Why?' she asked. 'For beating up Weez like I did.' 'It
happen sooner or later. Better sooner' she said. 'I'm not
like that' I said. 'Like what?' 'Going post office' I said.
'What's meant?' 'Like when people who work at the post
office go crazy and kill everybody they work with' I said.

'Understood' Iz said. 'I'm really not like that' I told her. 'Must be part a you like that otherwise it wouldn't show. It all right Lola just be careful that's all' Iz said. 'It's an awful part then' I said. 'People do awful things even nice people. That's life you know. I go post office sometime. Jude too. Weez, she a full time letter carrier.'

Iz laughed so hard that I started laughing too even though I felt bad about it. 'Post office. Shit girl you talk funny' Iz said. It was cooler than it had been earlier so we snuggled against each other. Iz felt so smooth and warm. 'Weez done ragging you I think' Iz said. 'I hope so but I wish she'd have just ignored me' I said. 'Gangstagirls better eye you close.' 'Why?' 'Cause you blood deadly girl way you move. You could be a DCon no prob' she said. 'Tell me about the DCons' I said. She put her mouth up to my ear. 'Listen now' she said. 'You listenin?' 'Yes' I said. Iz licked my ear with her tongue and got it all wet. 'Icky' I said jumping and sitting up. 'DCons suck your brains out your ears' Iz said. 'Do not' I said. 'Do.' We started giggling again and lay back down.

'Am I a Death Angel now?' I asked. 'Honey you wingin'' she said and laughed some more. She put her arms around my waist and without even thinking about it we started kissing little kisses. It was so sweet Anne and I felt so good again and so peaceful. We petted each other's faces with our hand. 'Pure process no kinkies' she said feeling my hair like she was combing it with her fingers. Her hair felt like dishwasher pads but in long thick ropes. My eyes were adjusted to the dark and I kept looking at her because she was so pretty, except when we were kissing and then we closed our eyes. 'You like this?' she asked me. 'Yes' I said. Then we just lay there for a while holding each other with our arms and with our legs wrapped together. 'Do you and Jude sleep together like this when you spend the night together?' I asked. 'Oh sure when we here' she said. 'Not at home though when it sleepytime Jude get on the floor cause Mama suspicious and come in to check' Iz said. 'Check what?' 'What we doing' Iz said. 'Sleepytime now. Stay here.' 'Good' I said holding her. I was so happy. There were dogs barking outside and they barked us to sleep.

When I woke up in the morning Iz had her arms and legs on top of me like Boob does sometimes and it was hard to get loose. Before I stood up I put my clothes back on in case anybody was looking in the window. The air was smoky and there were sirens going but it looked quiet. The sun was like a big red ball over Long Island because the air was so bad. I had to go to the bathroom real bad but didn't know what to do so I woke Iz up. She was sleepy and puffy eyed but she showed me where to go down the hall. When I came back she was sitting on the bed.

'What's your plans today?' she asked. 'I'd better go home I've got some studying to do' I said. Actually I wanted to go home because I was tired and still upset about the fight I had with Weezie. 'I see you home safe' she said. She got dressed and put her old clothes in her bag and we left. There was a little scab on my head I could feel but Iz said she couldn't see anything and I was glad. I didn't want to tell Mama and Daddy I'd been in a fight. We walked back down Broadway not saying much since Iz was still half zoned. Twice as many Army boys as there'd been were at the barricade at 138th and the bodega where the angry men had been was burned out but otherwise everything looked normal. The broken glass on the street sparkled like diamonds. When we got to 125th I said goodbye to Iz wishing she could come with me. 'Tell me if Weezie and Jude are all right' I asked her. 'I call you tomorrow. Careful now' she said and we hugged.

On the way upstairs to our apartment Anne I got scared that Mama and Daddy were going to notice that there was something different about me. At first I thought it had to be because I'd been acting street getting in that fight with Weez but the more I thought about it today once I got inside the more I realized it was because Iz and I slept together kissing and stuff. Because now that I think about it you could say that we were being queer even though it didn't seem that we were doing anything bad at all. Maybe we were being queer but I don't know because I haven't been before whatever the Brearley girls say.

Of course as it turns out I was just paranoid because Mama and Daddy didn't act like they saw anything different about me at all. They were sitting at the kitchen table with Boob having breakfast together for a change when I got in. 'Oh sweetie did you have a wonderful time last night?' Mama asked. 'Yes I did' I said which was true even with the fight. How far up does your friend live? Daddy asked. 'Only a few blocks' I said not saying how many. That's good Daddy said it gets very dangerous the farther up you go and I wouldn't want you to get hurt. I sat next to Boob and ate several pieces of buttered toast. Boob as usual now didn't say anything but just sat there fiddling with her bowl of cereal picking up her spoon and dropping it back into the milk.

Then I took a shower because I felt filthy dirty. The soap stung my cut. After that I went to our room and sat down and started writing you which is why this is so amazingly long today, just so much happened and I had to tell you all about it. I hope Weez doesn't bother me anymore and I hope Jude isn't mad at me for beating up Weez. I'd love to ask Iz to stay over here one night but it would be awful crowded with Boob sleeping with us so we'll have to see. I can't wait to see her again.

Death Angels rule!

MAY 3
Not much happened today Anne except the President's funeral. We watched a little of it but it wasn't as big this time plus it was all formality since they said there wasn't actually much of a body to speak of. This morning I woke up and discovered granny came for her visit. For a while this morning I sat at my desk finishing reading Tess and

Boob came over and hugged me. 'What's that for?' I asked her but she didn't say anything and wouldn't let go. 'Answer me Boob' I said. 'When are we going home?' she asked. 'We are home Boob.' 'When are we really going home?' 'What did I just say Boob?' She let go and curled up on the bed grabbing her My L'il Fetus which now has no arms and only half of one leg. 'What's wrong Boob please tell me' I said. 'Nothing' she said.

Iz called me late this afternoon. Her grandmother came over yesterday and so she had to spend the day in church today and couldn't go out tonight because they have to go back for more. 'Everybody get special holy when Meemaw come calling' Iz said. I asked if she'd talked to Jude or Weez. 'Jude call last night from downtown saying they got to Weezie's safe. Said she recovering but feeling low.' 'That's my fault' I said. 'Quit self abusing there no point' Iz said. 'I'm sorry' I said not wanting to upset her. 'Don't be sorry just don't fret' Iz said. She said she'd tab me on goings on during the week. 'What was Jude doing downtown?' 'She know people down there we go sometime.' 'You think Weez's still after me?' I asked and Iz laughed. 'No.' 'Jude's not mad at me?' 'No not about Weez like I say don't fret.' We talked and laughed for half an hour but then she had to get off the phone to eat before going back to church. It makes me feel so good and so happy to talk to Iz Anne I really love her. I mean I really love to be around her that's all.

This evening Mama and I watched the news. Boob refuses to come out of her room if the news is on I guess it scares her too much. The new President said he'd never expected to have the high office thrust on him and he'd do as good as the two dead Presidents. The TV people said the Army was controlling minor disturbances in troubled zones and everything was fine. That's what they said last night and I was surprised after what I'd seen on Friday night when Iz and I were going over to Jude's. I asked Mama if she'd heard about anything serious on the news Friday night and she shook her head. They're more than fudging Anne they're lying. You can hear the explosions uptown even where we live.

MAY 6

Not much homework tonight Anne so I wanted to write you while I had the chance. That'll change in a couple of weeks when it's finals time but for now everything's handleable.

School is the same as always. Miss Wisegarver said she was looking into going to live with her sister in England so she may not be back next year. Lori has stopped going to class. Since nobody who'd know talks to me anymore I don't know if she relapsed or if her parents took her out to send her to an institution or what but she's gone and the teachers don't call her name out in class anymore when doing attendance. Nobody's missing anything Anne because she never said anything in class since she came back, she'd just sit there like she was floating. I think they started her doing drugs at Kure-A-Kid because she always looked like Mama does when Mama takes too much.

Mister Mossbacher fired one of the night managers because the coins in the cash register drawers weren't arranged in even rows. So Daddy had to work again last night and has to again Friday night. He doesn't get overtime of course since now he's on salary. Daddy doesn't have to work this Sunday because otherwise he'd be working two weeks straight almost without a break and Mister Mossbacher is the only person who's in the store every day working ten hours. Mama says we'll do something to take advantage of Daddy's free weekend time if he feels like it. It's nice to be with Daddy but I hope he doesn't feel like it Anne. I want to do something with Iz. We'll see what happens. Iz called tonight and says Weez hasn't been in school either all week. Maybe she's with Lori.

Boob's about the same. Something

* * *

164

Last night I dropped pen when I did because Boob snuck up behind me and said 'What are you writing about me?' scaring me green. 'Just that you're unhappy and we don't know what's wrong with you Boob' I said. Actually I wouldn't have written that because it's known already Anne but that is what bothers us. 'Boob remember how you told me not to hold things in or I'd explode?' I asked her and she nodded. 'You can tell when I do that can't you?' 'Yes' Boob said. 'Well that makes two of us that have eyes' I said. 'I'm not holding things in' she said. 'Boob you're exploding inside I can tell and so can Mama and Daddy. So level Boob level and don't fake me.'

Boob cried and then she finally said what it is. It turns out her school friends are bad as mine except she still wants to hang with them. After we moved here they started calling her Ghetto Girl even though we're not ghetto people we just live in a poor neighborhood. They wrote welfare mother on her desk in Geography class in black magic marker and her teacher made her wash it off. They laugh at her clothes even though they're the same clothes she was wearing before we moved.

'Do they call you names all the time?' I asked and Boob nodded. 'What do you say?' 'I used to say quit but that just made them say it more' she said still crying. I rocked her while she boo hooed for ten minutes. I felt sorry for Boob but couldn't say anything she didn't already know. If that's all it had been though I'd have been glad because we thought she was going schizo.

'Do your teachers know that they do that?' 'They do but they don't do anything' she said. 'That's awful if they know' I said and she nodded. 'Are you sure they know have you told them?' 'I'm no tattletale' Boob said. 'When are we going to go back home?' 'Boob like I say they're broke we'll be staying here' I said not keen to upset her but I wasn't going to lie. 'I hate it here' she said. 'You never even go out up here Boob how can you hate it?' 'Because it's not home' she said. 'It is Boob anywhere we are is home' I said. That's kind of true though I hear what she means. It's not so bad up here I don't think but then I've made new friends and she hasn't that's the problem. Boob is a real snob though like her friends which is why she frets about them.

'Look the girls I knew at Brearley said the same sort of thing to me and so I freeze them when they do that. There's nothing you can do but ignore them they're idiots' I said. 'That's not all they said to you' Boob said. She cried so much she mumbled and it was hard to hear. 'What's meant Boob?' I asked. 'That's not all they say to you I know' she said. 'Who says?' I asked. 'Trish' she said. Trish is Tanya's sister and exactly like her but younger. 'Trish and Debbie and Gloria. They say you're queer and say you're going to rape me' Boob said.

Oh Anne I should have guessed it but I didn't know they'd tell the world what they thought I was. What worried me was what Boob thought and if it made her act the way she'd been acting. 'That's stupid Boob don't tell me you believed that' I said. 'Queers rape little kids that's what they told me' Boob said. 'They do not' I said. 'How do you know?' Boob asked. 'I do that's all. What do you think I am Boob?' I asked. 'My sister. You don't like boys do you' she said. 'Neither do you.' 'It's different. And I know you don't like babies.' 'I hate babies but so what. That doesn't mean I'm going to rape you that's stupid' I said. 'Don't call me stupid' Boob said. 'I said it's stupid if you think that.' 'Don't you call me names either' she said. 'I won't. Is this why you've been so quiet and achy the way they've been treating you?' I asked.

'Yes' Boob said. 'Well old friends of mine call me names like queer and say mean things to me but I don't clam like I'm cat tonguing' I said. 'I'm not a ghetto girl' Boob said. 'Of course not.' 'And you're not a queer?' 'I'm not going to rape you Boob that's disgusting' I said and she laughed. 'That's not why you've been so quiet here at home is it?' I asked and she shook her head. 'Why do you listen to them when they call you names like that?' I asked. 'Because they're my friends' Boob said. 'They're bad to you as Chrissie is to Mama' I said. 'Chrissie's not bad to Mama' Boob said. 'Yes she is' I said. 'No she's not.' We argued like that for a while but then ran out of words. Chrissie plies Boob with treats every Christmas whenever we visit them. 'Boob ignore them when they say mean things about us ignore all of them' I said.

She said yes but Boob fudges just like Mama and Daddy. I know that whatever they say she'll believe. I'm so sick of people saying things that they don't know anything about. Boob got tired after we talked and went back to sleep. I brushed my teeth and got in bed beside her and turned over pulling as far away from her as I could so she wouldn't think I was going to rape her.

Tonight I'm writing this in the living room. I'm facing the hall so Boob or no one can sneak up on me and see what I'm writing because it's NONE of their business. I'm going to start hiding you Anne because I bet Boob will try to pick your lock if she hasn't already.

Friday tomorrow. I can't wait to see Iz. Night night Anne.

MAY 9
Writing you early Saturday morning Anne because I was out last night with Iz and Jude and Esther. Not that late really because I was home by eleven long before Daddy was back. The curfew is over for now because they say the Army has everybody quieted down enough to suit them. They're still all over the place uptown though.

We helped Esther to move from Iz's building to 129th and Lenox in with her aunt. 'Esther relocatin cause her cousin came back in with them. While everthing deconstructin up here Brooklyn looked safer but it worse over there ever day' Jude said. 'If Esther lives with her mother why does she have to move and her cousin stay?' I asked.

167

'Small apartment and besides her cousin the one get her pregnant' Iz said. 'Juicin for more too. He straightface lie bout it but we pegged him' Jude said.

Esther's apartment was much smaller than Iz's, only three rooms. The furniture was fancier than Iz's though and looked like it was never used. Esther was sitting in the living room waiting for us. She had two bags as well as her backpack. Esther's mother didn't look much older than Esther. She stared at me when we came in but didn't say anything.

Her cousin was in the kitchen talking on a cellular phone. His name is Rodell and he's one of those little short guys that pump up so they're wider than they are high. Rodell wore a red shirt and shorts and had an X shaved in the back of his head. He watched us help Esther take her bags into the hall but kept talking to whoever he was talking to. Esther and Iz went into her mother's bedroom to say goodbye. Jude and I stayed in the living room by the door. Rodell was looking at us and whispering in the phone and laughing. Her mother was lying in bed watching TV with Esther's two younger sisters. 'Mind your aunt' her mother said not looking up. Esther said 'Yes ma'am' and that was it so we left.

Jude carried one bag and Iz carried the other. I offered to take Esther's backpack but she said she was okay. We walked east into deep Harlem. 'Esther how long he be hoggin space?' Jude asked. 'Don't know' Esther said. 'What's your auntie say bout your condition?' Iz asked. 'Not much' Esther said. Army greenasses were all over but not doing anything in particular. At every street intersection there were a few standing around with their guns eyeing everybody suspicious. Big Army trucks with barred windows zipped up the avenues. They were blindsided and we couldn't see who rode them.

'Where's Weezie?' I asked. Jude motioned uptown. 'Runnin streetwild with Mico and Bad Conrad and mucho bad boys' she said. 'Jude tell her what we doing tonight say

168

hey go along but she's no nursemaid she says' Iz said. 'Weezie's a bitch' Esther said and we laughed. 'Is she all right?' I asked Jude. Jude didn't act like she was mad at me and remembering what Iz said I didn't ask. 'She fed up with girls she say. Wants to tom it a while' Jude said. 'Why hang with boys?' I asked. 'Male attention make her strut limpin or not' Jude said. 'They all dogs too. Let her run with em but she have to do what they say in return.' 'She wanta lowlife let her she lowest low' Esther said. 'That's cruelty Esther' said Iz. 'Be handin herself over like that oughta pick better hands' Jude said. 'I wouldn't do anything a boy told me to do' I said. 'Depend on the boy' said Jude. 'Weez think she game like a boy that way. Shit she be whatever they want her to be.' 'Why?' 'Why else they want her round?' 'Why don't boys like girls as they are?' 'They bore easy cause they so deadhead. Sometimes they want you mami, sometimes sis, sometimes lovergirl. You game with boys you got to know who you are and not let them tell you' Jude said.

Esther's Aunt Naomi lived in an old brownstone building whose front was crumbling off. The hall smelled like everybody on the block peed there. Her apartment was rundown but clean though there was cat hair everywhere because she owned four cats. She looked ten years older than Esther's mother. We put Esther's bags in the living room because that was where Esther would sleep on the couch. 'Thank you girls' Naomi told us. 'You come see Esther anytime you want so long as it's daylight.' 'Can I go back out with my friends auntie?' Esther asked but her aunt shook her head. 'No running round in your condition you staying right here till that baby born and we take it to the adoption people' Aunt Naomi said. 'Nobody adoptin my baby' Esther said. 'Child you're too foolish for mothering we're not discussing it anymore' Aunt Naomi said. 'Auntie it my baby' Esther said and her aunt slapped her face.

We didn't say anything but started backing out toward the door. 'You having it but it's not yours and don't sass me' Aunt Naomi said. Esther didn't cry or anything just eyed her aunt like she wanted blood. 'We rollin' Jude said and we said goodbye.

'Her aunt shouldn't have slapped Esther she didn't say anything bad' I said. 'Bad enough for Esther's aunt' Jude said. 'Nada we can do let's go.' 'Lola's right though Jude that's evilness slapping a girl with a baby in her' Iz said. 'Detach Iz detach. Both of you detach. We do what doable but can't undo what's done. Come on' Jude said. 'Esther really wants to keep her baby' I said. 'That obvious' Jude said. 'Why?' 'Well it is hers' Jude said.

We walked down Lenox to 125th and then over toward Broadway. 125th is the main street of Harlem. People were all over walking but most kept looking over their shoulders. Most of the stores were closed shutter tight and the Apollo Theater was dark. The marquee had a number where you could send money to reopen it. Down the middle of the street Army greenasses had set up barricades of oil cans and barbed wire to make it harder to cross from one side to the other. They weren't checking anybody, it looked like they were doing it just to be bothersome. Halfway between Amsterdam and Broadway near where a bunch of homeless men were wrapped up in their blankets and boxes we saw a gang of boys. Jude and Iz recognized some of them and shouted.

'Yo what is?' Jude asked walking toward them. Some slapped her hand when she stuck it out but others kept theirs pocketed rocking on their heels like coolies on the move. They were black except one little kid who was white because he was albino. His skin was pasty light with freckles and he had orange hair and super black features. They were our age or younger I guessed, Jude and me were taller than most of them. Just out the tallest said. He wore a basketball top and was skinny but all muscles. 'Out for blood or out for trash?' Jude said. No bloodin round these boys he said nodding at the Army. The soldiers didn't have their guns up but they eyed close. We behavin said another boy. 'This is Lola. Lola that's Robert, Charles, Kwame' Iz said. Billy B said the tall boy. The albino didn't say anything. This ugly bastard he Choker Billy B said. Choker smiled showing a whole mouth of gold teeth. He had a big scar running up his cheek from his mouth to his ear. He wasn't just ugly Anne he was double ugly.

'Why you called Choker?' I asked. He kept grinning and then suddenly leapt on the back of Billy B putting his arms around his neck. They fell down and everybody laughed. He master yoker Billy B said as they stood up. 'Total deadhead' Iz said to me. Choker dusted off his jacket and wandered to where the homeless men were. 'You been uptown?' Jude asked. The boys said yes in that muttery way boys do. We been that way said Billy B. 'Whatchu see?' Saw Weez and Blood T. 'Doin what?' Loadin for action up in Washington Heights. She outgrow that blade didn't she Billy B said. 'What's meant?' She carryin now. 'Carryin what?' Heavy artillery 'What she pack?' Jude asked. Rifle said Billy B she's gunnin now. 'RIFLE?' Jude eyebugged and her mouth dropped open. 'What you think Jude?' Iz asked. 'Think hell know' said Jude. 'Weez wouldn't do that would she?' 'She more mindlost than I thought. Shit I gotta check this out she don't even know how to shoot that thing' Jude said. 'Heard. You better fly' said Iz. Jude looked cross street at the soldierline. 'Where's it passable?' she asked. Bway said Billy B. 'Later' Jude said running west and disappearing. She ran like a beautiful antelope going windfast.

There was a flash of light to our left and a commotion. Choker set a homeless man's pants on fire. The man rolled on the sidewalk trying to put them out while his friends looked at him. All the boys laughed except Billy B who slapped Choker on the head. Don't be doin that them greenasses ready for us Billy B said but none of the Army boys did anything but watch. 'Lola we better go. Later' Iz said to the boys and saying bye we walked toward Broadway. They went the other way down 125th laughing and yelling.

171

'Weez steal Jude's gun?' I asked Iz. 'Look that way Jude's checking now' Iz said. 'Jude said no one was supposed to touch it but her' I said. 'Known Jude wouldn't even let me finger it. That girl gonna get exed runnin around firepowered like that. And if Jude catch her watch out. Jude come by that Kalishnikov hard' Iz said. 'What's meant?' 'She had to trade heavy to get it' Iz said. 'Trade what?' I asked. 'You hear Jude wording you tonight bout picking the right hands to hand yourself into?' 'Sure.' 'Jude mean you let yourself out to trade you gotta trade equal or better. Jude had to do lowlife rough trade to get that heavy artillery. She usually aims for a higher class when she cats around but you do what's needed.' 'When she goes downtown by herself is that when she's trading and catting around?' I asked. Iz nodded. 'Understand?' she asked and I nodded. 'Should we go to Jude's house and see if she's there or wait for her?' I asked but Iz shook her head. 'She gotta solo this. I think we oughta just home it. Anything happen tonight gonna happen bad. Damn Weez's worthless ass' Iz said.

It was dark by the time we reached Broadway. Farther up I saw that the Army had put up big searchlights between the storage buildings and the subway on both sides that were aimed up at the sky but made the whole street a lot brighter. I couldn't tell how far up they went. 'Do you want to sleep over at my house?' I asked. 'Mama expectin me home and she don't like short notice. Otherwise I would. Sometime yeah.' Iz said. 'You don't think Weezie will shoot Jude do you?' I asked. 'Maybe' Iz said. 'Jude probably see her first though.' She held hands a minute and then she ran across 125th to her side. I walked home worrying scared that Weezie might shoot Jude and if she did she might want to shoot me next. Boob noticed and said 'What's wrong?' 'Nada. Nothing' I said. 'Now you're a pot calling kettles black again' she said and she was right but so what.

Iz called fifteen minutes ago. We'll hook later. She hasn't

heard from Weez or Jude so far. I'll tell more when it happens Anne.

MAY 10

Daddy didn't go to work today because it was his special Sunday off. We didn't do anything family because Mama got three manuscripts Friday she had to turn in tomorrow and she's working overtime. It's good when she's got a lot to do because it distracts her and she doesn't dope constant. In fact Anne Mama only takes one or two pills a day and only at night. Daddy sat at his computer and typed but I don't think he wrote anything just letters. Boob watched TV this morning. She's clamming again and scoots away if I touch her when she's sitting next to me. 'I'm not going to rape you dammit' I finally yelled pissed at how she acted. Boob went pale and I wonder how mean I looked when I said it. Mama and Daddy didn't hear me or didn't say anything if they did. It racks me the way her friends stuffed her empty head with these ideas. She still octopusses me come nightside and I wake up every morning covered with arms and legs. So that's home news which is usually as bad and boring as school news.

Weezie's somewhere but nobody knows where. Yesterday I met Iz and Jude at McDonald's. It's certified Weez has Jude's gun. 'She trash it up too. Slash the mattress. Toss all the candles out the window. Stole my box and my tapes. She's bitchin plain and that's one side but she overstepped jerkin my peacemaker' Jude said. 'Any leads?' Iz asked. 'Too much sideshow last night to trail and she been underground today. Her folks deadheaded me when I ask' Jude said. 'Jude if she with Bad Conrad and Blood T then you know where she be she must' Iz said. 'Where she maybe must be. Better in knowin not guessin' Jude said. 'It past that now. We got to go you know that' Iz said. 'Go where?' I asked. 'In with the Pit Bulls' Jude said. 'Her main men hang there nights doing their business' Iz said. 'Weez only

173

daytime the Pit. If she there last night she either been exed or banged thirty time runnin by the gangstaboys or worst a all she lost my long arm' Jude said. 'We got to check Jude what if Blood T prompted her action or what if they did the lifting theyselves?' Iz asked. 'She's your old one Jude you got to act.'

Jude sat there watching greenasses putting sandbags down the middle of 125th Street. 'Known known known. Well let's go fore it darkens' she said and then turned to me. 'Not you though.' 'Why?' I asked. 'Pit's nearly the worst of worst. You not goin there' Jude said. 'Weez blew at you because of me right?' I asked. 'Weez blow bout anything it just happened that way' Jude said. 'But I caused it and I should go too if it's dangerous. I'm a Death Angel too Iz said.' Jude looked over at Iz who nodded. 'Uh-uh. It's bad evilness in there.' 'I'm going' I said. 'I'll heart you sis. You goin for white reasons and I thought you above that. Goin cause you guilty, not cause you care' Jude said. 'Don't care about Weez no but I care about you. That's what is. And if it's a bad place if there's more of us aren't we safer?' I asked.

Jude stared at me for a long time without even blinking. At first I thought she was mad but then I could tell without knowing that she wasn't. 'As Death Angels go you not official just yet' Jude said and we stood up and walked out of McDonald's. 'She's willing and able Jude but it's up to you' Iz said. 'All right but you do the overseein, I can't interrogate and safeguard both in real time' Jude said. 'AO' Iz said. 'Only time I see you mayhem you went freehand. I spec you clean?' Jude asked. 'Clean how?' I asked. 'You weaponed?' I shook my head.

Jude eyed the dumpster by the side of the building. Going over to the side she picked up a round wooden pole that was about three feet long and gave it to me. 'Swing like a cane en route' Jude said. 'Swing like a bat if we call.' 'What do you carry?' I asked her holding the pole in one hand like a shepherd's crook. Jude pulled a switchblade knife from her jacket and clicked it open. 'Both sides bladed.

174

Unfeelable when it slip in' she said. Jude I expected but it surprised me to see Iz unpocket a bicycle chain out of her jacket. 'Iz a <u>qualified</u> plastic surgeon' Jude said and Iz smiled. They put their things back and we started across 125th Street walking by the soldiers like we were going to school. 'If the Pit's not the worst of the worst what's worst?' I asked. 'Where the DCons live' Jude said. 'Where's that?' 'Wherever they go' Iz said.

We walked east on 133rd Street which at first didn't seem any worse than any other up there. When we crossed Amsterdam Jude told us to keep in the street along the parked cars. We hadn't gone a hundred feet when a toilet bowl crashed on the sidewalk near us. Looking up we didn't see anybody. The buildings were abandoned like Jude's house, that is they were boarded up but you had the idea somebody housed there. The parked cars were either shiny new or stripped totally. The fire hydrants were open but empty.

'This the Free Enterprise Zone unofficial' Jude said as we crossed the street. In the next block were thousands of people standing around drinking and arguing and huddling in little groups. We edged lightfoot through them so they wouldn't notice us but I don't think they would have anyway they were so busy buying and selling. A row of trucks covered with graffiti was parked in a vacant lot and people sold TVs and VCs and stereos from them. Men wearing hoods over their heads and with rifles slung around their shoulders loaded brown paper packages into the trunks of cars. Black and white women in their underwear all with dyed blond hair were climbing into vans and being driven off. 'Pimps haulin loser lalas downtown to work tunnel trash' Jude said and she spit in their direction not hitting anybody. Two older women stood by a bookcase with cellular phones on the shelves for sale. 'Everbody needin fundin these days. They hustlin high that way look look' Jude said nodding across the street. Mercedes and BMWs were parked along the curb. The windows were dark so you couldn't eye who was riding. People got in and out of the cars patting their pockets. Two men lifted a blanket off the back of a pickup truck showing all sorts of big and small guns underneath. 'My peacemaker calmin three states distant by now' Jude said shaking her head. 'Let's hope so' Iz said and grabbed my arm whenever she caught me wandering. It wasn't as scary as I thought at first Anne because everyone was too busy. There weren't any greenasses in the Pit though people hustled Army equipment like gas masks and electrical equipment and boxes stamped with red crosses or yellow smiley faces. There were a lot of police cars around but the cops were busy buying and selling too all the way to St Nicholas Avenue. 'Glue tight now' Jude said. 'Jungleland next stretch.'

The next block was much more frightening Anne. Even though it was still daytime it felt like night. The cars parked along the curb there were old and beat up and had their radios on full. People sat in them with their feet stuck out the doors and sat on the roofs and hoods. We stepped over people nodded off in the middle of the sidewalk. There were men and boys standing on all the stoops of the buildings that were still standing. Almost as many people were in the street here as in the block before but they weren't selling anything large, they just milled around whispering saying Ten get you twenty I got that magic Good weight good weight. Everything smelled horrible like pee and vomit and worse.

The men on the stoops looked at us when we walked but didn't catcall. Everybody looked like serious junkies or people with AIDS. Whatever they were men or women they had droopy eyelids and scars and missing legs and teeth. The women were bony with blank faces usually. Some of the people had sores all over their faces and cuts that were still bleeding. 'Jude if she here she gone let's go' Iz said. 'Little further' Jude said and we kept walking east.

In the middle of the street a minister stood on the roof of a van holding a microphone. He shouted Wake up Wake up

Wake up but nobody even looked at him. On the side of the van was painted a devil with a smiley face and skeletons and they were throwing people into fire. Underneath were thousands of words like he drew the Bible on the van. Copters flew over and people threw rocks and bricks in the air but they didn't hit the copters, only the people who threw them. It was noisy when they were flying over but when they passed everything the crowd was saying mixed into kind of a hum like a machine that you hear so often you don't hear it anymore. 'Any signs?' Iz asked. 'Nada. This way then we fly' Jude said. We walked into another vacant lot and that was the worst Anne.

A bunch of men were ringed around people in the center watching chickens fight. On the other side were more men each leading pit bulls on long leather leashes. They were starting to look at us now and I held my piece of wood like a club. I saw Iz had her chain out. There were old bricked up buildings surrounding the vacant lot and people were lined up to get packages lowered on ropes outside from high windows. Some of them were shaking and they all looked sick. 'There's Blood' Jude said.

Blood T stood leaning against the side of a building with some other boys. He wore a hooded jacket and sunglasses and baggy pants stuffed into boots with sharp metal points. They weren't cowboy boots because they didn't have heels only thick soles with spikes in them. He wore rings that slipped over all the fingers of his hands and he fiddled with the strings that tightened his hood around his head.

'Word me Blood I want knowin' Jude said walking up to him. The others he was with walked away. Why you here slummin? Blood T asked with a deep growly voice. 'Where Weezie be?' Businessin somewhere mama what you aimin to trade? Blood T asked. 'Nada no way it Weezie I want cause she owe me for her thievin.' Break the girl mama none a my sayso said Blood T. How's little Izzie? he asked but Iz didn't do anything but nod and hold her chain tight. 'Don't string me Blood I know you know' Jude said. Not stringin not knowin. Say girls you get youself a new spic already? Blood T asked looking at me. 'Unlip' Jude said. Guess Weez right when she say she be replaced Blood T said. 'Once more I ask you' Jude said. Weez she prefer chorizo to liver I wonderin how this one feel Blood T said but then shushed. Jude moved fast and I hardly saw what she was doing till she'd done it. With one hand she hooked her fingers into his nose pulling his head forward and with the other she stuck her knifepoint against the side of his neck. Me and Iz stood in front of them so no one could see what was doing.

'Talk or bleed you decide' Jude said pinching her fingers together in his nose and keeping her knife at his neck. Blood T whimpered like a puppy and hopped up and down kicking his boots. 'Talk don't walk' Jude said. Yokay yokay yokay Blood T said. Jude took her fingers out wiping them on his shirt. 'Where Weezie roamin?' Jude asked not moving her knife. Inwood tonight Blood T said. 'Doin what?' Mayhem Blood T said. 'Who with?' Bad Conrad and that boy a hers Alonso they keen to pillage Blood T said. 'Gracias' Jude said shoving him against the wall. He stepped forward as if to grab her but before he could Jude slashed and he stopped and felt his stomach where his shirt was cut. When he took his hand away there was blood all over it.

'Straightaway' Jude said turning. We ran through the lot to 134th listening to them scream behind us. Rats ran ahead of us getting out of our way. At the entrance to the street a couple of men tried to nab us but Iz whipped one in the face with her chain and the other stopped where the first one fell. It was so exciting I forgot to be scared Anne it was amazing. Jude outraced us crossing Eighth Avenue as the light changed. So many cars and trucks were zipping uptown we had to wait and while we did a man ran out of the building at the corner grabbing Iz. He had his hand over her mouth and the other holding her arms and she dropped her chain. I swung out with my club without even thinking and hit his head. It broke in half making a whacking sound like if you dropped a watermelon. He fell down groaning and I took Iz's hand and we jumped out into traffic. We sidestepped the cars coming at us though they were coming fast. Before we reached the corner a gypsy cab almost hit us but stopped short. I hit the hood with what was left of my club as hard as I could and we kept running finally catching up with Jude. Then we ran and ran and ran the long blocks to Bway.

We couldn't stop and sit down when we got there not because there wasn't any place to sit because we could have sat on the curb but the Army wasn't letting anybody loiter. So we walked down Broadway catching our breath. It was getting dark and I was glad we weren't in the Pit anymore, I can't imagine what it must be like at night. 'What's planned then?' Iz asked Jude. 'Inwoodin' Jude said. 'How can you get up there?' I asked just as a subway went by on the elevated tracks. Jude laughed and said 'Greenasses wonder nothin's controlled enough and look. Motherfuckers let the trains roll on.' 'You know where Weez hanging?' 'Spec so.' 'Is it dangerous there?' I asked. 'Safer'n where we were' Jude said. 'Need help?' Iz asked. Jude shook her head. 'Gotta solo this' she said. 'Understood' Iz said.

At 125th Jude went upstairs to the station. We waved bye without saying anything. 'She'll be safe?' I asked. 'Nobody ever safe' Iz said. 'Are you feeling all right?' I asked. 'Oh yeah Lo thanks for assisting.' 'It's nothing' I said. 'Shit you shut up' she said and we hugged. I wanted to go home but I didn't want to let go of her Anne I was so glad we were both safe. 'You want to bedaway at my house next weekend? We'll have to sleep with my sister' I said. 'She wet the bed?' Iz asked. 'Of course not' I said. Boob hasn't done that since she was five. 'Sound good to me' Iz said.

We walked to Tiemann Place arm in arm talking about what we'd seen in the Pit. 'I never been there before either' she admitted. 'Never?' 'Round the edges like where they have the open air market but never down in the deep part.

I probably scared as you was. Were' Iz said. 'Let's never go back' I said. 'I still gotta getta new chain' she said and we laughed.

Iz said she'd call when and if Jude found Weezie. She hasn't called yet but I'm not surprised. Anyway that's the latest Anne. Night night.

MAY 11

Today I suddenly felt bad about hitting that guy like I did when he jumped out and put a hold on Iz. Anne what's the matter with me why didn't I think of it before now? Sure he could have hurt her and when I think about it I know I'd do it again if I had to but why did it take so long to rack me like this? It wasn't like he wasn't human or anything. I could have killed him and it took me till today to care. I still remember the sound his head made when I hit it.

That's all I just had to write it down to look at how I felt.

MAY 12

There's too much evil craziness now Anne. The chickens are roosting homeways. Tonight Boob and Mama and me were sitting in the kitchen watching TV when we heard a funny noise back in our bedroom. It didn't sound like anything scary and so Boob got up to see what it was. We've been glad that Boob's not staying in our room all the time lately like she was doing and we're so glad tonight you can't believe it.

Boob went to look and then came running back screaming 'Look look look.' Mama and me got up and followed her back down the hall to our room. There were feathers fluttering in the air like we'd had a pillow fight. Boob hid behind Mama and said 'Look' pointing to her pillow. There was a hole in it. I walked over and turned the pillow over and we saw a bigger hole on the other side and another hole in the wall behind our bed. There was a hole in our window

180

and the glass was cracked. Somebody shot our bedroom Anne. 'My God my God' Mama said holding Boob almost squeezing her to death. If Boob had been lying on the bed like she's been doing she'd have been shot right in the head.

I started to look out the window to see where they might have tried shooting from. Across the way are the Grant houses with the elevated tracks in between. Either they shot from the Grant houses or they snuck onto the tracks when the train wasn't coming through. 'Angel get down they might shoot again' Mama shouted at me and I ducked suddenly thinking. I couldn't believe I was so deadhead as to do that. I crawled out of the room on the floor and back into the hall. Mama was still holding Boob and we went into the living room where the windows face Tiemann Place. She tried to call Daddy at work but not only wouldn't Mister Mossbacher let Daddy come to the phone even when she told him what had happened but then he screamed at her not to ever call his employees at work for any reason.

Mama told us to sleep in their room tonight. I didn't want to sleep with everybody so I'm sleeping in the living room which is where I am now. That was the only shot Anne. I tried to call Iz and tell her but no one was home. Jude must not have found Weez yet. I know it must have been Weez who shot our bedroom Anne it had to have been. She still wants to kill me and now that she has Jude's rifle she can. I have to do something Anne and I don't know what.

MAY 13

Mama said Daddy blew today when she told him what Mister Mossbacher said when she tried calling him. 'Angel I told him he has to quit that horrible job whatever happens he just can't keep working for that maniac like that' Mama said. 'What'd he say?' I asked. 'He said that's what he intends to do' Mama said. 'But if he quits how

181

will we live?' 'I don't know my darling but we will little Boob or you could have been killed and he wouldn't even let Michael come to the phone it just isn't right it just isn't' Mama said. She said Daddy was going to give his two weeks notice to Mister Mossbacher today. We'll see what happens.

Chrissie called. She and stupid Alan have moved to the hills where they're guarded by guns and electrified security fences which probably also go Warning Warning all the time until you want to scream. Mama for some reason told Chrissie what happened the other night really letting herself in for it. She said Chrissie told her that if we're murdered in our beds Mama has no one to blame but herself since she insists on keeping us here surrounded by what Chrissie calls those people. Iz is those people and I love Iz she's my best friend. I would never leave New York Anne I could tell Mama was upset when she got off but she wouldn't say anything except for what I just told you. When I tried to cheer her up she hid her face in her hands and said 'Oh angel I know you're worrying but just go away please I can't deal with it.' I stopped trying to cheer her up.

Boob hid behind me the whole time we stood at the bus stop this morning waiting for the bus. She thinks we'll be shot any minute. I haven't told her I think it might be someone I know who shot at us. Boob blames me enough already I think that's all. Once we got on the bus Boob started crying and didn't stop until we transferred at 86th Street.

Where is Iz? Nobody answers the phone at their house. I know it's silly of me Anne but what if Weez went over and shot her and her mother. Maybe Weez is picking off everybody she's mad at. I wish Jude had a telephone. It's only Wednesday and I probably won't see them until the weekend though I'm scared deathless I might see Weez before then.

* * *

182

MAY 14

Too tired to write but I wanted to let you know Daddy did give notice to Mister Mossbacher. But he told Daddy that he couldn't quit. He said Daddy had to give a month's notice not two weeks so Daddy said then I quit in a month. Mama said Daddy told her that Mister Mossbacher grabbed him by the shirt and screamed at him in the store for five minutes in front of everybody and all the customers Anne and told him he was going to have to work six days every week until he quit. He also said that if Daddy quit before then he'd have to pay Mister Mossbacher the overtime salary he'd have to give other people who had to fill in for him. Daddy can't do that of course so he has to stay another whole month working till one in the morning and hearing Mister Mossbacher scream constant. That's so unfair Anne but there's nothing Daddy can do. If there's anyone I hate as much as I hate Weez it's Mister Mossbacher.

P.S. <u>Iz finally called me</u> !!! Not only is she not dead but she's going to stay over tomorrow night. No sign of Weez. Would write more but too tired Anne.

Iz Iz Iz Iz Iz Iz Iz Iz Iz Iz Iz Iz Iz Iz Iz Iz Iz Iz!

MAY 16

Weekend's here so Iz showed at six last night. Mama fixed us spaghetti carbonara. Boob kept eyeing Iz's dreads like they were alive and she expected them to bite her. 'Isabel dear do you specialize in school yet?' Mama asked. 'What's meant Ms Hart?' Iz asked. 'Is there some favorite subject of yours that you study exclusively?' 'I like English but we study what they give us' Iz said. 'What are you studying in English now?' 'Stephen King. Teacher likes him' Iz said. 'My' Mama said and then asked 'Do you?' 'No ma'am I just use the Cliff notes when it's time to test' Iz said. 'Who do you like dear?' Mama asked. 'Alice Walker's all right' Iz said. I haven't read her yet but I'll have to sometime.

'Do they shoot people at your school?' Boob asked. 'Sometimes' Iz said. 'Did you ever shoot anybody?' Boob asked. 'Oh my silly angel what sort of question is that to ask our guest?' Mama said. 'I been shot at but they missed' Iz said. 'Me too' said Boob. She'd been all right until then but after she said that she got nervous again. Mama and Boob like Iz a lot which makes me happy.

Last night I told Iz what happened. She doesn't think Weez shot our bedroom, she thinks it was just random. 'My Uncle Steve he walking through the park one day get hit in the chest with a rifle bullet' she said. 'Some deadhead be doing his target practice and catch him. Uncle Steve live, doctor called him luckiest man in New York. Mama say some luck going walking through the park and get plugged in the chest.' That frets me even more Anne that somebody we'd never ordinarily know could shoot us and we wouldn't even see them. If Weez shot us at least it would be for a reason.

After we ate we went outside to meet Jude who'd finally found where Weez went to hide. 'This week I call her house twice, both times her mama badmouth me bout it bein my fault Weez asshauled streetways' Jude said. 'She gone weeklong now. I run down Mico last night, worked him some. He spill once I did my convincin.' 'She still in Inwood?' Iz asked. 'Weez move downtown. Boy she used to bump with, he quartered in Loisaida now. They shack-in.' 'She still armed?' Iz asked. 'Till I catch her she is. Mico gettin me their address tonight, I get it tomorrow. Time to go visitin once that's got' Jude said. 'Tomorrow night?' Iz asked. Jude nodded. 'You need associates?' Iz asked. Jude nodded. 'No good catfootin solo downtown. Meet me here seven thirty. We skylark' she said. 'Mico say how Weez is?' 'She a DCon now' Jude said.

The three of us stood there not looking at each other. Maybe it's unreasoned but I felt bonecold and I think they did too. A subway train ran overhead and we dodged the bolts falling loose from the tracks. They rained iron on the cars parked under. 'You gonna be up my way later?' Jude asked. Iz shook her head. 'Mama not curfewin you again is she?' 'No' Iz said. 'Iz homing with me tonight' I said. Jude stared at Iz hard not like she was really mad but surprised. 'I didn't say?' Iz asked Jude. 'Don't recall' Jude said looking at Iz. 'Jude don't personalize you clicked off before I could tell' Iz said. 'Understood. I see you tomorrow night. AO?' Jude asked. We nodded and she turned around and walked up Broadway.

'Why's Jude so nervestrung?' I asked Iz as we went back to our apartment. 'Weez mostly' Iz said. 'Like I say they lifetime close. Weez bound to flip one day and now she has, Jude not taking it well. Jude, she too optimistic about people she know deep.' 'What's meant?' I asked. 'She always think they gonna do as she say constant that's all' Iz said. 'Will it be dangerous tomorrow night?' I asked. 'Stick round me when we cruise. Be all right.' 'Jude is upset with me over Weez isn't she?' I asked. 'Jude she overall upset right now. Once they done confronting we go on from there' Iz said.

Since Boob is still sleeping with Mama and Daddy Iz and I got to bed alone. Mama went into her room at ten thirty. Boob was already tucked and Daddy didn't home it until one thanks to deadhead Mister Mossbacher. We opened the sofa bed and put fresh sheets and pillows on the mattress which is lumpy but better than Jude's. It wasn't as hot as it's been but we took off our clothes anyway. Mama left the hall light on so Daddy wouldn't have to radar when he homed in so it was dark in the living room but light enough we could see each other's faces when we talked and kissed. Anne it was so nice just lying in bed with Iz holding and petting each other like kittens. If I closed my eyes it was like I was touching myself but I wasn't I was touching Iz which is a weird feeling but good. Maybe I am queer Anne but if I am it's not awful that's all.

We were still awake when Daddy came home. When the door opened we stopped giggling and playing and got real still pulling away from each other. We lay there like we were exed not moving until he came out of the bathroom and went into their bedroom. He snuffed the hall light and then it was dark dark except every once in a while helicopter lights came through the windows. We rolled back together but just talked in whispers because if we'd started goofing again Daddy might hear us and come back out.

'Why didn't you tell Jude you bedding here tonight?' I asked. 'Jude upsets easy I thought it might rack her overmuch' Iz said. 'Why?' I asked. 'Hear Lo Jude and me we been girls together since I come here and now you and me together sometimes too as well as hanging' she said. 'She's not jealous is she?' 'Don't think so but I don't do Jude's thinking.' 'Will she hate me more if she's jealous?' I asked. 'She don't hate you but she love me' Iz said. 'I love you too Iz' I said not surprised I said it but mindlost over what she'd say. She held me tighter and rubbed her face against mine. Her dreads were scratchy but nice.

'You're lovable' I said. 'You too' she said. 'Jude won't upset?' 'Weez be aching Jude now nada else. Don't fret' Iz said and then asked 'How you know you love me?' 'I just do that's all' I said. 'You mean like you love Cheryl?' Iz asked. 'Different I think' I said. Anne I really do I love Iz like I loved Katherine or Lori but more so. It's almost like I love Boob but different. I don't know how much she still loves me now that she's scared of me because I'm queer but she's my sister constant whatever. 'You think or you know?' Iz asked. 'How do people know they love each other really?' I asked. 'If they bed together and nobody die, that's love' Iz said.

It was late but I wanted to stay awake to be with Iz and know I was with her. 'Tell me about the DCons' I said. She necklaced me with her arms and put her lips on my ear and started whispering inbetween kissies. 'The DCons be bad evilness, the worst of worst' Iz said. 'They prime nightcrawlers, they soulslashers, they roll when it darken and nobody see their shadow. Everbody run when the DCons come. Naturals, Intercrime, Pit Bulls, all of em. Anything bad happen nightside gets done by DCons.' 'What do they do?' I asked. 'They steal the babies. They pack the crack. They do the driveby make everbody bleed. Nobody know who the first DCon be but whoever they was they did the king strut early on. DCons in total control in the end. When the streetlight blink they snuff it. When the rat sneak streetways they right behind. You get in the subway and you solo in the car you jump back out at that stop cause the DCons get you fore the next. Police can't catch the DCons. Army can't catch em. Gangstaboys couldn't catch em if they wanted. Nobody catch the DCons but even if they caught they still be round.'

'Jude said Weez was a DCon now. How did she join?' I remember asking feeling sleepier and sleepier. 'The DCons know where the lines be before people. The lines they never crossed before. They get you to cross your line. When you cross it, you with the DCons. You never come back' Iz said.

Even though Iz put the scare in me the way she did it rocked me eyeshut. When I woke up in the morning Boob was sitting on the foot of the mattress holding a pillow and looking at us. I pulled the sheet up so she wouldn't see we didn't have our clothes on. 'About time you woke up' Boob said shouting enough to wake Iz who groaned. 'Go away Boob' I said. 'Get enough sleep?' she asked. Iz sat up holding the sheet in front of her. 'Who plugged you in last night?' Boob asked looking at Iz. Iz's hair was sticking up in places and some of her dreads were bent. We all started laughing. 'Now go away Boob' I said and she did. I was glad she was acting like her old self again. Me and Iz put our shirts on under the covers and then we got up and Mama fixed breakfast for us before she went home. It was eleven by the time we woke up and Daddy of course had already had to go to work so he still hasn't met Iz.

I've been writing you this afternoon Anne but have to stop because it's time to meet and greet. Maybe we find Weez maybe not. I tell you tomorrow. I'm scared but I'll be with them so I'll be all right. I'll be with Iz.

Last night Anne we subwayed downtown changing trains twice. We had to bank on the way Jude said so we did even without Weezie. I did the lookout Iz did the lift and Jude boosted a man in a suit. He was dressed to strut but all his wallet had was fifty. We finally went street on Houston near Second Avenue walking into Loisaida which is also the Lower East Side. It always nerves you walking a neighborhood you haven't walked before and I was scared Anne. I've only been there once or twice before and always with Mama and Daddy never solo or with friends. Greenasses are all over Loisaida just like Harlem and Washington Heights. Since they aren't on the Upper East Side or below 125th I didn't think they were anywhere else but I was wrong.

It was darkening and everything hopped. There were as many people out as uptown and all dressed for action. Loisaida's mixed so there were whites and Asian and Spanish people as well as black. I didn't feel placeless but I was still more wrought cause everybody stared us down when we passed because they probably figured we were strangers come to harm. But Weez was the only one we were after. We took Avenue B to Tompkins Square which looked worse than the Pit Anne. Hundreds of people hang and bed in the park. They had fires burning and tents up and the trees had their limbs cut off. A big apartment building was cross the street. The entrance was razorwired and men with machine guns guarded the front. The first floor was graffitied so much it looked like they'd tried to paint it badly. Army trucks were curbsided with their soldiers all round. Loisaida's Army boys were testier than the ones in Washington Heights. They dissed us whistling and grabbing themselves like they had to pee and yelling hey sweetie come here and do me. Me and Iz and Jude stuck glue tight walking past. An old man stood in the street yelling over and over to himself I'm an American I'm an American like he just found out.

At the northeast corner of Ninth Street was an old tenement with broken out windows with newspaper curtains. 'That's it. Mico say Weez and her boy Guillermo home it right in front fourth floor' Jude said pointing to where lights made the newspaper glow. 'We heading up to call?' Iz asked. 'Not everbody no' Jude said. 'She eye all of us she might flip. You solo Iz in case they in the hall. Lola and me we backtrack.' 'How?' I asked. 'Roofways from the next buildin over, down the fire escape and then pop in. Window might be trapped.' 'What if Weez come up shooting?' Iz asked. 'We'll divert. Think it handleable?' Jude asked me. 'I got fingers. I can poke' I said. 'They be armin not fistin. Pack this' she said handing me a small meat cleaver she had tied on a loop inside her jacket. 'Swing it if they spring. Hit wherever but hit somethin' she said. Then she turned to Iz and said 'Start climbin once we in next door. Ear careful till you hear us then you pop too. Set?'

We nodded. Me and Jude ran up the stoop of the next door building kicking away beer bottles. Jude unpocketed a wire and poked the lock jiggling it till it opened. She nodded to Iz and we went inside. Fluorescent lights in the inside halls made everything look dead even the mice. The stairs were shaky and worn down in the middle. There were six flights and another door at the top. Downstairs we heard dogs bark and babies squall and salsa music loud as airplanes. Jude kicked the door open and we roofed.

'Foot careful' she said. My feet sank in the roof when we walked sagging boards but nothing gave. Loisaida buildings aren't high and we saw everything for blocks and farther, apartment lights and Tompkins Square trees and Brooklyn fires and white Army beams sticking up like needles all over town. Pigeons roosted topside not flying away when we lightfooted through them crossing to Weez's building. Jude shook the railings on the fire escape when we reached it. 'Tight solid that's good' she said. I'd never been on a fire escape before. It feared me to have nothing underneath but little bars. We started down looking in the windows we passed. The sixth floor looked empty and if anybody lived there they lived dark. The fifth floor window was wide open and the ceiling light was on. The room we saw was empty except for a dirty mattress and a suitcase. We didn't see anybody inside. Jude waited on the ladder before going down to the fourth floor. 'Gotta tizzy em. Gimme that' she said whispering and pointing at a flowerpot on the fifth floor landing. It was full of dirt. I gave it to her and she threw it like a ball into Weez's apartment hard as she could. The newspaper tore away and we heard the flowerpot break. When we didn't hear anything else she hopped the railing of the ladder and slid windowways inside.

'Iz you there?' I heard her ask. I was starting to climb down when I got yoked and pulled off my feet. For a second I thought I was falling and dropped the cleaver. I didn't fall though because somebody octopussed me yanking me up and then back through the window. I kicked the fire escape and wall as he dragged me hurting my feet like I broke my toes. He handed my mouth too tight to bite and shoved me on the mattress falling on me. Oh Anne it was so horrible I could hardly think I was so scared. The man who grabbed me was a Spanish guy in his twenties or thirties with an awful mustache that smelled. He smelled too like he never took a bath. One of my arms was loose and I hit his back but he didn't act like he felt it. He pushed himself in between my legs laying on me so I could hardly breathe and then he used his free hand to try and undo my pants. The man kept talking in Spanish which I hardly know. I wriggled and kicked and his hand slipped so I bit him real hard between his thumb and finger. For a second he let go and I sirened out help help. Cono he said sitting up on top of me so I could hardly wiggle. He sucked on the hand I bit and with the other hand he started slapping me in the face as hard as he could. It brainrattled me Anne he hit so hard and I cried I couldn't help it.

Then he got off me sudden like he'd jumped backwards

but when I looked I saw Jude had a rope round his neck yoking him. She dragged him up and then I saw Iz she had something she swung it and hit him on the head while Jude gripped tight with her knee in his back. He staggered and Jude let him long enough for Iz to start rib punching him. I lay there watching like it was a movie until I stopped crying. My feet were sore where I'd kicked them on the brick and my neck felt like he tried to tear my head off. When Jude and Iz got him down on the floor they started booting him full leg in the head and stomach not stopping or saying anything. His face was bloody and he moaned like they were breaking all his bones.

'Pile on Lola pile on' Iz shouted. I stood up getting off his filthy mattress and I felt headspun at first but then I started kicking him in the back as hard as I could really wanting to hurt him. Like the time it happened with Weez when I go post office like that Anne my reptile brain just thinks kill kill kill. And while I was kicking him the same thing happened again too, it was like there wasn't any time anymore everything just froze. The man was still moving some when we stopped kicking him but not much. 'We calmed him' Jude said out of breath and panting. 'Let's out.'

We ran down to the fourth floor and into Weez's place slamming the door behind us. All of us fell down trying to catch our breath and think ourselves clear again. It was like I was electrocharged Anne I saw everything so sharp I was dizzy and I could feel blood beating my neck and head. We just panted for about five minutes resting. Then Iz helped me sit up putting her arms around me. 'You viable?' she asked. 'Sure' I said not sure if I was. The more I settled the worse I felt Anne stomach sick like I was going to spew. He didn't rape me but I felt like he had. My skin didn't seem to be mine anymore it was like greasy all over. I hurt all over my neck and face especially and I wondered if he bruised me. Jude slid over hugging both me and Iz and that's how we sat for a while until we all felt safe again.

'Well here we come callin and nobody home' Jude said

looking around the room. 'No Weez. No gun. No nothin nada.' 'You think they've been here?' I asked. 'I spec they close. However circumstanced Weez not gonna leave her dress boots behind.' Weez's boots with the tape on them were thrown onto a pile of used yellowy bandages. 'Foot still achin her look like. She racked bodywide probably' Jude said. 'We waiting for em?' Iz asked. Some jeans were tossed on the mattress. Weez and her boyfriend didn't have sheets or pillows. There were empty soda cans and wine bottles piled in one corner. The flowerpot Jude threw in broke into a hundred pieces and sprayed the dirt round in a splash. Little empty glass crack capsules were all over the floor. The breeze coming in the window rattled the newspaper still ahang there. 'She gone' Jude said. 'Let's home it.'

Leaving the apartment we walked down the stairs. My legs were still wobbly but I managed. We couldn't tell how quiet it was upstairs because the salsa downstairs deafened so but I didn't think the man would chase us. Two little kids maybe eight years old sat on the stoop outside the building. They stood up when they heard us downstairing. One was a little girl with black hair. Her arms and legs were stubby like a dwarf's and she hissed at us like a snake. The other kid was a little boy who smiled at us. All three of us startled Anne because when he started smiling he didn't stop. He knew he scared us I think and did it deliberately. He could have put two or three oranges in his mouth it was so big going from ear to ear nearly.

We didn't talk much on the way to the subway we just tried to fade in. I kept itching I feared I got liced by the man though I didn't. I didn't know it then though. 'Did we exe him?' I asked Jude. 'Who's tellin?' she asked. Until she spoke and I heard her voice sound normal I couldn't tell if she was going to cry too. 'Keep minded it was him or you' Iz said. 'No choice. Happen to everbody' Jude said. Iz nodded.

The subway was like home sort of, at least it wasn't

Loisaida. We rode the conductor's car because that's always safest from mugs and thugs. At 125th we detrained and went down streetside again to our neighborhoods. Army trucks and police with sirens going headed uptown and we specked there was trouble due. 'Want to home it with me tonight?' I asked them but they shook their heads. 'Got that churching come morningside' Iz said. 'You sure Jude?' I asked hoping that she might want to, not in the same way as when me and Iz bed but to talk to her about whatever. 'Gracias no. I'm keen to solo' she said. Iz hugged and kissed me goodnight. Jude eyed us without seeming to care. So they went up and I went down.

It was ten thirty by the time I homed and Mama and Boob were asleep in their room. Running water in the tub I took a long hot bath scrubbing all over with lots of soap. Last night even when I tried to think of what happened I couldn't yet though I can today. Baths always feel so nice though they were better in our old place, there weren't any roaches there.

This afternoon Iz called. She met Jude after escaping from church and says she's moody but settled. Iz seemed more fixed on me, she probably heard trouble in my voice. 'You still fretting on last night?' she asked. 'Yes. I bring down too much evilness' I said. 'What's meant?' 'Maybe Weez'd be AO if not for me' I said. 'Weez caused Weez's troubles that's truth twice over. What else aching you?' Iz asked. 'What the man tried and how we did him. It sickens.' 'Mean what he did or what you done?' 'Both' I said. 'If punishment fit the crime everything evens out. You hear me? Let me truth you plain on this' Iz said and then she told me that she and Jude have both been raped. A boy Iz schooled with who she liked attacked and unvirgined her one night. His name was Kevin and he was two years older and housed downstreet from her in her old neighborhood. 'He was a class boy. Months after I think I musta made him do it but I didn't. Boys be that way unmattering if they street or not, they all got pokers and always wanta start a

193

fire goin' she said. 'I don't want them to stick me ever' I said. 'They don't have to but that won't stop em trying' Iz said. 'You must hate him' I said. 'Sometime. He gone though even fore I move. Lowlifing catch up soon or sooner. It's liveable these days' Iz said. 'What happened to Jude?' I asked. 'I shouldn't spill cause it shame her.' 'I'm safe' I said. 'I know that' Iz said. 'Then please tell me she'll never know' I said. 'It heartsicks, Lola. Her daddy like his little girls overmuch' Iz said. 'That why her little sister cracked last year, Jude was already homin solo and not around to deflect no longer. He work that peacemaker till memorial day. Jude, she took off first time he did her. Once be too much for Jude.'

As Iz levelled with me about Jude I started thinking about Katherine and my bad suspicions. I don't always think so Anne but me and Boob are lucked big no doubt at least that way. Daddy may not be father of the year but he's Daddy and nada else. Families wrong each other so bad even when they don't try it seems like. My home family's crazed but I love them and I love Iz too. I like Jude a lot but she's just not as lovable as Iz. 'Don't ever tell her I tell you Lola' Iz said. 'Don't fret' I said. 'You my best friends both of you and you especially Iz I love you' I said. 'Everbody need lovin' Iz said and we agreed. That happied our hearts but we boohooed all the same because however we thought of Weez whether hate or love it's unmattered now that she in the twilight zone with the DCons.

Night night Anne.

MAY 19
TV called this Black Tuesday Anne. It was on even before we schooled. They said this morning the money will be replaced with new money this week. It'll bankrupt drug pushers and ex out Mideast counterfeits like the one Daddy got stuck with at the store. The President said by making

the new money worth more that'll take care of inflation. Mama and Daddy were pale when he said that and I asked what fretted. They say that means everyone will have less real money than they do now and we don't have much as it is. They were torn Anne but they said we get by somehow.

It was all the teachers were talking about too they told us we were paid up through this term but adjustments would have to be made next fall. This afternoon we went to Civics class and Ms Boardman had the TV on and we news-watched some more. Nothing like schooling and doing nada but tube daylong. We watched the stock market collapse this afternoon and Ms Boardman excused herself to make a phone call. Boob was watching not booking today too she said when I met her after. Once we homed I asked Mama if we owned stocks. She laughed and said 'Not for years and years my angels we didn't keep them long even when we had them and a good thing it is too now.' The President said tonight that it'd be a little rough at first but in the long run everything would be the way it should be. The TV heads didn't know what else will happen and that's the first time I've seen them say they didn't know.

MAY 20

Everybody's mindlost Anne there's no fudging. The President was killed again right after he was on TV. A mob calmed him in Washington. He was trying to shoot out in his helicopter when air force planes grounded it. They yoked and stomped him flat. None of them have been caught but the FBI is arresting whole neighborhoods in Washington and the Home Army's surrounding it so the guilty won't fly. First I thought hooray no school but the office called to tell everyone class as usual today. Mama said it was cause people liked this President least of all but I spec now everybody's just used to them getting exed. The new President was a senator from New York before he was Vice

President Pro Tem. Mama gives him a week. He says he's disappointed in public reaction and it's time for America to readjust. Daddy was home today on his one day off and was tubing still when we homed. Daddy says the government's ready to dissolve the people. He stonefaced when he said that even though it was supposed to be joking.

There been sirens wailing nightlong and explosions north and a new noise like a low whoop that goes then stops then goes again. Also the Warning building's been going Warning Warning Warning for hours now. There's overmuch craziness Anne I think everybody's spinning. Mama was standing at the kitchen sink newswatching tonight when she started to spew. She looked healthy right before so we didn't do anything but watch till she finished. Then me and Boob cleaned her while Daddy held her. 'What's wrong?' we asked. 'My angels I'm so embarrassed I didn't mean to scare you but I couldn't help it it just came' she said. She broke then holding her head in her hands and hairpulling like to bald herself. Daddy took her back to their bedroom and shut the door. We thought they'd be out quick but no. We heard Mama flood tears and Daddy whispering saying things we couldn't hear. Boob knocked wanting in and Daddy stepped out asked if she'd sleep with me tonight for once. Boob howled and stormed but finally said okay. She took her pillow and slept on the floor in the living room saying 'I'm safe down here.' 'Safe from me?' I asked. 'Safe from everything close the windows Booz they'll kill us.' I shaded them all and then once she settled I kitchened myself wide eye and sleepless ever since.

Warning Warning finally stilled but it's loud outside. I tried calling Iz to sure myself that she's safe but nobody answers. Her mother probably wouldn't let me talk to her even if they were there. I tired sure now and have to wake come morningside. God please watch over Iz.

* * *

Iz is safe! but she worded me that the Army's creepcrawling
through Harlem and the Heights and Inwood housecalling.
Housecalling means they don't knock they just come
through. Sometimes they come with Swatters from midtown precinct and sometimes just blueboys which is what
Iz calls cops. When greenasses visited Iz and her mother
they emptied the drawers and closets and unzipped the
covers off the couch. Half the dishes they broke throwing
them on the floor. 'They do anything bad to you direct?' I
asked. 'Not to me or mama no they be gun collecting this
trip. That and digging up druggies and crackers' Iz said.
We spec they're aiming to certify nothing happens to the
new President but nobody gunned him on Monday night,
they calmed him silent which works best I think. I asked if
the greenasses were going into abandoned buildings too and
Iz said 'No they just burn those.' 'Jude's house too?' 'Not
yet. She'll house here if and when' Iz said. Once Iz awared
me of what was doing I realized why my eyes stung. The
smoke comes through our windows so faint it's hardly
seeable but now I know it's there I can't forget it. It's
noisy outside even though the subway's not running
tonight for the first time.

At school Miss Wisegarver said there'd still be finals next
week and we do our best though it may not be easy. On TV
they said they think the old President was buried today but
they didn't tell where.

MAY 22
Friday. Jude and Iz will bed here tomorrow night which
will mean all night party. I wish it was just me and Iz but
we'll be girls together anyway. Then one week of finals and
school's out and it's summer.

I wish we were vacationing this year but we're not of
course. New York is still New York but it's worse than ever.
It's roughened so it's getting like Brooklyn except there

aren't any planes and tanks in Manhattan yet. Our rooms are always smoky now. They've burned half of Harlem I think. Outside it's been dark daylong the past two the smoke heavies so. Cars and buses keep their lights on at noon. Boob and Mama cough constant and spit black sometimes. We keep the windows shut when we can but it's so hot we have to open them come night. The heat made Daddy's computer crash. Even if he was writing we're not moneyed enough to fix it so he's luckless present.

Mama got new money at the bank today all dollar bills. Now they're pink and blue and orange and have Martha Graham on the front and an eagle on the back. When you hold them up to the light you can see the watermark which is a smiley face. 'Our cash be like this now?' I asked her when me and Boob were eyeing them. 'Yes sweeties what little bit there is' Mama said. She said she doesn't know what we'll do if the prices don't adjust to fit the money. One new dollar is worth ten of the old ones but that's supposed to change again next week.

Stock market ran out weeklong and drained today nearly.

MAY 24

Sunday today and we've all been resting except for Daddy. Anne now that study time nears if I'm chanced I'll write you again before next Friday but I can't guarantee.

Iz and Jude came over last night at seven thirty when it was already darkening. Before they showed Mama said to me 'My angels we have so little food in the house I feel terrible for not being able to properly entertain your little friends.' 'Don't fret we'll adjust' I told her but Iz and Jude bettered that for us Anne. They'd banked and brought us two big bags of groceries including bologna and cheese and bread and milk and toilet tissue and much more. 'You be hostin us we got to supply' Jude said unpacking the groceries. Mama happied instant and hugged them both saying

198

'Oh angels you're so sweet it's so unnecessary you're sure you have enough at home?' Iz and Jude nodded and said don't fret. They're such good friends Anne and now Mama loves them as much as I do.

We pigged but didn't do much else but tube. We asked Boob if she wanted to hang with us but she said no and went into Mama's room. Iz and Jude scare her I think. It's unknowing if they scare her because they're black or because she thinks they're queer too. It didn't stop her from eating the food they brought though. Boob is changing Anne and I don't know into what. Every day this week she said 'Let's go live with Chrissie' and she meant it. Mama shudders hearing her.

There wasn't anything on the networks to watch except specials on EcoCrisis Day Five. 'Nada new on this news let's surf' Jude said running channels. There weren't any videos we hadn't seen before and the cartoons were bad and guys on the Christian stations were hopped raving about God's sword and the end at hand. We clicked off even before Mama and Boob bedded and then finished two bags potato chips and a bottle of Pepsi. 'You seen Esther?' I asked. 'Ever night cept Tuesday' Iz said. 'She thinking she gonna drop soon.' 'Drop what?' 'The baby.' 'It's time?' 'Close enough it'll drop when it ready to drop. We eyeing close to make sure she do good' Jude said. 'Her auntie be overlooking too just waiting being terrible the whole time though' Iz said. 'How?' 'Always be saying Esther being punished for being bad but not being punished enough' Iz said.

We unfolded the sofa and pajama partied without pajamas. Jude lay stomached looking at everything. 'This everything you own?' she asked. 'Most we stored or got rid of' I said. 'How many rooms in your old place?' 'The living room and study three bedrooms two baths kitchen pantry and foyer' I said. 'I been in bigger' Jude said. 'Where?' I asked. 'Around.' 'Much bigger?' 'Six bedroom terrace with dining room too. Jacuzzi and bidet in the bathroom' Jude said. 'What's a bidet?' Iz asked. 'You squat down on it and it hose you.' 'Get out' Iz said. 'It's true I've seen them but I never used one' I said. 'Don't they take baths?' Iz asked. 'Yeah but it's like for after you be bumpin nasty' Jude said. 'Whose apartment was it?' I asked. 'Friend' she said rolling over onto her back looking ceilingways.

'You want to play make believe?' I asked. 'Make believe what?' Iz asked. 'It's a fun game. I say imagine something and then you do. Like I say make believe you could have any apartment just the way you wanted it. What would your apartment be like?' I said. 'And we say?' Jude asked. 'That's it.' 'Hell I be happy with an apartment' Jude said. 'But if I do the architectin I want a penthouse two floors and a terrace. Big kitchen full a food. King size bed in my room and a bathtub big enough to swim in.' 'And a bidet to squirt you all night long' Iz said laughing. Jude tried to grab her ankles but Iz jumped rolling cross the bed.

'Iz make believe you could work doing anything you wanted. What would you do?' I asked. 'Be an artist' she said. 'Painting sculpting. Live in the country and do art.' 'What about you?' Jude asked. 'I'd be a writer' I said. 'Do movies and TV.' 'Like you daddy?' Jude asked. 'Exactly. And you?' I asked. 'I get some mogul to fund me and then when his back turn I take the wheel. Run the world way I wanted to run it.' We all laughed again.

'Make believe you could fly anywhere. Where you go?' Iz asked. 'I'd go to Europe' I said. 'Germany I think and then France after.' 'I go to England' Iz said. 'Get there say look here Queen it's me. What about you Jude?' 'New York do me fine. Got everthing needed if you know how to look' she said.

'Make believe one day you can do anything you want. What would you do?' I asked. 'I go wild shoppin' said Jude. 'Go to Bergdorf try on dresses then put em back sayin uh-uh you quality slipslidin. Then I taxi somewhere for a six course lunch with cloth napkins and waiters kissin my ass. After that go shop some more then go to a show then come home.' 'What then?' Iz asked. 'You know what I be doin then difference bein I be the one doin the pickin' Jude said giggling. 'You too nasty Jude you are' Iz said and they smacked each other. 'I be lowkey' Iz said. 'In the morning I get up and do some art and then read some. Have a big lunch and then go hang in the park.' 'Sound like you do the same then you do now. Little nerdy girl' Jude said laughing some more. 'I'd sleep till noon cause there's nothing better' I said. 'That all?' Jude asked. 'No I'd get up at night and go out. Anything's doable come nightside and I do anything and everything' I said. 'I bet. You crazy girl. Crazy Lola that your name now' Iz said. 'I'm not crazy' I said. 'You are sometime darlin you mindlost complete' Jude said. 'Am not' I said and smacked her foot. She smacked me back hard on the shoulder and I jumped her. We tumbled laughing and wrestling on the bed. Jude is so strong I couldn't pin her and finally she fixed my head between her legs and squeezed till I squeaked. We wilded so Iz whispered saying 'You wake Mrs Hart you keep on now come on settle.' Jude unclamped me and we sat up again hot and breathless.

'Make believe you have you own boy' Jude said leaning against the back of the sofa. 'What you make him do for you?' Iz got up and closed the curtains though she left the windows open for breeze. 'Boys are ickola I'd never want one' I said. 'You say' Jude said. 'I mean' I said. 'Boys nothing but big babies and I never want a baby either like I say.' 'Way you play boys is get em to baby you' Jude said. 'And how you play yours then?' Iz asked. 'You seen me you oughta know' Jude said. Iz shook her head and sat down. 'My boyfriend be big and strong' she said. 'Be smart and able to talk. Not be grossin me out daylong like they tend.' 'And what else?' Jude asked. 'Begone with you Jude' Iz said.

I got jealous when Iz talked about boys and I didn't expect to. It weirded me Anne but I couldn't help it however mindlost it seems. If I had to share Iz with some boy instead of Jude I think I'd be edged constant. 'What

201

else Iz? You missin your essential' Jude said. 'I don't think
so' Iz said. 'Better be cloud white don't he?' Jude asked.
'Don't matter I'm not after boys now anyway' she said. 'Do
tell' Jude said looking at her. 'Iz she like em pale long as
they red where it count' she added to me. 'And how often
you go native Jude?' Iz said looking mad. 'If I'm businessin
I trade the upscale market that's known. Not enough
cleanheads round for girls wantin to climb' Jude said.
'And when you're not businessing?' Iz asked. 'Boys gotta
wait they turn then' Jude said. 'Got better ways spendin my
time.'

'This game too sharp it getting like doin dozens' Iz said.
'We just gamin Iz' Jude said. 'It suit me. My turn now I
spec. Make believe you could do revenge on whoever
wronged you most. Who they be and what you do to em?'

Me and Iz sat muted waiting for someone else to spill
first. Jude eyed us close and smiled like a cat not showing
her teeth. 'Awful quiet now' she said. 'Kevin' Iz said. 'I
hear you. How you treat?' Jude asked. 'Bad' Iz said. 'How
bad?' 'So bad he wish he was black' Iz said. 'She tell you
who Kevin was?' Jude asked me. I nodded. 'What she tell?'
'Jude stop' Iz said. 'Nada' I said hoping Jude would stop.
'Keep minded Iz sorta racist when it come to brothers.
Even when she a little girl, seem like' Jude said. 'She fancy
that ice people skin whoever it on' Jude said eyeing me and
crooking her grin. 'Jude you lying not truthing hush up' Iz
said looking pissed. 'Kevin he be a gold boy. Greek or
something but light. He lead her off to play doctor. Doctor
hell he an afrogyno' Jude said. 'Iz be callin it rape now but
it sound different to me.'

Iz swung out her hand to hit Jude but Jude caught it.
She didn't do anything but hold onto it staring at Iz and in
a second or two Iz took her arm down. 'She know why it
sound different to you too long as we spilling' Iz said to her.
'However you call it that's what it was. And that's why he
never suffer bad enough. Now you ask the question Jude,
your turn to answer.' 'Answer what how?' she asked. 'Who

202

you want to revenge on most. She already know who and why Jude so let's keep gaming. What you do to him?'

'Done enough already' Jude said. 'Never nohow and you know it' said Iz. Jude sat not looking at us for a minute not saying anything. Then she lay down putting her head on one of the pillows. 'What you do to him if you could?' Iz asked again. 'Rope his feet and hang him from the roof. Swing him till he go sailing. Watch him bounce when he hit and let the rats eat him. No more Milton Glastonbury. But he gone now anyway from my view' Jude said saying it all very calm. 'I hate this damn game. Crazy you tell yours and then we done with it.'

They looked at me. I'd been so headset on what they said to each other and the way Jude was saying what she didn't say that I hadn't thought of who I'd revenge on most. Weez hadn't really done that much to suffer me and now that she was gone I heartfelt for her. Besides she and Jude were longtime close and I knew Jude still saddened over it, that was probably why she was so spiky. There were plenty of people I was mad at at school mostly Lori and Katherine but I wouldn't want to hurt them either really. 'Mister Mossbacher' I finally said. 'He teach you?' Iz asked. 'He owns Excelsior Bookstore. Daddy works for him and wrongs him daylong' I said. 'Who did you most wrong Lola not daddy' Jude said. 'He did me wrong because he wrongs Daddy' I said. 'Uh-uh. When you revenge serious on some-body they got to have wronged you direct and not just sideswipe' Jude said. 'She right Lola that don't count. You can't think a nobody?' Iz asked. I shook my head. 'Well I pick Weez if I be you but so be it' Jude said. 'Game over.'

A little later we snuffed the lights. I was sorry we gamed after we did. Make believe doesn't always go like you'd want it to. We lay in bed side by side with Iz in the middle listening to the noise outside and talking some. Jude could tell the kinds of guns people were shooting from the sounds they made and did for a few minutes listening. 'What do you want when you grow up? Not make believe' I asked whispering. 'Go to college get married. Work doing something I like' Iz said. 'Once I get situated I make sure you workin Iz' Jude said. 'Something I like' Iz repeated and then she said 'Be nice to get babied once I settle and pay. Then I just take it from there after that.' 'What about you Jude? What do you want?' I asked. 'Everthing' she said. 'How bout you?' Iz asked me. 'I don't know' I said. 'You have to' she said. 'I used to think I knew but I don't. It's all far away' I said. 'What is?' Iz said. 'Everything. College work whatever. It's all dreamy. Mostly I want to live that's all' I said.

When Daddy homed I woke. He bathroomed and I lay wide eye hearing water run and distanced sirens sounding like trains in the country. I thought Iz and Jude were dead out but they weren't and they must have figured the same about me. Once Daddy bedded Iz got on top of Jude and they kissed. I heard their lips smack when they started kissing big slurpy kisses. I turned over pressing the side of my head in my pillow and my hand over my open ear so I couldn't listen.

It wasn't the listening but the wanting that racked me Anne I wanted to be kissing Iz. But she and Jude have been girls together longtime though and I shouldn't be jealous even though I was. They were moving a lot making little gurgling sounds and shook like they chilled. The bed overheated with three of us on it so they couldn't have been cold I knew. I wished I was doing what Jude was doing with Iz even though it's queer. That aches me too because they prefer boys I can tell even if they don't want them now and I don't like boys at all. There's nothing wrong with me there isn't but everyone else thinks so when they know even if they don't know. Sometimes I fear I'll never happy proper.

It seemed like hours before they finished playing and Iz rolled off. They were breathing hard like they'd been running and I could hear them even though I was trying not to. I wanted to sleep but couldn't and then I started crying. It was so deadhead there wasn't any reason for boohooing I was just sad. I hate crying Anne it uglies your face and doesn't settle you and it shames me when I cry. I never do it noisy I just drop tears. It was awful and I wished I was millions of miles away but I wasn't and I didn't want them to know I heard them so all I could do was lay there dead. I was glad they couldn't hear me cry but I think Iz could tell anyway because before I fell asleep she touched my back with her hand and petted me. It was so nice to have her do that that I settled and slept then.

This morning they left. Jude went rambling and Iz went churching and here I am writing you before I study. It'll heart me to have finals over. I used to like school so much back in September I loved going. But that was past and now I can't wait till it's done. My friends were fun and I loved them but they threw me. At least I have new friends now but they could go too sometime you never know though. Look what happened to Weez and Jude and they'd known each other as long as me and Lori. You don't know who your friends are Anne until you're not like them anymore.

I walked with Iz and Jude to 125th Street. The greenasses are stacking concrete blocks down the middle of the street making a wall with openings to let cars and buses through. That'll easy their keeping people in or out we guessed. Then after I left Iz and Jude and before I came back here to write and now study I walked down Broadway thinking and looking skyhigh. That's when I saw it Anne I think it was an angel up airways cloudfloating but not so high I couldn't see her. Nobody else streeted acted like they eyed her so I peg her for my very special own angel. She was white and gold and bewinged like a bird. Even though she was far distant I saw her smile at me. Maybe it was a cloud but it didn't dress like one it looked like an angel in a book like by William Blake. At first I thought seeing an angel signed good but now when I rethink it's more clear and worrisome. Maybe my new name Crazy Lola is right. I didn't tell

Mama or Boob that I saw the angel and I won't tell Daddy or Iz or Jude either, I'll just tell you. It nerves me thinking about it.

I'll write when I can Anne.

MAY 26

Just here quick because I'm set to blow. Miss Wisegarver told me her test I took yesterday has to be redone before she grades me. She says it's obvious I didn't know what I was doing and hadn't studied. She'll incomplete me she says and let me take it again Thursday. I did study for it I did but something racked and my mind wouldn't hold any more. I don't know how I'll redo but we'll see. Usually I do best in her class so it fears me about how I'm doing in everything else. But enough gnash back to studying now.

MAY 28

What's wrong with me Anne. I got C on my final in Math and B minus in History. Today I took Miss Wisegarver's test over and I spec I redid it better but I thought I aced first time through. Tomorrow's the last test day and I'm heart-happy. Monday we find out our grades and then we gone till September rolls and I won't have to think school till then.

Granny showed today worsening my mood twiceover but what's to be done with her. What's to be done with me. It's hateful Anne it is.

MAY 29

Friday and the last real day of school and the last test in Sociology class. It's done and I'm happied. Weekend's here and tomorrow I'm set to meet Iz and Jude. We'll do something somewhere though I don't know what. Banking essential so watch out guys. Daddy's kitchened present working over his résumé and the bills figuring what we'll do once he's jobless. That won't be soon soon though because Mister Mossbacher told him yesterday he hasn't been able to get a capable replacement yet so Daddy has to work another extra week before he's free. Mister Mossbacher says he'll time and a half him for every hour over fifty Daddy slaves. That's something considering with the new money he only hauls forty a week. Mama and Boob they're dead out already even though it's just nine.

Daddy's quieted overmuch and I think I better check him I be right back Anne.

JUNE 2

I didn't come back like I said I would the other night and I haven't writ before now because of what went down. Forgive me Anne.

When I went kitchenways I eyed Daddy chaired at tableside laying his head on his arms like he sleepied. He never drops like that but Mister Mossbacher had worked him so I think maybe it caught up and felled him. I didn't know he had slept away yet. I shook his shoulder but he sat statued.

'Daddy?' I said shaking him harder but he didn't move he just stilled. It nerved me and so I touched his head and it rolled sideways and I spied how he was, he looked but didn't see. I knew he was dead Anne even though there wasn't any certifying. I don't know why and how I knew but I did. Screaming's called for when you find people dead I always thought but I didn't. I zipped hallways running in Mama's room waking her trying not to stir Boob.

'Angel sweetie what is it did you have a bad dream?' Mama asked. 'No Mama come here' I said whispering. 'I don't understand' she said. 'In the kitchen please Mama lipstill and come here.' 'My darling you're in such a state what is it what's wrong?' 'Daddy' I said. Mama unbedded and robed and tripped misfooting through the dark hallways. When she eyed Daddy she knelt down next to him putting her hand on his neck and then on his wrists pulsefeeling but there weren't feelables. 'Mama?' I asked when she didn't speak she statued too. 'Angel call 911 please hurry.' She chaired next to him holding his hand crying while I called.

The police showed and medtechs and suit people taking an hour to get there. Daddy was moldcold by then. The doctors poked and thumped and awared Mama he had a massive heart attack she told me later. 'My darling precious it was the best way he was there one minute and gone the next' Mama said sounding it like Daddy did what everybody do. Right before the place filled Mama had me go in their bedroom and babysit Boob keeping her in there. She woke wide eye when she heard their big boots come in going thump thump thump.

I baldfaced her Anne I said something was wrong with Daddy but I didn't say how wrong. 'Is he sick I want to see him' she said. 'No Boob they're taking him to the hospital you can't talk to him now' I said. 'What's wrong with him?' she asked. 'Can't say' I said. 'Can we see him tomorrow?' 'I don't know Boob.' 'Why can't I see him?' 'Because you can't.' 'Is he dead?' she asked surprising me because sharp as Boob is I didn't spec she'd figure so quick. 'He's doing bad Boob just settle yourself' I said. 'Did somebody shoot him?' 'No Boob' I said. 'Then why can't I see him?' 'Boob please please' I said and she started boohooing and trying to push me off but I was unbudging finally sitting on her to keep her bedded. She howled like a monkey and a blueboy opened the door. He eyed us like we'd been caught wronging like he hated us. 'Where's my daddy?' Boob shouted at him. He shut the door. Boob shoved hard and pushed me off yelling 'I hate you I hate you.' She didn't unbed though she just pillowed her face crying. I sat there trying to blank my mind it was too much. I saddened fast but it wasn't for Daddy, that wasn't real yet. I ached deepdown because Boob never said she hated me even when she maddened before. However I tried to deafen to everything I heard her saying that. Finally after an hour or longer everybody left and then Mama came back shutting the door behind her.

'Oh my angels' she said and then told us about Daddy even though we knew. We held her and cried and then we bedded though we didn't really sleep. I know I lay there hours eyeing ceilingways thinking it was awful and bizarre. Just a few hours earlier Daddy was there with us and now he was gone and we'd never see him again. However much I tried to blank I couldn't Anne everything about Daddy blurred into his face it wouldn't go away. What was the last thing he said to me I kept trying to remember I think he asked if I'd help him wash the dishes later and I said yes but never did. Even though I never thought about heaven before I started wondering where Daddy had gone now that he'd died, that is if he went anywhere. I felt my face getting wetter and wetter and finally I stomached flat so I couldn't see anything even Daddy's face.

The funeral was Sunday morning. Daddy still had Guild coverage for funerals which heartened because otherwise we'd have had to dump him somewhere I think. He was cremated in a plain wood box at the funeral home. The chimney was smoking when we got there. When ash rains grounddown now I think I'm still getting sprinkled with Daddy. Mama told me they'd had a family space clear in a mausoleum in Queens but now it's off limited thanks to the warring so she got a new space in Woodlawn in the Bronx. Besides us and the funeral people and the Society For Ethical Culture speaker there were other friends of Mama and Daddy who came. Some were teachers and some writers and some I didn't know. His agent couldn't come because Mama said he was closing with Paramount. No one from Excelsior showed. Mama called Mister Mossbacher to say Daddy wouldn't be in because he was dead. She said he sounded like he craved to shout but didn't. Daddy was supposed to get paid Saturday because payday was shifted two days up due to cashflow problems he'd said and Mama told Mister Mossbacher we needed it. He said he'd express it and then he hung up on her.

We rode six cars going up sticking close. It took an hour and a half because the greenasses checked all running detectors over the cars before passing us through. The cars had mirror windows so we could eye without being eyed. Washington Heights and Inwood look like I expected all torched and blasted except round City College and Columbia Presbyterian. They have those rounded bout with razorwire and soldiers. Hardly any businesses are left anywhere except liquor stores and bodegas. There aren't any cars but you see buses. It's all Serbia up there and the people walk stoopbacked like they had enough. Army's got the streets lined with tanks even though they're not supposed to let them in and everywhere you look there's thousands of soldiers armed and itchy. They're building another wall down the middle of Dyckman Street in Inwood.

Once we Bronxed we rode a parkway to Woodlawn. At the mausoleum we sat in a little chapel and the Ethical Culture man raved on about translating goodness. Some friends of Daddy told everybody how lucked they were since they knew him. They may be lucked sure they still alive. We held each other's hands, me and Mama and Boob. We didn't cry except Mama did at the very end. I'd never been to a funeral before. It weirded me Anne I kept wishing it was done not because it ached me so but because I went deadhead halfway through hearing them blather and fudge. I couldn't help it if they missed him so much why didn't they do more to help him? Maybe they did maybe I'm just being unfair but so what. Instead of thinking of Daddy my mind fixed on Mister Mossbacher and how I hated him. If he hadn't wronged Daddy it probably wouldn't have happened I thought and I know I'm right. I just wanted to leap and run far away leaving them all it dizzied me so. Oh Anne if there is hell like on Christian commercials I guess I'm bound for it.

Chrissie and Mama phone each other every day since Daddy died. Mama told me today they've been talking about us. Boob was so unhappy even before and now Mama says it's all so uncertained she just doesn't know. 'Sweetie you're a toughie aren't you you think we can be all right?' she asked me. 'Plenty so' I said. 'Oh angel I know you can make it and I think I can too but I just don't know about that poor little Boobster she was already so feathery and now this' Mama said. Boob's chubola I think so I don't think feathery when I think Boob but I knew what was meant. 'Do you think she'll be all right living with Chrissie if it can be worked out?' Mama asked me. 'I spec she'll be a Chrissie clone in no time' I said. 'My darling that's such a dreadful thought and you're probably right. But think of how things are here the Army everywhere and people shooting at us and our money running out don't you think it'd be safer there?' Mama said. 'If they're moneyed so why don't they trickle us?' I asked. 'Sweet darling they'd help by providing a better environment for Boob don't you see?' she said. 'Safer maybe better maybe not' I said. 'Chrissie wanted me to ask if you wanted to come out there too and live with the rest in the bunker' Mama said. 'Nada never' I said. 'That's what I told her sweetie but you know Chrissie. She knows better than to ask if I want to because it would be inviting murder' Mama said. 'We're still housing here then?' I asked. 'Yes angel I don't know what we'll do though it's going to be so much harder' she said. I told her it would be all right but she just looked at me and half-smiled. I stayed floating while Mama told. It'll never be hard enough I have to live with Chrissie.

Daddy didn't have insurance because he'd cashed it in earlier. There was a little money we got from the Guild that he'd set aside but translated into new money it's even less than it would have been. We're choiceless in the matter in any event that's all so we'll have to earplay it and see what goes.

Iz called me Saturday to see when we could meet and I

told her we couldn't and why. She saddened having only met Daddy last week and then only momentslong before he went to work. When I talked to Iz I started crying loud but not for long, tears don't help you. She said she understood. 'What happened to your father Iz?' I asked. 'He was cancered' she said. 'I was little. Three or four. I hardly remember him except he had big hands and smiled.' 'You loved him?' 'Sure why you ask?' Iz said. 'Maybe I didn't love Daddy enough' I said only half believing it but thinking it possible enough. 'Girl you mindlost what a thing to say' said Iz. 'I know but I wonder' I said. 'Lola you so crazy' she said. 'I know that's my name Crazy Lola' I said.

It's all breaking Anne I better stop now.

JUNE 4

We've settled. Boob is going to stay with Chrissie. She and Mama talked and they detailed what they had to. Dopey Alan is using frequent flier miles to pay for Boob's ticket to San Francisco. She leaves tomorrow from Newark Airport which is the only one open. She'll be gone then. It's not forever Mama says but who knows how long that'll be everything's forever when you don't know when it'll end. I spec one day we will regroup but there'll be meantime changes and what we'll be when we see each other again, that's unknowable. I'll miss Boob so much all the times I wished she was somewhere else but when it downcomes I don't. But what's to do?

This evening me and Boob. 'What will you do out there besides school?' I asked. 'I don't know but I'll be safe' Boob said. She held her My L'il Fetus which is just about gone now, it's nada but a lump with a head. 'Nobody's safe Boob that's truthed plain' I said. 'That's what you say but I'll be safe with Aunt Chrissie.' 'Maybe maybe not' I said. 'Nobody will get me' she said. 'Nobody who?' I asked. 'Nobody in New York. Nobody at school and nobody on the street and none of my friends and none of your friends' Boob said.

'Me too?' I asked. 'I said everybody didn't I?' she said. 'What's meant Boob?' 'I mean you won't do anything to me' she said. 'What you think I do to you?' I asked getting mad. 'Don't know but you'd do something someday I know' she said.

Boob is going to turn into Chrissie whatever we do I think. It's not so much that Chrissie has her own Kure-A-Kid program like what was done to Lori, it's more genetic. Maybe Chrissie won't harass Mama as much once she's got Boob to rebuild. Mama said when she talked to Chrissie the other day Chrissie was again saying she was a terrible mother for wanting to keep me here with her. 'I told her you didn't want to go sweetie but you know Chrissie she knows everything' Mama said. Mama said she told Chrissie she wished to God she knew what to do and she said Chrissie told her God hears the prayers of Jews but not if they live in New York. 'She's become so peculiar out there in the outback sweetie she was always awful to me but now it's like she's not even human' Mama said. 'But you want Boob to be with her' I said. 'Boob's so fragile my darling she'll wither if she's here much longer she takes so after her poor father' Mama said. 'She's not too withery' I said. 'Inside sweetie inside.' 'I take after you' I said pleased because even though she flutters and she's too medicated Mama can tough it better than Daddy could that was always how it was. 'Oh my angel I hope not I hope not' Mama said. After I hugged her longtime she finally dried and went on.

JUNE 5

We bussed out to Newark Airport today from Port Authority. It's one of the worst places in town and always has been Anne. It's on 42nd which is all abandoned and empty now to start with and wilders hang there in and out constant. City claim it safer now but there's more living there now than there were last year. Men layabout eyeing women till they find the new ones and then make them prostitutes dog ugly ones worse than the tunnel tramps on Eleventh Avenue. Port Authority is horror plus Anne you feel greasy just walking through it.

We put Boob on the plane to San Francisco at the airport. Actually Boob put herself on the plane because the antiterrorist police wouldn't let us terminal too far in. I wanted to word her this morning before she flew but I tonguetied and she kept forgetting making Mama doublecheck what she hauled so we never talked. I said I'd write but I don't know what I'll say. She won't be there a month before she's Chrissiesized and it's racked me overmuch already Anne the way people like Lori and Katherine sideshift. Knowing somebody so long and then they sudden change disrupts so it's not handleable anymore or at least I spec not for me. I kissed her goodbye and she statued when I did, I think she's already season changed and it's too late.

Me and Mama rode back lipstilled the whole way. She vizzed sad like I know I do but nothing was sayable so I hushed and just remembered Boob like I knew her back when we homed in our old place. The ride wasn't long enough. I hadn't been out of New York all year so even Jersey counted this trip. Everything there was ugly as always and didn't look different. The ride was only a quarter for each of us both ways but that would have been ten dollars not long ago. That's one whole dinner gone on the road. Mama reloaded in the bathroom once we homed that much's known but I can't tell what's zoned her tonight. She's sitting couched in the living room with manuscripts round her waiting to be read. I think she's better but it's hard to tell.

JUNE 6
Saturday today. I'm still a family girl though because instead of meeting Iz and Jude I went with Mama to

Excelsior Bookstore to see Mister Mossbacher. Guess what? You guessed he hadn't sent Daddy's last paycheck.

The guards brisked us when we went in. Guards are worse than blueboys they're always either middle age fat white guys who don't shave but once a week or else they're Spanish and peachfuzz young like the ones who sexmouth us in our neighborhood. They eye our purses and make us raise our arms and then they do the laying on of hands always patting my butt. Guards don't rub up men as much cause if they did they'd likely find them armed and then they'd shake not knowing what to do.

The store was packed but it wasn't people buying books as much as it was people trying to get cash refunds wanting that new cash of course. The managers screamed blood murder at them and they threw books at the managers saying I want my money. We hotfooted to the info counter where Mama asked to see Mister Mossbacher. He's in the back unpacking books the man said nodding his head. Mama had to ask twice to replay before she heard him. They walled in info with token booth lucite so customers couldn't torch them I guessed.

Mister Mossbacher wasn't hitting his head on the dumb-waiter this time. He unpacked books from a box and stacked them on a table making sure each stack was neat even with the rest. He dressed so bumly Anne dirty pants and a tee and nerd perps Daddy told me once he'd heard he'd never had a girlfriend and that reasoned cause nothing animal would want him. The louder the customers yelled the louder they volumed the radio at info so everybody deafened in time I guessed. Mama waited a second before going over to him. 'Come on' I said leading. 'All right angel he can't be as bad as your father said' Mama said. 'He is' I said remembering the only other time I'd seen him. I knew she feared him but turning back time was done.

'Oh excuse me Mister Mossbacher my name is Faye Hart and my husband Michael worked for you until he died' Mama said. Maybe he didn't hear her firstoff but I bet he did. He didn't even blink, it was like we'd gone homeless invisible. 'Please excuse me but Mister Mossbacher?' she asked. I heard you he said sounding mad. Then he went mute again still unpacking books. 'You said you'd mail us his last paycheck but we haven't received it yet and we need it' Mama said. He stopped unpacking and raised to glare lasers at us. What do you expect? he asked holding his hands out and pointing all around him. Look at this I hate my fucking life he said and then he unpacked some more like we'd left. 'What about my husband's last pay-check Mister Mossbacher?' Mama asked quieting her voice. I eyed her hands shake so I knew she feared overmuch but I couldn't tell if he knew. The longer we were there the more he boiled though that showed plain. I was left in a bad position when your husband died Mister Mossbacher said. The managers who covered for him put in overtime and it equalled out.

Mister Mossbacher picked up a boxcutter and slit a new box. 'What do you mean equalled out?' Mama asked. That paycheck had to go to pay overtime for the managers who had to cover for him. 'You mean we don't get it?' Mama asked. What is it aren't I being clear enough for you to understand? Mister Mossbacher said gripping the boxcutter like he was going to stick us. 'He earned that money the last week he was here you can't do that' Mama said. Goddamit I'm trying to run a business here if you can't fucking see that so don't tell me what I can't do Mister Mossbacher said. 'You told me you'd send it along' Mama said. I was wrong Mister Mossbacher said. 'He died it wasn't deliber-ate God help him I need that money for my children' Mama said. Can't you understand I've got problems here it's not my fault he died that screwed up my schedule like you wouldn't believe Mister Mossbacher said shouting.

Boxcutter or no I readied to lunge cause I didn't like the way he worded her. He was smaller than Weezie was wiry but I was reddened like Mama. 'You're a horrible man' Mama said. 'You worked him to death and you talked to him like he was a dog and now you're stealing money from his children.' Get the fuck out of my fucking store Mister Mossbacher yelled screaming in her face and waving the boxcutter. I prepped but before there was jumping one of the guards showed and he was packing like all of them. 'There's no reason for you to talk to me this way' Mama said. Get the fuck out of here or I'm calling the police Mister Mossbacher said. Your husband couldn't work for shit anyway take them out Felix and don't ever let them in again he told the guard.

'You'll be hearing from my lawyer' Mama told Mister Mossbacher. Lady if you're hounding me for checks how the fuck will you pay a lawyer? he said laughing and taking books out of the box again. Felix the guard took our arms and marched us down the aisle not saying anything. He held us at the entrance while other guards looked in our purses and brisked us updown rough. Mama closed her eyes while they felt her and I keened to blow oh Anne it was like with Weez I was set to go post office but it scares me so when I do I didn't. I wanted to ex Mister Mossbacher and pain him through and through. There's nobody I hate as much as I hate Mister Mossbacher.

When they finished copping feels the guards shoved us outside. Mama started crying. People onceovered us and kept walking. 'Mama it's all right' I said trying to hearten her. 'No it's not all right it's never all right' she said pushing me away. That almost did it Anne I almost ran back storeways. First he killed Daddy I thought and now he'd torn Mama so she was after me. She hugged me then saying 'Oh my angel I'm so sorry I'm so so sorry that awful man just upset me so' and if she hadn't distracted I aimed to get him. Mister Mossbacher doesn't deserve to have a store Anne he doesn't deserve to walk like normal people he doesn't deserve to live. I hate him hate him hate him.

We came back home and kitchened ourselves and tried to figure how to money ourselves but it doesn't longrun good. 'Angel I was counting on that money I don't know what we'll do I'm beside myself trying to pay rent and utilities I don't know how we'll eat' she said. 'Don't fret yourself Mama we'll eat' I said. Mama has manuscripts but she's only being paid now for ones she did in April and being paid new money besides. I better stay far from Excelsior cause if I ever see him again that'll be judgment day for Mister Mossbacher.

Mama cried and cried. Sometimes I wish I could drip when I wanted. Time to bedaway Anne I'm deepdown tired.

JUNE 7

Met Jude and Iz today shorttime because Iz churched this morning and again tonight and Jude was meeting a friend downtown. It startled Anne she was business dressed almost. She wore a wig with long straight Barbie hair except it was black and makeup and a short tight black dress that showed her legs. She looked ten years older. 'You're sure it's you?' I asked. 'Somewhere in here' she said. 'Are you partying?' I asked. 'We going to a restaurant so I can stuff then whatever' she said. Iz told me Jude dudes when she goes downtown but I didn't know how much. She prettied so we just sat and eyed her updown. It's not how I'd ever want to look but it suits her.

'Before I church I'm gonna run by Esther and see her again wanta come?' Iz asked me. 'I think I should stay Mama she's upping and downing' I said. 'Our last school day's Wednesday let's get together then' Iz said. 'Okay' I said. 'We busy on Wednesday Iz' Jude said. 'Doing what?' Iz said. 'We busy' Jude said. 'You say we busy but I don't know what we busy at.' 'Think about it' Jude said staring at Iz. Iz put her head down a second and then said 'That's right Lola I forgot.' 'That's all right' I said. 'Maybe Thursday or Friday.' 'Maybe' Iz said. I willied some watching Jude eye Iz and I thought I better lipstill. A little later we said goodbye. Iz said she'd call.

218

I am worried about Mama Anne. Tonight we watched the news some but she finally made me turn it off it depressed so. She read over papers that had to do with Daddy in the kitchen but didn't mail anything out. She has manuscripts to proofread but didn't work on them tonight. I don't spec that'll money us enough either but Mama doesn't tell and I don't ask. The new rent is only twenty new dollars a month but it's still more than we probably have. I miss Boob a lot but I miss Daddy the most.

JUNE 9

A new bill collector called today huffing like he was going post office even before I said hello. This is about the payment due where's your father? he asked. 'Dead' I said. Don't you know you'll go to hell if you tell lies he said. 'Maybe but I'm truthing he's cold dead and if he owed you you're fucked' I told him. That worked in shushing him Anne maybe because I said it so little girl like. He lipstilled for a second and I hung up before he could start in again. He didn't recall so I spec he guiltied enough to cave at least for now.

Bad dreams stir me nightlong Anne. The one last night was nothing but bad craziness. I was sitting in my room with a Siamese cat. The cat eyed me and nodded its head. Though it kept wordless I heard it say rat. I scoped Mama's bedroom where she bedded there naked. A dog ugly rat facecrawled her. When I stood doorways it hopped down and walked past me kitchenways while I stilled. Then I took a hammer from a drawer and got behind the rat. I fullarm hammered its head five or six times. While I was swinging it turned into a turtle and moved its head round to stare at me. I heard it crack when I hit it and I stopped hitting and then I woke up shaking in wet sheets.

When Iz called tonight I told her my dream. 'Crazy girl' she said and she's dead on. She says she can bed here Friday night. Oh Anne that hearthappies me nobody else hears when I word except you problem is you don't talk back.

Pardon my writing you being so on again off again Anne but now that it's summer I sleep in and then daylong I busy myself and then come night it's just like schooltime I don't feel keen to pen. Today I went walking starting down Broadway and fastfooting till I midtowned. When I hit Excelsior I stopped outside cause when I looked in I saw him. Mister Mossbacher stood windowsided by the cashiers and he screamed blood murder at them like he'd been deepdown hurt but I knew he was just looning. He was wildeyed and shouted so you could hear him through the glass. For a second I thought I should go in but then I thought how the guards would be giving me a layon of hands so I rounded the block instead. If I'd gone in or if he'd come out I don't know what I'd have done but I'd have done something.

I subwayed home. Greenasses march through the trains now slinging their guns up like their dicks so big they got to throw them over their shoulder. After they leave the cars riders mutter but otherwise do nada I spec they like me and think if there's going to be shooting they don't keen on being the ones being shot. It's occupatory democracy they call it on TV but I say these Army boys hang where they shouldn't be hanging myself. They irked but didn't madden what most racked me on the way back was the way Mister Mossbacher did Mama and Daddy. There's no excusing it Anne. I boiled so that when a man accidentally footstomped me coming out I nearly hopped up to hit him but didn't. My unreasoning fretted me so I ran inside when I got here and started writing so I could blow safe.

Iz gets here in another hour or so and I watch the minutes change on the clock wishing I could doubletime them and speed her here. It's like waiting for Christmas Anne when I think of Iz I almost stop seeing Mister Mossbacher's puss. I love her Anne I really do. Fifty three minutes to Iz exact but she always lates.

* * *

Damn it Anne damn it damn it damn it. There's no wording proper what downed last night. The world brutalizes however you live it whatever you do. Everything started so good Anne Iz came and we ate dinner and tubed and talked and just had heaven time. Before she showed I feared Jude might come too because she has a standing invite too but she didn't. Iz said she was with a downtown friend so she was occupied.

Mama headed bedways early. She never tells but I spec she's upped her dose this week she's giddied some and nods easy. It frets me but her docs know best I imagine and if she hadn't been medicated tonight I can't say how she'd have done. In any event once she faded me and Iz hit the sheets and played till we were drippy wet. As usual once we settled again we lay in the dark talking all the air out. 'What was it you couldn't remember you were doing with Jude?' I asked. 'When?' Iz said and it's goofed but true Anne I can already tell when she fudges and when she doesn't and she was. 'We were going to hang Wednesday night and Jude said you couldn't because of something doing. What?' I asked. 'Jude can't schedule for shit we were open as it turned out' Iz said. 'Can I pin you?' I asked. 'You can try' Iz said. 'Did Jude say that so you and me wouldn't be girls together?' I asked. 'There's no mindreading Jude Lola you know that. She always reasoned one way or the other' Iz said. 'I think she's getting jealous of me' I said. 'And she was already upset cause of me and Weez.' Iz shook her head but only a little and I guessed she knew more than she was saying. 'Jude in a funny pass right now even fore Weez fade away. She up one day, down the next. Thing is Jude never be thinking a day ahead or a week ahead but always be aiming for twenty years away. That longterms good but shortterms bad. Each day right today has to be like she want it or she frets overmuch she won't reach payday. Once it's past it's past that's why she don't drain her brain bout Weez. But for the right now, she want everything placed where she think it ought to be placed' Iz said stopped and then went on. 'She not jealous about you yourself Lola. She jealous about the time I solo with you.' 'But she's running with her other friends tonight' I said. 'That's more work than play' Iz said. 'It's hard to word it. She know we not always going to be girls together but even when we apart me and Jude, we're <u>together</u> together. That's our way, then now and ever.' 'When you and Jude are girls together that's because it's how you like it right?' I asked thinking about something fretsome. 'Uhhuh' Iz said. 'And when we're girls together like now it's because you like it with me too right?' I asked. 'Why else I be bedding here what's aching you girl?' she asked and kissed me. 'But you and Jude like boys too even if you don't want to be around them now right?' 'I spec so I can't say for Jude I think she likes herself best of all' Iz said. 'But I don't think I'll ever like boys or want to be with them like this' I said. 'Well that's you there's nothing wrong there' Iz said. 'I think I <u>love</u> love you Iz. You know what's meant?' I said. She nodded. 'That's AO' she said. 'What are you circling round?' 'That means I'm different' I said feeling sad because even if Iz didn't leave me to fulltime with Jude again one day she'd meet some boy more like and then I'd be left. 'Everybody different Lo. Jude's Jude and I'm me and you're you however you are. That's how it is that's all so don't let em break you for it' Iz said. 'Long as there's hearting there's loving whoever's heart's involved.'

'How do you love me really?' I asked. She started kissing me again Anne and then it happened. Somebody shouted and we heard the front door smashing in and people heavyfooting inside. My bedroom door crashed open and then these helmet wearing flashlight swinging gun aiming blueboys ran in yelling don't move or you're dead freeze freeze freeze. They prepped to gun us shoving barrels against our heads before we could move. We blinded when they switched on the overhead and I felt humiliated so we weren't sheeted we were just lying there tangled and they could see everything. They dragged Mama out of her bedroom we could hear her screaming and them shouting at her to shut up. They stood us up and grabbed our arms shoving us forward while others upturned the furniture and emptied my drawers and closet. Once they halled us we saw they floored Mama facedown yanking her arms behind her back hard enough to break them. They had guns at her head too and kept screaming shut up shut up. One kicked her in the leg when she wouldn't still. More blueboys were ripping up the living room unzipping the sofa cushions knocking over tables and pulling down the curtains. Iz statued like she wasn't inside herself anymore and I wondered if this was how they did her when they came calling on her and her mother. The one grappling me stuck his gun in my ear and I thought it was endtime Anne I did.

'Don't hurt us please don't' I shouted but they didn't. Mama cried and screamed and they stopped kicking her. Where are they? Where? one of them kept asking her you gonna answer or what? Blueboys who'd kitchened themselves banging pots and pans on the floor like to deafen. A gasmasked hulker smashed in the TV with his gun and it popped and fizzed. Answer us where are they where where? the one on top of Mama kept shouting and he put his gun at the back of her head. I didn't fight to loose myself because I specked they'd flash trigger so I stood there staring them down. The ones who weren't busy eyed me and Iz updown. You could see their little brains click and their tongues drooling and I hated them like I hate Weez and the bill collectors and Aunt Chrissie and Brearley and Boob and Mister Mossbacher.

'Oh God please stop what do you want what please stop' Mama shouted finally able to word clear even though they kept pulling her arms back. 'Stop it quit hurting my mother' I yelled feeling set to blow and thank goodness I didn't because they'd have killed me in seconds but I was almost careless Anne I wasn't taking much more. Where are the men hiding we have a warrant the man atop Mama said answer or you won't see them again.

Then one of them ran up and shook the man's shoulder saying sergeant sergeant this is apartment nineteen. What the fuck do you mean this is apartment sixteen. No sir it's not the number slipped. 'It's apartment nineteen and we're the Harts who do you want?' I shouted. They still held us tight but they took the guns down. Jesus Fucking Christ the sergeant said uprighting and looking around the apartment. Jesus Fucking Christ listen up stop stop it stop he yelled to the others Jesus fucking Christ let them go. When they released me and Iz ran to my bedroom and wrapped sheets around us so they couldn't fisheye us anymore. 'Why did you want to arrest us?' I asked going over to where Mama was still lying and holding her. Iz started to come toward us but one of the blueboys grabbed her arm. She tried to hold onto her sheet but it was slipping. Not so fast the one who did the grabbing said. This ain't your sister who is she? he asked me. 'She's my friend let her go' I said. Damn close friends this young another one said and several of them laughed and I wanted to ex every one of them then. 'What is it with you people what are you doing to us?' Mama shouted up asking the sergeant. Look there's been a mistake ma'am you got to excuse us he told her. 'Some mistake you nearly shot us up you fat fucks' I said and a cop aimed at me. Another one grabbed his arm though not enough to make him shoot accidentally which was good. 'What mistake?' Mama asked. Wrong apartment the sergeant said look it happens. 'You could have killed us' Mama said. Lady you want a safe neighborhood it's the only way to go said the sergeant come on boys.

What about her? one asked pointing at Iz who looked ready to go post office herself right then. Probable perp take in for preventative said another. 'No one here has done anything she's my daughter's friend leave her alone' Mama said. All right that wraps it the sergeant said. What about apartment sixteen? another asked. Jesus Fucking Christ we've done enough here they'll get the picture the sergeant said turning. 'What about our apartment?' Mama asked as they started walking out crunching things they hadn't broke underfoot. Just like Mister Mossbacher they acted like she wasn't there. 'I want your badge numbers' she said but none of them stopped. They left not shutting the door behind them of course. The doorknob was broken off and the door was caved in and barely hung on the hinges. In the hall they'd spraypainted BEWARE BEWARE THE MOTTO OF A BOY SCOUT IS BE PREPARED.

Almost everything was trashed. Mama sat on the floor and starting crying without sounding and it feared me Anne she shook and wouldn't stop. We floored with her and held her until she settled. Then we took her into her room and after pulled in a chest from the living room shoving it against the door so no one else could get in. We rebedded her mattress and sheeted it fresh while Mama sat in her chair where I'd dreamed the rat crawled. 'Do you want us to sleep with you Mama?' I asked and she nodded eyeballing us direct I guess for the first time since we were assaulted. 'Oh God my angels what did they do to you?' she asked. 'Nothing overmuch why what's wrong?' I asked. 'Where are your pajamas sweetie you're naked as babies' she said. 'It was so hot we weren't wearing any' I said helping her lie down.

Then we crawled in too me next to Mama Iz next to me. We were played out certain and all three of us were shaky scared and I couldn't sleep. I lay there thinking God God it's death in life what did we do why did it happen and finally I went coma not dreaming or anything. Come morningside the first thing Mama asked was did I want to go live with Chrissie but however bad it is here that would be worse I know. The second thing she did was medicate and then back to bed she went. I dressed and found the super Gus. He said he'd come fix the door but hasn't been up yet. He said if we're raided again we'd have to go and I told him we were faultless but he just stonefaced me like I wasn't worth hearing.

Iz and I spend so little solo time and we finally did this

happened. I fixed us breakfast that is cold cereal and we talked some. She was AO but nervestrung still and I bet she doesn't home it here any more even though last night happenstanced and nada else. She had to go and I stayed with Mama. While I've been writing she's been screaming whenever she wakes like the cops are still in the room with her. Anne the future's unknowable but I wish I knew it even if it was hateful. It's stopping time now so that's all till later. Bye bye.

JUNE 15

Mama was in recovery yesterday so we started cleaning the apartment proper finishing today. Actually I did the cleaning while she worked on manuscripts. She phoned some publishers who owe her and they word nice claiming the checks are processing there's always delays. One check she's waited on nine weeks now because the managing editor lost it on his desk and they had to redo it.

The blueboys trashed us total nearly. We can't tube anymore and Daddy's old computer got bashed too. After flooring our clothes they stomped muddy boots over them so the dry cleaner calls but there's no money for it. It's unmattered all the dry cleaners close by have bankrupted. All the stores are closing Anne no one can afford to buy they offerings and they won't lower their prices enough to match the new money. Excelsior's open still.

This afternoon I spied out the window longtime minding Iz and nobody else. I started fresh maddening cause I spec she's charged to see me like me her but she won't like she wants because of Jude. She hasn't called today. It puzzles and racks I sametime get misty and drippy when I brainfix on Iz Anne I don't know what's doable these days. It's my fault and it's not my fault I think she wants to bide with me more but maybe I dream maybe she suits Jude better maybe I'm real and they're not and that's all. But I hearten when I eye her Anne I fly off this evil world.

226

Last night it overheated in here way much and my hair matted and clung bugging me so till I wanted to yank it out. I didn't though I scissored it off down short it's goofed but cooler now and I got tired being a babydoll. Mama went openmouthed when she lay look and said 'My darling angel you don't look like you anymore' and I said 'You mean I don't look kiddy now.' 'Sweetie you know your head if that's how you want your hair that makes me happy' she said but she hardly looked at me when she said it. I hope Iz likes it I spec she won't but I do.

JUNE 17

We got lettered from Brearley today telling the new tuition costs for September and asking us to go ahead and money them. Tuition's down from forty thousand a year to six hundred but it's the same after all. 'Angel the one thing your father and I always wanted was to make sure you and little Boob went to good schools because it's so important' Mama said. 'Known' I said. She was bedded again and playing with her hair twirling it around her fingers while she worded. 'But sweetie I don't see how we can now we don't have the money to pay them it's all we can do to pay the expenses.' 'Is that doable?' I asked wondering how behind we were getting. 'Barely just' she said which means no. 'Are they checking you like they ought?' I asked. 'Sometimes sweetie but it's never enough and never on time' she said. 'What about Daddy's royalties?' 'They've downsized my darling and only come in twice a year besides the next aren't due until December and who knows where we'll be by then?' Mama said. 'So I won't go back to Brearley' I said glad at first because I tired of them so but then I thought deeper and it evidenced clear Anne I'll have to go to public school. Iz and Jude say the teachers at theirs are all deadhead and nobody works and somebody's shot up every day. Plus there'll be constant dealings with other Weezies and nasty gangstaboys forever

227

wanting to hop and pop. I'm not going to public school Anne whatever happens.

'Angel I don't see any way around it I just don't' Mama said. 'That's all right' I said. 'It's not sweetie it's not all right oh angel I hate to say it but won't you reconsider going to stay with Chrissie for a while just a while?' 'No never nada' I said. 'She's horrible yes but could be worse' Mama said. 'What would you do if I went out there? You wouldn't go.' 'No I wouldn't but I don't have school to worry about' Mama said. 'Sweetie at this rate I think we're heading for the street I don't want you there.' 'I'd rather be there than with Chrissie she won't even let Boob talk to us' I said. 'Oh angel the last time I called Chrissie said little Boob was out or couldn't come to the phone I don't know what she told me but it was something' Mama said starting to cry. 'She's tonguing false Mama it's plainfaced' I said and I know she knew but she didn't say, she boohooed loud and lay down pillowing her face. There's only so much that's handleable Anne and I limited just then so I ran into my room unable to bear and closed the door quiet behind me wishing something was doable knowing nothing was.

So it's bye bye to Brearley Anne. I can't public school it though I just can't. I'd get exed too quick there and it's living I want.

JUNE 19

Another ratty dream Anne. How it went was I was sitting with Iz in my room reading magazines like Boob and me did. Suddenly a big rat crawled over the bed. Iz looked bored but I hated the rat and taking my magazine which turned into a boot I smashed it. It lay bloodless like a little mouse after I calmed it. Iz picked it up by the tail and swung it and then she put it back on the bed tucking it in. I prepped to heave so I pulled it out and windowtossed it but it wouldn't go through. 'Don't' Iz said and then I woke.

I wish these dreams decoded. I think I have them even when I don't remember. I told Mama about this one to see what she thought but she just shook her head with preoccupations. She was supposed to ready a manuscript yesterday but she didn't and the publisher called often as a bill collector. I eyed today's bills when the mail showed and saw a cutoff notice for the phone. Unless it's paid we won't get any calls. That's how Iz and me contact sole fifty percent of the time lately so something needs doing now.

JUNE 20

Iz and me went boosting today solo and lucked though it was close. We didn't do any buttrubbing like Jude though because Iz fears doing that and I don't want boy germs so I won't. What we did was subway downtown ankling trainlong til we pegged our chicken. Iz can pick them but she was fearing I could tell. He looked middle age and wasn't little but wasn't big. We parked next to him and waited till he moved. At Houston Street he started out and we trailed close. The station was near empty and once we certified it safe we acted. I moved on him one side bumping him hard saying 'Sorry' while Iz did the lifting. She quick worked him but he knew something upped and as she started off he armed her holding on. Iz shouted and I circled back. He looked like he prepped to hit her and I wasn't having that I lunged and jumped him and brought him down hard. His head cracked on the concrete and he was out but moving. We raced to the turnstile looking back eyeing him sitting up and once we saw he was viable we went on. Once we streeted we sped north back to Christopher.

I shook sure but not like the times before when we'd gone boosting I spec cause this time it was needed money and not just frosting. Iz though was strung wired and pissed. 'No more a that no more' she kept saying. 'Two's not enough three's needed and only like we do it.' 'It essentialled how we did' I said opening the wallet. It had a hundred new

dollars Anne that's a fortune now. 'You hear his head I
know it fractured he coulda been exed Lo and then what
then what?' Iz said almost yelling. 'Shush Iz we're moneyed
now come on' I said because if we'd had a dry run the
phone'd go and there'd be nothing home eating but rice
and beans and I can't stomach it overmuch. 'That's bad
craziness Lo. Next time you go you better do a solo yoke if
we don't go boosting with Jude' Iz said. 'Jude Jude Jude if
Jude'd been with us she'd have third wheeled the take' I
said. 'If she'd been with us sure that's right' Iz said. 'It's
needed money Iz and needed now if her schedule don't suit
there's nada to do but move' I said. Iz was all adrenalized
so I spec that's why she raged so but when it came time to
divvy she took her split just the same.

We uptowned and homed separate. She settled by the
time we got back and when we byebyed we kissed like usual
but not deep since we were streeted and the layabouts could
see.

Fifty dollars covers the phone bill and more. When I gave
it to Mama she happied full and didn't ask who dropped it.

JUNE 22

Last night Iz phoned and we talked deep. I fretted she still
maddened and Anne I thought true. 'Boosting's one thing
yoking's another specially yoking for blood. If blood's called
for they got to know why they bleeding otherwise it's a gone
deed' she said. 'If he hadn't grabbed you I wouldn'ta
jumped him' I said. 'You should have seen your face glow
when you lit him. It feared me' Iz said. 'That's untruthed' I
said. 'It's so' Iz said and the way she said it certified she told
true. 'But Iz if we're not moneyed we won't pass the weeks
and Mama's on the slope sinking. What's optioned other-
how?' I asked. 'There always something better. Yoking like
that's what gangstaboys do and you got to line the limit
somewhere' Iz said. 'Your Mama fulltime works and you
get state aid anyway there's no comparing' I said. 'They cut

the state aid and the federal aid Lo we suffering like all do. There's still other ways to money shit' said Iz.

'Like Jude does?' I asked knowing what she uses to get her funding. 'Jude does what Jude wants to do and she's picky choosy besides it's not like she streetwhores' Iz said and I heard her steaming. 'That's not my way and not yours either I know that and you know it too' I said. 'Yeah but yoking for blood's not mine either' Iz said. 'He'da had you and he'da hurt you less I acted quick' I said almost yelling. She lipstilled a second and I feared she prepped to click but she didn't. 'Iz you there?' I asked. 'Here' she said. 'I know you intended right girl but we actioned wrong from the getgo. We ran down trouble's path. That street leads direct to DCon turf, you hear?' 'Heard' I said and softened not wanting her mad at me. 'Forgive me Iz.' 'Forgiven' she said. We sweettalked some until we had to get off or try to come through the phone. It rages me though still Anne I know what happened troubled her but there's no other way to bank right now. If I knew how she'd feel I'd have tried solo though because I don't want to rack her even if it costs me. I love her overmuch Anne I do and I almost did it in not even knowing or expecting. Everthing that hangs you come endtime is something you don't expect I think that's all.

JUNE 24

I'm worsening when it comes to writing Anne but my energy drains too quick sometimes. Mama's sleepless nearly ever night now and I sometimes sit with her hourslong handholding her and saying it's all right Mama it's all right. She's breaking Anne and I'm no nurse I don't know what's doable. Iz and Jude help coming by with groceries and stuff but I'm losing what I've got. I paid the phone bill but rent's coming due. I can't remember what I used to be like Anne it fears me.

* * *

231

Friday last night and Iz came over. This time at least no
blueboys barged through and we were safed and all to
ourselves for awhile. Lately I spec ever time we get together it might be the last and I can't say why it's just
my soul telling me. So as it circumstances I let worry slip as
it may and happy while I can. We played and bedded hot
hour on hour last night Anne. Why can't life be more like
that more times, it unreasons so that it doesn't. People
throw together for a time whether thinking they want and
usually they flare eventually but sometimes they blend and
when they do there's nada topping it no because when they
don't they just grind and groan and moan they lives away
and there's no point to living like that.

'How you living?' Iz asked when we settled and comftied
up against each other. 'Just' I said. 'Your mama call the aid
people?' she asked. 'We're unqualified' I said which was
true. Not even Mama could explain it but it's so, we're left
to our own. 'You gone yoking anytime?' Iz asked. I headshook. 'That's good it's a losing prop less you're beyond
caring.' 'I'm not yet' I said. 'That's good' Iz said.

'Where's Jude tonight?' I asked knowing some time she'd
rise up like she was there with us and figuring I might as
well do the rising and be done with her. 'Housing downtown' Iz said. 'With one of her friends?' I asked and Iz
nodded. 'How long's Jude been doing that?' 'She was eleven
first time she say. Jude's a fast grower' Iz said. 'Where's she
meet her friends?' I asked. 'One know another know
another and she daisy chain down the run' Iz said. 'Who
are they?' 'Bigscale shakers. Corporation boys. The ones
who do the owning, you know. As told, Jude's picky choosy.
She don't go with just any of them and the ones she goes
with have to put plenty gravy on the plate' Iz said. 'They
fund her?' 'Usually.' 'Does she always have to sex them?'
'Not always some of em get off easier and she know all their
ways.' 'They know how young she is?' I asked. 'No as told
she claim she ten year older. She still got the look they think

and she say once she thirty she still claim she be twenty. Go up now, go down later' Iz said. 'Isn't it hellbound?' I asked. 'No more than living Jude say. It's not for me, I couldn't bear those old men she tosses' Iz said. 'She say she'll make the best of it one day so we'll see.' 'How much do they fund her?' I asked. 'Enough I spec' Iz said. 'Reason she be busying so now cause of the changeover and also cause you remember when Weez degunned her?' 'Sure' I said. 'That's not all Weez ripped. Jude had a stash a cash in her mattress and it flyaway too. Don't know how much funding went but Jude, she'd been talking bout getting a real apartment not long before' Iz said. 'She lipstilled about that' I said. 'Cause it something between just me and her, Lo. We confidence each other bout some things nobody else knows about' Iz said and that saddened because I knew that meant some things about her I'd never know even though I'd never tell either. 'Weez knew about the gun but happenstanced on the money' Iz said kissing me. 'That's why Jude fulltilt went after Weez and why once Weez went over Jude swallowed her loss so easy. They had a cord tween em but when she took that money Weez snipped it. It evidences plain, Lo, once people start footing the DCon trail they mindlose total and there's no going back.'

Something racked me just then Anne and inside I felt total alone like I orbited solo eyeing everybody earthed below. It unreasoned my feeling that way but I did just the same. 'How'll we endtime Iz?' I asked. 'What's meant?' she asked back. 'What'll happen. To you, me, Jude' I said. 'Unknown' Iz said. 'Spilling tomorrow into today's suited sometime but not once it darkens. Nada's changeable come nightside and all it does is waken overmuch. Got to think deep in the sun sole, you hear me?' 'Yeah' I said loosing my hold on her so sleep could come easy. 'I love you sis' I said and she didn't answer but she kissed me again night night. Night night. Night night.

* * *

233

I mailed the rent check this morning and good timing too because of something's downing and it fears me big. Mama wouldn't rise and shine after she woke her alarm rang and rang and she didn't mute it. I sat bedded myself thinking what if it rang endless because she died in midnight? Finally I hauled up and eyed round her door to see but she was still here just silenced that's all. 'Mama what's aching you?' I asked and she just shook her head. 'Oh angel I just can't get up anymore' she finally said. 'There's no ending it there's no changing it there's no nothing.' 'That's stupid talk' I said taking her hands which were icecold. Mama lidded her eyes while wording and I knew she'd medicated and that fears me so Anne cause I spec she'll overgo sometime the way she is and then what? 'It's all right' I kept saying, 'It's all right.' I don't know if she believed but she sleepied eventually and once she was out I hid her extra pills between my bed and mattress. She wasn't as supplied as I thought ten to one the blueboys confiscated plenty for resale when they rocked our house. If she exes I don't know what would downcome.

Then Chrissie called and lucky me I got to word her and give ear. 'Does she sleep all day every day?' she asked when I told her Mama was bedded and incommunicado. 'No she's just racked' I said. 'What are you saying get her up' Chrissie said. 'She's too tired tell what needs telling and I'll pass on' I said. 'My God Lola Cheryl was right you've become completely unreasonable that's what she told me and she's absolutely right go get your mother' Chrissie said. 'She's asleep' I said fixing to boil. 'I can't believe your disobedience you won't be that way with me you know' Chrissie said. 'Known cause I never be with you' I said. 'Can't you even speak English?' Chrissie asked. 'I want to word Boob where is she?' I asked. 'Cheryl doesn't want to speak to you she's told me what you've become and let me tell you I was horrified. You know where you're going when you die young lady and you're not going to like it believe me' Chrissie said. 'Maybe I will' I said and hung up sick of hearing her. I knew Boob would say something but who knows what between her fearing and Chrissie twisting whatever she tells well they can sky high with what's imagined about what they think I am. I almost go mind-lost thinking how Chrissie said I was hellbound and maybe so but if she's not there that plusses going there twiceover. God Anne I hate Chrissie I hate Chrissie.

Mister Mossbacher came out under his rock to letter us today. He wrote saying his accountant accidentally moneyed Daddy an extra five in a May paycheck and that if we didn't reimburse the lawyers would have us. Five dollars Anne and he's after us for blood. I took the letter kitchenways and torched it on the burner. Then I put it in the sink watching it burn crispy black and then I drained the ash. Let his lawyers come they'll regret. Oh Anne it aches me thinking that growing adult grinds you so that it's certified you old enough to run loose you be thereafter constant beset by evil craziness. Every adult I know is mindlost and worsening daylong and I'm crazy enough now.

JULY 2

This morning Mama started coming kitchenways while I was sitting there eating cereal. First off I thought how she looked better but I erred. She sudden went floorways and momentslong it seemed like she'd gone away but she hadn't. I hopped to help her running over seeing if she'd hurt herself tumbling but it didn't seem so she just said 'Oh darling I'm done there's no getting around it.' 'You're not done that's crazed don't lie like that' I said. 'My legs are numb sweetie it's almost as if I didn't have them anymore though I know they're there' Mama said. I touched her knee saying 'Feel that?' 'Sort of angel but it might be because I see your hand there' she said. 'We should call the doctor' I said but Mama stood up saying 'Angel it's

235

nothing and besides we owe him too much he'll bar his door if we were to show up.' 'That's deadhead' I said. 'Yes sweetie but that's the way of the world I'll be all right I just feel a little funny that's all' she told me. Propping herself doorways she hung there a second headshaking and then she smiled. 'There now see good as new however it may have seemed at first oh darling I'm sort of itchy do I have anything crawling on me?' She turned and dropped her robe and I eyed her back seeing nada. 'No' I said. 'You're sure angel I think I can feel big bugs are you sure there's nothing?' Mama asked. 'Mama there's not no' I said. 'Very well sweetie but I think there are' she said smiling and scratching herself. She bled in one or two places where she dug too deep. 'I think there are.'

I rebedded her Anne and then rang her main doc. Nurse said less we advance paid the old bills and new bill full it'd be pointless showing though. 'Mama's crazy sick I think' I said but she wouldn't slack nurse just said that wasn't their responsibility. Then I buzzed 911 but nobody answered and I finally got a disconnect every time I tried. Spying on Mama I saw she'd gone bellywhite and shook till she rattled. 'Mama should we hospital you?' I asked. 'Oh sweetie you know hospitals I'll go in and then never come out again once you're in you're in' Mama said.

The way she was feared me so I gritted and then called Iz hoping her mother wouldn't answer the phone though of course she did. When she worded me I shorttalked to try and throw her but who knows if it did. 'Izthere?' I mumbled. 'Just a minute' she said sounding beset. Iz picked up momentslong. 'Mama's shaping bad and needs to hospital can you help Iz?' I asked. 'Which hospital I meet you there' she said. 'St Luke's' I told her since that was closest. 'You get there AO?' Iz asked. 'Should.' 'I be in ER don't fret' she said and got off.

Mama and me taxied to the hospital and we shoved up to the linehead where they admitted. Nurses triaged Mama through cause they saw she looked like she was skirting the boneyard. While they processed her I detailed the facts I knew for the nurses telling where born where live where who why. I'd pocketed Daddy's Guild insurance papers when we rolled and once I gave them over they smoothed and stopped shouting questions at me. Trouble was once they quieted I couldn't give ear as well cause the screams were so loud. The room was full of sickies and oldsters and hospital guards packing Army arms and all of them bigmouthed at once till my head rang. Emergency workers ran through constant shouting watch your back carrying in shootees and bloody babies and brokenhead people who somebody bashed. Worst of all while I hung there telling what they wanted I eyed a big rat creepcrawling along the wall behind seats where people sat. A guard spotted it too and before it could escape he caved it in with his gunbutt splattering everywhere.

When everything was documented I eyed round to see if Iz had come but she hadn't. While they worked over Mama not telling how she was I waited and waited and waited but Iz didn't show. I squeezed in to an old man who slept they kept him so long. He slumped forward until his magazine slipped his hands. I handed it back sliding it on his lap. I ached and maddened that Iz hadn't showed yet cause she claimed she would and a claim's nearly promise. Before I could mope it though I got distracted by another familiar.

'They testing your mama or what?' Jude asked me springing behind me like to yoke. 'It's unsaid' I said. 'Where's Iz?' 'Iz be booked familyways half the time and got her own life you hear? She had to company her Meemaw this morning' Jude said. 'She didn't say when I called' I said. 'Iz hear you upset bout you own so she not gonna throw hers onto you. She try being too much to too many and that's bad for her' Jude said. 'What's meant?' I asked. 'Nada just facing fact' Jude said but she was lying not truthing, it evidenced plain.

'When Iz beds over at my place does that ache you or what Jude?' I asked. She eyed ceilingways while she worded me and that closed it I knew she jealoused over us or me in particular. 'I know she tell you how we be,' she said. 'You awared but you keep on wedging in. Maybe I'm not faultless but nobody here is. See there's lines and when they get crossed too much spills.' 'Iz likes coming over she likes seeing me' I said. 'Known. But you both young girls and you besides never gonna know how Iz really is' Jude said. 'What's meant?' I asked. 'Way you are' Jude said. 'How's that?' I asked. 'Don't need saying it's already known' Jude said. 'Say' I said. But before she could the old man thudded floorways. Jude and me moved to help but guards shoved us away. Holding his wrist they checked to see if he pulsed and signalled a nurse while we eyed what downwent. Two orderlies came out and carried him off. I think he slept all the way away Anne but nobody said and we didn't ask.

'They keeping your mama long as they kept him?' Jude asked. I headshook not knowing but hoping not. 'Hear' I said. 'Nada's wrong with me cause I girl exclusive. If you and Iz like boys too that's your life. She help me with that and there's no denying.' Jude stared me updown like I dumbfounded her. 'Girl that's not what's meant' she said. 'We're tribal. You're not. Her flinging with you's a catkiller nada more. Am I incoming or not?'

She uprighted before me with noselifting attitude. 'That's racist' I said. 'That's fact' she told me. 'I gotta appointment this after so I better go. Look we call you later see how you be. AO?' I nodded and she left. I sat myself and thought and thought about what she said. Maybe it's true that what's blooded tops all but if so it's a worse world than I ever specked Anne that limits who's close overmuch and divides and conquers just like the big boys want. Love's love whoever's loving Anne it always seemed to me and I've been wrong so much I can't be wrong there too. Maybe I never will know Iz like Jude knows her but maybe it works two ways and she'll never know Iz like I know her either who's to say. Anyway as it circumstanced that's how that went and it left me clouded over like deep December. There's no comfort to it no hope no Iz if that's how it really be.

An hour later the nurse told me Mama would have to hospital a few days for observation. I asked when I could see her. She asked my age and I told twelve and she said I wasn't old enough I needed to come back with my father. 'He's dead' I said but she'd already turned and that was that. 'Can I call?' Another nurse nodded and I hoped she spoke true and not just gas. They'll aware me I spec once she's ready to home it but otherwise it's beyond anything doable for me. I homed after that and kitchened myself to write

Excuse my dropping pen so hasty Anne but Iz just called and we talked long. 'What Jude said is that truthed?' I asked her and I could tell she squirmed but I was careless. 'Jude fears overmuch sometime she only takes so much however it seems' Iz said. 'But was what she said truthed?' I asked again. 'It is and it isn't' Iz said. 'How's that?' I asked. 'I don't know but that's how it is that's all. There's no reason just sense' she said. 'That means we're splitting?' I asked feeling tears prepping but not letting them fall. 'No no no no way' Iz said. 'Way Jude is though I better not overnight there anytime soon. That's not saying forever till endtime just not for now. But Lo we can hang constant otherwise but we keep doing what we been doing it's only so long till we be burned you hear me?' 'Yes' I said hearing but wanting to deafen. 'Lo it's just a shifting that's all' she said and I said yes again and then I said 'I love you Iz.' 'Baby I know you do just peace yourself for now please try and peace yourself' Iz said. 'We get together tomorrow.' 'With Jude?' I asked. 'Tomorrow yeah but not always Jude track her own private schedule you know' Iz said. 'That'll be nice' I said fudging. 'There be something downcoming soon you know. Everything's charged' she said. 'Everything where?' I asked hardly hearing myself sounding little girly. 'Streetways. Something's downcoming. Evil craziness of the

worst kind I spec. Set yourself to toe the line or rub it one'
Iz said. 'You know?' I asked. 'I feel' Iz said. 'I feel too love
you' I said again and she cried I gave ear to her tears a long
time. 'See you come morning baby night night' she said and
clicked.

I'm unsoulled Anne I'm racked total now constant I
never felt so lone bereft lifelong. It's an evil year when
everybody skips me first my Brearley friends then Daddy
Boob and now Mama and Iz gone gone the same day.
Rethinking what's already downgone my aching breaks
me open like I'm bleeding everywhere an allover visit from
granny. We lived right one time Anne and then it all
popped there's no knowing why there's not. What did I
do to bring down this what. When I solo now I feel constant
set to blow like I could bloody everbody I see unreasoned I
know but that's that. I don't see how it's handleable but
everybody bypasses somehow they say but it's hard to think I
will there's too much I hate now. What did I do Anne what
did I do.

JULY 3
I rang Mama today and we worded as much as we could.
They'd doped her full it was clear so she slurred and blurred
when she talked and sometimes she didn't sense however
close I gave ear. 'Angel thank you so much for bringing me
here don't know what I'd done if you hadn't' Mama said.
'They stopped me from seeing you' I told. 'Sweetie I know I
asked for my baby but they said sorry no exceptions whatever the case it's a question of infection and safety' Mama
said. 'They say I'm infective?' I asked unsurprised they'd so
claim cause that's my feeling now that I'm bad news to
whoever and all. 'Sweetie no rather if you're infected
coming to visit then you could sue' she said. 'You better?'
I asked. 'I think so darling but it's hard to tell sometimes'
Mama said. Her voice sounded like she was half asleep so
we didn't go on long. She says they'll out her in a few days

240

she just needs more checking. It fears me cause you always read about people who hospital and then never come out but as usual there's nada doable.

This afternoon Iz and Jude and me hooked up not for long. It weirds me Anne now it's almost as if we never bedded close almost like we were two worlded. They worded some about greenasses closing ranks like they waited the volcano anyday and told about Esther and how she hasn't dropped yet but nada else about nothing. After a while I took leave and homed solo sitting here and wishing it would darken. When badness settles why does everbody after act like whatever happened didn't happen? I mean not that it's forgiven forgotten but that nada bad ever downwent ever. That's how it seemed Anne we all stood round wording bout mindlost things and the true importants never rose. It's like painting shit gold it show pretty but it still shit.

Mister Mossbacher's accountant rang tonight wanting that five dollars. I clicked him dead and then kitchened myself feeling full ready to go post office Anne I took a pot and beat it on the table breaking it and the table fearing me plenty and worst of all Anne worst of all once I was done I felt no better like I still wanted blood. It crazes me having those notions but it livens me too like I couldn't go without them anymore. When I eye myself mirrored I don't see me anymore it's like I got replaced and didn't know it but I'm still here underneath I'm still here.

JULY 4

Iz and Jude and me prepped to downtown tonight to see fireworks but they got cancelled because of worsening situations. So I'm homing giving ear to noise out and boiling in. There's naught to be done except rack and rage there's no ridding the feel. When I let myself memory it helps but then I hit a bad one and start dwelling and then everthing circles round again. City fireworks would have topped all Anne I looked forward to seeing them. Summers past we were on the Island and watched them out there Boob called them fireflowers when she was little. It's long gone now so it's unmattered.

Holidays pain your soul so Anne you always think where you've been and who with every year counting back and when they're gone like this year the ache won't stop. Even when we weren't moneyed here everthing safed long as Daddy lived once he went it all crumbled fast. He glued it somehow and it roughed but worked and now no. If Daddy was alive it wouldn't be like this it wouldn't. He'd be here if the store didn't ex him if Mister Mossbacher didn't ex him. If not for him we'd be safer we would. If not for him.

JULY 5

Everthing downcame today Anne the world's spinning out and I spec we finally all going to be riding raw. Morningside when I woke it was ninety already and I was swimming. A half hour passed and then Iz phoned saying 'Meet us at 125th there's gonna be heavy action.' 'What is it?' 'Looks like we're gonna be doing some occupying ourselves' she said. 'Dress down.'

I wore heavy jeans and my cowboy boots and a tight tee that was hard to grab onto. Jude and Iz had cornered at the elevated station when we met up. Thousands of people were streeted Anne most of them unarmed but some packing homemade product. The armed ones slung bats and axes and bags of rocks and bricks. Nobody was acting they just stood round in midstreet stopping traffic. The crowd was pulling down the wall built in the center of 125th breaking up the cement block. Horns blared and sirens flared and lights flashed downstreet but nobody moved far they just waited.

'What's up?' I asked. 'Madness plainfaced that's all' said Iz. 'Everbody aiming to march downtown tell em to get the greenasses out. Give em their own medicine.' 'Bad news on the front page it's a mean bunch we got here' said Jude. 'I been giving ear nightlong to what's downcoming. Time's come.' 'Is it everybody or just some?' I asked. 'Not everbody. Pit Bulls they happy with things that are so they're lowlaying today. Older gangstaboys don't want no messin either but they've handed off now' said Jude.

People continued gathering like they were concert going. Broadway filled topfull as far uptown as was seeable and 125th all the way east. When you firstglanced it showed like a black ocean but when you closed in you saw all types in on it, black white Asian and Latin. They waved banners reading ENOUGHS ENOUGH and STOP THE KILL and NO JUSTICE NO MERCY. I eyed round for Army or blueboys but didn't spot either they must have been hiding with the Pit Bulls I thought. 'We joinin in?' I asked. 'We're right to protest we have to say what's seen' said Iz. 'It's bad news' Jude said headshaking. 'What's fretting you Jude what's feared?' Iz asked. 'Everybody do this they just gonna come back bad twiceover and worsen things even more than they are' Jude said. 'Maybe so but enough's enough Jude' Iz said and I specked most everyone talked this way but of course I couldn't give ear to them all. 'I say let's go too. They just marching what's doable about that?' Iz asked. Jude headshook but didn't leave. 'Bad news' she kept saying.

We were total surrounded by then like on the rush hour train. A minute later we felt the press behind us as people started footing down Broadway and we moved with them sticking close. 'Don't separate whatever happens' Jude said taking our hands. As everyone crowded off they took up both sides of Broadway from curb to curb even under the el tracks. Everybody steamed and heated it was so hot already. The sun shined up buildings westways making them gold but you couldn't see five blocks straightfaced, the sky hazed so. All through Morningside Heights everybody stillipped pacing off slow. People in the buildings above looked out their windows and then shut themselves in. Around Columbia the security guards lined tight arm in arm walling off the campus. Eyeballing past them through the gates I saw a crowd like ours bearing down Amsterdam. 'See we just marching that's all' Iz said. 'How far?' I asked. 'City Hall I spec if they let us midtown certain' she said. We lowspoke even in the crowd cause just then it was almost like we'd be shouting in church if we'd worded normal.

At 96th Street is a hill that goes up five blocks before Broadway slopes slow down to midtown. Once we hit 90th everyone buzzed and started pacing faster. It weirded Anne I didn't notice we hustled up till we were briskfooting, not overmuch but like when you hurry for the bus after school. The talking upvolumed and we heard chants farther back. Ahead of us people raised their banners and sticks. Cars stopped at the side streets honking unable to pass. Down the park in midstreet marchers crunched through the bushes hacking at the trees. My forehead beaded sweat and I happied I'd hacked my hair cause if I hadn't I'd have been dying it was so hot and when I looked at Jude and Iz I saw their faces shine.

There were Army boys at 86th positioned on either side lifting their guns but not shooting. They lined the sidewalks eyeing us not moving. 'Maybe we better break' Jude said to us. 'Howso Jude we're bounded' Iz said and she truthed we were in midcrowd several blocks from the head but moving through gradual. We started trotting feeling our heels getting bumped by those coming up and we held up our elbows to keep a distance and not get split up. The chants loudened and we joined in saying Fight the Power Fight Fight. Soon I heated so I started cooling again feeling my face be breezed as we zipped on and after 79th it was like I air raced Anne I didn't effort I just held Jude's hand tight and we sailed on.

At 72nd the Army boys had personnel carriers blockading the cross streets and Amsterdam south of Broadway that's where they meet up. The crowd coming that way mixed into ours everbody making room as they could. Nobody stood streetside now we took the sidewalks rushing down hotfooting almost faster and faster. Just before we reached Lincoln Center we heard glass break somewhere close but far. We clung tighter and moved faster running now though we weren't in a flat sprint. 'Shit this getting bad' I heard Jude say. 'Prep yourself to bolt' she told us. We kept together but it wasn't easy since people were heading every which way jumping the stores and smashing the windows they hadn't smashed and pushing over the cars blocked off in the side streets. Cops blued the plaza at Lincoln Center watching us walling off Columbus south of where it cuts through Broadway. I dumbfounded Anne seeing another huge crowd coming down Columbus and mixing in with us moving as fast.

Somebody bricked a window with a smash and that did it. Seconds after that first brick flew everybody updown heaved whatever they carried if they carried. All the windows in those blocks sounded to break at once and even in midcrowd glass rained us. People fired the trees in the squares in front of the Center and started trashing stores and restaurants. We kept running almost full tilt now still holding on to one another. Looking left I saw that Central Park West was jammed topfull too heading to where we'd mix total at Columbus Circle. We must have emptied uptown Anne and there was no saying who joined on the way. Looking skyways we saw dozens of copters police and Army overhead whirring and swinging low. Midtown showed dead ahead all its towers fuzzed and hazed in the bad air. It thrilled so Anne we sped free listening to breaking glass sound like all the windows were blowing sametime. I adrenalized and near started jumping while I went running crazy daywild.

Then we hit Columbus Circle which is opened up full. One corner is the park and where Central Park West comes through along with 59th and Broadway shoots through the middle. On the other side is a big vacant lot which was blanketed over with police. It evidenced plain the Army set to stop everybody there before they rocked midtown. We didn't see right off what downwent but we heard. The crowd was shouting deaf loud and then the Army started shooting. They set machine guns along the south end of the circle and once the north end filled with people they let loose.

Usually you floor yourself when you hear guns go and lots did but they were stomped flat when everybody frontways circled round ungripping me and Iz and Jude. Everybody screamed to madden and then they went. A man pushed me over and momentslong I specked I'd be tramped too but I landed high and pulled back up. Then I shoved back going over under aiming sideways. The copters started buzzing and strafing and there was nowhere they didn't aim even shooting out the glass in the buildings. Everybody pressed so my feet lost their boots. I was thoughtless Anne there was nothing doable but haul and fly whoever I stomped getting out and I did. I punched back when I got punched and kicked and cursed and finally sidewalked myself. I came out on the west side by the Bible Society building which was all shot up and started eyeing round for Iz and Jude. The cops started north clubbing handy heads and shouting through their bullhorns yelling go to your homes go to your homes while they swung. I sided myself against the building watching blueboys beat and maim and marchers drop and tumble. It nervestrings me now rethinking it Anne but just then I froze myself unable to move I was so hopped. Soon I thought I was safed cause Broadway started emptying mostly. Hundreds must have headed parkways but there were plenty more still lying there. The street wasn't seeable because of the bodies shot and stomped flat. The copters kept swooping down shooting and the blueboys kept swinging and then Army trucks and hummers brought up the rear aiming north. Some Army boys packed bazookas and flamethrowers and I couldn't believe they used them but I spec they did. Every siren citywide must have been awail. Then I saw a stupefying

246

thing Anne. Through the midst of everything a limo drove through aiming uptown. It passed broad as day on Broadway like nada troubled bumping over the streeted bodies like potholes. It was like all limos wide as my room and black and with midnight windows you couldn't see through. On the driver door was a bloodspattered smiley face.

It's certified that nobody got through the riot glass clear and sure enough I didn't Anne. While I sat there a cop ran up wearing his mirrorglass riot helmet and holding his club. I did nada but that was unmattered as he went by me he swung hitting me upside my head and running on. I didn't coma but I pitched and minuteslong I lay sidewalked feeling drippy warm and I wondered if I was prepping to cool permanent. I was careless if I did or not.

Soon but not too soon I felt my brain replace itself proper and I groaned up blinking and touching where I got whapped fearing what I'd find. I settled quick once I saw I bled some but not much if it had been a granny visit I wouldn't have thought twice. The cop sideswiped me and didn't skull so I lucked plain though tonight my head racks me like I want to tear it off but I can't drop pen I can't you have to know. I can't feel a split though maybe I'm healed already it's untellable. Once I finally raised I giddied and spun thinking I was going to kiss street again but no. I ached so bodywide it surprised but I could live. The copters buzzed off. Broadway was beset by roamers and blueboys and Army stompers so I hauled down the street to Columbus and then uptowned far from the mob stopping sometimes to lean against buildings. Explosions distanced and I wondered what got blown up why. Dozens crawled off my direction holding their sides and heads but I didn't see Iz and I didn't see Jude.

But I did see somebody I willed to see. Going up Amsterdam that's when I saw him Anne. Mister Mossbacher gawked along unmindful scratching his beard and it plainfaced simple he hadn't been rioted on. Once my eyes fixed him I wanted to lunge but I couldn't I pained too

much and I lacked arming anyhow. Daddy told us he
homed near the store but I didn't know where and now I
keened to find out. He went along and I trailed him to an
old corner building and that's where he drew his keys and
unlocked. Right then I had him radared and it happied me
he missed the riot cause if anybody headbashes Mister
Mossbacher I mean it to be me. I'm set now Anne I'm
priming and prepped. Mister Mossbacher brought us down
he fucked over Daddy he fucked over us all and everybody
besides. There's no excusing anymore Anne it just waits for
the doing. When I eyeclose I see his place and see where I
be waiting for him one time real soon now.

It racks me to think on him so here I stop.

To pick up where I dropped Anne so once I recovered I
homed straightaway. I had enough of Broadway so I took
West End instead back to Morningside Heights. Others
ideaed likewise and footed the same route you could tell
them by the blood. The whole West Side updown sounded
livewired with gunshots and sirens and shouts and all the
effects you get up here but now they played down the
length. Each cross street I eyed right seeing what scored
and every block looked bad till I topped 96th. Once West
End merged up with Broadway there was no scaping but it
was all peace up there by then. Burned out cars blocked
some lanes and a bus was crashed into the front of Sloan's at
110th but otherwise it all seemed normal. The subway had
closed tight and Army boys guarded the exits there and at
Columbia and at the elevated where we are. Rioters scared
most stores shut it looked they'd curtained their windows
with plywood like the hurricane was coming. Broadway
filled with cruisers as usually but they didn't windowshop
cause there was nada seeable, everybody just wandered
blankfaced like they all got hit.

Before reaching it I started fearing that our building be
gone but it lasted tall no worse than before. The city must
have shut the bridges cause no cars traveled only Army and
police on the roam staring everbody updown cruel. Most

showed worse than me so nobody closed in which pleased. Finally I homed insiding and checking round to certify all safed. It was like nothing downwent inside Anne it was plain still. I bedded myself hourslong wishing I could sleepaway wishing Mama wasn't hospitalled wishing we never left 86th. No calls from Iz or Jude so there's no saying how they did or if they viable still. That aches me but I can't dwell on bad till I be sure it's bad. They hang tough usual so that's how I keep them minded safe but somewhere else. It's nothing I can think on now I'm not set yet to be total alone.

When night came I rose refreshed and eyed my pillow where I headlaid. It spotted red but not over so, I was unbloodied finally. It stung when the water rinsed it in the shower. After I dried I started penning cause you had to know what happened today it's what they'll never tell and memories don't flypaper everything.

JULY 6

Mama called from the hospital today saying 'Angel they tell me I can get out the day after tomorrow I'm on the mend and now they're keeping me here for observation they say but I think they just want to run the bill up.' 'Is it all Guild payable?' I asked. 'In theory sweetie but about cleans us out so we'll both have to stay healthy from now on' she said blurring her words and I wondered how heavy they doped her before she called.

Later Iz called. It heartened to hear her and I overjoyed listening. 'They nailed us too' she told explaining what downwent once we split. They broke out of the crowd only a block south of where I landed. Second they curbsided cops circled round hammering. 'You'd think young girls be safe from such but once blueboys go wilding there's no hiding away' said Iz. They whopped Iz and Jude headlong breaking one of Iz's ribs and concussioning Jude. Just like with me after they toyed they sallied on uptown slinging

249

their beat leaving Iz and Jude sidewalked and bleeding long with everbody else.

'Jude squeak out saying go phone this number then she told it to me' Iz said. 'I slump off bent over barely breathing finally found a working booth and punched in. Corporation woman answered and I do like Jude said, told her where we were and what happened. She say sit tight.' 'What did she do?' I asked. 'They sent a car up for us and then we hospitalled' Iz said. 'That's true?' 'Why wouldn't it be?' Iz asked. 'Whose car?' I asked. 'One a Jude's friend's company cars' Iz said. 'Good thing too cause we was in bad shape.' Iz didn't word it direct but rethinking it I spec that limo I saw must have had them in it and it racked me Anne that I lay there painfull and they cruise past not even wondering. 'I looked for you' I said. 'Yeah well if you'd have stuck with us you'da got driv too what they do to you?' Iz asked. 'Nada' I said not wanting to admit. 'Weren't you fretting what happened to me?' I asked. 'Sure but you were somewhere else so what was doable?' Iz asked. 'We were both aching Lo we couldn't go looking.' 'Guess not and you had Jude to watch over too' I said. 'Don't be jealousing me Lo it's unreasoned' Iz said and I gave ear to her maddening but I raged too the more I thought on it. 'Just I coulda been exed total and what'd you do or care?' I asked. 'I'd cared plenty but if that happened it was unchangeable Lo and Jude needed me then' she said. 'Jude could get that car too.' Well Anne that racked me total when she said that and I bit my lip bleeding it trying to keep her from knowing it did. 'You'd driven over me too if I'd been in front of you' I said. 'What's meant what are you talking about?' Iz asked but she'd know if she thought but she deadheaded on this one. I clicked off and when she rerang I didn't answer just let it go.

Once Mama homes it'll be nursemaid time for me again so I better do what needs to be done tomorrow I think. He needs the fear put in him Anne and I need to let it out.

* * *

250

Tonight I prepped dressing black in a shirt of Mama's and black jeans and sneakers packing Daddy's softball bat. Mister Mossbacher always stored late ever night Daddy once told hanging there till eight. On riot day he must have closed early or else homed it for lunch and it lucked so that I saw him or at least that's how I thought when I outset for him. My brain fixed on Mister Mossbacher all the way downtown I footed it cause the West Side subway's still out. By the time I reached his building it was eight coming on sunset time and I readied for it to darken deep dark.

While I waited I hid the bat alongside the stoop between trash cans then stairsat watching cars swoop past. His street wasn't much for walkers and that pleased cause I didn't keen interference. The light outside his building burned out and that heartened cause the darker the better when it all downcomes. Sitting there I photoed his puss in my head the way he cursed Daddy and Mama and lied on Daddy's paycheck and his billing five dollars and I steamed set to boil. There was no excusing what he did none nada none. Every time I heard the clipclop I eyed round but it never was him even after nine. I didn't leave though.

Bells rang ten right before he showed. I was standing curbside stretching my legs when he clumped along muttering to himself. Mister Mossbacher been out on a jog and he wore shorts and I saw his skinny ugly hairy legs. When he almost stooped himself I slid up my bat seeing he paid me no mind. He upstaired and I trailed direct keeping the bat behind me. At the door he circled round like he suspected a yoking but seeing me just smiled. Evening he said not recognizing me but I didn't spec he would. 'Evening' I said eyeing the street. Nobody showed and no cars neither. You new in the building? he asked unlocking the door. It was an old place sans doorman and I saw through the glass nobody was halled either. 'Yes' I said as he opened up. When he go in I stuck close and when the door shut behind I took up the bat. Which field you play on in the park? he started to ask but he was just finishing when I swung down on his head.

Jesus no he said eyeing me like he was at a surprise birthday party. My first connect didn't raise much blood but the second hit softness and he spurted. Why who are you he said but I aced him again wanting to deafen myself. He dropped floorways and once he downed I worked his sides and legs listening to the crack crack whack. Up to then I reasoned full Anne but when I started giving double ear I went general post office updowning him again and again and again. There's no denying I was mindlost till I watched him lift his arm saying why and I batted it hard. When I eyed him full color again it sickened but there was no end to swinging till my arms tired and he was all broke up.

If anybody buildingwide heard they didn't show. Momentslong I stared knowing sure I'd gone over now. Before I went down I told and retold myself I'd hurt but not ex but I lied fullface once it started there was no stopping till it was done. It all seemed in dreamtime Anne nada moved and I froze there holding the bat. The hall was all yellowy light and smelled like cabbage. It weirded me sudden that Mister Mossbacher owned a store but housed in a building like ours. What got me most was that my hands looked like somebody else's it's true when that's said. The walls were all spattery and red and I specked I was too but I was careless it unmattered. Then I circled fast to go footsliding in the blood. Rebalancing I kept from tumbling and walked out like I was going to the store. Nobody showed outside and I briskfooted round the corner and up the avenue wiping my face till my hands were red too. Ten blocks distant I spotted an uncovered manhole so I dropped the bat down hearing a splash. Then I homed full tilt blanking my mind all the while getting there by midnight.

Clock shows three thirty Anne it's when my pen looses freest once my night mind's loose but it's lost the leash now and there's no rehanding it. Mama's let out tomorrow at eleven so sleep essentials but I'm all wide eye. There's no denying Anne I can say I mindlost but I didn't not really. Now that he's done I'm glad but still I thought I'd hearten more than this, the feeling rushed then faded out blue and now I feel low low down. It's like nada's changed but certain it has, it's so much worse. What worsens most is that if I was reweaponed and Mister Mossbacher still walked I'd do it again Anne I know I would. And if I did one why wouldn't I do another and who would I do?

JULY 8

They sprung Mama this morning and I went to meet. She looked better though tired but she smiled with full teeth all set to go. 'My angel I'm so proud of you' she said. 'Why?' I asked. 'Because you helped so much getting your poor sick mother to the hospital oh my darling' she said hugging me. I still felt sticky with blood like I feel with granny sometime but now an allover feel that doesn't wash.

'How'd they do you?' I asked helping her out and into a cab so we could home it.

'I'm so much better now my darling' Mama said but I didn't like how she eyeshut while she worded. 'How?' I asked. 'Sweetie they checked with my doctor about my prescriptions and then made sure I was properly dosed, they think I must have gotten my train off the track or something' Mama said. I thought about her extra pillbottles still mattressed in my bed. 'What's meant?' 'I have to be more careful' Mama said. 'They gave me shots and told me I'd be feeling much better shortly and sure enough I did.' 'What kind of shots?' I asked. 'Medication sweetie good medication that helps me get through the day' she said.

Now this is the root of it Anne. This certifies on one hand I be nursing from here out till she hospitals again or counts out before I can get her there. On the other hand it's chanceless she can keep us moneyed, even before she went in publishers stopped calling. If we're not going to wind up street housing then I'll have to do whatever funding essentials to keep the bank open. I'm no burger pusher and I've got to school somewhere I guess so what's left it's either going to be yoking or taking up Jude's line if we overmuch keen on living which I still am. It's unreasoned Anne it's unfair but there's naught to do it's mapped out now. I blank when I try thinking on it but I have to now I have to.

Mama stiffened on the way over so I had to unbend her gentle getting her out of the cab. She groaned and moaned but I finally loosened her up and helped her doorways. Her hair got grayer while she was in. Maybe she just needs dying I spec she does. 'Oh God my angel what a drag it is getting old' Mama said.

JULY 10

Mama says she missed me while she clinicked. She nearly comaed this morning till I walked her backforth and poured the coffee down her. Now she's bedded eyeing ceilingways like if she looks long and hard enough she'll viz what's downcoming with time enough to duck.

Then this afternoon Iz called. 'How's Jude?' I asked. 'Recuperating' Iz said. 'You nursing her or her friends keeping her downtown?' I asked. 'They overlooking her at their place she'll get kept proper there' Iz said. 'What about your rib?' I asked. 'It's achy but I'm all right' Iz said. 'How's your head?' 'It pains me' I told her. I hadn't aimed to but then I told her about Mister Mossbacher how I trailed him what happened when I caught the way he slumped and wiggled. It's unsayable now what made me spill like I did but it racks me when I retell it mindways and if anybody could read everthing I wrote I knew it would be Iz.

'What's thought Iz?' I asked once I done the tell. 'That's senseless Lo' she said. 'Not total though' I said defending. 'Senseless enough what'd he ever do to you direct?' 'He fazed Daddy till Daddy had his heart attack and then he stole our money' I said. 'Known but what he do to you direct not indirect?' Iz asked. 'Nada direct' I said. 'He know who you were?' Iz said. 'No' I said certified that he didn't and now rethinking it that was something that livened it most. 'That's bad craziness, Lo, if revenging's called for it's got to be reasoned and it's got to be for something somebody did direct. Otherwise better let it slide, it all just worsens longterm if you don't' Iz said. 'I'm sorry' I said. 'You didn't do nothing to me' Iz said. 'Can I see you?' I asked missing her wanting to be with her wanting her to hold me. 'Better not. You awful mixed now Lo you better see how you sort' she said. That ached me but not as much as before I spec I'm adjusting to going solo when it essentials that's all that needs doing. I reason total how I'm going to sort. 'Maybe sometime' I said. 'Maybe. I do love you Lola' Iz said. 'Love you too' I told her and I'm truthing I do and always will but that's matterless mostly both ways these days. We've walled apart not for Jude not cause I love love her but cause I crossed over and you can't come here less you want. Night's darkened full now and I spec I'm finally set to ride. Take me street take me.

Bye bye Anne. You're my best friend but I've penned myself dry with all I writ. You give ear when everybody deafs and lend me shoulder constant if tears need dropping. I know you're always with me but time shorts and I have to solo present. Deathpeace still be a undone deal but I set now ready when it come whenever it come. I do the warning first though so nobody sully you fore I close out.

Lookabout people. Beef me overlong and I groundbound you express. Down down down you go down and I be bottomed out set to catch. Snatch your whispers and tape what plays then hit rewind and scream you to sleep, siren you ass and then ex you proper. Lookabout all you. Spec your mirror and there I be. Crazy evilness be my design if that's what needs wearing. All people herebound be evilsouled heartside, no ho they sweet talk. Shove do push and push do shove and everbody in this world leave lovelost hereafter. Lookabout. Chase me if you want. Funnyface me if you keen but mark this when I go chasing I go catching. Eye cautious when you step out people cause I be running streetwild come nightside and nobody safes when I ride. I bite. Can't cut me now. Can't fuck me now. Can't hurt me now. No more. No more.

Night night Anne. Night night. I'm with the DCons now.

CPSIA information can be obtained
at www.ICGtesting.com
Printed in the USA
LVHW040342040321
680411LV00001B/1